A POLITICIAN IS DEAD...

- His mistress had threatened to kill him.
- His doctor had said he'd murder him if he ever got the chance.
- His wife had hated him.
- The anarchists had been plotting to assassinate him.
- His sister had liked him, but she was a little crazy...

...and, for once, Roderick Alleyn has plenty of suspects!

THE NURSING HOME MURDER

NGAIO MARSH

THE NURSING HOME MURDER

NGAIO MARSH

WITH DR. H. JELLETT

A JOVE BOOK

For
"THAT ONE"

This Jove book contains the complete
text of the original hardcover edition.
It has been completely reset in a type face
designed for easy reading, and was printed
from new film.

THE NURSING HOME MURDER

A Jove book / published by arrangement with
Little, Brown and Company

PRINTING HISTORY
Little, Brown and Company edition published 1963
Jove edition / June 1978
New Jove edition / February 1982

ISBN: 0-515-05967-6

Jove books are published by Jove Publications, Inc.,
200 Madison Avenue, New York, New York 10016.
PRINTED IN THE UNITED STATES OF AMERICA

CONTENTS

CHAPTER I

10 DOWNING STREET

Friday, the fifth. Afternoon.

THE Home Secretary, with an air of finality, laid down the papers from which he had been reading and glanced round the table. He was struck, not for the first time, by the owlish solemnity of the other members of the Cabinet. "Really," he thought, "we look for all the world like a Cabinet Meeting in a cinema. We are too good to be true." As if to confirm this impression, the Prime Minister flung himself back in his chair, laid the palms of his hands on the table, and cleared his throat.

"Well, gentlemen," he said portentously, "there we have it."

"Strong!" said the Foreign Secretary. He folded his arms and stared at the ceiling.

"Drastic!" added the Lord Chancellor. "I venture to think—drastic."

"But in my opinion," the Postmaster-General said, "neither too strong nor too drastic." He fidgeted with his tie and became almost human. "Damn it all," he said irritably, "we've got to do something."

There was a pause. The Home Secretary drew in his breath sharply.

"Well," repeated the Prime Minister, "we have talked

a great deal, gentlemen, and now we've heard the
proposed Bill. We have all the facts. To put it briefly,
we are perfectly well aware of the activities of these
anarchistic personages. We know what they are about
and we know they mean to take definite action. We are
agreed that the importance of the matter can hardly be
overstated. The reports from the F.O., the Secret Service and the C.I.D. are sufficiently conclusive. We
have to deal with a definite menace and a growing
menace. It's a bad business. This Bill"—he made a
gesture towards the Home Secretary—"may be drastic.
Does anyone think it too drastic? Should it be mod-
ified?"

"No," said the Postmaster-General. "No."

"I agree," said the Attorney-General.

"Has it occurred to you," asked the Lord Chancellor,
looking across the table to the Home Secretary, "that
you yourself, Sir Derek, have most cause to hesitate?"

The others looked at him. The Home Secretary
smiled faintly.

"As sponsor for this Bill," continued the Lord
Chancellor, "you will get a lot of limelight. We know
what these people are capable of doing. Assassination is
a word that occurs rather frequently in the reports."
The Home Secretary's smile broadened a little. "I
think I do not exaggerate if I say their attention will
be focused on yourself. Have you considered this possibility, my dear fellow?"

"I quite appreciate your point," answered the Home
Secretary. "The Bill is my child—I'll not disclaim
parentship and I'll look after myself."

"I think the Home Secretary should be given proper
protection," said the Chancellor of the Exchequer.

"Certainly," agreed the Prime Minister warmly.
"We owe it to the country. Her valuable assets must
be guarded. The Home Secretary is an extremely
valuable asset."

Sir Derek made a curious grimace.

"I can assure you," he said, "that I'm in no hurry to play the hero's part in a theatrical assassination. On the other hand, I really don't feel there is any necessity for me to walk down to the House surrounded by policemen dressed up as private secretaries and journalists."

"I met Roderick Alleyn of the C.I.D. yesterday," said the Prime Minister ponderously, "and discussed this business quite unofficially with him. He's had these gentry under his eye for some time. He's the last man on earth to exaggerate a position of this sort. He considers that the Minister who introduces a Bill to deal with them will be in real danger from the organisation. I strongly urge you to let the Yard take any measures it thinks necessary for your protection."

"Very well," said Sir Derek. He moved uneasily in his chair and passed his hand over his face. "I take it," he added wearily, "that the Cabinet approves the introduction of the Bill?"

They fell to discussing again the suggested measures. Their behaviour was weirdly solemn. They used parliamentary phrases and politicians' gestures. It was as though they had so saturated themselves with professional behaviourism that they had lost the knack of being natural. The Home Secretary sat with his eyes fixed on the papers before him, as though sunk in a profound and unwilling meditation.

At last the Prime Minister put the matter to the vote—did the Cabinet consider the introduction of the Home Secretary's Bill advisable? It did.

"Well," said the Prime Minister, "that is as far as we need go."

The Home Secretary groaned slightly.

They all turned to him. His face was extremely white and he was leaning forward over the table.

"O'Callaghan!" exclaimed the Postmaster-General. "What's the matter? You're ill?"

"It's all right. Pain. Pass off in a moment."

"Brandy," said the Prime Minister and stretched out his hand to a bell.

"Water," whispered Sir Derek. "Just water." When it came he drank it greedily and then mopped his face.

"Better," he told them presently. "I'm sorry."

They looked uncomfortable and concerned. The Lord Chancellor hovered uncertainly over him. The others eyed him with that horrified ineptitude with which we observe sudden illness in our fellow men.

"I must apologise," said Sir Derek. "I've had one or two bouts like this lately. Appendix, I imagine. I'll have to get vetted. It's an infernal bore for myself and everyone else. I want to stave it off until after this business if I can." He drew himself up in his chair, paused a moment, and then got slowly to his feet.

"Everything settled?" he asked.

"Yes, yes. Won't you lie down for a little?" suggested the Prime Minister.

"Thank you so much, P.M.—no. I'll go home, I think. If someone could tell my chauffeur——" A secretary was summoned. O'Callaghan turned to the door. The Postmaster-General made as if to take his arm. Sir Derek nodded his thanks, but walked out independently. In the hall the secretary took his coat from the butler and helped him into it.

"Shall I come out to the car, Sir Derek?"

"No, thank you, my boy. I'm my own man again." With a word of farewell to the Prime Minister he went out alone.

"He looks devilish ill," said the Prime Minister irritably. "I hope to heaven it's not serious."

"It'll be damned awkward if it is," said the Postmaster-General. "Poor old O'Callaghan," he added hurriedly.

In his car the Home Secretary looked out of the window drearily. They turned out of Downing Street into Whitehall. It was a cold, gusty evening. The faces of the people in the streets looked pinched and their clothes drab and uneventful. Their heads were bent to the wind. A thin rain was driving fitfully across the window-pane. He wondered if he was going to be very ill. He was overwhelmed with melancholy. Perhaps he would die of this thing that seized him with such devastating agony. That would save the anarchists and the C.I.D. a lot of trouble. It would also save him a lot of trouble. Did he really care tuppence about his Bill or about the machinations of people who wanted to revolutionise the system of British government? Did he care about anything or anybody? He was conscious only of a pallid indifference and an overwhelming inertia. He was going to be ill.

At the top of Constitution Hill his car was held up by a traffic jam. A taxi drew up close beside it. He could see that there was a fare inside, but no more than that. The driver looked several times at O'Callaghan's chauffeur and called out something which his man answered gruffly. O'Callaghan had the feeling that the person inside the taxi stared in at his window. He was being watched. He had experienced this sensation many times lately. He thought, with a sort of amusement, of the Prime Minister's anxiety. He pulled a cord and the inside of the car was flooded with light.

"Give them a good view while I'm about it," he thought grimly.

To his surprise the windows of the taxi were lit up as if in answer. He peered across, shading the pane with his hand. The taxi's fare was a solitary man in a dinner-jacket. He sat with his hands resting on the knob of a stick. His silk hat was worn at a slight angle, revealing a clear-cut and singularly handsome profile. It was an intelligent and well-bred face, with a straight nose, firm mouth and dark eyes. The man did not turn his head, and while Sir Derek O'Callaghan still watched him, the ranks of cars moved on and the taxi was left behind.

"That's someone I know," thought O'Callaghan with a kind of languid surprise. He tried for a moment to place this individual, but it was too much bother. He gave it up. In a few minutes his chauffeur pulled up outside his own house in Catherine Street and opened the door of the car.

The Home Secretary got out slowly and toiled up the steps. His butler let him in. While he was still in the hall his wife came downstairs. He stood and contemplated her without speaking.

"Well, Derek," she said.

"Hullo, Cicely."

She stood at the foot of the stairs and watched him composedly.

"You're late," she observed after a moment.

"Am I? I supposed I am. Those fellows jawed and jawed. Do you mind if I don't change? I'm tired."

"Of course not. There's only Ruth dining."

He grimaced.

"I really can't help it if your sister likes to see you occasionally," remarked Lady O'Callaghan tranquilly.

"All right," said her husband wearily. "All right."

He glanced at her inimically and thought how tiresomely good-looking she was. Always so perfectly groomed, so admirably gowned, so maddeningly remote. Their very embraces were masked in a chilly patina of good form. Occasionally he had the feeling that she rather disliked him but as a rule he had no feeling about her at all. He supposed he had married her in a brief wave of enthusiasm for polar exploration. There had been no children. Just as well since there was a taint of insanity in his own family. He supposed he was all right himself. His wife would have brought out any traces of it, he reflected sardonically. Cicely was an acid test for normality.

She walked away from him towards the drawing-room. At the door she paused for a moment to ask:

"Have you been worried at all by that pain today?"

"Oh, yes," said O'Callaghan.

"What a bore it is," she murmured vaguely, and went into the drawing-room.

He looked after her for a moment and then crossed the little hall and entered his own study, a companionable room with a good fireplace, a practical desk and deep square-angled chairs. Cedar logs blazed in the grate and a tray with glasses and a decanter of his particular sherry waited near his particular chair. She certainly saw to it that he was adequately looked after.

He poured himself out a glass of sherry and opened his afternoon post. It was abysmally dull. His secretary had dealt with the bulk of his letters and had evidently considered that these were all personal. Most of them were so marked. One writer begged for money, another for preferment, a third for information. A typewritten envelope had already been opened by his secretary. It contained an anonymous and threatening message and was merely the latest of a long series of such communications. He picked up the last letter, glanced at the envelope, raised his eyebrows, and then frowned. He finished his sherry and poured out another glass before he opened the letter and read it.

It was from Jane Harden.

From Jane. He might have known he wouldn't hear the end of that business in a hurry. He might have known he was a fool to suppose she would let him go without making difficulties. That week-end in Cornwall —it had been pleasant enough but before it was over he'd known he was in for trouble. Damn it all, women were never fair—never. They talked about leading their own lives, said they wanted to get their experience like men, and then broke all the rules of the game. He glanced again over the letter. She reminded him that she had "given herself" to him (what nonsense that was. She'd wanted it as much as he had!), that their families had been neighbours in Dorset for generations before her father went bankrupt. He flinched away from the imputation of disloyalty which, since he was a tolerably honest and conservative man, made him profoundly uncomfortable. She said he'd treated her as though she was a suburban pick-up. He wished fretfully that she had been. She wrote that she was going to a post in a private nursing-home. Would he write to her at the Nurses' Club? Up to this point the letter had apparently been written with a certain amount of self-control but from then onwards O'Callaghan saw, with something like horror, that Jane's emotions had run away with her pen. She loved him but what had she left to offer him? she asked. Must they both forget? She was fighting for her soul and nothing was too desperate. There was a devil tearing at her soul and if she lost him it would get her. She added again that she loved him and that if he persisted in ignoring her she would do something terrible. With a sudden petulant gesture he crumpled up the sheet of paper and threw it on the fire.

"Blast!" he said. "Blast! Blast! Blast!"

There was a light tap on the door which opened far enough to disclose a large nose, a vague mouth, a receding chin, and a gigantic ear-ring.

"Affairs of state, Derry?" asked a coy voice. "Affairs of state?"

"Oh, come in, Ruth," said Sir Derek O'Callaghan.

CHAPTER II

INTRODUCES A PATENT MEDICINE

Friday, the fifth. Evening.

DURING the following week the Home Secretary followed his usual routine. He had become more or less accustomed to the attacks of pain. If anything they occurred more often and with increasing severity. He told himself that the day after he had introduced his Bill, he would consult a doctor. Meanwhile he took three tablets of aspirin whenever the pain threatened to become unendurable, and grew more and more dispirited and wretched. The memory of Jane Harden's letter lurked at the back of his thoughts, like a bad taste in the conscience.

His sister Ruth, an advanced hypochondriac, with the persistence of a missionary, continually pressed upon him strange boluses, pills and draughts. She made a practice of calling on him after dinner armed with chemist's parcels and a store of maddening condolences and counsels. On Friday night he retreated to his study, begging his wife to tell Ruth, if she appeared, that he was extremely busy, and not to be interrupted. His wife looked at him for a moment.

"I shall ask Nash," she said, "to say we are both out."

He paused and then said uncomfortably:

"I don't think I quite like——"

"I too," said his wife, "find myself bored by Ruth."

"Still, Cicely—after all she is exceedingly kind. Perhaps it would be better——"

"You will see her then?"

"No, damn it, I won't."

"Very well, Derek. I'll tell Nash. Has your pain been worrying you lately?"

"Quite a lot, thank you."

"That, of course, is why you are irritable. I think you are foolish not to see a doctor."

"I think I told you I would call in John Phillips as soon as this Bill was through."

"It's for you to decide, of course. Shall I ask Nash to take your coffee into the study?"

"If you please."

"Yes." She had a curiously remote way of saying "Yes," as though it was a sort of bored comment on everything he uttered. "Good night, Derek. I am going up early and won't disturb you."

"Good night, Cicely."

She stepped towards him and waited. By some mischance his kiss fell upon her lips instead of her cheek. He almost felt he ought to apologise. However, she merely repeated "Good night" and he went off to study.

Here his secretary Ronald Jameson awaited him. Jameson, just down from Oxford, was an eager but not too tiresomely earnest young man. He did his work well, and was intelligent. Normally, O'Callaghan found him tolerable and even likeable. To-night, the sight of his secretary irritated and depressed him.

"Well, Ronald?"

He sank down into his chair, and reached for a cigar.

"Sir John Phillips has rung up, sir, and would like to come and see you this evening if you are free."

"Phillips? Has anyone been talking about me to Phillips? What does he want? Is it a professional visit?"

"I don't think so, sir. Sir John didn't mention your—indisposition."

"Ring him up and say I'll be delighted. Anything else?"

"These letters. There's another of the threatening variety. I do wish, sir, that you'd let me talk to Scotland Yard."

"No. Anything else?"

"Only one, marked personal. It's on your desk."

"Give it to me, will you?"

Jameson brought the letter and handed it to him. He looked at it and experienced the sensation of going down in a lift. It was from Jane Harden. O'Callaghan let his arm swing down by the side of his chair. The letter hung from his fingers. He remained staring at the fire, the unlighted cigar between his lips.

Ronald Jameson waited uncomfortably. At last he produced his lighter and advanced it towards O'Callaghan's cigar.

"Thank you," said O'Callaghan absently.

"Is there anything I can do, sir?"

"No, thank you."

Jameson hesitated, looked uneasily at his employer's white face, reflected that Sir John Phillips still awaited his message, and left the room.

For some time after the door had shut behind his secretary O'Callaghan sat and stared at the fire. At last, with an enormous effort, he forced himself to read through the letter. Jane Harden had written a frantic, bitter arraignment, rather than an appeal. She said she felt like killing herself. A little further on, she added that if an opportunity presented itself she would not hesitate to kill him: "Don't cross my path. I'm warning you for my own sake, not for yours. I mean it, Derek,

for you and all men like you are better out of the way.
This is my final word.—Jane Harden."

O'Callaghan had a swift mental picture of the letter
as it would appear in the columns of the penny Press.
Rather to his surprise O'Callaghan heard his wife speak
to the secretary in the hall outside. Something in the
quality of her voice arrested his attention. He listened.

"—something seems to be worrying him."

"I think so too, Lady O'Callaghan," Jameson murmured.

"—any idea—any letters?" The voice faded away.

"Tonight—seemed to upset—of course this Bill——"

O'Callaghan got up and strode across the room. He
flung open the door.

His wife and Ronald Jameson stood facing each other
with something of the air of conspirators. As he opened
the door they turned their faces towards him. Jameson's
became very red and he looked swiftly from husband to
wife. Lady O'Callaghan merely regarded Sir Derek
placidly. He felt himself trembling with anger.

"Hitherto," he said to Jameson, "I have seen no
reason to suppose you did not understand the essen-
tially confidential nature of your job. Apparently I have
been mistaken."

"I'm—I'm terribly sorry, Sir Derek—it was only
because——"

"You have no business to discuss my letters with
anyone. With *anyone*. You understand?"

"Yes, sir."

"Please don't be absurd, Derek," said his wife. "I
asked Mr. Jameson a question that he could not avoid
answering. We are both very worried about you."

O'Callaghan jerked his head. Jameson made a
miserable little bow and turned away. At the door of
his own room he paused, murmured "I'm extremely
sorry, sir," and disappeared.

"Really, Derek," said Lady O'Callaghan, "I think

you are unreasonable. I merely asked that unfortunate youth if you had received any letter that might account for your otherwise rather unaccountable behaviour. He said a letter in this evening's mail seemed to upset you. What was this letter, Derek? Was it another threat from these people—these anarchists or whatever they are?"

He was not so angry that he did not hear an unusual note in her voice.

"Such threats are an intolerable impertinence," she said hastily. "I cannot understand why you do not deal with these people."

"The letter had nothing whatever to do with them, and my 'unaccountable behaviour,' as you call it, has nothing to do with the letter. I am unwell and I'm worried. It may satisfy you to hear that John Phillips is coming in this evening."

"I'm delighted to hear it."

The front door bell sounded. They looked at each other questioningly.

"Ruth?" murmured Lady O'Callaghan.

"I'm off," he said quickly. Suddenly he felt more friendly towards her. "You'd better bolt, Cicely," he said.

She moved swiftly into his study and he followed her. They heard Nash come out and open the door. They listened, almost in sympathy with each other.

"Sir Derek and my lady are not at home, madam."

"But there's a light in the study!"

They exchanged horrified glances.

"Perhaps Mr. Jameson——" said Nash.

"*Just* the man I want to see."

They heard Nash bleating in dismay and the sound of Miss Ruth O'Callaghan's umbrella being rammed home in the ship's bucket. With one accord they walked over to the fireplace. Lady O'Callaghan lit a cigarette.

The door opened, and Ruth came in. They had a

brief glimpse of Nash's agonised countenance and then were overwhelmed in embraces.

"*There* you are, darlings. Nash said you were out."

"We're only 'not at home,' Ruth darling," said Lady O'Callaghan, very tranquilly. "Derek expects his doctor. It was too stupid of Nash not to realise you were different."

"Ah-ha," said Ruth, with really terrifying gaiety, "you don't defeat your old sister like that. Now, Derry darling, I've come especially to see you, and I shall be very cross and dreadfully hurt if you don't do exactly what I tell you."

She rummaged in an enormous handbag, and fetched up out of its depths the familiar sealed white parcel.

"Really, Ruth, I can *not* swallow every patent medicine that commends itself to your attention."

"I don't want you to do that, darling. I know you think your old sister's a silly-billy"—she squinted playfully at him—"but she knows what's good for her big, famous brother. Cicely, he'll listen to you. Please, please, persuade him to take just one of these teeny little powders. They're too marvellous. You've only to read the letters——"

With eager, clumsy fingers she undid the wrapping and disclosed a round green box decorated with the picture of a naked gentleman, standing in front of something that looked like an electric shock.

"There are six powders altogether," she told them excitedly, "but after the first, you feel a *marked* improvement. 'Fulvitavolts.' Hundreds of letters, Derry, from physicians, surgeons, politicians—*lots* of politicians, Derry. They all swear by it. Their symptoms were precisely the same as yours. Honestly."

She looked pathetically eager. She was so awkward and vehement with her thick hands, her watery eyes, and her enormous nose.

"You don't know what my symptoms are, Ruth."

"Indeed I do. Violent abdominal seizures. Cicely —do read it all."

Lady O'Callaghan took the box and looked at one of the folded cachets.

"I'll give him one to-night, Ruth," she promised, exactly as though she was humouring an excitable child.

"That's topping!" Ruth had a peculiar trick of using unreal slang. "I'm most awfully bucked. And in the morning all those horrid pains will have *flown* away." She made a sort of blundering, ineffectual gesture. She beamed at them.

"And now, old girl, I'm afraid you'll have to fly away yourself," said O'Callaghan with a desperate effort to answer roguishness with brotherly playfulness. "I think I hear Phillips arriving."

"Come along, Ruth," said his wife. "We must make ourselves scarce. Good night again, Derek."

Ruth laid a gnarled finger on her lips and tiptoed elaborately to the door. There she turned and blew him a kiss.

He heard them greet Sir John Phillips briefly and go upstairs. In his relief at being rid of his sister, O'Callaghan felt a wave of good-fellowship for John Phillips. Phillips was an old friend. It would be a relief to tell him how ill he felt—to learn how ill he really was. Perhaps Phillips would give him something that would help him along for the time being. He already felt a little better. Very likely it was a trifling thing after all. Phillips would know. He turned to the door with an air of pleased expectancy. Nash opened the door and came in.

"Sir John Phillips, sir."

Phillips entered the room.

He was an extremely tall man with an habitual stoop. His eyes, full-lidded and of a peculiarly light grey, were piercingly bright. No one ever saw him without his single eye-glass and there was a rumour that he wore it

ribbonless while he operated. His nose was a beak and
his under lip jutted out aggressively. He was unmarried,
and unmoved, so it was said, by the general tendency
among his women patients to fall extravagently in love
with him. Perhaps next to actors medical men profit
most by the possession of that curious quality that
people call "personality." Sir John Phillips was, very
definitely, a personage. His rudeness was more glam-
orously famous than his brilliant ability.

O'Callaghan moved towards him, his hand extended.

"Phillips!" he said, "I'm delighted to see you."

Phillips ignored the hand and stood stockstill until
the door had closed behind Nash. Then he spoke.

"You will be less delighted when you hear my business," he said.

"Why—what on earth's the matter with you?"

"I can scarcely trust myself to speak to you."

"What the devil do you mean?"

"Precisely what I say. I've discovered you are a
blackguard and I've come to tell you so."

O'Callaghan stared at him in silence.

"Apparently you are serious," he said at last. "May
I ask if you intend merely to call me names and then
walk out? Or am I to be given an explanation?"

"I'll give you your explanation. In two words. Jane
Harden."

There was a long silence. The two men stared at
each other. At last O'Callaghan turned away. A kind
of mulish huffiness in his expression made him look
ridiculous and unlikeable.

"What about Jane Harden?" he said at last.

"Only this. She's a nurse at my hospital. For a very
long time her happiness has been an important thing
for me. I have asked her to marry me. She has refused,
over and over again. To-day she told me why. It seems
you made capital out of a friendship with her father
and out of her present poverty. You played the 'old

CHAPTER III

SEQUEL TO A SCENE IN THE HOUSE

Thursday, the eleventh. Afternoon.

THE Home Secretary paused and looked round the House. The sea of faces was blurred and nightmarish. They were playing that trick on him that he had noticed before. They would swim together like cells under a microscope and then one face would come out clearly and stare at him. He thought: "I may just manage it— only one more paragraph," and raised the paper. The type swirled and eddied, and then settled down. He heard his own voice. He must speak up.

"In view of the extraordinary propaganda——"

They were making too much noise.

"Mr. Speaker——"

A disgusting feeling of nausea, a kind of vapourish tightness behind his nose.

"Mr. Speaker——"

He looked up again. A mistake. The sea of faces jerked up and revolved very quickly. A tiny voice, somewhere up in the attic, was calling: "He's fainted."

He did not feel himself pitch forward across the desk. Nor did he hear a voice from the back benches that called out: "You'll be worse than that before you've finished with your bloody Bill."

"Who's his doctor—anyone know?"

"Yes—I do. It's bound to be Sir John Phillips—they're old friends."

"Phillips? He runs that nursing-home in Brook Street, doesn't he?"

"I've no idea."

"Somebody must ring Lady O'Callaghan."

"I will if you like. I know her."

"Is he coming round?"

"Doesn't look like it. Tillotley went to see about the ambulance."

"Here he is. Did you fix up for an ambulance, Tillotley?"

"It's coming. Where are you sending him?"

"Cuthbert's gone to ring up his wife"

"God, he looks bad!"

"Did you hear that fellow yell out from the back benches?"

"Yes. Who was it?"

"I don't know. I say, do you think there's anything fishy about this?"

"Oh, rot!"

"Here's Dr. Wendover—I didn't know he was in the House."

They stood back from O'Callaghan. A little tubby man, Communist member for a North Country constituency, came through the group of men and knelt down.

"Open those windows, will you?" he said.

He loosened O'Callaghan's clothes. The others eyed him respectfully. After a minute or two he looked round.

"Who's his medical man?" he asked.

"Cuthbert thinks it's Sir John Phillips. He's ringing his wife now."

"Phillips is a surgeon. It's a surgical case."

"What's the trouble, Dr. Wendover?"

"Looks like an acute appendix. There's no time to be lost. You'd better ring the Brook Street Private Hospital. Is the ambulance there? Can't wait for his wife."

From the doorway somebody said: "The men from the ambulance."

"Good. Here's your patient."

Two men came in carrying a stretcher. O'Callaghan was got on to it, covered up, and carried out. Cuthbert hurried in.

"Yes," he said, "It's Phillips. She wants him taken to Phillips's nursing-home."

"He's going there," said little Dr. Wendover, and walked out after the ambulance men.

O'Callaghan climbed up, sickeningly, from nowhere into semi-consciousness. Grandiloquent images slid rapidly downwards. His wife's face came near and then receded. Somebody groaned close to him. Somebody was in bed beside him, groaning.

"Is the pain very bad?" said a voice.

He himself was in pain.

"Bad," he said solemnly.

"The doctor will be here soon. He'll give you something to take it away."

He now knew it was he who had groaned.

Cicely's face came close.

"The doctor is coming, Derek."

He closed his eyes to show he had understood.

"Poor old Derry, poor old boy."

"I'll just leave you with him for a minute, Lady O'Callaghan. If you want me, will you ring? I think I hear Sir John." A door closed.

"This pain's very bad," said O'Callaghan clearly.

The two women exchanged glances. Lady O'Callaghan drew up a chair to the bed and sat down.

"It won't be for long, Derek," she said quietly. "It's your appendix, you know."

"Oh."

Ruth had begun to whisper.

"What's Ruth say?"

"Never mind me, Derry-boy. It's just silly old Ruthie."

He muttered something, shut his eyes, and seemed to fall asleep.

"Cicely darling, I know you laugh at my ideas but listen. As soon as I heard about Derry I went and saw Harold Sage. He's the *brilliant* young chemist I told you about. I explained *exactly* what was the matter and he gave me something that he says will relieve the pain *at once* and can do no harm at all. It's an invention of his own. In a few months all the hospitals will use it."

She began a search in her handbag.

"Suggest it to Sir John if you like, Ruth. Of course nothing can be done without his knowledge."

"Doctors are so bigoted. I *know,* my dear. The things Harold has told me——!"

"You seem to be very friendly with this young man."

"He interests me enormously, Cicely."

"Really?"

The nurse came back.

"Sir John would like to see you for a moment, Lady O'Callaghan."

"Thank you. I'll come."

Left alone with her brother, Ruth dabbed at his hand. He opened his eyes.

"Oh, God, Ruth," he said. "I'm in such pain."

"Just hold on for one moment, Derry. I'll make it better."

She had found the little package. There was a tumbler of water by the bedside.

In a few minutes Phillips came back with the nurse.

"Sir John is going to make an examination," said

Nurse Graham quietly to Ruth. "If you wouldn't mind joining Lady O'Callaghan for a moment."

"I shan't keep you long," said Phillips and opened the door.

Ruth, with a distracted and guilty look at her brother, gathered herself up and blundered out of the room.

O'Callaghan had relapsed into unconsciousness.

Nurse Graham uncovered the abdomen and Phillips with his long inquisitive fingers pressed it there—and there—and there. His eyes were closed and his brain seemed to be in his hands.

"That will do," he said suddenly. "It looks like peritonitis. He's in a bad way. I've warned them we may need the theatre." The nurse covered the patient and in answer to a nod from Phillips fetched the two women. As soon as they came in, Phillips turned to Lady O'Callaghan but did not look at her. "The operation should be performed immediately," he said. "Will you allow me to try to get hold of Somerset Black?"

"But you, Sir John, won't you do it yourself?"

Phillips walked over to the window and stared out.

"You wish me to operate?" he said at last.

"Of course I do. I know that sometimes surgeons dislike operating on their friends but unless you feel— I do hope—I beg you to do it."

"Very well."

He returned to the patient.

"Nurse," he said, "tell them to get Dr. Thoms. He's in the hospital and has been warned that an operation may be necessary. Ring up Dr. Grey and arrange for the anæsthetic—I'll operate as soon as they are ready. Now, Lady O'Callaghan, if you don't mind leaving the patient, nurse will show you where you can wait."

The nurse opened the door and the others moved away from the bed. At the threshold they were arrested by a kind of stifled cry. They turned and looked back to the bed. Derek O'Callaghan had opened his eyes and was staring as if hypnotised at Phillips.

"Don't——" he said. "Don't—let——"

His lips moved convulsively. A curious whining sound came from them. For a moment or two he struggled for speech and then suddenly his head fell back.

"Come along, Lady O'Callaghan," said the nurse gently. "He doesn't know what he is saying, you know."

In the anteroom of the theatre two nurses and a sister prepared for the operation.

"Now you mustn't forget," said Sister Marigold, who was also the matron of the hospital, "that Sir John likes his instruments left on the tray. He does *not* like them handed to him."

She covered a tray of instruments and Jane Harden carried it into the theatre.

"It's a big responsibility," said the sister chattily, "for a surgeon, in a case of this sort. It would be a terrible catastrophe for the country if anything happened to Sir Derek O'Callaghan. The only strong man in the Government, in my opinion."

Nurse Banks, an older woman than her superior, looked up from the sterilising apparatus.

"The biggest tyrant of the lot," she remarked surprisingly.

"Nurse! What did you say?"

"My politics are not Sir Derek O'Callaghan's, matron, and I don't care who knows it."

Jane Harden returned from the theatre. Sister Marigold cast an indignant glance at Nurse Banks and said briefly:

"Did you look at the hyoscine solution, nurse, and the anti-gas ampoule?"

"Yes, matron."

"Gracious, child, you look very white. Are you all right?"

"Quite, thank you," answered Jane. She busied herself with tins of sterilised dressings. After another glance at her, the matron returned to the attack on Nurse Banks.

"Of course, nurse, we all know you are a Bolshie. Still, you can't deny greatness when you see it. Now Sir Derek is my idea of a big—a *really* big man."

"And for that reason he's the more devilish," announced Banks with remarkable venom. "He's done murderous things since he's been in office. Look at his Casual Labour Bill of last year. He's directly responsible for every death from under-nourishment that has occurred during the last ten months. He's the enemy of the proletariat. If I had my way he'd be treated as a common murderer or else as a homicidal maniac. He ought to be certified. There is insanity in his blood. Everybody knows his father was dotty. That's what I think of your Derek O'Callaghan with a title bought with blood-money," said Banks, making a great clatter with sterilised bowls.

"Then perhaps"—Sister Marigold's voice was ominously quiet—"perhaps you'll explain what you're doing working for Sir John Phillips. Perhaps his title was bought with blood-money too."

"As long as this rotten system stands, we've got to live," declared Banks ambiguously, "but it won't be for ever and I'll be the first to declare myself when the time comes. O'Callaghan will have to go and all his blood-sucking bourgeoisie party with him. It would be a fine thing for the people if he went now. There, matron!"

"It would be a better thing if you went yourself, Nurse Banks, and if I had another theatre nurse free, go you would. I'm ashamed of you. To talk about a patient like that—what are you thinking of?"

"I can't help it if my blood boils."

"There's a great deal too much blood, boiling or not, in your conversation."

With the air of one silenced but not defeated, Banks set out a table with hypodermic appliances and wheeled it into the theatre.

"Really, Nurse Harden," said Sister Marigold, "I'm ashamed of that woman. The vindictiveness! She ought not to be here. One might almost think she would——" Matron paused, unable to articulate the enormity of her thought.

"No such—thing," said Jane. "I'd be more likely to do him harm than she."

And that's an outside chance," declared matron more genially. "I must say, Nurse Harden, you're the best theatre nurse I've had for a long time. A real compliment, my dear, because I'm very particular. Are we ready? Yes. And here come the doctors."

Jane put her hands behind her back and stood to attention. Sister Marigold assumed an air of efficient repose. Nurse Banks appeared for a moment in the doorway, seemed to recollect something, and returned to the theatre.

Sir John Phillips came in followed by Thoms, his assistant, and the anæsthetist. Thoms was fat, scarlet-faced and industriously facetious. Dr. Roberts was a thin, sandy-haired man, with a deprecating manner. He took off his spectacles and polished them.

"Ready, matron?" asked Phillips.

"Quite ready, Sir John."

"Dr. Roberts will give the anæsthetic. Dr. Grey is engaged. We were lucky to get you. Roberts, at such short notice."

"I'm delighted to come," said Roberts. "I've been doing a good deal of Grey's work lately. It is always an honour, and an interesting experience, to work under you, Sir John."

He spoke with a curious formality as if he considered each sentence carefully and then offered it to the person he addressed.

"If I may I'll just take a look at the anæsthetising-room before we begin."

"Certainly."

The truculent Banks reappeared.

"Nurse Banks," said the matron, "go with Dr. Roberts to the anæsthetising-room, please."

Dr. Roberts blinked at Banks, and followed her out.

Sir John went into the theatre and crossed to a small table, enamelled white, on which were various appliances concerned with the business of giving hypodermic injections. There were three syringes, each in a little dish of sterile water. Two were of the usual size known to the layman. The third was so large as to suggest it was intended for veterinary rather than human needs. The small syringes held twenty-five minims each, the larger at least six times as much. An ampoule, a bottle, a small bowl and a measure-glass also stood on the table. The bottle was marked:*"Hyoscine solution. 0.25 per cent. Five minims contains $^1/_{100}$ of a grain."* The ampoule was marked: *"Gas-Gangrene Antitoxin (concentrated)."* The bowl contained sterile water.

Phillips produced from his pocket a small hypodermic case from which he took a tiny tube labelled: *"Hyoscine gr. $^1/_{100}$."* The tube being completely covered by its label, it was difficult to see the contents. He removed the cork, examined the inside closely, laid down the tube and took another, similarly labelled, from his case. His fingers worked uncertainly, as though his mind was on something else. At last she took one of the smaller syringes, filled it with sterile water, and squirted its contents into the measure-glass. Then he dropped in the hyoscine, stirred it with the needle of the syringe, and finally, pulling back the piston, sucked the solution into the syringe.

Thoms came into the theatre.

"We ought to get washed up, sir," he said.

He glanced at the table.

"Hullo!" he shouted. *"Two* tubes! You're doing him proud."

"One was empty." Phillips picked them up automatically and put them back in his case.

Thoms looked at the syringe.

"You use a lot of water, don't you?" he observed.

"I do," said Phillips shortly. Taking the syringe with him, he walked out of the theatre into the anæsthetic-room. Thoms, wearing that air of brisk abstraction which people assume when they are determined to ignore a snub, remained staring at the table. He joined the others a few minutes later in the anteroom. Phillips returned from the anæsthetic-room.

Jane Harden and Sister Marigold helped the two surgeons to turn themselves into pieces of sterilized machinery. In a little while the anteroom was an austere arrangement in white, steel, and rubber-brown. There is something slightly repellent as well as something beautiful in absolute white. It is the negation of colour, the expression of coldness, the emblem of death. There is less sensuous pleasure in white than in any of the colours, and more suggestion of the macabre. A surgeon in his white robe, the warmth of his hands hidden by sleek chilly rubber, the animal vigour of his hair covered by a white cap, is more like a symbol in modern sculpture than a human being. To the layman he is translated, a priest in sacramental robes, a terrifying and subtly fascinating figure.

"Seen this new show at the Palladium?" asked Thoms. "Blast this glove! Give me another, matron."

"No," said Sir John Phillips.

"There's a one-act play. Anteroom to a theatre in a private hospital. Famous surgeon has to operate on man who ruined him and seduced his wife. Problem— does he stick a knife into the patient? Grand Guignol stuff. Awful rot, I thought it."

Phillips turned slowly and stared at him. Jane Harden uttered a little stifled cry.

"What's that, nurse?" asked Thoms. "Have you seen it? Here, give me the glove."

"No, sir," murmured Jane, "I haven't seen it."

"Jolly well acted it was, and someone had put them right about technical matters, but, of course, the situation was altogether too far-fetched. I'll just go and see——" He walked out, still talking, into the theatre, and after a minute or two called to the matron, who followed him.

"Jane," said Phillips.

"Yes?"

"This—this is a queer business."

"Nemesis, perhaps," said Jane Harden.

"What do you mean?"

"Oh, nothing," she said drearily. "Only it is rather like a Greek play, don't you think? 'Fate delivers our enemy into our hands.' Mr. Thoms would think the situation very far-fetched."

Phillips washed his hands slowly in a basin of sterilised water. "I knew nothing of this illness," he said. "It's the merest chance that I was here at this hour. I'd only just got in from St. Jude's. I tried to get out of it, but his wife insisted. Evidently she has no idea we—quarrelled."

"She could hardly know *why* you quarrelled, could she?"

"I'd give anything to be out of it—anything."

"And I. How do you think I feel?"

He squeezed the water off his gloves and turned towards her, holding his hands out in front of him. He looked a grotesque and somehow pathetic figure.

"Jane," he whispered, "won't you change your mind? I love you so much."

"No," she said. "No I loathe him. I never want to

see him again, but as long as he's alive I can't marry you."

"I don't understand you," he said heavily.

"I don't understand myself," answered Jane, "so how should you?"

"I shall go on—I shall ask you again and again."

"It's no good. I suppose I'm queer, but as long as he's there I—I'm in pawn."

"It's insane—after his treatment of you. He's—he's discarded you, Jane."

She laughed harshly.

"Oh, yes. It's quite according to Victorian tradition. I'm a 'ruined girl,' you know!"

"Well, stick to the Victorian tradition and let me make an honest woman of you."

"Look here," said Jane suddenly, "I'll try and be an honest woman *with* you. I mean I'll try and explain what's inexplicable and pretty humiliating. I told him I wanted to live my own life, experience everything, all that sort of chat. I deceived myself as well as him. In the back of my mind I knew I was simply a fool who had lost her head as well as her heart. Then, when it happened, I realised just how little it meant to him and just how much it meant to me. I knew I ought to keep up the game, shake hands and part friends, and all that. Well—I couldn't. My pride wanted to, but—I couldn't. It's all too grimly commonplace. I 'loved and hated' him at the same time. I wanted to keep him, knew I hadn't a chance, and longed to hurt him. I wrote to him and told him so. It's a nightmare and it's still going on. There! Don't ask me to talk about it again. Leave me alone to get over it as best I may."

"Couldn't I help?"

"No. Someone's coming—be careful."

Thoms and Roberts returned and washed up. Roberts went away to give the anæsthetic. Phillips stood and watched his assistant.

"How did your play end?" he asked suddenly.

"What? Oh. Back to the conversation we first thought of. It ended in doubt. You were left to wonder if the patient died under the anæsthetic, or if the surgeon did him in. As a matter of fact, under the circumstances, no one could have found out. Are you thinking of trying it out on the Home Secretary, sir? I thought you were a pal of his?"

The mask over Phillips's face creased as though he were smiling. "Given the circumstances," he said, "I suppose it might be a temptation."

He heard a movement behind him and turned to see Nurse Banks regarding him fixedly from the door into the theatre. Sister Marigold appeared behind her, said: "If you please, nurse," in a frigid voice, and came through the door.

"Oh, matron," said Phillips abruptly, "I have given an injection of hyoscine, as usual. If we find peritonitis, as I think we shall, I shall also inject serum."

"I remembered the hyoscine, of course, Sir John. The stock solution had been put out, but I saw you had prepared your own injection."

"Yes, we won't need the stock solution. Always use my own tablets—like to be sure of the correct dosage. Are we all ready?"

He went into the theatre.

"Well," said Sister Marigold, "I'm sure the stock solution is good enough for most people."

"You can't be too careful, matron," Thoms assured her genially. "Hyoscine's a ticklish drug, you know."

The sickly reek of ether began to drift into the room.

"I must say I don't quite understand why Sir John is so keen on giving hyoscine."

"It saves anæsthetic and it has a soothing effect after the operation. I give it myself," added Thoms importantly.

"What is the usual dose, sir?" asked Nurse Banks abruptly.

"From a hundredth to a two-hundredth of a grain, nurse."

"As little as that!"

"Oh, yes. I can't tell you the minimum lethal dose —varies with different cases. A quarter-grain would do anyone in."

"A quarter of a grain," said Nurse Banks thoughtfully. "Fancy!"

CHAPTER IV

POST-OPERATIVE

Thursday, the eleventh. Late afternoon.

SIR JOHN waited in the theatre for his patient.

The matron, Jane and Nurse Banks came in with Thoms. They stood near the table, a group of robed and expressionless automata. They were silent. The sound of wheels. A trolley appeared with Dr. Roberts and the special nurse walking behind it. Dr. Roberts held the anæsthetic mask over the patient's face. On the trolley lay the figure of the Home Secretary. As they lifted it on the table the head spoke suddenly and inconsequently.

"Not to-day, not to-day, not to-day, damn the bloody thing," it said very rapidly.

The special nurse went away.

The reek of ether rose up like incense round the table. Dr. Roberts wheeled forward his anæsthetising apparatus, an object that, with its cylinders of compressed gases carried in an iron framework, resembled a gigantic cruet. A low screen was fixed across the patient's chest to shut off the anæsthetist. Thoms looked at the patient curiously.

"He's a striking-looking chap, isn't he?" he remarked lightly. "Curious head. What do you make of it, Roberts? You're a bit of a dog at that sort of thing, aren't you? Read your book the other day. There's insanity somewhere in the racial makeup here, isn't there? Wasn't his old man bats?"

Roberts looked scandalised.

"That is so," he said stiffly, "but one would hardly expect to find evidence of racial insanity clearly defined in the facial structure, Mr. Thoms."

The sister arranged the sterile coverings over the abdomen. With the head screened, the patient was no longer an individual. A subject for operation lay on the table—that was all.

Sir John took up a scalpel and made the first incision.

"Peritonitis, all right," said Thoms presently.

"Hull-lo!" he added a little later. "Ruptured abscess. He's made a job of it."

"Accounts for the attacks of pain," Phillips grunted.

"Of course, sir. Wonder he kept going so long—look there."

"Nasty mess," said Phillips. "Good God, matron, are you deaf! I said forceps."

Sister Marigold bridled slightly and gave a genteel cough. There was silence for some time. Sir John's fingers worked, nervously, inquisitively, and with a kind of delicate assurance.

"The pulse is weak, Sir John," said Roberts suddenly.

"Oh? Look at this, Thoms."

"I don't like this pulse."

"What's the matter, Roberts? Pulse?"

"Yes. It's rather weak. I don't like his looks. Get me an injection of camphor, will you, nurse?"

Nurse Banks filled the second small hypodermic syringe and brought it to him.

"Give it, nurse, at once, please."

She did so.

"Serum," grunted Phillips.

"Serum, Nurse Harden," murmured the sister.

Jane crossed to the table of apparatus. There was a little delay.

"Well—well, where is it?" asked Phillips impatiently.

"Nurse!" called Thoms angrily. "What are you doing?"

"I'm sorry—but——"

"It's the large syringe," said Nurse Banks.

"Very well," said Jane faintly.

She bent over the table.

Phillips finished sewing up the incision.

"Nurse," repeated Thoms, *"will* you bring me that syringe! What's the matter with you?"

An agitated drop appeared on the end of his nose. Sister Marigold cast an expert glance at it and wiped it off with a piece of gauze.

Jane came back uncertainly, holding the tray. Phillips straightened his back and stood looking at the wound. Thoms put on the dressing and then gave the injection.

"Well," he said, "that's that. Very nasty case. I suppose he's neglected it."

"I believe so," answered Phillips slowly. I saw him the other evening and I had no idea he was ill—no idea of it."

"How's the condition now, Roberts?" asked Thoms.

"Not too brilliant."

"Well—take him to bed," said Phillips.

"And take that tray away," added Thoms irritably to Jane who still stood at his elbow.

She turned her head and looked into Phillips's eyes. He seemed to avoid her gaze and moved away. She turned towards the other table. Her steps grew more uncertain. She stopped, swayed a little, and fell forward on the tiled floor.

"Good God, what's the girl up to now!" shouted Thoms.

Phillips strode across the theatre and stood staring down at her.

"Fainted," he said behind his mask. He looked at his blood-stained gloves, pulled them off and knelt beside her. Sister Marigold "Tut-tut-tutted" like a scandalised hen and rang a bell. Nurse Banks glanced across and then stolidly helped Thoms to cover the patient and lift him back on the trolley. Dr. Roberts did not even look up. He had bent over the patient in an attitude of the most intense concentration. Two nurses came in.

"Nurse Harden's fainted," said the matron briefly.

They managed to get Jane to her feet. She opened her eyes and looked vaguely at them. Between them they half carried her out of the theatre.

The patient was wheeled away.

Phillips walked off into the anteroom followed by Thoms.

"Well, sir," remarked Thoms cheerfully, "I think the usual state of things has been reversed. You are the fierce member of the party as a rule, but to-day you're a perfect sucking-dove and I damned that poor girl to heaps. I'm sorry about it. Suppose she was feeling groggy all through the op."

"I suppose so," said Phillips, turning on a tap.

"I'm sorry about it. She's a nice girl and a good nurse. Attractive. Wonder if she's engaged."

"No."

"Not?"

"No."

Thoms paused, towel in hand, and stared curiously at his senior. Sir John washed up sedately and methodically.

"Unpleasant game, operating on your friends, isn't it?" ventured Thoms, after a pause. "And such a distinguished friend, too. Jove, there are lots of Bolshie-minded gentlemen that wouldn't be overwhelmed with grief if O'Callaghan faded out! I can see it's hit you up a bit, sir. I've never before seen the faintest tremor in your hands."

"Oh—I'm sorry."

"Nothing to be sorry about." He took off his gown and cap and brushed his hair. "You're quite right," he said suddenly, "I didn't enjoy the operation."

Thoms grinned good-naturedly and then looked sympathetic.

The door opened and Dr. Roberts came in.

"I just looked in to report, Sir John," he began. "The patient's condition is rather disquieting. The camphor injection helped matters at the time but the pulse is still unsatisfactory." He glanced nervously from one surgeon to the other and polished his glasses. "I must confess I feel rather anxious," he said. "It's—it's such an important case."

"All cases are important," said Phillips.

"Of course, Sir John. What I meant to convey was my possible over-anxiety, occasioned by the illustriousness of the patient."

"You speak like your book, Roberts," said Thomas facetiously.

"However," continued Roberts with a doubtful glance at the fat little man. "However, I *am* anxious."

"I'll come and look at him," answered Philips. "I can understand your concern. Thoms, you'd better come along with us."

"I won't be a minute, sir."

"There's something about his condition that one doesn't quite expect," Roberts said. He went into details. Phillips listened attentively. Thoms darted a complacent glance at the mirror.

"I'm ready," he told them.

He turned to Roberts.

"That's a rum-looking old stethoscope you sport, Roberts," he said jovially.

Roberts looked at it rather proudly. It was an old-fashioned straight instrument of wood with a thick stem, decorated by a row of notches cut down each quadrant.

"I wouldn't part with that for the latest and best thing on the market, Mr. Thoms," said Roberts.

"It looks like a tally-stick. What are the notches in aid of?"

Roberts looked self-conscious. He glanced deprecatingly at Phillips.

"I'm afraid you'll set me down as a very vain individual," he said shyly.

"Come on," said Thoms. "Spill the beans! Are they all the people you've killed or are they your millionaire patients?"

"Not that—no. As a matter of fact, it is a sort of tally. They represent cases of severe heart disease to whom I have given anæsthetic successfully."

Thoms roared with laughter and Roberts blushed like a schoolboy.

"Are you ready?" asked Phillips coldly.

They all went out together.

In the theatre Sister Marigold, Nurse Banks, and a nurse who had appeared to "scally," cleaned up and prepared for another operation, an urgent broncho-scopy, to be performed by a throat specialist. Jane had been taken off to the nurses' quarters.

"Two urgent ops. in one evening!" exclaimed the matron importantly; "we *are* busy. What's the time, nurse?"

"Six thirty-five," said Banks.

"Whatever was the matter with Harden, matron?" asked the scally.

"I'm sure I don't know, nurse," rejoined Sister Marigold.

"I do," said Nurse Banks grimly.

Sister Marigold cast upon her a glance in which curiosity struggled with dignity. Dignity triumphed. Fortunately the scally was not so handicapped.

"Well, Banks," she said, "come clean. Why *did* she faint?"

"She knew the patient."

"What! Knew Sir Derek O'Callaghan? Harden?"

"Oh, yes! Their people were neighbours down in Dorset, don't you know," aped Banks with what she imagined to be the accent of landed proprietorship.

Sister Marigold's starch seemed to crackle disapproval.

"Nurse Harden comes of a very nice family," she said pointedly to the scally.

"Oh, most fraytefully nayce," jeered Banks. "Yes, she knew O'Callaghan all right. I happened to say, about a month ago it was, that he was probably the most completely unscrupulous of the Tories and she didn't half flare up. Then she told me."

"Thank you, Nurse Banks, that will do," said matron icily. "The theatre is not the place for politics. I think we are ready now. I want a word with the doctor about this case."

She rustled out of the theatre.

"You've got a nerve, Banks," said the scally. "Fancy talking like that about Sir Derek. I think he looks lovely in his photos."

"You think because he's got a face like Conrad Veidt he's a suitable leader of the people—a man to make laws. Typical bourgeois ignorance and stupidity! However, he's probably the last of his species and he'll be the first to go when the Dawn breaks."

"Whatever are you talking about?"

"I know what I'm talking about."

"Well, I'm sure I don't. What Dawn?"

"The Dawn of the Proletariat Day."

"What's that? No, don't lose your hair, Banks. I'd like to know."

"You will know," said Banks. "Very shortly."

Upon which the throat specialist appeared and inquired if they were all ready for him. In ten minutes' time the figure of a child was wheeled into the theatre and once again the fumes of anæsthetic rose like incense about the table. In another ten minutes the child was taken away. Nurse Banks and the scally began to clear up again. The throat specialist whistled as he washed up in the anteroom. He thrust his head in at the door, remarked: "No rest for the wicked, nurse," and took himself off.

The two women worked in silence for a little while. Nurse Banks seemed preoccupied and rather morose.

"Hullo," said the scally, "there's Pips growling on the stairs." ("Pips" was hospital slang for Sir John Phillips.) *"And* Thomcat. Wonder how he is now. Sir Derek, I mean."

Nurse Banks did not answer.

"I don't believe you care."

"Oh, I'm quite interested."

The voices grew louder but neither of the two nurses could hear what was said. They stood very still, listening intently.

Presently there seemed to be some kind of movement. A woman's voice joined in the conversation.

"Who's that?" asked the scally.

"Sounds like Marigold," said Banks. "God, that woman infuriates me!"

"Ssh! What's it all about, I wonder?"

Sir John Phillips's voice sounded clearly above the others.

"I'd better attend to that," it said.

"Pips sounds absolutely *rampant*," breathed the scally.

"Yes," said Thoms clearly. "Yes."

A sound of footsteps. Then suddenly the door into the theatre opened and O'Callaghan's special nurse burst into the room.

"Isn't it frightful!" she said. "Oh, isn't it frightful!"

"What? What's the matter with you?"

"He's dead—Sir Derek O'Callaghan's dead!"

"Nurse!" The scally gazed at her speechless.

"It really is awful," said Nurse Graham. "Lady O'Callaghan is there now—she wanted to be left alone with him. I felt I simply must tell somebody."

There was a dead silence and then, prompted perhaps by some kind of mental telepathy, they both turned and stared at Banks.

The older woman's head was tipped back. She held her arms stiffly at her sides. Her eyes shone and her lips worked convulsively.

"Banks!" said the scally, "Banks! How can you behave like that? I believe you're glad he's gone!"

"If I hadn't cast off the wornout shackles of religion," said Banks, "I should say 'Praise the Lord for He hath cast down our Enemy.'"

"You disgusting old horror," said the special, and went out of the theatre.

CHAPTER V

LADY O'CALLAGHAN INSISTS

Friday, the twelfth. Afternoon.

"LADY O'CALLAGHAN, I'm terribly sorry to bother, but may I speak to you for a moment?"

Ronald Jameson paused and looked apologetically at the widow of his late employer. She was very handsome in black. Her hair—he could never make up his mind whether it was a warm white or a white blonde— looked as though it had been ironed into place. Her hands, thin and elegant, hung relaxed against the matt surface of her dress. Her pale blue eyes under their heavy lids regarded him with a kind of polite detachment.

"Yes," she said vaguely. "Come into my room, Mr. Jameson."

He followed her into that place of frozen elegance. She sat down leisurely, her back to the light.

"Yes," she repeated. "Sit down, Mr. Jameson."

Ronald said: "Thank you so much," nervously, and sat on the most uncomfortable chair.

"I've just come back from the House," he began. "The Prime Minister saw me in his room. He is terribly distressed about—about yesterday. He wished me to tell you that—that he is entirely at your service should there be anything——"

"Here is the letter I spoke of," she said. "You will see that they threaten to poison him."

"Yes. I see."

"You still do not believe me, Mr. Jameson?"

"I'm sorry. I'm afraid I don't."

"I shall insist upon an inquiry."

"An inquiry? Oh Lord!" said Ronald involuntarily. "I mean—I wouldn't, really, Lady O'Callaghan. It's—we've no grounds for it."

"Are you taking these notes to the Prime Minister to-day?"

"Yes."

"Will you tell him, if you please, what I propose to do? You may discuss it with him. In the meantime I shall go through the private letters. Have you the keys of those drawers?"

Ronald took a bunch of keys from the desk, and with an air of reluctance put them in her hand.

"When is your appointment?"

"For three o'clock."

"It is now only half-past two. Please come and see me before you leave."

As he left her she was fitting a key to the bottom drawer.

To anybody who had the curiosity to watch him—Nash, the butler, for instance—Ronald Jameson would have appeared to be very much upset. He went up to his bedroom, wandered aimlessly about, smoked three cigarettes, and finally sat on the bed, staring in a sort of trance at a wood-engraving that hung above his dressing-table. At last he looked at his watch, went downstairs, got his hat and umbrella, and returned to the study.

He found Lady O'Callaghan seated at the desk with a neatly arranged pile of letters in front of her. She did not turn her head when he came in. She simply stared very fixedly at a paper she held in her hand. It

struck him that she had sat like that for some time—
while he himself had done much the same thing upstairs
in his room. Her face was always pale—she did not use
rouge—but he thought now that it was deadly white.
There was a thin ridge, like a taut thread, linking her
nostrils with the corners of her mouth.

"Come here," she said quietly.

He went and stood by the desk.

"You told me that night, a week ago, I think, that
my husband had received a letter that seemed to upset
him. Was this the letter?"

He glanced at it and then looked away.

"I did not see the letter," he stammered. "Only the
envelope."

"Is that the envelope?"

"I—I think so. I can't be sure."

"Read it."

With an expression of extreme distaste he read the
letter. It was Jane Harden's.

"If an opportunity presented itself," Jane had written, "I would not hesitate to kill you."

Ronald put it down on the desk.

"Now read this."

The second letter was from Sir John Phillips. Phillips had written it at fever-heat on the night he got
home from his interview with O'Callaghan, and had
posted it before he had time to cool down.

"I gather you're going to cut your losses and evade
what, to any decent man, would be a responsibility.
You talked of sending Jane a cheque. She will, of
course, either tear it up or return it. I cannot force your
hand, for that would do still more harm to a lady who
is already deeply wronged. I warn you, however, to
keep clear of me. I've a certain devil in me that I
thought was scotched, but you have brought it to life
again, and I think I could very easily kill you. This

may sound like hyperbole; as a matter of fact, it is a
meiosis.   JOHN PHILLIPS."

"Have you seen that before?" asked Lady O'Callaghan.

"Never," said Ronald.

"You notice the signature? It was written by the man
who operated on my husband."

"Yes."

"Who is this woman—Jane Harden?"

"Honestly, I have no idea, Lady O'Callaghan."

"No?" A nurse, evidently. Look at the address, Mr.
Jameson."

"Good God," said Ronald. "It's—it's the nursing-
home."

"Yes. We sent him to a strange place for his operation."

"But—"

"Will you please take these letters with you?"

"But, Lady O'Callaghan, I can't possibly show them
to the P.M.—the Prime Minister—really!"

"Then I shall have to do so myself. Of course, there
must be an inquest."

"Forgive me, but in the shock of reading these letters
and—realising their inferences, have you considered the
effect any publicity would have on yourself?"

"What do you mean? What shock? Do you suppose
I did not know he had mistresses?"

"I've no idea, I'm sure," said poor Ronald unhappily.

"Of course I knew," she said composedly. "That
seems to me to have nothing to do with the point we
are discussing. I knew he had been murdered. I thought
at first that these other people——" She made a slight
gesture towards the neat little pile on the desk. "Now I
find he had bitter enemies nearer to him than that." Her
hand closed over the letters on her knee. "He has been

murdered. Probably by this nurse or by Sir John Phillips; possibly by both of them in collaboration. I shall demand an inquest."

"An inquest! You know, I doubt very much if you would be given permission."

"To whom does one apply?"

"One can't just order an inquest," Ronald said evasively.

"Who can do so, Mr. Jameson?"

"The—well, the coroner for the district, I imagine."

"Or the police?"

Ronald winced.

"I suppose so—yes."

"Yes. Thank you, Mr. Jameson."

Ronald, in a panic, took himself off to the House.

Lady O'Callaghan put a jade paper-weight on the little heap of letters and opened the telephone directory. The number she wanted was printed in large letters on a front page. She dialed it, and was answered immediately.

"Is that New Scotland Yard?" she asked, pitching her voice in a sort of serene falsetto. "It is Lady O'Callaghan speaking. My husband was Sir Derek O'Callaghan, the late Home Secretary. I want to speak to someone in authority, in reference to the death of my husband. No, not on the telephone. Perhaps someone would call? Immediately, if possible. Thank you."

She hung up the receiver and leant back in her chair. Then she rang for Nash, who came in looking like a Stilton in mourning.

"Nash," she said, "an officer from Scotland Yard is calling in ten minutes. It is in reference to the funeral. I wish to speak to him myself. If Miss O'Callaghan calls, will you tell her I am unable to see her? Show the officer in here when he comes."

"Very good, m'lady," breathed Nash and withdrew.

Cicely O'Callaghan then went to the room where her

husband lay, awaiting his last journey down Whitehall. She was an Anglo-Catholic, so candles burned, small golden plumes, at the head and foot of the coffin. The room, a large one, was massed heavily with flowers. It smelt like a tropical island, but was very cold. A nun from the church that the O'Callaghans attended knelt at a little distance from the coffin. She did not look up when Lady O'Callaghan came in.

The wife knelt beside her for a moment, crossed herself with a thin vague movement of her hand, and then rose and contemplated her husband.

Derek O'Callaghan looked impressive. The heavy eyebrows, black hair, jutting nose and thin wide mouth were striking accents in the absolute pallor of his face. His hands, stiffly crossed, obediently fixed a crucifix to the hard curve of his breast. His wife, only a little less pale than he, stared at him. It would have been impossible to guess her thoughts. She simply looked in the direction of the dead face. In the distance a door opened and shut. She turned away from the bier, and walked out of the room.

In the hall Nash waited gloomily, while a tall, thickly built man handed him hat and umbrella.

"Inspector Fox, my lady."

"Will you come in here?"

She took the inspector into the study. Nash had lit the fire, and she held her thin hands towards it.

"Please sit down," she murmured. They sat facing each other. Inspector Fox regarded her with respectful attention.

"I asked you to come and see me," she began very quietly, "because I believe my husband to have been murdered."

Fox did not speak for a moment. He sat stockily, very still, looking gravely before him.

"I'm sorry to hear that, Lady O'Callaghan," he said at last. "It sounds rather serious."

Apparently she had met her match in understatement.

"Of course, I should not have called you in unless I had material evidence to put before you. I believe the police are aware of the activities of those persons against whom my husband's Anarchy Bill was directed?"

"We know a good deal about them."

"Yes. My husband had received many threatening letters which were believed to come from these people. I wished him to let the police see the letters, but he refused."

"We were informed of the matter from another source," said Fox.

"The Prime Minister, perhaps?"

Fox regarded her placidly, but did not reply.

"I have the letters here," she continued, after a moment, "and would like you to read them." She took them from the desk and gave them to him.

Fox took a spectacle case from an inner pocket and put on a pair of gold-rimmed glasses. He looked extremely respectable. He read the letters through stolidly, laying them down neatly one on top of the other. When the last was finished, he clasped his enormous hands together and said:

"Yes. That's the sort of thing these people write."

"Now, will you read these?"

She gave him the letters from Sir John Phillips and Jane Harden. He read them carefully, in exactly the same way.

"Sir John Phillips is the surgeon who operated upon my husband. I understand the other letter is from a nurse in the hospital."

"Is that so, Lady O'Callaghan?" said Fox politely.

"My husband had peritonitis but I believe he died of poisoning. I believe he was poisoned."

"In view of these letters? These two, or the others?"

"I do not know. I am inclined to regard the personal ones as being more important. They definitely threaten his life."

"Yes. Very vindictive, they seem to be."

"I wish to have an inquest."

"I see," said Fox. "Now that's quite a serious matter, Lady O'Callaghan."

A faint redness appeared in her cheeks. Another woman would possibly have screamed in his face.

"Of course it is serious," she said.

"I mean, if you understand me, that before an order is made for an inquest, the coroner who makes it has to be certain of one or two points. What about the death certificate, for instance?"

"What do you mean?"

"Well, was one signed?"

"Yes."

"By Sir John Phillips?"

"I don't know. Possibly. Mr. Thoms, the assistant surgeon, may have signed it."

"Yes. Well, now, Mr. Thoms is a well-known surgeon. Sir Derek was a distinguished patient. He would take every care before he signed. I think that would be considered sufficiently conclusive by the coroner."

"But these threats! I am convinced he was murdered. I shall demand an inquest."

Fox stared gravely into the fire.

"Perhaps," he said, rather ponderously, "perhaps you would like me to ring up the coroner, and put the case before him."

"Certainly, if you will."

"It would be better if you could tell him, definitely, who signed the certificate."

"Mr. Jameson, my husband's secretary, may know. He had an appointment with the Prime Minister at three."

Inspector Fox consulted a large, bland watch.

"It's fifteen minutes to four."

"I shall ring up the House," she said, and did.

She got Ronald at last and asked her question.

"It was Mr. Thoms?" she said into the telephone. Ronald's voice quacked audibly in the room. "Yes. Thank you. Have you discussed the matter? I see. No, I think not, Mr. Jameson; I am communicating directly with the police."

She hung up the receiver and informed Fox that Thoms had signed the certificate.

Inspector Fox then rang up the coroner. He held a long and muffled conversation. The coroner talked a great deal and appeared to be agitated. Lady O'Callaghan listened. Her fingers drummed bonily on the arm of her chair. For her, it was a terrific gesture. At last Fox rang off.

"It's as I thought," he said. "He says he cannot interfere."

"Then I shall go direct to the Prime Minister."

He got rather ponderously to his feet.

"I don't think I'd do that, Lady O'Callaghan—at least not yet. If you'll allow me to I'd like to talk it over with my superior, Chief Detective-Inspector Alleyn."

"Alleyn? I think I've heard of him. Isn't he——" She paused. Cicely O'Callaghan had nearly dropped a brick. She had been about to say "Isn't he a gentleman?" She must have been really very much perturbed to come within hail of such a *gaffe*. Inspector Fox answered her very simply.

"Yes," he said, "he's rather well known. He's a very highly educated man. Quite a different type from me, you might say."

Again a faint pink tinged her cheeks.

"I am grateful to you for the trouble you are taking," she told him.

"It's all in the day's work," said Fox. "If you'll excuse me, Lady O'Callaghan, I'll get along. I'll speak to the chief at once. If you're agreeable, I'll show him the correspondence."

"Yes."

"Thank you very much. I'll wish you good afternoon."

"Will you have something to drink before you go?"

"No, thank you. Very kind of you, I'm sure." He tramped to the door, turned and made a little bow.

"I hope you'll allow me to offer my sympathy," he said. "It's a great loss to the nation."

"Thank you."

"Good afternoon, Lady O'Callaghan."

"Good afternoon, inspector."

So Inspector Fox went to the Yard to see Alleyn.

CHAPTER VI

CHIEF DETECTIVE-INSPECTOR ALLEYN

Friday, the twelfth. Afternoon and evening.

"Hullo, Brer Fox," said Alleyn, looking up from his desk. "Where've you been in your new bowler?"

"Paying a call on the Snow Queen," replied Fox with unexpected imaginativeness. "And when I say 'Snow Queen' I don't mean cocaine, either."

"No? Then what do you mean? Sit down and have a smoke. You look perturbed."

"Well, I am," said Fox heavily. He produced a pipe and blew down it, staring solemnly at his superior. "I've been to see the wife of the late Home Secretary," he said.

"What! You *are* coming on."

"Look here, chief. She says it's murder."

"She says what's murder?"

"Him. Sir Derek O'Callaghan."

Alleyn put his pipe down and swung round slowly in his chair.

"Oh!" he said. He raised one eyebrow to an excruciating height and twisted his mouth sideways. This trick invested his handsome face with a kind of impish fastidiousness.

"What sort of woman is she?" he asked.

"A very cold fishy sort of lady," answered Fox. "A

Snow Queen, in fact. Not the hysterical sort, if that's what you mean."

"She was a Rattisbon. All the Rattisbons are a bit frosty. I was at school with her brother—who was, of course, called 'Ratsbane.' I speak like Mr. Gossip, don't I? A very churlish fellow, he was. Well, let's have the whole story."

Fox told him the whole story, dwelling a little on the letters.

"I see," said Alleyn. "And she's hell-bent on an inquest?"

"That she is. If we won't do anything, she's going to the Prime Minister. He's a friend of yours, isn't he, sir?"

"I know the old creature, yes. As a matter of fact, he summoned me to the presence on another matter about a fortnight ago and we had an Oppenheimian conversation about anarchists. He was very perturbed and asked me if I didn't consider O'Callaghan would be in personal danger if he pushed the Bill. Well, one never knows, and I said so. Some bright young Communist might bowl a bomb. As a matter of cold fact, I greatly doubt it. They do a certain amount of mischief, they're an almighty nuisance, but as murderers I've no real faith in the British anarchist. Anarchist! The word is *vieux jeu.*"

"I suppose that's French?"

"Quite right, Fox. I always said you had a flair for languages."

"I'm teaching myself with the gramophone. All the same, sir, these anarchists are no joke."

"Of course they're not. The P.M., as I believe the member for Little Squidgemere calls him, thought O'Callaghan ought to have police protection. I quite agreed. I couldn't very well do anything else. O'Callaghan pooh-poohed the idea. As you know, we were look-

ing after him in our unassuming way. On the afternoon
of the Cabinet Meeting, when they decided to introduce
the Bill, I went along to Downing Street myself. I'd got
wind of that insufferable nuisance Nicholas Kakaroff,
and found him standing about in the street, dressed up
as something rather ridiculous—a photographer, I
think. He made off, with all his infra-red rays and
whatnot, as soon as he saw me. I took a taxi and followed O'Callaghan home. We were alongside each other
at one moment. He turned up the lights in his car and
I returned the compliment."

"His servants are all right, aren't they?" asked Fox.

"Oh, yes; we went as far as that. But, of course,
we couldn't do much without O'Callaghan's permission
or knowledge."

"No. I think her ladyship suspects the surgeon or the
girl."

" 'The Surgeon or the Girl'—it sounds like a talkie.
Sir John Phillips is a very able man and handy, so I
understand, with the knife. She thinks he dug it into
an unlawful spot, because O'Callaghan had been interfering with his girl—is that it?"

"She thinks Sir Derek was poisoned, otherwise that
seems to be the general idea, but of course his letter
isn't very explicit."

"Have you got the letters?"

"Yes. Here they are."

Alleyn read them carefully.

"You know, Fox, hundreds of people write letters
like these without planning murder."

"Isn't that what I tried to tell her!"

"My poor Foxkin! See if you can find the Press
report of his death."

Fox produced a paper.

"I brought it with me," he said.

"You think of everything. Here we are. He died an

"Lady O'Callaghan?" asked Alleyn.

"Her ladyship is expecting you, sir." Alleyn gave him his hat and overcoat. Nash said: "Thank you, sir," and waddled off towards the study. Alleyn followed him. Nash opened the door.

"Mr. Alleyn, m'lady," he said. Obviously the degrading titles were better omitted.

Alleyn walked in.

Cicely O'Callaghan sat before the fire in her husband's arm-chair. As Alleyn came in she rose to her feet and looked serenely at him.

"How do you do?" she said.

"How do you do? I am extremely sorry to bother you, Lady O'Callaghan."

He thought: "Golly, she *is* like Ratsbane!"

"But I wished to see you. It is good of you to come so promptly."

"Not a bit." This was an exceedingly polite introduction to a murder story.

"Do sit down. I suppose the man who came here this afternoon has told you my reason for communicating with the police?"

"I believe Inspector Fox gave me a full account of your conversation."

"Yes. I am convinced that my husband was murdered —probably poisoned."

"I am sorry that in addition to your grief you should suffer the pain occasioned by such a suspicion," said Alleyn and wondered how long they were to make speeches at each other.

"Thank you. Do you agree with me that the circumstances warrant an inquest?"

"I think I should like to hear a little more about them. I have read the letters."

"Surely they, in themselves, are enough to arouse anybody's suspicion?"

"Lady O'Callaghan, it is extremely unusual for a

person contemplating homicide to write such letters. I do not say it is unknown, but it *is* very unusual. I expect Fox told you that."

"I believe he said something of the sort. My point is this: I do not think the murderer contemplated homicide when writing the letter. I do think that a person capable of writing such a letter would also be capable of seizing the opportunity when it presented itself."

"So it *is* Phillips and the girl she's after," thought Alleyn.

"I see your point, of course," he said slowly.

"There is another incident which I did not go into with—Inspector Fox. Before my husband's operation I was in his room with him. He did not realise where he was or what had happened to him. I tried to explain about the appendix. Then Sir John Phillips came into the room. When my husband saw him he exclaimed: 'Don't—don't let——' and then he collapsed. He seemed terrified by the presence of Sir John Phillips and I am certain that he tried to say: 'Don't let him touch me.' I must tell you that a week before this Sir John called on my husband. I hoped that it was for a consultation about his pain, which was then very severe. Next morning I asked my husband if Sir John had examined him. He evaded my question, and seemed very much upset. I had met Sir John in the hall and had thought his manner most unusual. His letter was written that same night, evidently as a result of the interview."

"You definitely connect Sir John's letter with the other, signed Jane Harden?"

"Yes. She is a nurse in the hospital where my husband was a patient. After your man left, this afternoon, I rang up the hospital and under pretext of wishing to thank the nurses concerned in the case, I found out their names. She was actually present in the operating theatre and I dare say assisted Sir John."

She drawled all this out in her serene, high-pitched voice, exactly as though she was reading aloud.

"Forgive me," said Alleyn, "but did you know anything about this business? I hope you will understand that I only ask because———"

"Because you wonder if I am prejudiced?"

"Exactly."

"I knew my husband was unfaithful to me from time to time. I also believed these incidents to be more or less casual encounters."

"You were unaware of this Miss Harden's existence?"

"Quite."

Alleyn was silent for a little while. Then he rose to his feet.

"I think, with you, that there should be an inquest," he told her.

She made a slight movement and the heavy folds of her dress stirred. It was as though she had suddenly gone tense all over. When she spoke, however, it was with her customary equanimity.

"You have, I am sure, made a very wise decision."

"I'm afraid we shall have difficulty with the coroner. Naturally he is rather chary about starting such an alarming hare. It will be impossible to keep the thing even moderately quiet. The papers already have wind of these threatening letters from Sir Derek's political enemies."

He watched her closely, but beyond a faint expression of distaste, could find no evidence of any sort of emotion.

"That will be rather disagreeable," she murmured.

"I am afraid so. Is there anything else that you would like to discuss?"

"I was going to suggest that you speak to Mr. Ronald Jameson, my husband's secretary. He will, I think, confirm what I have said about Sir Derek's reaction to these letters."

"If you wish it, I will see him. Of course, if the post-mortem shows that poison has been given, it will then be my duty to make very exhaustive inquiries."

"Of course," she agreed.

Evidently she had made up her mind Alleyn should see Jameson, because she sent for him then and there. Ronald came in looking very perturbed and uneasy.

"This is my husband's secretary—Mr. Jameson, Mr. Alleyn."

"How do you do, sir?" said Ronald. "You won't have the foggiest recollection of me, I'm afraid, but we have met before."

"I've a filthy memory," declared Chief Inspector Alleyn.

"It was at Nigel Bathgate's."

"Oh, yes." Alleyn was polite, but non-committal.

"Really?" murmured Lady O'Callaghan. "Yes. I thought too that perhaps I had seen you—that your face——" She seemed uncertain how to go on.

"People often find they are familiar with the faces of the police," said Alleyn gravely.

"It's not that, sir." Ronald turned to Lady O'Callaghan. "Mr. Alleyn is in some of Mr. Rattisbon's photos in the study at Karnelly."

"Ratsbane's cricketing groups," thought Alleyn. "Oh, Lord!"

"Oh," said Lady O'Callaghan. "Yes." She stared rather blankly at him.

"Mr. Jameson," Alleyn began, "I believe Lady O'Callaghan wants me to speak to you about an incident that took place here a week before Sir Derek's operation."

Ronald jumped and glanced nervously at the lady.

"I have spoken to Mr. Alleyn about my suspicions. He agrees that there should be an inquest."

"Really, sir? Look here—I mean, of course, you

know best, but, well—it's—it's a pretty ghastly thought, isn't it?"

"You remember the evening my husband had the letter signed Jane Harden?"

"Yes," said Ronald very reluctantly.

"You remember that you told me the letter seemed to upset him very much?"

"Yes—but——"

"And when he overheard you speaking of it he was quite unreasonably angry?"

"I don't think *unreasonably,* Lady O'Callaghan," Ronald protested. "Sir Derek was quite right. I should not have mentioned his correspondence. I had never done so before."

"Why did you do so then?" she asked him.

"Really," thought Alleyn, "she might be an Attorney-General."

"Because—well, because it seemed to upset him so much." Ronald saw the fence too late and crashed into it.

"Yes," said Lady O'Callaghan.

"Would you describe him as being alarmed?" Alleyn asked.

"Well—more sort of disturbed and distressed. After all, sir, it *was* an unpleasant letter to get."

Ronald seemed to be in a perfect agony of embarrassment.

"Certainly," Alleyn agreed. "You were not present, were you, at any time during the interview between Sir Derek and Sir John Phillips?"

"No. I—no, I wasn't."

"What were you going to say? Was anyone else there?"

"Nash, the butler, took in the tray."

"Has he spoken to you on the subject?" asked Alleyn casually.

"Er—yes. Servants' gossip. I rather snubbed him, sir."

"What did he say before you'd snubbed him?"

"He's an awful old woman—Nash. He seemed to think Sir John had used some sort of threatening expression. Honestly, sir, he's a fearful ass."

"I see. I think that's all, Lady O'Callaghan. Perhaps the apprehensive Nash will make an appearance when I go."

She rang the bell.

"He should have come in with the tray by this time," she said vaguely.

When Nash appeared it was with the tray, which he set down delicately.

"Mr. Alleyn, will you——?"

"No, thank you so much. I must be off. Good-bye, Lady O'Callaghan. I'll ring you up if I may."

"Yes. Thank you. Good-bye."

Nash opened the door and followed Alleyn into the hall. Jameson made as if to see the inspector out.

"Oh—Mr. Jameson," said Lady O'Callaghan. He hesitated and then returned to the study, closing the door.

As he took his hat and coat from the butler Alleyn paused and looked directly at him.

"Perhaps you realise why I am here?" he said.

"Not altogether, sir," murmured Nash composedly.

"It is in connection with Sir Derek's death."

Nash bowed very slightly.

"If I ask you a question," Alleyn continued, "you must understand there is no obligation to answer if you don't want to. I particularly do not wish the matter mentioned in or out of the servants' hall. You understand?"

"Certainly, sir," said Nash quietly.

"I believe I can depend on you. How long have you been with Sir Derek?"

"Twenty years, sir. I was footman to his father."

"Yes. Did you hear Sir John Phillips say anything to your master the last time he came here?"

"Yes, sir."

"What was it?"

" 'If the opportunity presented itself, I should have no hesitation in putting you out of the way.' Those were the exact words, sir."

"I see. Have you told anyone about this?"

"Mr. Jameson, sir. I considered it my duty. No one in the hall has any idea of the incident, sir."

"What did Mr. Jameson think about it?"

"He appeared to attach no importance to it, sir."

"No? Thank you, Nash."

"Thank you very much, sir. Shall I get you a taxi, sir?"

"No, I'll walk. Good night."

"Good evening, sir."

Nash opened the door and Alleyn went out into the street. He paused a moment to light a cigarette. He had taken a few steps along the pavement when he heard something that made him pause and turn.

Ronald Jameson had come out of the house and hurried after him, bareheaded.

"Please forgive me, sir," he said hurriedly, "but I felt I must have another word with you. It was rather difficult with Lady O'Callaghan present. About these ideas of hers. I'm certain there's nothing in it. Sir Derek was a man of the world and—and, of course, he had his relaxations. She seems very cold and all that, but I believe she was frightfully jealous and she wants to punish this girl. I'm sure that's all it is."

"Oh. Why should she want to punish Sir John Phillips as well as Miss Harden?"

"Oh, Lord knows. You can't tell with women, sir, can you?"

"I haven't tried," said Alleyn.

"I expect you think it frightful cheek, my butting in like this, but, you see, I—well, Sir Derek was rather a marvellous person to me, and I simply loathe the idea of everything being dragged out and made public. It's a ghastly thought."

Something of Ronald's semi-diplomatic air of winning tactfulness still appeared in his rather dishevelled manner. He gazed with anxious deference into Alleyn's sardonic face. The inspector cocked an eyebrow.

"And yet," he said, "I imagine, if Sir Derek was actually killed, you would rather the murderer didn't get off scot-free?"

"Yes, but, you know, I'm sure he wasn't. Those two letters didn't mean anything—I thought so at——"
Ronald stopped short.

"Were you about to say 'at the time'?" inquired Alleyn.

"I meant at the time Lady O'Callaghan found them."

"Where were the letters kept, Mr. Jameson?"

"In his private drawer," said Ronald with a very red face.

"And the keys?"

"Er—oh, usually in the desk."

"I see. Well, we must pursue the subject no more until we discover whether Sir Derek was murdered."

"I'm absolutely certain there's nothing in it, sir."

"I hope you are right. Good night."

"Thank you *so* much, sir," said Ronald, all eager and charming. "Good night."

Alleyn swung his stick up, turned on his heel, and walked away. Ronald gazed after the long, elegant figure for some seconds. His fingers fidgeted with his tie. Then he looked up at the windows of the house, slightly shrugged his shoulders, and ran up the steps and through the door.

Alleyn heard the door slam. As he turned out of

Catherine Street towards Buckingham Gate he began
to whistle Ophelia's song:

> "He is dead and gone, lady,
> He is dead and gone;
> At his head a grass-green turf,
> At his heels a stone."

CHAPTER VII

POST-MORTEM

Monday, the fifteenth. Afternoon.

"EVERYBODY talks to me about 'P.M.s,'" complained Chief Detective-Inspector Alleyn to Inspector Fox on Monday afternoon, "and I never know whether they mean post-mortem or Prime Minister. Really, it's very difficult when you happen to be involved with both."

"It must be," said Fox dryly. "How's the case going?"

"It's too young to be called a case. So far it's only a naughty thought. As you know, Lady O'Callaghan urged the inquest and threatened to appeal to the P.M. However, the coroner ordered the inquest, which opened on Saturday a.m. and was adjourned for a P.M. which has been going on during the week-end p.m. and a.m. You see how tricky it all is?"

"I can see you're worried, chief."

"When you call me 'chief,' Fox, I feel like a cross between an Indian brave and one of those men with jaws and cigars in gangster films."

"Okay, chief," said Fox imperturbably. "It's a big job, this," he added somberly.

"It is," said Alleyn. "I don't mind admitting I was nervous over the inquest. I should have looked remarkably silly if it had gone the other way and no P.M. had been ordered."

"It might very easily have happened. Phillips did his best to put the kybosh on a post-mortem."

"You thought so?"

"Well—didn't you?"

"Yes, I suppose so. Oh, yes."

"Of course," said Fox slowly, "an innocent man in his position would have been anxious for a P.M."

"Not if he thought someone else had done the trick."

"Oh," Fox ruminated. "That's the big idea, is it, sir?"

"It's only one idea—possibly a silly one. What did you think of the matron's contribution to the evidence? Sister Marigold?"

"Couldn't make her out at all and that's a fact. She seemed to welcome the inquest. She obviously resented any hint of criticism against Sir John Phillips."

"She made one or two very acid remarks about the other nurse—Nurse Banks."

"Yes. Now, that struck me as rum, too, sir. No suggestion of anything as regards the Harden girl, but when Nurse Banks was mentioned——"

"She bridled like a Persian," said Alleyn. "I know—'rum's' the word, Fox."

"The medical witnesses are always a bit trying in a case like this," reflected Inspector Fox. "On the defensive, as you might say. They all pull together."

"Now that's exactly what I thought they did *not* do. I've just read over the shorthand report of the inquest and the thing that struck me all of a heap was that the hospital gang seemed to be playing a sort of tig-in-the-dark game. Or rather tug-of-war in the dark. They wanted to pull together, but didn't know which way to pull. Here's the report. Let us go over it, shall we? Where's your pipe?"

They lit up. Alleyn shoved a carbon copy of the verbatim report on the inquest across to his subordinate.

"First you get straight-out evidence on the operation. Phillips said Sir Derek O'Callaghan, suffering from a ruptured abscess of the appendix, was admitted to the Brook Street hospital. He examined the patient, advised an immediate operation, which, at Lady O'Callaghan's request, he undertook to perform himself. Peritonitis was found. The anæsthetist was Dr. Roberts, engaged for the job because the usual man was unavailable. Phillips says Roberts used all possible care and he can find no fault in that department. Thoms, the assistant, agrees. So do Sister Marigold and the two nurses. Before he began, Phillips injected hyoscine, his usual procedure for all operations. For this injection he used tablets he brought with him, saying that he preferred them to the solution in the theatre, as hyoscine is an extremely tricky drug. 'All care taken, no responsibility accepted,' one feels moved to remark. He prepared the syringe himself. At the end of the operation a concoction prettily named 'Concentrated Gas-Gangrene Antitoxin,' used in cases of peritonitis, was injected. The serum, together with a large syringe, was laid out by Nurse Banks before the operation. It was a commercial preparation kept in an ampoule from which she simply filled the syringe. Nurse Harden fetched the syringe and gave it to Thoms, who injected the stuff. Meanwhile Roberts, the anæsthetist, had got all hot and hectic about the patient's heart and had asked for an injection of camphor, which was prepared and given by the elder nurse. They then tacked up the tear in the tummy and away went the patient. He died an hour later, presumably, one longs to say, of heart-failure, but my medical friends tell me that's as good as saying 'he died of dying.' So we can only murmur humbly 'he died as the result of an operation which, apart from this little incident, was a howling success.'"

"Well," said Fox, "so far they all agree."

"Yes, but did you notice that where it came to the bit about Jane Harden fetching the syringe with the anti-gas, as they call it for short, they all went rather warily. She herself looked pretty sick when the coroner asked her about it. Here it is:

" 'The coroner: I understand you brought the syringe containing the anti-gas, to Dr. Thoms?

" 'Nurse Harden (after a pause): Yes.

" 'The Coroner: There was no unusual delay, or anything of that sort?

" 'Nurse Harden: I—I did hesitate a moment. The syringe was already full and I paused to make sure it was the right one.

" 'The Coroner: Did you not expect to find it prepared?

" 'Nurse Harden: I was not sure. I—I wasn't well, and for a moment I hesitated and then Nurse Banks said it was the large syringe and I brought it to Dr. Thoms.

" 'Sir John Phillips, recalled, said that the delay was of no significance. Nurse Harden was unwell and had subsequently fainted.

" 'The Coroner: I understand you were personally acquainted with the deceased?

" 'Nurse Harden: Yes.' "

Alleyn laid down the report.

"That's the incident," he said. "It's all perfectly natural, but I smelt high tension among the expert witnesses, whenever it was mentioned."

He waited for a movement and then said slowly:

"That incident would never have come out if it hadn't been for Thoms."

"I noticed that, sir. Mr. Thoms let it out during his evidence and then looked as if he wished he hadn't."

"Yes," said Alleyn dryly.

Fox eyed him cautiously and then went on:

"That girl must have been in a pretty good fatigue—in the light of what we know, I mean. There was this man to whom she'd been writing—the man she'd gone off with, as far as we can tell. She'd reckoned on some sort of permanent understanding, anyway, according to her letter, and when there was nothing doing she'd said she'd like to kill him and—there he was."

"Very dramatic," said Alleyn. "The same line of chat, with a difference, may be applied to Sir John Phillips."

"That's so," admitted Fox. "They may have been in collusion."

"I'm entirely against any sort of speculation until we get the analyst's report, Fox. I have not interviewed any of these people. As you know, I thought it best to start no hares before the inquest. I wanted the inquest to be as colourless as possible. The post-mortem may be a wash-out, in which case we'll want to fade away with the minimum amount of publicity."

"That's right," said Fox heavily.

"We're only noting any points of interest in the evidence that may come in handy for future reference. Exhibit A—Nurse Harden and the anti-gas. Exhibit B—curious behaviour of Nurse Banks while giving evidence. The woman closely resembled a chestnut on the hob. She might have spontaneously combusted at any moment. However, she didn't, more's the pity perhaps, but I think she managed to fill the minds of the jury with strange surmises. It struck me that she hadn't exactly hero-worshipped the late Home Secretary. There was more than a suspicion of a snort in her references to him."

"Bolshie-minded, perhaps," ruminated Fox.

"Dare say. She looks like that."

"He may have carried on with her too."

"Oh, Fox! She does *not* look like that."

"People take very strange fancies sometimes, sir."

"How true that is. No speculations, Foxkin."

"All right, sir, all right. What about Exhibit C?"

"Exhibit C. *In re* above. Heavy restraint of the matron, Sister Marigold, when Banks was mentioned.

Marigold seemed to me to seethe with suppressed information. 'Wild horses wouldn't get me to tell, but, my oath, if wild horses could——?' "

"And Sir John himself?"

"*Agitato ma non troppo,* and unnaturally *ppp*. This abbreviation business is insidious. Sir John was so anxious to let everybody know he had prepared the hyoscine injection, wasn't he?"

"Very straightforward of him, I thought," remarked Fox doubtfully.

"Oh," said Alleyn vaguely, "so did I. As honest as the day."

Fox regarded him suspiciously.

"Lady O'Callaghan gave her evidence well," he said.

"Admirably. But, oh, lummie, how we did hover on the brink of those letters. I'd warned the coroner, who had, of course, read them and thought they were sufficient grounds for a post-mortem. However, he agreed it was better they should not come out. He was very coy about the whole thing, anyway, and would have repressed pints of hyoscine——"

"Hyoscine!" shouted Fox. "Aha—you are thinking of hyoscine!"

"Don't shriek at me like that; I nearly bit my pipe-stem in half. I'm not thinking particularly of hyoscine. I was about to remark that I was in deadly fear Lady O'Callaghan would drag in the letters. I'd warned her, advised her, implored her not to, but she's not a Rats-bane for nothing, and you never know."

"And Thoms?"

"Thoms took the line that the whole show was unnecessary, but he gave his evidence well, appeared to have nothing to conceal apart from his regret over divulging the fainting episode, and seemed to resent the slightest criticism of Phillips."

"Yes," Fox agreed, "I noticed that. Roberts took

much the same line. That's what I mean about the experts sticking together."

"Oh, quite. They wanted to pull together, but I'm pretty certain they were not all agreed. I did rather feel that they were uneasy about Nurse Harden's delay over the anti-gas syringe, and that there was something about Nurse Banks that both Sister Marigold and Jane Harden shied away from."

"There were three injections altogether," said Fox thoughtfully. He held up as many short fingers. "The hyoscine, prepared and injected by Phillips; the camphor, prepared and injected by Nurse Banks, and the anti-gas, prepared by Nurse Banks and injected by Mr. Thoms."

"Sounds like a petrol station. Well, there it is. If his tummy turns up a natural, we can forget all about it. If dirty weather sets in, it'll be with a vengeance. Do you like cocktail metaphors?"

"I've been talking to Inspector Boys about the political side," said Fox. "He's got all the Kakaroff crowd taped out and he doesn't think there's much in it."

"Nor do I. Since the Krasinky lot were roped in they've piped down considerably.[1] Still, you never know with these people. They may mean business. If that Bill goes through next week, it'll larn 'em. I hope there's no nonsense at the funeral to-morrow. We're making elaborate enough arrangements for burying the poor chap—shutting the stable door with a gold padlock. They might possibly choose the moment to celebrate at the funeral, but, no, I don't think they were in on the murder. I'm inclined to think they would have staged something more spectacular—a suitable echo to the Yugoslavia affair. Hyoscine doesn't sound their cup of tea at all."

"Why hyoscine?" asked Fox with massive innocence.

---

[1] See *A Man Lay Dead*.

"You old devil," said Alleyn, "I refuse to discuss the case with you. Go and catch pickpockets."

"Sorry, sir."

"And if anything comes of this P.M. business, you can jolly well deal with Lady O'Callaghan yourself. That makes you blanch. What's the time?"

"Three o'clock, sir. The results of the post-mortem ought to come in fairly soon."

"I suppose so. Our famous pathologist is going to ring me up himself as soon as he has informed the coroner."

Alleyn got up and walked about the room hunching up one shoulder and whistling under his breath. The desk telephone rang. Fox answered it.

"It's a Miss O'Callaghan asking for you," he said stolidly.

"Miss——? Who the devil——? Oh, all right. *Now* what's in the wind, do you suppose?"

"Send her up," said Fox to the telephone. "I'd better push off, sir," he added.

"I suppose you had. This is all very rum—very rum indeed."

Fox departed. Alleyn knocked out his pipe, opened the window, and sat behind the desk. A woman's voice sounded in the passage outside. The door was opened by a police-constable, who said:

"Miss O'Callaghan, sir," and withdrew.

Ruth O'Callaghan walked into the room. She appeared to be dressed in a series of unrelated lengths of material. Her eye-glasses were canted over the top angle of her enormous nose. Her handbag and umbrella, wedded by an unhappy confusion of cords and leather thongs, dangled from a gaunt wrist. Her face, exclusive of the nose, was pale. She seemed to be grievously agitated.

Alleyn rose and waited politely.

"Oh!" said Ruth, catching sight of him. "Oh!" She

came towards him at a kind of gallop and held out the hand that was encumbered with the umbrella and hand-bag. Alleyn shook it.

"How do you do?" he murmured.

"So good of you to see me," Ruth began. "I know how busy you must be. The statistics of crime are so appalling. Too kind."

"I am making no arrests this afternoon," said Alleyn gravely.

She gazed at him dubiously and then broke into a sort of whooping laugh.

"Oh, no, no, no," said Ruth. "That's very funny—no, of course, I didn't suppose——" She stopped laughing abruptly and looked disconcertingly lugubrious.

"No," she repeated. "But it *is* kind, all the same, when I expect you think I'm a jolly old nuisance of an interfering woman."

"Do sit down," said Alleyn gently, and pulled forward a chair. Ruth shut up rather like a two-foot rule. He pushed the chair under her and returned to his own. She leant forward, resting her elbows on his desk, and gazed earnestly at him.

"Mr. Alleyn," Ruth began, "what is this dreadful, dreadful suspicion about my brother's death?"

"At the moment, Miss O'Callaghan, it can scarcely be called a suspicion."

"I don't understand. I've been talking to my sister-in-law. She said some dreadful things to me—terrible—appalling. She says my brother was"—Ruth drew in her breath noisily and on the crest of the intake uttered the word "murdered."

"Lady O'Callaghan attaches a certain amount of importance to threatening letters which were sent to Sir Derek. You have heard of these letters, I expect."

"You mean from those horrible anarchist people? Of course, I know they behaved very badly, but Derry —my brother, you know—always said they wouldn't do anything, and I'm quite certain he was right. Nobody else could have any reason for wishing him harm." ("She hasn't heard about the other letters, then," thought Alleyn.) "Everybody adored him, simply adored him, dear old boy. Mr. Alleyn, I've come to *beg* you not to go on with the case. The inquest was bad enough, but the other—the—you know what I mean. I can't endure the thought of it. Please—please, Mr. Alleyn——" She fumbled desperately in the bag and produced a colossal handkerchief.

"I'm so sorry," said Alleyn. "I know it's a beastly idea, but just think a little. Does it matter so much what they do to our bodies when we've finished with them? I can't think so. It seems to me that the impulse to shrink from such things is based on a fallacy. Perhaps it is impertinent of me to speak so frankly." Ruth gurgled and shook her head dolefully. "Well then, suppose there was no post-mortem, what about your feelings then? There would always be an unscotched suspicion whenever you thought of your brother."

"He was ill. It was his illness. If only he had followed my advice! Mr. Alleyn, I have a friend, a brilliant young chemist, a rising man. I consulted him about my brother and he—generously and nobly—gave me a wonderful remedy, 'Fulvitavolts,' that would have cured my brother. I *begged* him to take it. It *would* have cured him; I know it would. My friend assured me of it and he *knows*. He said——" She broke off abruptly and darted a curiously frightened glance at Alleyn. "My brother always laughed at me," she added quickly.

"And he refused to try this 'Fultitavolts'?"

"Yes—at least—yes, he did. I left the tablets there but, of course—he just laughed. My sister-in-law is not very——" Here Ruth floundered unhappily. "I'm sure he didn't take them."

"I see. People are generally very conservative about medicine."

"Yes, *aren't* they?" agreed Ruth eagerly and then stopped again and blew her nose.

"The lack of interest shown in chemical research must be very discouraging to a young man like your friend," Alleyn went on. "I know a brilliant fellow— only twenty-five—who has already——" He stopped and bent towards her. "I suppose we can't possibly be speaking of the same person?"

Ruth beamed at him through her tears.

"Oh no," she assured him.

"Now, how do you know, Miss O'Callaghan?" said Alleyn gaily. "I'm a very great believer in coincidence. My man is James Graham."

"No, no." She hesitated again, oddly, and then in another burst of confidence: "I'm talking about Harold Sage. Perhaps you've heard of him too? He's getting quite famous. He's—he's practically thirty."

"The name seems to strike a chord," lied Alleyn thoughtfully. The desk telephone rang.

"Will you excuse me?" he asked her, and took off the receiver.

"Hullo? Yes, speaking. Yes. Yes. I see. Thank you very much. I'm engaged at the moment, but if I may I'll come round and see you to-morrow? Right." He hung up the receiver. Ruth had just got to her feet.

"I mustn't keep you, Mr. Alleyn. Only before I go— please, please let me beg you to go no further with these investigations. I've—I've got a reason—I mean I'm so sure Derry died naturally. It is all so dreadful. If I could be sure you were satisfied——" She made an ineffectual movement with her hands, a clumsy gesture of entreaty. "Tell me you'll go no further!" begged Ruth.

"I am extremely sorry," said Alleyn formally, "but that would be impossible. The post-mortem has already been held. That message gave me the result."

She stood gaping at him, her mouth half open, her big hands clutching at her bag.

"But what—what is it? What do they say?"

"Your brother died of an overdose of a dangerous drug," said Alleyn.

She stared at him in utter dismay and then, without another word, turned and blundered out of the room.

Alleyn wrote the name "Harold Sage" in a minute notebook that he carried. Having done so, he stared at it with an air of incredulity, sighed, shut up his book and went to find Fox.

CHAPTER VIII

HYOSCINE

Tuesday, the sixteenth. Afternoon.

ON the following afternoon, five days after his death,
Derek O'Calaghan was buried with a great deal of
pomp and ceremony. Alleyn was right about the funeral
—there was no demonstration from the late Home
Secretary's obscure opponents, and the long procession
streamed slowly down Whitehall without disturbance.
Meanwhile the inquest had been resumed and concluded. After hearing the pathologist's and the analyst's
report, the jury returned a verdict of murder against "a
person or persons unknown." Alleyn had had a few
words in private with the pathologist before the inquest
opened.

"Well," said the great man, "there wasn't much doubt
about the hyoscine. The usual dose is a hundredth to a
two-hundredth of a grain. My calculations, based on
traces of hyoscine found in the organs, show that more
than a quarter of a grain had been given. The minimum
lethal dose would be something very much less."

"I see," said Alleyn slowly.

"Did you expect hyoscine, Alleyn?"

"It was on the *tapis*. I wish to heaven you hadn't
found it."

"Yes. Unpleasant business."

"Do they ever put hyoscine in patent medicines?"

"Oh, yes. Had Sir Derek taken patent medicines?"

"I don't know. It's possible."

"The dosage would be too small to enter into the picture."

"If he swallowed an entire packet?"

The pathologist shrugged his shoulders. "Would he take an entire packet?" Alleyn did not answer. "I can see you've got something in mind," said the pathologist, who knew him.

"Sir John Phillips injected hyoscine. Suppose O'Callaghan had taken a patent medicine containing the drug?" Alleyn suggested.

"The average injection, as I have said, is about, say, a hundredth of a grain. The amount in patent medicines would be very much less. The two together, even if he had taken quantities of his rot-gut, could scarcely constitute a lethal dose—unless, of course, O'Callaghan had an idiosyncrasy for hyoscine, and even if there was an idiosyncrasy, it wouldn't account for the amount we found. If you want my private opinion, for what it is worth, I consider the man was murdered."

"Thank you for all the trouble you have taken," said Alleyn glumly. "I shan't wait to hear the verdict; it's a foregone conclusion. Fox can grace the court for me. There's one other point. Were you able to find the marks of the injections?"

"Yes."

"How many were there?"

"Three."

"Three. That tallies. Damn!"

"It's not conclusive, Alleyn. There might be a fourth injected where we couldn't see it. Inside the ear, under the hair, or even into the exact spot where one of the others was given."

"I see. Oh, well, I must bustle away and solve the murder."

"Let me know if there's anything further I can do."

"Thank you, I will. Good-bye."

Alleyn went out, changed his mind and struck his head round the door.

"If I send you a pill or two, will you have them dissected for me?"

"Analysed?"

"If you'd rather. Good-bye."

Alleyn took a taxi to the Brook Street home. He asked a lugubrious individual in a chastened sort of uniform if Sir John Phillips was in the hospital. Sir John had not yet come in. When would he be in? The lugubrious individual was afraid he "reely couldn't say."

"Please find someone who can say," said Alleyn. "And when he's free give Sir John this card."

He was invited to wait in one of those extraordinary drawing-rooms that can only be found in expensive private hospitals in the West End of London. Thick carpet, subfusc curtains of pseudo-empire pattern and gilt-legged chairs combined to disseminate the atmosphere of a mausoleum. Chief Inspector Alleyn and a marble woman whose salient features were picked out embarrassingly in gilt stared coldly at each other. A nurse came in starchily, glanced in doubt at Alleyn, and went out again. A clock, flaunted aloft by a defiant bronze-nude, swung its pendulum industriously to and fro for twenty minutes. A man's voice sounded somewhere and in a moment the door opened and Phillips came in.

He was, as usual, immaculate, a very model for a fashionable surgeon, with his effective ugliness, his eyeglass, his air of professional cleanliness, pointed by the faint reek of ether. Alleyn wondered if the extreme pallor of his face was habitual.

"Inspector Alleyn?" he said. "I am sorry to have kept you waiting."

"Not a bit, sir," said Alleyn. "I must apologise for

bothering you, but I felt you would like to know the report of the post-mortem as soon as it came through."

Phillips went back to the door and shut it quietly. His face was turned away from his visitor as he spoke.

"Thank you. I shall be relieved to hear it."

"I'm afraid 'relieved' is scarcely the word."

"No?"

Phillips faced round slowly.

"No," said Alleyn. "They have found strongly marked traces of hyoscine in the organs. He must have had at least a quarter of a grain."

"A quarter of a grain!" He moved his eyebrows and his glass fell to the floor. He looked extraordinarily shocked and astonished. "Impossible!" he said sharply. He stooped and picked up his monocle.

"There has been no mistake," said Alleyn quietly.

Phillips glanced at him in silence.

"I beg your pardon, inspector," he said at last. "Of course, you have made certain of your facts, but— hyoscine—it's incredible."

"You understand that I shall be forced to make exhaustive inquiries."

"I—I suppose so."

"In a case of this sort the police feel more than usually helpless. We must delve into highly technical matters. I will be quite frank with you, Sir John. Sir Derek died of the effects of a lethal dose of hyoscine. Unless it can be proved that he took the drug himself, we are faced with a very serious situation. Naturally I shall have to go into the history of his operation. There are many questions which I should like to put to you. I need not remind you that you are under no compulsion to answer them."

Phillips took his time in replying to this. Then he said courteously:

"Of course, I quite understand. I shall be glad to tell you anything that will help—anxious to do so. I owe it to myself. O'Callaghan came here as my patient. I operated on him. Naturally I shall be one of the possible suspects."

"I hope we shall dispose of your claims to that position very early in the game. Now, first of all—Sir Derek O'Callaghan, as you told us at the inquest, had been given hyoscine."

"Certainly. One-hundredth of a grain was injected prior to the operation."

"Exactly. You approved of this injection, of course?"

"I gave it," said Phillips evenly.

"So you did. I'm afraid I know absolutely nothing about the properties of this drug. Is it always used in cases of peritonitis?"

"It had nothing to do with peritonitis. It is always my practice to give an injection of hyoscine before operating. It reduces the amount of anæsthetic necessary and the patient is more comfortable afterwards."

"It is much more generally used nowadays than, say, twenty years ago?"

"Oh, yes."

"Do you mind telling me just how, and at what stage of the proceedings, it is given? This was not stated specifically at the inquest, I think.

"It was given in the anæsthetising-room immediately before the operation and after the patient was under the anæsethetic. A hypodermic syringe was used."

"Prepared, I imagine, by the nurse in charge of the theatre?"

"In this instance, no. I thought this was all perfectly clear, inspector. I prepared the injection myself."

"Yes, of course—how stupid I am!" Alleyn exclaimed. "That makes it much simpler for me. What exactly did you do? Dip the syringe in a blue bottle and suck up a dram?"

"Not quite." Phillips smiled for the first time and

produced a cigarette-case. "Shall we sit down?" he said. "And will you smoke?"

"Do you mind if I have one of my own? Good cigarettes are wasted on me."

They sat on two incredibly uncomfortable chairs under the right elbow of the marble woman.

"As regards the actual solution," said Phillips, "I used a tablet of a hundredth of a grain. This I dissolved in twenty-five minims of distilled water. There was a stock solution of hyoscine in the theatre which I did not use."

"Less reliable or something?"

"It's no doubt perfectly reliable, but hyoscine is a drug that should be used with extreme care. By preparing it myself I am sure of the correct dosage. In most theatres nowadays it's put out in ampoules. I shall see," added Phillips grimly, "that this procedure is followed here in future."

"In this instance you went through the customary routine?"

"I did."

"Were you alone when you prepared the syringe?"

"There may have been a nurse in the theatre—I don't remember." He paused and then added: "Thoms came in just as I finished."

"Did he go out with you?"

"I really don't know. I rather think he returned to the anteroom a few moments later. I left him in the theatre. I went to the anæsthetic-room and gave the injection."

"Of course, you have no doubt in your own mind about the dosage?"

"I know quite well what you are thinking, Inspector Alleyn. It is a perfectly reasonable suspicion. I am absolutely assured that I dissolved one tablet and one tablet only. I filled the syringe with distilled water, squirted it into a measuring-glass, shook one tablet into my hand, saw that it *was* a single tablet, and dropped it into the glass."

Phillips leant back, looked steadily into Alleyn's eyes, and thrust his hands into his pockets. "I am prepared to swear to that," he said.

"It's perfectly clear, sir," said Alleyn, "and although I had to consider the possibility of a mistake, I realise that even if you had dropped two tablets into the water it would have only meant a dosage of a fiftieth of a grain. Probably the entire contents of the tube would not be a quarter of a grain—the amount estimated."

For the first time Phillips hesitated. "They are packed in tubes of twenty," he said at last, "so an entire tube would contain a fifth of a grain of hyoscine." He felt in his coat pocket and produced a hypodermic case which he handed to Alleyn.

"The actual tube is still in there. I have since used one tablet."

Alleyn opened the case and took out a glass tube completely covered by its paper label. He pulled out the tiny cork and looked in.

"May I?" he asked, and shook out the contents into his hand. There were eighteen tablets.

"That settles it," he said cheerfully. "Do you mind if I take these for analysis? Purely a matter of routine, as one says in crime fiction."

"Do," said Phillips, looking rather bored.

Alleyn took an envelop from his pocket, put the tablets back into the tube, the tube into the envelope, and the envelope into his pocket.

"Thank you so much," he said. "You've been extremely courteous. You've no idea how scared we are of experts at the Yard."

"Indeed?"

"Yes, indeed. This must have been a distressing business for you."

"Very."

"I believe Sir Derek was a personal friend."

"I knew him personally—yes."

"Had you seen much of him recently?"

Phillips did not answer immediately. Then, looking straight in front of him, he said: "What do you call recently?"

"Well—a fortnight or so."

"I called at his house on the Friday evening before the operation."

"A professional call?"

"No."

"Did you think he was heading for a serious illness then?"

"I did not know there was anything the matter with him."

"He did not mention a patent medicine?"

"No," said Phillips sharply. "What is this about patent medicines?"

"Merely a point that arises."

"If there is any question of his taking a drug," said Phillips more cordially, "it should be gone into most thoroughly."

"That is my view," Alleyn answered coolly.

"He may," Phillips went on, "have had an idiosyncrasy for hyoscine and if he had been taking it——"

"Exactly."

The two men seemed to have changed positions. It was the surgeon who now made the advances. Alleyn was polite and withdrawn.

"Is there any evidence that O'Callaghan had taken a patent medicine?"

"It's possible."

"Damn' fool!" ejaculated Phillips.

"Strange he didn't tell you he was ill on the Friday."

"He—I—we discussed another matter altogether."

"Would you care to tell me what it was?"

"It was purely personal."

"Sir John," said Alleyn mildly, "I think I should let you know at once that I have seen your letter to Sir Derek."

Phillips's head jerked up as though he had come suddenly face to face with a threatening obstacle. He did not speak for perhaps half a minute and then he said very softly:

"Do you enjoy reading other people's private correspondence?"

"About as much as you enjoy glaring into a septic abdomen, I should think," rejoined Alleyn. "It has a technical interest."

"I suppose you've spoken to the butler?"

"Would you like to give me your own explanation of the business?"

"No," said Phillips. "No."

"Speaking unofficially—a thing I am far too prone to do—I am extremely sorry for you, Sir John."

Phillips looked at him.

"Do you know, I think I believe you," he said. "Is there anything else?"

"No, I've kept you quite long enough. Would it be an awful bore for everyone if I had a word with the nurses who attended the case?"

"I don't think they can tell you very much further."

"Probably not, but I think I ought to see them unless they are all heavily engaged in operations."

"The theatre is not in use at the moment. The matron and the nurse who assists her—Nurse Banks—will be free."

"Splendid. What about Sir Derek's personal nurse and the other one from the theatre—Nurse Harden, wasn't it?"

"I will find out," said Phillips. "Do you mind waiting?"

"Not at all," murmured Alleyn with an involuntary glance at the marble woman. "May I see them one by one—it will be less violently embarrassing for all of us?"

"You do not impress me," rejoined Phillips, "as a person who suffers from shyness, but no doubt you would rather sleuth in secret. You shall see them one by one."

"Thank you."

Alleyn waited only a few minutes after Sir John left him and then the door reopened to admit Sister Marigold, in whose countenance gentility, curiosity and resentment were exquisitely reflected.

"How do you do, matron?" said Alleyn.

"Good afternoon," said Sister Marigold.

"Won't you sit down? Here? Or under the statue?"

"Thank you very much, I'm sure." She sat with a rustle, and eyed the inspector guardedly.

"Perhaps Sir John has told you the report on the post-mortem?" Alleyn suggested.

"It's terrible. Such a loss, as I say, to the country."

"Unthinkable. One of the really strong men in the right party," said Alleyn with low cunning.

"Just what I said when it happened."

"Now look here, matron, will you take mercy on a wretched ignorant policeman and help me out of the awful fog I'm wallowing in? Here's this man, perhaps the foremost statesman of his time, lying dead with a quarter of a grain of hyoscine inside him, and here am I, an abysmally incompetent layman, with the terrific task before me of finding out how it got there. What the devil am I to do about it, matron?"

He smiled very charmingly into her competent spectacles. Her very veil seemed to lose starch.

"Well, really," said Sister Marigold, "I'm sure it's all very trying for everybody."

"Exactly. You yourself must have had a great shock."

"Well, I did. Of course, in the ordinary way we

nurses become accustomed to the sad side of things.
People think us dreadfully hard-hearted sometimes."

"You won't get me to believe that. Of course, this
discovery——"

"That's what makes it so dreadful, Mr.—er—I
never could have believed it, never. Such a thing has
never happened in the whole of my experience. And for
it to be after an operation in my own theatre! Nobody
could have taken more care. Nothing went wrong."

"Now you've hit the nail right on the head!" exclaimed Alleyn, gazing at her as if she was a sort of
sibil. "I felt assured of that. You know as well as I do,
matron, that Sir Derek was a man with many bitter
enemies. I may tell you in confidence that at the Yard
we know where to look. We are in close touch with the
Secret Service"—he noted with satisfaction the glint of
intrigue in her eye—"and we are pretty sure how the
land lies. In our midst—in our very midst, matron—
are secret agents, secret societies, powers of evil known
to the Yard but unsuspected by the general public.
Mercifully so." He stopped short, folded his arms, and
wondered how much of this the woman would swallow.
Apparently the whole dose.

"Fancy!" breathed Sister Marigold. "Just fancy!"

"Well—that's the position," said Alleyn grandly,
throwing himself back in his chair. "But here's my difficulty. Before we can fire point-blank we've got to
clear away the other possibilities. Suppose we made an
arrest now—what would be the defense? An attempt
would be made to throw suspicion on innocent persons,
on the very people who fought to save Sir Derek's life,
on the surgeon who operated, and on his assistants."

"But that's terrible!"

"Nevertheless it is what would happen. Now to meet
that position I must have the actual history of Sir
Derek's operation, in all its details, at my fingers' ends.

That is why I have laid my cards on the table, matron, and that is why I have come to you."

Sister Marigold stared at him so long that he wondered nervously if he had been inartistic. However, when she did speak, it was with the greatest air of earnestness.

"I shall consider it my duty," she said, "to give you what help I can."

Alleyn thought it better not to shake hands with her. He merely said with quiet reverence:

"Thank you, matron, you have made a wise decision. Now to come down to tin tacks. I understand Sir John performed the operation, assisted by Mr. Thoms and with Dr. Roberts as anæsthetist. Sir John gave the hyoscine injection and prepared it himself."

"Yes. Sir John always does that. As I always say, he's so conscientious."

"Splendid, isn't it? And Mr. Thoms gave the anti-gas injection. Nurse Harden brought it to him, didn't she?"

"Yes, she did. Poor Harden, she was dreadfully upset. Sir Derek was a great friend of her own family, a very old Dorsetshire family, Mr.—er——"

"Really? Strange coincidence. She fainted afterwards, didn't she, poor girl?"

"Yes. But I assure you she did her work all through the op., quite as usual—really." Sister Marigold's voice trailed away doubtfully.

"Someone said something about a delay over the anti-gas injection."

"It was only for a moment. She told me afterwards she was so faint she had to pause before she brought it across."

"Yes, I see. Frightful bad luck. Nurse Banks gave the camphor injection, didn't she?"

"She did." Sister Marigold's thin lips closed in a whippy line.

"And prepared the serum?"

"That is so."

"I suppose I'll have to see her. Between you and me and the Marble Lady, matron, she rather alarms me."

"H'm" said Sister Marigold. "Really? Fancy!"

"Still, it *is* my duty and I *must*. Is she on the premises?"

"Nurse Banks is leaving us to-morrow. I believe she is in the hospital this afternoon."

"Leaving you, is she? Does she frighten you too, matron?"

Sister Marigold pursed up her lips.

"She is not a type I care to have nursing for me," she said. "As I say, personal feelings should not interfere with a nurse's work, much less political opinions."

"I *thought* she looked as if she was suffering from High Ideals," Alleyn remarked.

"Call them high ideals! Beastly Bolshevik nonsense," said Sister Marigold vigorously. "She had the impertinence to tell me, in my own theatre, that she would be glad if the patient——" She stopped short and looked extremely uncomfortable. "Not, of course, that she meant anything. Still, as I say——"

"Yes, quite. They'd say anything, some of these people. Of course with those views she'd loathe the very sight of O'Callaghan."

"How she dared!" fumed Sister Marigold.

"Tell me about it," said Alleyn winningly.

After a little hesitation she did.

CHAPTER IX

THREE NURSES

Tuesday, the sixteenth. Afternoon.

THE unbosoming of Sister Marigold was almost an epic. Once the floodgates of her wrath were opened the spate of disclosure flowed turbulently. Alleyn decided that in the Marigold's eye Banks was a murderess. Derek O'Callaghan's nurse had told Sister Marigold of Banks's triumph at the news of his death. The theatre scally had lost her head and told everybody. At first, prompted no doubt by her anxiety to stifle the breath of scandal in her hospital, Sister Marigold had determined to say as little as possible about the unspeakable Banks. Alleyn's hints that Phillips, his assistants, even she herself, would come under suspicion had evidently decided her to speak. She now said that Banks was obviously an agent of Sir Derek's political enemies. Alleyn let her talk and talk, and contrived to remain brilliantly non-committal. He discovered that she had an excellent memory and, by dint of careful questioning, he arrived at the procession of events during, and immediately before, the operation. It appeared that the only members of the party who had been alone in the theatre were Phillips, herself, Thoms, and possibly one of the nurses. Mr. Thoms, she thought, had come out of the theatre into the anteroom a few moments after Sir John had prepared his syringe. When she had told him everything two or three times over, Alleyn said that he was a brute to keep her so long and could he see the private nurse and the scally. He asked her not to mention the result of the post-mortem. The scally came first. She was alarmed and inclined to shy off his questions, but quietened down presently and stuck to her story of Banks's indecent rejoicing. She said Banks was always dinning Soviet teaching into the other nurses. She added nervously that Banks was a good nurse and would never forget her duty to a patient. She described the impedimenta that was put out on a side table before the operation—a full bottle of hyoscine solution, an ampoule of anti-gas serum, syringes, a bowl of distilled water. She was quite sure the bottle of hyoscine solution had been full. She believed that a small amount had since been used. She hadn't looked at it immediately after the operation. This tallied with information already given by the matron. The scally herself had put all the things away and had cleaned the outsides of all the jars carefully. Matron was so particular. "No use looking for prints on this job," thought Alleyn with a sigh. He thanked her and let her go.

Nurse Graham, O'Callaghan's special, was then sent into the room. She came in quietly, smiled at Alleyn and stood with her hands behind her back waiting. She had blue eyes, set far apart, a wide humorous mouth, slightly prominent teeth and a neat figure. She had an air of repose and efficiency which pleased the inspector.

"Do sit down, won't you?" Alleyn invited her. She sat down comfortably and didn't fidget.

"You nursed Sir Derek, didn't you?" he began.

"Yes."

"How long was it from the time he was admitted until the operation?"

"Nearly an hour, I think. He came in soon after I

went on duty at five o'clock. The operation was at a quarter to six."

"Yes. Look here, Nurse Graham, will you tell me the whole story of that hour as though you were writing it down in detail?"

She looked gravely at him for a moment or two.

"I'll try," she said at last. Alleyn took out a notebook and with an uneasy glance at it she began: "Soon after I came on duty a message came up that he was on his way and I was to 'special' him. I met the stretcher, put him to bed, and prepared him for operation."

"Did you give an injection of any sort?"

"No. The usual injection of morphia and atropine was not given. Sir John's injection of hyoscine took its place."

"I see. Well, nurse?"

"While that was being done Lady O'Callaghan and Sir Derek's sister arrived, and when the preparation was over they went into his room. He was semi-conscious. Am I doing this properly?"

"Admirably. Please go on."

"Well, let me think. I was in the room with them at first. Lady O'Callaghan was very good—quiet, and didn't upset the patient. Miss O'Callaghan was rather distressed. They sat down by the bed. I went out to speak to Sir John. When I came back they were talking together. Sir Derek was lying with his eyes closed, but he opened them for a moment and groaned. I think he was conscious just then and he seemed very uncomfortable. Lady O'Callaghan came out and spoke for a minute to Sir John. Then we all returned and Sir John made an examination. The patient seemed much easier, but I thought that now he was quite unconscious, more deeply so than he had been since he came in. Sir John diagnosed ruptured appendix abscess and offered to get Mr. Somerset Black to operate immediately. Lady O'Callaghan begged him to do it himself and he finally said he would. I took Lady O'Callaghan and Miss O'Callaghan out."

Nurse Graham paused and looked very earnestly at the inspector.

"Was there any further incident before they left the room?" Alleyn asked.

"You mean——? There was something else, but please, Inspector Alleyn, do not attach too much importance to it. The patient, I am sure, did not realise in the least what he said."

"What did he say?"

"He opened his eyes and said 'Don't—don't let——' and then relapsed again."

"Did you get any idea of what he was trying to say?"

"It might have been anything."

"At what was he looking?"

"He looked at Sir John, who was nearest the bed."

"How would you describe his look? Appealing? Entreating? What?"

"N-no. He—he seemed frightened. It might have been anything. He looked rather like a patient who had been given a drug—morphia, for instance. It's a kind of frowning stare—I have often noticed it appear when the drug is beginning to take effect."

"And yet you tell me he had not had anything of the sort."

"I gave him nothing," Nurse Graham said.

"There's a curious inflexion in your voice, nurse. *You* gave him nothing? Now of what are you thinking?"

She moved uneasily and her face became rather pink.

"I have said nothing about this to anybody," she told him. "It seemed to me a dangerous thing to speak of what was—was—not absolute fact."

"Quite right. Don't you think, though, that you should tell me? Nurse Graham, Sir Derek O'Callaghan was murdered." He watched her closely. She seemed both startled and shocked. She gave a quick look as if she hoped she had mistaken what he'd said. After a moment he went on:

"He was given a lethal dose of hyoscine. At least four people come under the possibility of suspicion. The very incident you are shying away from might be the one to save an innocent person. I am too old a hand to jump at asinine conclusions. Do you really think you can do any good by keeping me in the dark?"

"Perhaps not."

"Let me help you. You think, don't you, that someone had given O'Callaghan something—a drug of some sort?"

"It looked like it, and yet it was too soon for a drug to act."

"What happened when you returned to your patient? What did you find?"

"You are—very acute," she said. "When I went back I tidied the room. The patient seemed to be asleep. I lifted his eyelid and he was quite unconscious. The pupil was not contracted. I knew then that he could not have had morphia. Then I saw under a chair by the bed a small piece of white paper. I picked it up and noticed that it had broken pieces of sealing-wax on it. It was certainly not there when Sir Derek was admitted."

"Have you kept it?"

"I—yes, I have. I wondered then if he had been given anything, and when the room was done out I put the paper into a drawer in his dressing-table. It will still be there."

"I'll look at it later on if I may. Who had sat in the chair?"

"Miss O'Callaghan," she said uneasily.

"And Miss O'Callaghan was alone with the patient for—how long? Three minutes? Five minutes?"

"Quite five, I should think."

"Notice anything else? Had he had a drink of water, do you think?"

"The glass on the bedside-table had been used."

"You are a model witness. I suppose this glass has also been cleaned? Yes. A hospital is a poor hunting-ground for the likes of me. Now don't worry too much about this. It may be quite beside the point. In any case it would have been criminal to withhold it. Consciousness of having done the right thing brings, I understand, solace to the troubled breast."

"I can't say it does to mine."

"Nonsense. Now will you be very kind and get your scrap of paper for me? Bring Nurse Banks back with you, and don't mention homicide. By the way, what did you think about her reception of the glad tidings— I gather she looked upon them as glad?"

"She's an ass," answered Nurse Graham unexpectedly, "but she's no murderer."

"What did she say exactly?"

"Oh, something out of the Bible about praising the Lord for He hath cast down our enemies."

"Good lack!" apostrophised Alleyn. "What an old— I beg your pardon, nurse. Ask the lady to come here, will you? And if you hear me scream come in and rescue me. I've no desire to die at the feet of that marble goddess there—who is she, by the way— Anæsthesia?"

"I've no idea, inspector," said Nurse Graham with a sudden broad smile. She went out briskly and returned in a few minutes to give him a small square of white paper such as chemists use in wrapping up prescriptions. Fragments of red sealing-wax remained on the margins and the creases suggested that it had contained a round box. Alleyn put it in his pocketbook.

"Nurse Banks is waiting," remarked Nurse Graham.

"Loose her," said Alleyn. "Good-bye, nurse."

"Good-bye, inspector."

Miss Banks made a somewhat truculent entrance. She refused a chair and stood uncomfortably erect, just inside the door. Alleyn remained politely on his feet.

"Perhaps Nurse Graham has told you of my business here?" he suggested.

"She said something about Scotland Yard," sniffed Banks. "I didn't know what she was talking about."

"I am investigating the circumstances of Sir Derek O'Callaghan's death."

"I said all there was to say about it at that inquest."

Alleyn decided that finesse was not indicated.

"You didn't mention it was murder," he remarked.

For a moment he thought she looked frightened. Then she said woodenly:

"It is?"

"Yes. What do you think of that?"

"How do you know?"

"The post-mortem revealed indications of at least a quarter of a grain of hyoscine."

"A quarter of a grain!" exclaimed Banks. He was reminded of Phillips. Neither of these two had ejaculated "Hyoscine!" as one might have expected, but had exclaimed at the amount.

"Wouldn't you have expected that to kill him?" he asked.

"Oh, yes. Mr. Thoms said——" She stopped short.

"What did Mr. Thoms say?"

"Heard him say before the op. that a quarter-grain would be a fatal dose."

"How did the subject arise?"

"Don't remember."

"I understand you prepared and gave the camphor injection and prepared the anti-gas injection."

"Yes. I didn't put hyoscine in either if that's what you're thinking."

"No doubt there will be some means of proving

that," said Alleyn smoothly. "I shall have the matter investigated, of course."

"You'd better," snorted Banks.

"Sir John prepared and gave the hyoscine."

"Well, what if he did? Sir John Phillips wouldn't poison his worst enemy in the theatre. Too much the little surgeon."

"I'm glad you think so," said Alleyn mildly.

Banks was silent.

"I hear you look upon the affair as a dispensation of Providence," he added.

"I am an agnostic. I said 'if'."

" 'If'?"

"If I wasn't, I would."

"Oh," said Alleyn. "It's cryptic, but I get you. Can you tell me which members of the party were alone in the theatre before the operation?"

"No, I can't."

"Do try. Do you remember if you were?"

"No. Phillips was. Thoms was."

"When?"

"Just before they washed up. We were in the ante-room. Phillips came in first and that little fool followed him."

"Meaning Mr. Thoms?"

"I said so, didn't I?"

"Are you going to hear Nicholas Kakaroff speak to-night?"

This was a shot in the dark. Kakaroff was to address a large meeting of Soviet sympathisers. The Yard would think it worth while to put in an amiable appearance. Nurse Banks threw up her chin and glared at him.

"I shall be proud to be there," she said loudly.

"That's the spirit!" cried Alleyn.

Inspired perhaps by fiery recollections of former meetings, Nurse Banks suddenly came out strong with a speech.

"You may stand there with a smile on your lips," she stormed, "but you won't smile for long. I know your type—the gentleman policeman—the latest development of the capitalist system. You've got where you are by influence while better men do bigger work for a slave's pittance. You'll go, and all others like you, when the Dawn breaks. You think I killed Derek O'Callaghan. I didn't, but I'll tell you this much—I should be proud—proud, do you hear, if I had."

She reeled all this out with remarkable fluency, as though it was a preposterous recitation. Alleyn had a swift picture of her covering her friends' suburban tea-parties with exquisite confusion. Small wonder the other nurses fought shy of her.

"Do you know, nurse," he said, "until the Dawn does break I rather think I'd pipe down a bit if I were you. Unless you really fancy the martyr's crown, you're talking like a remarkably silly woman. You had as good a chance as anyone else of pumping hyoscine into the deceased. You're now shrieking your motive into my capitalist face. I'm not threatening you. No, you'd better not say anything more at the moment, but when the mantle of Mr. Kakaroff is laid aside you may think it advisable to make a statement. Until then, Nurse Banks, if you'll forgive me the suggestion, I should really pipe down. Will you tell Nurse Harden I'm ready?"

He opened the door for her. She stood for a moment staring above his head. Then she walked to the door, paused, and looked directly at him.

"I'll tell you this much," she said. "Neither Phillips nor Harden did it. Phillips is a conscientious surgeon and Harden is a conscientious nurse. They are hidebound by their professional code, both of them."

With which emphatic assertion she left him. Alleyn screwed his face sideways and opened his notebook.

Here, in an incredibly fine and upright hand he wrote: "Thoms—conversation about hyoscine," and after a moment's hesitation: "P. and H.—hidebound by their professional code, says the B."

He wrote busily, shut his little book, glanced up, and gave a start of surprise. Jane Harden had come in so quietly that he had not heard her. There she stood, her fingers twisted together, staring at the inspector. He had thought at the inquest that she was very good-looking. Now, with the white veil behind it, the extreme pallor of her face was less emphatic. She was beautiful, with that peculiar beauty that covers delicate bone. The contour of the forehead and cheek-bones, the little hollows of the temples, and the fine-drawn arches of the eyes had the quality of a Holbein drawing. The eyes themselves were a very dark grey, the nose absolutely straight and the mouth, rather too small, with dropping corners, was at once sensuous and obstinate.

"I beg your pardon," said Alleyn; "I did not hear you come in. Please sit down."

He pulled forward the nearest of the preposterous chairs, turning it towards the window. The afternoon had darkened and a chilly sort of gloom masked the ceiling and corners of the room. Jane Harden sat down and clasped the knobs of the chair-arms with long fingers that even the exigencies of nursing had not reddened.

"I expect you know why I'm here?" said Alleyn.

"What was the—is the post-mortem finished?" She spoke quite evenly, but with a kind of breathlessness.

"Yes. He was murdered. Hyoscine."

She seemed to stiffen and became uncannily still.

"So the hunt is up," added Alleyn calmly.

"Hyoscine," she whispered. "Hyoscine. How much?"

"At least a quarter of a grain. Sir John injected a hundredth, he tells me. Therefore someone else gave the patient a little more than a fifth of a grain—six twenty-fifths, to be exact. It may have been more, of course. I don't know if the post-mortem can be relied upon to account for every particle."

"I don't know either," said Jane.

"There are one or two questions I must ask you."

"Yes?"

"I'm afraid this is all very distressing for you. You knew Sir Derek personally, I believe?"

"Yes."

"I'm terribly sorry to have to bother you. Let's get it over as soon as possible. As regards the anti-gas injection. At the close of the operation Sir John or Mr. Thoms asked for it. Sister Marigold told you to get it. You went to a side table, where you found the syringe. Was it ready—prepared for use?"

"Yes."

"At the inquest it appeared that you delayed a little while. Why was this?"

"There were two syringes. I felt faint and could not think, for a moment, which was the right one. Then Banks said: 'The large syringe,' and I brought it."

"You did not hesitate because you thought there might be something wrong with the large syringe?"

This suggestion seemed to startle her very much. She moved her hands nervously and gave a soft exclamation.

"Oh! No. No—— Why should I think that?"

"Nurse Banks prepared this syringe, didn't she?"

"Yes," said Jane.

Alleyn was silent for a minute. He got up and walked across to the window. From where she sat his profile looked black, like a silhouette with blurred edges. He stared out at the darkening roofs. Something about a movement of his shoulders suggested a kind of distaste. He shoved his hands down into his trouser pockets and swung round, facing the room. He looked shadowy, but larger than life against the yellowish window-pane.

"How well did you know Sir Derek?" he asked suddenly. His voice sounded oddly flat in the thickly furnished room.

"Quite well," she said after another pause.

"Intimately?"

"I don't know what you mean."

"Well—did you meet often—as friends, shall I say?"

She stared at his darkened face. Her own, lit by the sallow light from the window, looked thin and secret.

"Sometimes."

"Recently?"

"No. I can't see what my acquaintanceship with him has to do with the matter."

"Why did you faint?"

"I was—I wasn't well; I'm run down."

"It had nothing to do with the identity of the patient? It wasn't because Sir Derek was so ill?"

"Naturally that distressed me."

"Have you ever written to him?"

She seemed to shrink back into the chair as though he had actually hurt her.

"You need not answer any of these questions if you think it better not to," he announced. "Still, I shall, of course, go to other people for the information."

"*I* have done nothing to hurt *him*," she said loudly.

"No. But have you ever written to him? That was my question, you know."

She took a long time to answer this. At last she murmured: "Oh, yes."

"How often?"

"I don't know——"

"Recently?"

"Fairly recently."

"Threatening letters?"

She moved her head from side to side as though the increasing dusk held a menace.

"No," said Jane.

He saw now that she loked at him with terror in her eyes. It was a glance to which he had become accustomed, but, since in his way he was a sensitive man, never quite reconciled.

"I think it would be better," he pronounced slowly, "if you told me the whole story. There is no need, is there, for me to tell you that you are one of the people whom I must take into consideration? Your presence in the operating theatre brings you into the picture. Naturally I want an explanation."

"I should have thought my—distress—would have given you that," she whispered, and in that half-light he saw her pallor change to a painful red. "You see, I loved him," added Jane.

"I think I understand that part of it," he said abruptly. "I am extremely sorry that these beastly circumstances oblige me to pry into such very painful matters. Try to think of me as a sort of automaton, unpleasant but quite impersonal. Can you do that, do you think?"

"I suppose I must try."

"Thank you. First of all—was there anything beyond ordinary friendship between you and O'Callaghan?"

She made a slight movement.

"Not——" She paused and then said: "Not really."

"Were you going to say 'Not now'? I think there had been. You say you wrote to him. Perhaps your letters terminated a phase of your friendship?"

She seemed to consider this and then answered uneasily: "The second did."

He thought: "Two letters. I wonder what happened to the other?"

Aloud, he said: "Now, as I understand it, you had known Sir Derek for some time—an old family friendship. Recently this friendship changed to a more intimate association. When was this?"

"Last June—three months ago."

"And it went on—for how long?"

Her hands moved to her face. As if ashamed of this pitiful gesture she snatched them away, and raising her voice, said clearly: "Three days."

"I see," said Alleyn gently. "Was that the last time you saw him?"

"Yes—until the operation."

"Had there been any quarrel?"

"No."

"None?"

"No." She tilted her head back and began to speak rapidly.

"It was a mutual agreement. People make such a fuss about sex. It's only a normal physical experience, like hunger or thirst. The sensible thing is to satisfy it in a perfectly reasonable and natural way. That's what we did. There was no need to meet again. We had our experience."

"My poor child!" Alleyn ejaculated.

"What do you mean!"

"You reel it all off as if you'd learnt it out of a textbook. 'First Steps in Sex.' 'O Brave New World,' as Miranda and Mr. Huxley would say! And it didn't work out according to the receipt?"

"Yes, it did."

"Then why did you write those letters?"

Her mouth opened. She looked pitifully ludicrous and, for a moment, not at all pretty.

"You've seen them—you've——"

"I'm afraid so," said Alleyn.

She gave a curious dry sob and put her hands up to the neck of her uniform as though it choked her.

"You see," Alleyn continued, "it would be better to tell me the truth, really it would."

She began to weep very bitterly.

"I can't help it. I'm sorry. It's been so awful—I can't help it."

Alleyn swung round to the light again.

"It's all right," he said to the window-pane. "Don't mind about me—only an automaton, remember."

She seemed to pull herself together quickly. He heard a stifled sob or two and a rustle as if she had made a violent movement of some sort.

"Better," she murmured presently. When he turned back to the room she was sitting there, staring at him, as though there had been no break in their conversation.

"There's not much more," he began—very business-like and pleasant. "Nobody accuses you of anything. I simply want to check up on the operation. You did not see Sir Derek from June until he was brought into the theatre. Very well. Beyond these two letters you did not communicate with him in any way whatever? All right. Now the only place where you step into the picture is where you fetched the syringe containing the anti-gas concoction. You delayed. You were faint. You are positive you brought the right syringe?"

"Oh, yes. It was much bigger than the others."

"Good enough. I'll look at it presently if I may. Now I understand that the jar, bottle, or pot containing the serum——"

"It was an ampoule," said Jane.

"So it was—and the pipkin, cruse, or pottle contain-ing hyoscine were on the table. Could you, feeling all faint and bothered, have possibly sucked up hyoscine by mistake?"

"But, don't you understand, it was ready!" she said impatiently.

"So I am told, but I've got to make sure, you know. You are positive, for instance, that you didn't squirt out the contents and refill the syringe?"

"Of course—positive." She spoke with more assurance and less agitation than he had expected.

"You remember getting the syringe? You were not so groggy that you did it more or less blindly?"

That seemed to get home. She looked frightened again.

"I—I was very faint, but I *know*—oh, I *know* I made no mistake."

"Right. Anyone watch you?"

He watched her himself, closely. The light was now very dim, but her face was still lit from the window behind him.

"They—may—have. I didn't notice."

"I understand Mr. Thoms complained of the delay. Perhaps he turned to see what you were doing?"

"He's always watching—— I beg your pardon; that's got nothing to do with it."

"What were you going to say?"

"Only that Mr. Thoms has rather an offensive trick of staring."

"Did you happen to notice, before the operation, how much of the hyoscine solution there was in the bottle?"

She thought for some time.

"I think it was full," she said.

"Has it been used since?"

"Once, I believe."

"Good."

He moved away from the window briskly, found the light switch and snapped it down. Jane rose to her feet. Her hands shook and her face was a little marked with tears.

"That's all," said Alleyn brightly. "Cheer up, Nurse Harden."

"I'll try."

She hesitated a moment after he had opened the door, looked as if she wanted to say something further, but finally, without another word, left the room.

After she had gone Alleyn stood stockstill and stared at the opposite wall.

At last, catching sight of himself in an ornate mirror, he made a wry face at his own reflection.

"Oh, damn the doings," said Alleyn.

CHAPTER X

THOMS IN THE THEATRE

Tuesday, the sixteenth. Afternoon.

IT *was* Mr. Thoms who took Alleyn into the theatre.
After Jane left him the inspector had wandered into the
hall and run into the plump little surgeon. Alleyn had
explained who he was, and Thoms instantly assumed an
expression of intense seriousness that made him look
rather like a clown pulling a mock-tragic face.

"I say!" he exclaimed. "You're not here about Sir
Derek O'Callaghan's business, are you?"

"That's it, Mr. Thoms," Alleyn rejoined wearily.
"The man was murdered."

Thoms began to babble excitedly. Alleyn held up a
long hand.

"Hyoscine. At least a quarter of a grain. Wilful
murder," he said briefly.

"Lor'!" ejaculated Thoms.

"Lor' it is. I've been badgering nurses and now I
want to see the theatre of operations. It never struck
me till just then what a localised implication that
phrase has."

"See the theatre?" said Thoms. "Yes. Of course.
Look here. It's not in use now. Sir John's gone out.
I'll show you round if you like."

"Thank you so much," said Alleyn.

Thoms talked excitedly as he led the way. "It's the most amazing thing I ever heard. Damn' nasty business, too. I hope to God you don't think I pumped hyoscine into the man. Thought you police chaps must have something up your sleeves when you pushed the inquest. Yes. Well, here we are. This is an anteroom to the theatre, where we wash and dress ourselves up for the business. Along there's the anæsthetising-room. Here's the theatre."

He butted open the swing-doors.

"Wait a bit," said Alleyn. "Let's get a sort of picture of the proceedings, may we? Before the operation you and the other medical men forgathered in here."

"That's it. Sir John and I came in here together. Dr. Roberts came in for a moment and then went off to the anæsthetising-room, where the patient was brought to him."

"Anyone else in here during that time?"

"With Phillips and me, you mean? Oh, yes—the matron, Sister Marigold, you know. She does theatre sister. It's only a small hospital, and she rather fancies herself at the job, does old Marigold. Then, let me see, the other two nurses were dodging about. Thingummy, the Bolshie one, and that pretty girl that did a faint—Harden."

"What did you all talk about?"

"*Talk* about?" echoed Thoms. He had a curious trick of gaping at the simplest question as though much taken aback. His eyes popped and his mouth fell open. He then gave a short and, to Alleyn, tiresome guffaw.

"What did we *talk* about?" he repeated.

"Well, let's see. Oh, I asked Sir John if he had seen the show at the Palladium this week and——" He stopped short and again his eyes bolted.

"Well—what about it?" asked Alleyn patiently.

"He said he hadn't," said Thoms. He looked ridiculously uncomfortable, as though he had nearly said something frightfully improper.

"I missed the Palladium this week," Alleyn remarked. "It's particularly good, I hear."

"Oh," Thoms mumbled, "not bad. Rather rot really." He seemed extraordinarily embarrassed.

"And had Sir John seen the show?" asked Alleyn lightly.

"Er—no, no, he hadn't."

"Did you discuss any particular part of it?"

"No. Only mentioned the show—nothing particular."

There was a long pause during which Thoms whistled under his breath.

"During this time," said Alleyn as last, "was any one member of the theatre party alone?"

"In here?"

"In here."

"Let me think," begged Thoms. Alleyn let him think. "No—no. As far as I remember, we were all here. Then one of the nurses showed Roberts to the anæsthetising-room. That left Sir John and the other two nurses and myself. I went with Marigold into the theatre to look round. That left Sir John and the other nurse—the pretty one—in this room. They were here when I got back. Then Roberts and I washed up while Sir John went into the theatre to fix his hyoscine injection. He always does that and gives it himself. Rum idea. We usually leave all that game to the anæsthetist. Of course, in this instance everything had been very hurried. The patient had not been given the usual morphia and atro-pine injection. Well, let's see. The females were dodging about, I suppose. I remember the—what's-her-name— the Banks woman asked me why Sir John didn't use the stock solution."

"Why didn't he?"

"Oh—well, because he wanted to be sure of the dosage, I suppose."

"And then?"

"I went into the theatre."

"Where you joined Phillips?"

"Yes. He'd just put the hyoscine tablet into the water, I think."

"Did you notice the little bottle—how many tablets were left? I simply want to check up, you understand."

"Of course. Well, it's a tube; you can't see the number of tablets unless you peer into it, and then you can only guess, but, of course, there would be nineteen, because it was a new lot."

"How do you know that, Mr. Thoms?"

"Well, as a matter of fact, I saw he had two tubes and said something about it, and he said one of them was empty, so he'd opened another."

"What happened to the empty one?"

"Eh? Search me. Chucked it away, I suppose. I say —er—look here, what *is* your name?"

"Alleyn."

"Oh. Well, look here, Alleyn, you're not attaching any importance to the second tube, are you? Because you jolly well needn't. It's all perfectly simple. Phillips uses a hypodermic case which holds two of these little phials. He'd obviously used the last tablet on a previous case without realising it was the last. Very easy thing to do."

"I see that. All this business is merely by way of checking up."

"Yes, but——"

"For my own sake I've got to account for every movement of the game, Mr. Thoms. It's all frightfully muddling and I've got to try to learn it like a lesson. Do you remember anything that was said just then?"

"Well, I—well, I chaffed him about the two tubes— said he was doing Sir Derek proud, and then I—I remarked that he used a lot of water."

"Did this seem to upset him at all?"

"Oh, Lord—no. I mean, Sir John always stands a bit on his dignity. I mean, he rather shut me up. He hasn't got what I call a sense of humour."

"Really? Did you go out together?"

"Yes. I went into the anteroom and Sir John into the anæsthetic-room to give the injection. I went first."

"Sure, Mr. Thoms?"

"Oh, yes," said Thoms, opening his eyes very wide. "Why?"

"I only want to get the order of events. Now let's look at the theatre, shall we?"

Once again Thoms butted the swing-doors with his compact little stern, and this time Inspector Alleyn followed him through.

The theatre was scrupulously, monstrously immaculate—a place of tiles and chromium and white enamel. Thoms turned on a switch and for a moment an enormous high-powered cluster of lights poured down its truncated conical glare on the blank surface of the table. The theatre instantly became alive and expectant. He snapped it off and in its stead an insignificant wall bracket came to life over a side table on rubber castors.

"Is this how it was for the operation?" asked Alleyn. "Everything in its right place?"

"Er—yes, I think so. Yes."

"Which way did the patient lie?"

"Head here. Eastward position, eh? Ha ha!"

"I see. There would be a trolley alongside the table, perhaps?"

"It would be wheeled away as soon as the patient was taken off it."

"That's the side table, over by the windows, where the syringes were set out?"

"That's it."

"Can you show me just where you all stood at the time each of the injections was given? Wait a bit—I'll make a sort of plan. My memory's hopeless. Damn, where's my pencil?"

Alleyn opened his notebook and produced a small rule from his pocket. He measured the floor space, made a tiny plan and marked the positions of the two tables, and, as Thoms instructed him, those of the surgeons and nurses.

"Sir John would be here, about half-way along the table, isn't it? I stood opposite there. Marigold hovered round here, and the other two moved about a bit."

"Yes. Well, where, as near as you can give it, would they all be for the operation?"

"The surgeons and anæsthetist where I have shown you. Marigold on Sir John's right and the other two somewhere in the background."

"And for the camphor injection?"

"As before, except for the Bolshie, who gave it. She would be here, by the patient's arm, you see."

"Did you watch Nurse Banks give this injection?"

"Don't think so. I wouldn't notice. Probably wouldn't see her hands—they'd be hidden by the little screen across the patient's chest."

"Oh. I'll take a look at that afterwards if I may. Now the anti-gas injection."

"That was after Sir John had sewed him up. I dressed the wound and asked for the serum. I damned that girl to heaps for keeping me waiting—felt rather a brute when she hit the floor two minutes later—what? I stood here, on the inside of the table; Sir John was opposite; Marigold had moved round to my side. Roberts and Banks, if that's her name, were fussing round over the patient, and Roberts kept bleating about the pulse and so on. They were both at the patient's head."

"Wait a bit. I'll fix those positions. Perhaps I'll get you to help me to reconstruct the operation later on. You have no doubts, I suppose, about it being the correct syringe—the one you used, I mean?"

"None. It seemed to be perfectly in order."

"Was there any marked change in the patient's condition after this injection?"

"Roberts is the man to ask about that. My own idea is that he was worried about the patient for some time before I gave the injection. He asked for camphor, remember. Naturally, you'll think, I want to stress that point. Well, inspector, so I do. I suppose the serum injection is the dangerous corner as far as I'm concerned. Still, I did *not* prepare the syringe and I could hardly palm it and produce another from behind my left ear. Could I? What? Ha ha ha!"

"Let's have a look at it," said Alleyn imperturbably, "and we'll see."

Thoms went to one of the shelves and returned with a syringe at the sight of which the inspector gave a little shout of horror.

"Good God, Mr. Thoms, are you a horse-coper? You don't mean to tell me you jabbed that horror into the poor man? It's the size of a fire extinguisher!"

Thoms stared at him and then roared with laughter. "He didn't feel it. Oh, yes, we plugged it into him. Well, now, I could hardly produce a thing like that by sleight of hand, could I?"

"Heavens, no! Put it away, do; it makes me feel quite sick. A disgusting, an indecent, a revolting implement."

Thoms made a playful pass at the inspector, who seized the syringe and bore it away. He examined it, uttering little noises of disgust.

"This is the type used for the other two injections," explained Thoms, who had been peering into the array of instruments. He showed Alleyn a hypodermic syringe of the sort familiar to the layman.

"Sufficiently alarming, but not so preposterous. This would be the kind of thing Dr. Roberts handled?"

"Yes—or rather, no. Roberts didn't give the camphor injection. The nurse gave it."

"Oh, yes. Is that usual?"

"It's quite in order. Generally speaking, that injection is given by the anæsthetist, but there's nothing in his asking the nurse to give it."

"This needle's a delicate-looking thing. I suppose you never carry a syringe about ready for use?"

"Lord, no! In the theatre, of course, they are laid out all complete."

"Would you mind filling this one for me?"

He gave Thoms a small syringe. The surgeon poured some water into a measuring-glass, inserted the needle and pulled back the piston.

"There you are. If a tablet's used, the usual procedure is to squirt the syringe half full into the glass, dissolve the tablet, and then draw it up again."

"The whole business only takes a few seconds?"

"Well—the tablet has to dissolve. In the case of the serum and the camphor the stuff was there ready."

"Yes, I've got that. May I see the bottle the serum is kept in?"

"It's not kept in a bottle, but in ampoules which hold the exact amount and are then thrown away. There aren't any kicking about in the theatre. I'll beat some up for you to see if you like."

"Very good of you, Mr. Thoms. I'm being a crashing bore, I'm afraid."

Thoms protested his freedom from boredom and fussed away. Alleyn prowled meditatively round the theatre until the fat man returned.

"Here we are," said Thoms cheerfully. "Here are ampoules of oil and camphor. Here's the antigas serum and here's the hyoscine solution. All labelled, as you see. Tell you what I'll do. I'll set out the table as it would have been for the op. How will that do you?"

"Splendid!"

"Let's see now—ampoules here, serum there. Here's the bottle of hyoscine solution; thought you'd want to see that too. Old-fashioned idea—it should be in ampoules, but matron's a bit of a dug-out."

"The bottle's nearly full, I see."

"Yes. I believe one injection had been given."

Alleyn noted mentally that this tallied with Nurse Harden's and the scally's impression that the bottle had been full before the operation and had since been used once.

"Can anyone have access to this bottle?" asked Alleyn suddenly.

"What? Oh, yes—any of the theatre staff."

"May I have a small amount—I may have to get it tested?"

He produced a tiny bottle from his pocket and Thoms, looking rather intrigued, filled it with the solution.

"There you are. Now—where were we? Oh! Along here, small syringe for the camphor, another small syringe for the hyoscine—they hold twenty-five minims each. That would be the one Sir John would use for his tablet. Now the whopper for the serum. It holds ten c.c.'s."

"Ten c.c.'s?"

"That's about a hundred and sixty minims," explained Thoms.

"What's that in gallons?"

Thoms looked at the inspector as if he had uttered something in Chinese and then burst out laughing.

"Not quite as solid at that," he said. "One hundred and sixty minims is equal to two and two-thirds drachms. That any better?"

"Not much," grumbled Alleyn. "The dawn may break later on. I'm talking like Nurse Banks. What's the strength of this hyoscine?"

"Quarter per cent."

"But—what does that mean? They'll have to get someone cleverer than me for this game."

"Cheer up. It's one grain in one point one ounces of water."

"That sounds as though it means something. I must look up those horrid little things at the end of an arithmetic-book. Wait a moment, now. Don't say a word, Mr. Thoms, if you please," begged Alleyn. "I'm doing sums."

He screwed up his face and did complicated things with his fingers. "Twenty-fives into ones, you can't. No, anyway you don't want to. Drat. Wait a bit." He opened his eyes suddenly and began to speak rapidly. "The twenty-five-minim syringe could hold a twentieth of a grain of hyoscine, and the vet's pump could hold eleven thirty-seconds of a grain. There!" he added proudly.

"Quite correct—good for you!" shouted Thoms, clapping the inspector on the back.

"There's more to come. I can do better than that. Eleven thirty-seconds is three thirty-seconds more than a quarter, which is only eight thirty-seconds. How's that?"

"Brilliant, but I don't see the application?"

"Don't you?" asked Alleyn anxiously. "And yet I know I thought it rather important a moment ago. Ah, well—it's gone now. I'll just write the others down."

Mr. Thoms moved to his elbow and looked curiously at his tiny hieroglyphics.

"I can't see," complained Alleyn and walked over to the light.

Mr. Thoms did not follow and so did not see the last of his minute entries, which read:

"The large syringe could hold a little over the amount found at the P.M."

He shut his little book tenderly and put it in his pocket.

"Thank you a thousand times, Mr. Thoms," he said. "You've made it very easy for me. Now there's only one more person I've got to see to-day and that's Dr. Roberts. Can you tell me where I'll find him?"

"Well, he's not the usual anæsthetist here, you know. He does a lot of Dr. Grey's work for him. Hasn't been in since this affair. I should think at this time you'd find him at his private address. I'll ring up his house if you like."

"That's very good of you. Where does he live?"

"Not sure. His name's Theodore. I know that because I heard Grey calling him Dora. Dora!" Mr. Thoms laughed extensively and led the way to a black hole with a telephone inside it.

He switched on a light and consulted the directory.

"Here we are. Roberts, Roberts, Roberts. Dr. Theodore. Wigmore Street. That's your man."

He dialled the number. Alleyn leant patiently against the door.

"Hullo. Dr. Robert's house? Is he in? Ask him if he can see Inspector——" He paused and put his hand over the receiver. "Alleyn, isn't it? Yes—ask him if he can see Inspector Alleyn if he comes along now."

Thoms turned towards Alleyn. "He's in—that'll be all right, I expect. Hullo, is that you, Roberts? It's Thoms here. Inspector Alleyn has just been over the O'Callaghan business with me. They've found hyoscine —quarter of a grain. That makes you sit up. What? I don't know. Yes, of course it is. Well, don't get all agitated. They're not going to arrest you. Ha ha ha! What! All right—in about twenty minutes, I should think. Look out, my boy—don't give yourself away— what!"

He hung up, and taking Alleyn by the elbow, walked with him to the front door.

"Poor old Roberts is in an awful hum about it, spluttering away down the telephone like I don't know what. Well, let me know if there's anything more I can do."

"I will indeed. Thank you so much. Good night."

"Good night. Got a pair of handcuffs for Roberts? Ha ha ha!"

"Ha ha ha!" said Alleyn. "Good night."

CHAPTER XI

THE ANÆSTHETIST

Tuesday, the sixteenth. Afternoon and evening.

DR. ROBERTS lived in a nice little house in Wigmore Street. It was a narrow house with two windows on the first floor, and on the street level was a large vermilion frond door that occupied a fair proportion of the wall.

A man-servant, small and cheerful to suit the house, showed Alleyn into a pleasant drawing-room-study with apple-green walls and bookshelves, glazed chintz curtains, · and comfortable chairs. Above the fireplace hung an excellent painting of lots of little people skating on a lake surrounded by Christmas trees. A wood fire crackled on the hearth. On a table near the bookcase was a sheaf of manuscript weighted down by the old wooden stethoscope that Mr. Thoms had found so funny.

After an appreciative glance ·at the picture, Alleyn walked over to the bookcase, where he found a beguiling collection of modern novels, a Variorum Shakespeare that aroused his envy, and a number of works on heredity, eugenics and psycho-analysis. Among these was a respectable-looking volume entitled *Debased Currency,* by Theodore Roberts. Alleyn took it out and looked at the contents. They proved to be a series of papers on hereditary taints. Roberts evidently had read them at meetings of the International Congress on Eugenics and Sex Reform.

Alleyn was still absorbed in this evidence of Roberts's industry when the author himself came in.

"Inspector Alleyn, I believe," said Roberts.

With a slight effort Alleyn refrained from answering "Dr. Roberts, I presume." He closed the bok over his thumb and came forward to meet the anæsthetist. Roberts blinked apprehensively and then glanced at the volume in the inspector's hand.

"Yes, Dr. Roberts," said Alleyn, "you've caught me red-handed. I never can resist plucking from book-shelves and I was so interested to see that you yourself wrote."

"Oh," answered Roberts vaguely, "the subject interests me. Will you sit down, inspector?"

"Thank you. Yes, the problems of heredity have an extraordinary fascination, even for a layman like myself. However, I haven't come here to air my ignorance of your country, but to try and fill out some of the blanks in my own. About this O'Callaghan business——"

"I am extremely sorry to hear of the result of the autopsy," said Roberts formally. "It is terribly distressing, shocking, an irreplaceable loss." He moved his hands nervously, gulped, and then added hurriedly: "I am also exceedingly distressed for more personal reasons. As anæsthetist for the operation I feel that I may be held responsible, that perhaps I should have noticed earlier that all was not well. I *was* worried, almost from the start, about his condition. I said so to Sir John and to Thoms."

"What did they answer?"

"Sir John was very properly concerned with his own work. He simply left me to deal with mine, after, I think, commenting in some way on my report. I do not remember that Thoms replied at all. Inspector Alleyn, I sincerely hope you are able to free Sir John from any possibility of the slightest breath of suspicion. Any doubt in that direction is quite unthinkable."

"I hope to be able to clear up his part in the business as soon as the usual inquiries have been, made. Perhaps you can help me there, Dr. Roberts?"

"I should be glad to do so. I will not attempt to deny that I am also very selfishly nervous on my own account."

"You gave no injection, did you?"

"No. I am thankful to say, no."

"How was that? I should have imagined the anæsthetist would have given the camphor and the hyoscine injections."

Roberts did not speak for a moment, but sat gazing at Alleyn with a curiously helpless expression on his sensitive face. Alleyn noticed that whenever he spoke to Roberts the doctor seemed to suppress a sort of wince. He did this now, tightening his lips and drawing himself rigidly upright in his chair.

"I—I never give injections," he said. "I have a personal and very painful reason for not doing so."

"Would you care to tell me what it is? You see, the fact that you did not give an injection is very important from your point of view. You did not see the patient while he was conscious and so—to be frank—could hardly have poured hyoscine down his throat without someone noticing what you were up to."

"Yes. I see. I will tell you. Many years ago I gave an overdose of morphia and the patient died as the result of my carelessness. I—I have never been able to bring myself to give an injection since. Psychologically my behaviour has been weak and unsound. I should have overcome this repulsion, but I have been unable to do so. For some time I even lost my nerve as an anæsthetist. Then I was called in for an urgent case with heart disease and the operation was successful." He showed Alleyn his stethoscope and told him its history. "This instrument represents an interesting experiment in psychology. I began to mark on it all my successful cases of heart disease. It helped enormously, but I have never been able to face an injection. Perhaps some day I may. Sir John is aware of this—peculiarity. I told him of it the first time I gave an anæsthetic for him. It was some time ago in a private house. He very thoughtfully remembered. I believe that in any case he prefers to give the hyoscine injection himself."

He turned very white as he made this unhappy confession, and it was curious to see how, in spite of his obvious distress, he did not lose his trick of formal phraseology.

"Thank you so much, Dr. Roberts," said Alleyn gently. "We need not trouble any more about that. Now, you say you were worried almost from the start about Sir Derek's condition. Would you describe this condition as consistent with hyoscine poisoning?"

"Ever since Thoms rang up I have been considering that point. Yes, I think I should. In the light of the autopsy, of course, one is tempted to correlate the two without further consideration."

"Did you notice any definite change in the patient's condition, or did the same symptoms simply get more and more acute, if that's the right way of putting it?"

"The pulse was remarkably slow when I first examined him in the anæsthetising-room. The condition grew steadily more disquieting throughout the operation."

"But, to stress my point, there was no decided change at any time, only a more or less gradual progression."

"Yes. There was perhaps a rather marked increase in the symptoms after Sir John made the first incision."

"That would be after he had given the hyoscine injection, wouldn't it?"

Roberts glanced at him sharply.

"Yes, that is true," he said quickly, "but do you not

see, the small amount Sir John injected—a hundredth
of a grain, I think it was—would naturally aggravate
the condition if hyoscine had already been given?"

"That's perfectly true," agreed Alleyn. "It's an important point, too. Look here, Dr. Roberts, may I take
it that it's your opinion that hyoscine—a fatal amount—
was somehow or other got into the man before the
operation?"

"I think so," Roberts blinked nervously. He had
that trick of blinking hard, twice—it reminded Alleyn
of a highly strung boy. "Of course," he added uneasily,
"I realise, inspector, that it would probably be to my
advantage if I said that I thought the lethal dose was
given when the patient was on the table. That, however,
is, in my opinion, most improbable."

"I must here trot out my customary cliché that it is
always to an innocent person's advantage to tell the
truth," Alleyn assured him. "Do you know, it's my
opinion that at least two-thirds of the difficulties in
homicidal cases are caused by innocent asses lying for
all they're worth."

"Indeed? I suppose there is no possibility of suicide
in this instance?"

"It seems very unlikely so far. Why? How? Where's
the motive?"

"There need not necessarily be any usual motive."
Roberts hesitated and then spoke with more assurance
than he had shown so far. "In suggesting this," he said,
"I may be accused of mounting my special hobbyhorse. As you have seen, I am greatly interested in
hereditary taints. In Sir Derek O'Callaghan's family
there is such a taint. In his father, Sir Blake O'Callaghan, it appeared. I believe he suffered at times from
suicidal mania. There has been a great deal of injudici-
ous inbreeding. Mark you, I am perfectly well aware
that the usual whole-hearted condemnation of inbreeding is to be revised in the light——"

He had lost all his nervousness. He lectured Alleyn roundly for ten minutes, getting highly excited. He quoted his own works and other authorities. He scolded the British public, in the person of one of their most distinguished policemen, for their criminal neglect of racial problems. Alleyn listened, meek and greatly interested. He asked questions. Roberts got books from his shelves, read long passages in a high-pitched voice, and left the volumes on the hearthrug. He told Alleyn he should pay more attention to such things, and finally, to the inspector's secret amusement, asked him flatly if he knew, if he had taken the trouble to find out, whether he himself was free from all traces of hereditary insanity.

"I had a great-aunt who left all her money to a muffin-man with coloured blood," said Alleyn. "She was undoubtedly bats. Otherwise I have nothing to tell you, Dr. Roberts."

Roberts listened to this gravely and continued his harangue. By the time it was over Alleyn felt that he had heard most of the theories propounded at the International Congress on Sex Reform and then some more. They were interrupted by the man-servant, who came in to announce dinner.

"Inspector Alleyn will dine," said Roberts impatiently.

"No—really," said Alleyn. "Thank you so much, but I must go. I'd love to, but I can't." The man went out.

"Why not?" asked Roberts rather huffily.

"Because I've got a murder to solve."

"Oh," he said, rather nonplussed and vexed. Then as this remark sank in, his former manner returned to him. He eyed Alleyn nervously, blinked, and got to his feet.

"I am sorry. I become somewhat absorbed when my pet subject is under discussion."

"I too have been absorbed," Alleyn told him. "You must forgive me for staying so long. I may have to reconstruct the operation—perhaps if I do you will be very kind and help me by coming along?"

"I—yes, if it is necessary. It will be very distasteful."

"I know. It may not be necessary, but if it is———"

"I shall do my part, certainly."

"Right. I must bolt. This has been an unpropitious sort of introduction, Dr. Roberts, but I hope I may be allowed to renew our talk without prejudice some time. The average bloke's ignorance of racial problems is deplorable."

"It's worse than that," said Roberts crisply. "It's lamentable—criminal. I should have thought in your profession it was essential to understand at least the rudiments of the hereditary problem. How can you expect———" He scolded on for some time. The servant looked in, cast up his eyes in pious resignation and waited. Roberts gave Alleyn his book. "It's the soundest popular work on the subject, though I do not pretend to cover a fraction of the ground. You'd better come back here when you've read it."

"I will. Thank you a thousand times," murmured the inspector and made for the door. He waited until the servant had gone into the hall and then turned back.

"Look here," he said quietly. "Can I take it you think the man committed suicide?"

Again Roberts turned into a rather frightened little man.

"I can't say—I—I sincerely hope so. In view of his history, I think it's quite possible—but, of course, the drug—hyoscine—it's very unusual." He stopped and seemed to think deeply for a moment. Then he gave Alleyn a very earnest and somehow pathetic look. "I hope very much indeed that it may be found to be suicide," he said quietly. "The alternative is quite unthinkable. It would cast the most terrible slur conceivable upon a profession of which I am an insignificant unit, but which I deeply revere. I would hold myself in part responsible. Self-interest is at the bottom of most motives, they say, but something more than self-interest, I think, prompts me to beg most earnestly that you explore the possibility of suicide to its utmost limit. I have kept you too long. Good night, Inspector Alleyn."

"Good night, Dr. Roberts."

Alleyn walked slowly down Wigmore Street. He reflected that in some ways his last interview had been one of the oddest in his experience. What a curious little man! There had been no affectation in that scientific outburst. The inspector could recognise genuine enthusiasm when he met it. Roberts was in a blue funk over the O'Callaghan business, yet the mere mention of his pet subject could drive any feeling of personal danger clean out of his head. "He's very worried about something, though," thought Alleyn, "and it rather looks as thought it's Phillips. Phillips! Damn. I want my Boswell. Also, I want my dinner."

He walked to Frascati's and dined alone, staring so fixedly at the tablecloth that his waiter grew quite nervous about it. Then he rang up Fox and gave him certain instructions, after which he took a taxi to Chester Terrace to call on his Boswell.

"And I suppose the young ass will be out," thought Alleyn bitterly.

But Nigel Bathgate was at home. When the front door opened Alleyn heard the brisk patter of a typewriter. He walked sedately upstairs, pushed open the sitting-room door and looked in. There was Nigel, seated bloomily at his machine, with a pile of copy-paper in a basket beside it.

"Hullo, Bathgate," said Alleyn. "Busy?"

Nigel jumped, turned in his chair, and then grinned.

"You!" he said happily. "I'm glad to see you, inspector. Take a pew."

He pushed forward a comfortable chair and clapped down a cigarette-box on the broad arm. The telephone rang Nigel cursed and answered it. "Hullo!" A beatific change came over him. "Good evening, darling." Alleyn smiled. "Who do you imagine I've got here? An old friend of yours. Inspector Alleyn. Yes. Why not hop into a taxi and pay us a visit? You will? Splendid. He's probably in difficulties and wants our help. Yes. Right." He hung up the receiver and turned, beaming, to Alleyn.

"It's Angela," he said. Miss Angela North was Nigel's betrothed.

"So I imagined," remarked the inspector. "I shall be delighted to see the minx again."

"She's thrilled at the prospect herself," Nigel declared. He made up the fire, glanced anxiously at his desk and made an effort to tidy it.

"I've just been writing you up," he informed Alleyn.

"What the devil do you mean? What have I got to do with your perverted rag?"

"We're hard up for a story and you've got a certain news value, you know. 'The case is in the hands of Chief Detective-Inspector Roderick Alleyn, the most famous crime expert of the C.I.D. Inspector Alleyn is confident——' Are you confident, by the way?"

"Change it to 'inscrutable.' When I'm boxed I fall back on inscrutability."

"Are you boxed?" asked Nigel. "That, of course, is why you've come to me. What can I do for you, inspector?"

"You can take that inordinately conceited look off your face and compose it into its customary mould of startled incredulity. I want to talk and I can think of no one who would really like to listen to me. Possibly you yourself are too busy?"

"I've finished, but wait until Angela comes."

"Is she to be trusted? All right, all right."

Nigel spent the next ten minutes telling Alleyn how deeply Miss Angela North was to be trusted. He was still in full swing when the young woman herself arrived. She greeted Alleyn as an old friend, lit a cigarette, sat on the hearth, and said:

"Now—what have you both been talking about?"

"Bathgate has talked about you, Miss Angela. I have not talked."

"But you will. You were going to, and I can guess what about. Pretend I'm not here."

"Can Bathgate manage that?"

"He'll have to."

"I won't look at her," said Nigel.

"You'd better not," said Angela. "Please begin, Inspector Alleyn."

"Speak!" said Nigel.

"I will. List, list, oh list."

"I will."

"Don't keep interrupting. I am engaged on a murder case in which the victim is not a relation of yours, nor yet, as far as I know, is the murderer your friend. In view of our past experiences, this is very striking[1] and remarkable."

"Come off the rocks. I suppose you mean the O'Callaghan business?"

"I do. The man was murdered. At least three persons assisting at his operation had sufficient motive. Two of them had actually threatened him. No, that is not for publication. No, don't argue. I'll let you know when it is. I have reached that stage in the proceedings when, like heroines in French dramas, I must have my confidante. You are she. You may occasionally roll up your eyes and exclaim 'Hélas, quelle horreur!' or, if you prefer it, 'Merciful Heaven, can I believe my ears?'

---

[1] See *Enter a Murderer* and *A Man Lay Dead.*

Otherwise, beyond making sympathetic noises, don't interrupt."

"Right ho."

Alleyn smiled amiably at him.

"You're a patient cove, Bathgate, and I get much too facetious. It's an infirmity—a disease. I do it when I'm bothered and this is a bothering case. Here's the cast of characters, and, look here, the whole conversation is confidential."

"Oh murder!" said Nigel. This was a favourite ejaculation of his. "It hurts, but again—— Right you are."

"Thank you. As you know, O'Callaghan either took or was given an overdose of hyoscine. At least a quarter of a grain. He never recovered consciousness after his operation. As far as the experts can tell us, the stuff must have been given within the four-hours preceding his death, but I'm not fully informed on that point. Now—dramatis personæ. You'll know most of them from the inquest. Wife—the ice-maiden type. Knew her husband occasionally kicked over the traces. Too proud to fight. Urged inquest. Sister—rum to a degree and I think has gone goofy on a chemist who supplied her with patent medicines. Urged patent medicines on brother Derek on bedder-sickness in hospital prior to operation. Now very jumpy and nervous. Private secretary—one of the new young men. Semi-diplomatic aroma. All charm and engaging manners. Friend of Mr. Bathgate, so may be murderer. Name, Ronald Jameson. Any comment?"

"Young Ronald? Gosh, yes. I'd forgotten he'd nailed that job. You've described him. He's all right, really."

"I can't bear the little creature," said Angela vigorously. "Sorry!" she added hurriedly.

"Surgeon—Sir John Phillips. Distinguished gent. Friend of victim till victim took his girl away for a week-end and then dropped her. Severed friendship. Visited victim and scolded him. In hearing of butler

expressed burning desire to kill victim. Wrote letter to
same effect. Subsequently operated on victim, who then
died. That makes you blanch, I see. Injected hyoscine
which he prepared himself. Very unusual in surgeons,
but he always does it. No real proof he didn't give overdose. No proof he did. Assistant surgeon—Thoms.
Comedian. Solemn warning to Inspector Alleyn not to
be facetious. Injected serum with thing like a pump.
Was in the theatre alone before operation, but said he
wasn't. This may be forgetfulness. Could have doctored
serum-pump, but no known reason why he should.
Anæsthetist—Dr. Roberts. Funny little man. Writes
books about heredity and will talk on same for hours.
Good taste in books, pictures and house decoration.
Nervous. Very scared when murder is mentioned. In
past killed patient with overdose of morphia, so won't
give any injections now. Matron of hospital—Sister
Marigold. Genteel. Horrified. Could have doctored
serum, but imagination boggles at thought. First theatre
nurse—Banks, a Bolshie. Expressed delight at death of
O'Callaghan, whom she considered enemy of proletariat.
Attends meetings held by militant Communists who had
threatened O'Callaghan. Gave camphor injection. Second theatre nurse—Jane Harden. Girl friend mentioned
above. Spent weekend with deceased and cut up rough
when he ended affair. Brought anti-gas syringe to
Thoms. Delayed over it. Subsequently fainted. You may
well look startled. It's a rich field, isn't it?"

"Is that all—not that it isn't enough?"

"There's his special nurse. A nice sensible girl who
could easily have given him poison. She found out
about Miss O'Callaghan handing out the patent medicine."

"Perhaps she lied."

"Oh, do you think so? Surely not."

"Don't be facetious," said Nigel.

"Thank you, Bathgate. No, but I don't think Nurse

Graham lied. Jane Harden did, over her letters. Well, there they all are. Have one of your celebrated lucky dips and see if you can spot the winner."

"For a win," Nigel pronounced at last, "the special nurse. For a place the funny little man."

"Why?"

"On, the crime-fiction line of reasoning. The two outsiders. The nurse looks very fishy. And funny little men are rather a favourite line in villains nowadays. He might turn out to be Sir Derek's illegitimate brother and that's why he's so interested in heredity. I'm thinking of writing detective fiction."

"You should do well at it."

"Of course," said Nigel slowly, "there's the other school in which the obvious man is always the murderer. That's the one you favour at the Yard, isn't it?"

"Yes, I suppose it is," agreed Alleyn.

"Do you read crime fiction?"

"I dote on it. It's such a relief to escape from one's work into an entirely different atmosphere."

"It's not as bad as that," Nigel protested.

"Perhaps not quite as bad as that. Any faithful account of police investigations, in even the most spectacular homicide case, would be abysmally dull. I should have thought you'd seen enough of the game to realise that. The files are a plethora of drab details, most of them entirely irrelevant. Your crime novelist gets over all that by writing grandly about routine work and then selecting the essentials. Quite rightly. He'd be the world's worst bore if he did otherwise."

"May I speak?" inquired Angela.

"Do," said Alleyn.

"I'm afraid I guess it's Sir John Phillips."

"I've heard you say yourself that the obvious man is usually the ace," ruminated Nigel after a pause.

"Yes. Usually," said Alleyn.

"I suppose, in this case, the obvious man *is* Phillips."

"That's what old Fox will say," conceded Alleyn with a curious reluctance.

"I suppose it's hopeless to ask, but have you made up your mind yet, inspector?"

Alleyn got up, walked to the fireplace, and then swung round and stared at his friend.

"I regret to say," he said, "that I haven't the foggiest notion who killed Cock Robin."

CHAPTER XII

THE LENIN HALL LOT

Tuesday, the sixteenth. Night.

"Of course," said Angela suddenly, "it may be the matron. I always suspect gentily. Or, of course——" She stopped.

"Yes?" asked Alleyn. "There's still some of the field left."

"I knew you'd say that. But I *do* mistrust people who laugh too much."

Alleyn glanced at her sharply.

"Do you? I must moderate my mirth. Well, there's the case, and I'm glad to have taken it out and aired it. Shall we go to the Palladium?"

"Why?" asked Nigel, astonished.

"There's a sketch on the programme that I am anxious to see. Will you both come? We'll only miss the first two numbers."

"We'd love to," said Angela. "Are you up to one of your tricks?" she added suspiciously.

"I don't know what you mean, Miss Angela. Bathgate, will you ring up for seats?"

They went to the Palladium and enjoyed themselves. Mr. Thoms's sketch was the third number in the second half. It had not run three minutes before Nigel and Angela turned and stared owlishly at the inspector.

The sketch was well cast and the actor who played the surgeon was particularly clever. Alleyn sensed a strange feeling of alertness in the audience. Here and there people murmured together. Behind them a man's voice asked: "Wonder if Sir John Phillips goes to the Palladium?" "Ssh," whispered a woman.

"The great British public twitching its nose." thought Alleyn distastefully. The sketch drew to a close. The surgeon came back from the operating theatre, realistically bloody. A long-drawn "Ooooo" from the audience. He pulled off his mask, stood and stared at his gloved hands. He shuddered. A nurse entered up-stage. He turned to face her: "Well, nurse?" "He's gone." The surgeon walked across to a practical basin and began to wash his hands as a drop curtain, emblazoned with an enormous question-mark, was drawn down like a blind over the scene.

"So that's why we came?" said Angela, and remained very quiet until the end of the show.

They had supper at Alleyn's flat, where Angela was made a fuss of by Vassily.

"Curious coincidence, that little play, didn't you think?" asked Alleyn.

"Very rum," agreed Nigel. "When did you hear about it?"

"Thoms told me that he and Phillips discussed it before the operation. Thoms seemed so anxious not to talk about it I thought it might be worth seeing. I can't help wondering if he meant to convey precisely that suggestion."

"Had Sir John seen it?" inquired Angela.

"No. Thoms told him about it?"

"I say," said Nigel. "Do you think that could have given Phillips the big idea?"

"It might be that."

"Or it might be—something quite different," added Angela, watching him.

"I congratulate you, Miss Angela," said Alleyn.

"Did Mr. Thoms tell you quite frankly about their conversation?"

"No, child, he didn't. He flustered like an old hen."

"And what did you deduce from that?" asked Angela innocently.

"Perhaps he was afraid of incriminating his distinguished colleague and senior."

"Oh," she said flatly. "What's he like in other ways?"

"Besides being a bit of a buffoon? Well, I should say either rather forgetful or a bit of a liar. He says he came out of the theatre with Phillips after the latter had prepared the hyoscine injection. Phillips, matron and Banks say he didn't."

"Oh," said Angela, "they do, do they."

"I haven't the least idea what you're driving at, Angela," complained Nigel. "I should like to hear more about the funny little man. Didn't he behave at all queerly?"

"He behaved very queerly indeed," said Alleyn. "He was as scary as a rabbit whenever the murder was mentioned. He's obviously very frightened whenever he thinks of it. And yet I don't think his alarm is purely selfish. He said it was, I believe. Thoms, in that asinine way of his, made very merry over Roberts's alarm when he rang up."

Alleyn looked steadily at Angela.

"Roberts is the man, depend upon it," pronounced Nigel. "I'll back him with you for a quid."

"I won't," said Angela. "I'll back——"

"I'm afraid the official conscience won't allow me to join in this cold-bloomed gamble," said Alleyn. He looked at them both curiously. "The attitude of the intelligent layman is very rum," he observed.

"I lay you two to one the field, bar Roberts, Angela," said Nigel.

"Done," said Angela. "In guineas," she added grandly. "And what were you saying, inspector?"

"I was only reflecting. Does the decision rest with the judge?"

"What do you mean?"

"Well—if it does, you are betting on a man or woman who, if you're right, will presumably be hanged. I can't imagine you doing this over any other form of death. That's what I mean about the attitude of the layman."

Angela turned red.

"That's the second time in our acquaintanceship you've made me feel a pig," she said. "The first was because I was too sensitive. The bet's off, Nigel."

"You can be pretty cold-blooded yourself, Alleyn," said Nigel indignantly.

"Oh, yes," said Alleyn, "but I'm an official."

"Anyway," argued Angela, "I was betting on Dr. Roberts's innocence."

"So you were."

"And, anyway," said Nigel, "I think he did it."

"How?"

"Er—well—somehow. With an injection."

"He gave no injections."

"Who *could* have done it?" asked Angela. "I mean who had the opportunity?"

"Phillips, who prepared and gave an injection. The special, who was alone with the patient. Ruth, ditto. Banks, who prepared and gave an injection. Thoms gave an injection, but did not prepare it. He was alone in the theatre for a few minutes if Phillips and the matron are telling the truth. He used the big syringe, and as he quite frankly pointed out, he could hardly have palmed another. Jane Harden had time to empty it and refill with hyoscine."

"Which of them do you say were alone in the theatre before the operation?"

"All the nurses, Thoms and Phillips had the chance to be there, I suppose."

"Not Roberts?" asked Nigel.

"I think not. He went straight to the anæsthetic-room, where he was joined by the special with the patient."

"Bad luck, darling," said Angela. "It really looks as though he's the only man who couldn't have murdered Sir Derek."

"Then he's a certainty," declared Nigel. "Isn't it true that when there's a cast-iron alibi the police always prick up their ears?"

"Personally, I let mine flop with a thankful purr," said Alleyn. "But you may be right. This is scarcely an alibi. Roberts was there; he merely had no hypodermic to give and no syringe to use."

"And no motive," added Angela.

"Look for the motive," said Nigel.

"I will," said Alleyn. "There's precious little else to look for. Has it occurred to you, if the lethal injection *was* given during the operation, how extraordinarily favourable the *mise en scène* was for the murderer? As soon as a patient is wheeled away they set to work, and as far as I can see, they literally scour out the theatre. Nothing is left—everything is washed, sterilised, polished. The syringes—the dishes—the instruments—the floor—the tables. Even the ampoules that held the injections are cast into outer darkness. If you wanted to think of a perfect place to get rid of your tracks, you couldn't choose a likelier spot." He got up and looked at his watch.

"He wants us to go," remarked Angela calmly.

"It's only eleven o'clock," murmured Alleyn. "I wondered if you'd both care to do a job of work for me?"

"What sort of job?" they asked.

"Attend a Bolshevik meeting at midnight."

"To-night?"

"To-night."

"I'd adore to," said Angela quickly. "Where is it? What's the time? What do we do?"

"It'll be a bit of copy for you, Bathgate," said Alleyn. "Mr. Nicholas Kakaroff, agent of a certain advanced section of Soviet propagandists, is holding a meeting at Lenin Hall, Saltarrow Street, Blackfriars. Lenin Hall is a converted warehouse. Mr. Kakaroff is a converted minor official, originally from Krakov. I feel sure Kakaroff is a made-up name. 'Kakaroff of Krakov'—it's too good to be really true, don't you feel? There's an air of unreality about his whole gang. As far as we know, they are not officially recognised by Russia or any other self-respecting country. Your genuine Soviet citizen is an honest-to-God sort of chap in his own way, once you get past his prejudices. But these fellows are grotesques—illegitimate offsprings of the I.W.W. You'll see. Nurse Banks attends the meeting. So do we. Myself disguised and feeling silly. Banks might penetrate my disguise, which would not be in the great tradition, so you sit next to her and get her confidence. You have been given your tickets by one Mr. Marcus Barker, who will not be there. He's an English sympathiser at present in custody for selling prohibited literature. He has a bookshop in Long Acre. Don't talk about him; you'd get into a mess if you did. I want you to pump the lady. You are enthusiastic converts. Let her hear that from your conversation together and leave it to her to make friends. If you can do it artistically, rejoice over O'Callaghan's death. Now wait a moment—I want to ring Fox up. Here, read this pamphlet and see if you can get down some of the line of chat."

He looked in his desk, produced a pamphlet bound in a vermillion folder, entitled "The Soviet Movement in Britain, by Marcus Barker." Angela and Nigel sat side by side and began to read it.

Alleyn rang up Fox, who was at the Yard.

"Hullo, Brer Fox. Any news?"

"Hullo, sir. Well, I don't know that I've got any thing much for you. Inspector Boys checked up on that heredity business. It seems to be quite O.K. Sir Derek's father was what you might call a bit wanting, very queer old gentleman he seems to have been. There's a great-uncle who fancied he was related to the Royal Family and did himself in a very peculiar manner with a hedger's knife, and a great-aunt who started some religious affair and had to be shut up over it. She was always undressing herself, it seems."

"Really? What about Ruth?"

"Well, as soon as you rang off, I called at Miss O'Callaghan's house to inspect the hot-water cistern and I had a cup of tea with the cook and the housemaid. They were both rather talkative ladies and full of *l'affaire O'Callaghan*," said Fox with one of his excursions into French. "They like Miss O'Callaghan all right, but they think she's a bit eccentric. It seems she was very much attached to her brother and it seems she's very thick with this chemist affair—Mr. Harold Sage. It seems he visits her a great deal. The housemaid gave it as her opinion that they were courting. Miss O'Callaghan takes a lot of his medicines."

"Say it with soda-mints? Anything more?"

"One useful bit of information, sir. Mr. Sage is a Communist."

"The devil he is! Bless me, Fox, that's a plum. Sure?"

"Oh, yes—quite certain, I should say. He's always leaving his literatur about. Cook showed me a pamphlet. One of the Marcus Marker lot, it was."

Alleyn glanced through the study door at Nigel and Angela sitting very close together, their heads bent over the vermilion leaflet.

"Did you gather if Miss O'Callaghan sympathised with these views?" he asked.

At the other end of the telephone Fox blew his nose thoughtfully.

"Well, no; it seems not. Nina, that's the housemaid, said she thought the lady was trying to influence him the other way. She gave it as her opinion that Sir Derek would have had a fit if he'd known what was going on."

"Highly probable. You've done a good bit of work there, Fox. What a success you are with the ladies!"

"I'm more at home below-stairs," said Fox simply, "and the cook was a very nice sort of woman. Is that all, sir?"

"Unless you've any more gossip. See you later."

"That's right, sir. *Aw revoir*."

"Bung-oh, you old devil."

Alleyn returned to the study and repeated the gist of Fox's information. "See if you can hear anything of this Sage who is Miss O'Callaghan's soul-mate," he said. "He may be there to-night. Bathgate, I'm just going to change. Won't be five minutes. Ask Vassily to call a taxi and give yourself a drink."

He vanished into his tiny dressing-room, where they heard him whistling very sweetly in a high key.

"Darling," said Nigel, "this is like old times. You and I on the warpath."

"I won't have you getting into trouble," said Angela. "You did last time, you know."

"That was because I was so much in love I couldn't think."

"Indeed? And I suppose that no longer applies?"

"Do you? Do you?"

"Nigel—darling, this is no moment for dalliance."

"Yes, it is."

Alleyn's whistling drifted into the silent room. "Hey, Robin, jolly Robin, tell me how thy lady does," whistled the inspector. In a very short time he was back again, incredibly changed by a dirty chin, a very ill-cut shoddy suit, a cheap-smart overcoat, a cap, a dreadful scarf, and pointed shoes. His hair was combed forward under the cap.

"Oh!" exclaimed Angela, "I can't bear it—you always look so frightfully well turned out and handsome."

To Nigel's amusement Inspector Alleyn turned red in the face, and for the first time in their acquaintance seemed at a loss for an answer.

"Has no one ever told you you are handsome, inspector?" pursued Angela innocently.

"Fox raves over me," said Alleyn. "What are you standing there for Bathgate, with that silly grin on your face? Have you ordered the taxi? Have you had a drink?"

Nigel had done neither of these things. However, this was soon remedied and in a couple of minutes they were in a taxi, heading for the Embankment.

"We'll walk the last part of the way," said Alleyn. "Here are your tickets. We got these three with a good deal of difficulty. The brethren are becoming rather exclusive. Now do be careful. Remember *The Times* criticised me for employing Bright Young People in the Frantock case. Repeat your lesson."

They did this, interrupting each other a good deal, but giving the gist of his instructions.

"Right. Now it's only eleven-twenty. We're early, but there will be plenty of people there already. With any luck I'll spot Banks and you may get near her. If not, drift in her direction afterwards. I'll be near the door. As you come out brush up against me, and if you've been shown the Sage, point him out to each other so that I can hear you. See? Good. Here's where we get out, for fear of seeming proud."

He stopped the taxi. They were still down by the river. The air felt chilly and dank, but exciting. The river, busy with its night traffic, had an air of being apart and profoundly absorbed. There were the wet black shadows, broken lights, and the dark, hurried flow of the Thames towards the sea. London's water-world was about its nightly business. The roar of the streets became unimportant and remote down here, within sound of shipping sirens and the cold lap of deep water against stone.

Alleyn hurried them along the Embankment for a short way and then turned off somewhere near Black-friars Underground Station. They went up a little dark street that resembled a perspective in a woodcut. A single street lamp, haloed in mist, gave accent to shadows as black as printer's ink. Beyond the lamp a flight of stone steps led dramatically downwards. They followed these steps, came out in a narrow alley, took several more turns and fetched up at last by an iron stairway.

"Up you go," said Alleyn. "We've arrived."

The stairs ended in an iron landing which rang cold-ly under their feet. Here, by a closed door, stood a solitary man, who struck his hands together and blew on his fingers. Alleyn showed him his ticket, which he inspected by the light of an electric torch. Nigel and Angela followed. The man flashed his torch on their faces, a disconcerting business.

"New, aren't you?" he said to Nigel.

"Yes," said Angela quickly, "and terribly excited. Will it be a good meeting?"

"Should be," he answered, and opened the door behind him. They went through and found themselves in a narrow passage lit by a solitary globe at the far end. Under this lamp stood another man, who watched them steadily as they came towards him. Angela took Nigel's arm.

" 'Evening," said Alleyn.

" 'Evening, comrade," said the man self-consciously. "You're early to-night."

"That's right. Many here?"

"Not many yet. Show your tickets, please." He turned to the others. "You newcomers?"

"Yes," said Nigel.

"I'll have to take your names, comrades."

"That's new," remarked Alleyn.

"Instructions from headquarters. We've got to be more careful."

"Just as well. I'm bringing Miss Northgate and Mr. Batherston. Friends of Comrade Marcus Barker." He spelt the names while the man wrote them down. "They come from Clearminster-Storton, Dorset, and are both right-minded."

"Anything doing in your part of the world?" asked the man.

"Gosh, no!" said Nigel. "All landed gentry, bourgeoisie and wage-slaves."

"Bone from the eyes up," added Angela perkily.

The man laughed loudly.

"You've said it! Just sign these cards, will you?"

With an effort they remembered their new names and wrote them at the foot of two pieces of pasteboard that seemed to be inscribed with some sort of profession of secrecy. Angela felt rather guilty. While they did this someone came in at the outside door and walked along the passage. The man took their cards, pulled open the door and turned to the newcomer. Led by Alleyn, they all walked through the door, which immediately was shut behind them.

They found themselves in a large room that still looked like a warehouse. Six office lamps with china shades hung from the ceiling. The walls were unpapered plaster in bad condition. A few Soviet propagandist posters, excellent in design, had been pasted on the walls. The Russian characters looked strange and out of place. At the far end a rough platform had been run up. On the wall behind it was an enlarged photograph of Lenin draped in a grubby festoon of scarlet muslin. There were some thirty people in the room. They stood about in small groups, talking quietly together. One or two had seated themselves among the chairs and benches that faced the platform. Nigel, who prided himself on this sort of thing, tried to place some of them. He thought he detected a possible newsagent, two undergraduates, three Government school teachers, compositors, shopkeepers, a writing bloke or two, and several nondescripts who might be anything from artists to itinerant hawkers. There were one or two women of the student type, but as Alleyn made no sign, Nigel concluded that none of these was Nurse Banks. Evidently the inspector had been to former meetings. He went up to a middle-aged, vehement-looking man with no teeth, who greeted him gloomily and in a little while began to talk very excitedly about the shortcomings of someone called Sage. "He's got no guts," he repeated angrily, "no guts at all."

More people came in at intervals; a few looked like manual labourers, but the majority seemed to belong to that class abhorred of Communists, the bourgeoisie. Nigel and Angela saw Alleyn point them both out to his gloomy friend, who stared morosely at them for a moment and then burst into an offensive guffaw. Presently Alleyn rejoined them.

"My friend has just come in," he said quietly. "She's that tall woman in a red hat."

They looked towards the door and saw the tall woman. Her face, as well as her hat, was red, and was garnished with pince-nez and an expression of general truculence. Banks was a formidable out of uniform as she was in it, Alleyn reflected. She glanced round the room and then marched firmly towards the second row of chairs.

"Off you go," murmured Alleyn. "Remember, you come from O'Callaghan's county, but are not of it."

They walked down the centre aisle and seated themselves alongside Nurse Banks.

She produced an uncompromising mass of wool, grey in colour, and began to knit.

"Don't you feel ever so excited, Claude?" asked Angela loudly in a very second-rate voice.

Nigel suppressed a slight start and checked an indignant glance.

"It's a wonderful experience, Pippin," he replied.

He felt Angela quiver.

"I wish I knew who everyone was," she said. "We're so out of touch. These are the people who are really getting things done and we don't know their names. If only Mr. Barker had been here."

"Ye gods, it makes me wild!" apostrophised Nigel. "And they call this a free country. Free!"

Angela, who was next to Banks, dared not look at her. Banks's needles clicked resolutely.

"Do you think," ventured Angela after a pause, "do you think we could ever make any headway down in the dear old village?"

"The dear old village, so quaint and old-world," gibed Nigel. "So typically English, don't you know. No, I don't. The only headway you could make there would be with a charge of dynamite. God, I'd like to see it done!"

"They'll all be in heavy mourning now, of course."

"Yes—for Sir Derek Bloody O'Callaghan."

They both laughed uproariously and then Angela said: "Ssh—be careful," and glanced apprehensively at Banks. She was smiling.

"I wonder if he's here yet?" whispered Angela.

"Who?"

"Kakaroff."

"There's someone going on to the platform now."

"Claude! Can it be he?"

This exclamation sounded so incredible that she

instantly regretted it and was infinitely relieved to hear Miss Banks remark in a firm baritone:

"Comrade Kakaroff isn't here yet. That's Comrade Robinson."

"Thanks ever so," said Angela brightly. "We're strangers ourselves and don't know anybody, but we're terribly keen."

Banks smiled.

"You see," continued Angela, "we come from the backwoods of Dorset, where everything died about the time Anne did."

"The counties," said Banks, "are moribund, but in the North there are signs of rebirth."

"That's right!" ejaculated Nigel fervently. "I believe it will come from the North."

"I hope you were not very shocked at what my gentleman-friend said just now about O'Callaghan?" Angela ventured.

"Shocked!" said Banks. "Scarcely!" She laughed shortly.

"Because, you see we come from the same place as his family and we're about fed to the back teeth with the mere name. It's absolutely feudal—you can't imagine."

"And every election time," said Nigel, "they all trot along like good little kids and vote for dear Sir Derek once again."

"They won't do that any more."

The other seats in their row filled up with a party of people engaged in an earnest and rather blood-thirsty conversation. They paid no attention to anyone but themselves. Nigel continued the approach of Banks.

"What did you think about the inquest?" he asked blandly.

She turned her head slowly and looked at him.

"I don't know," she said. "What did you?"

"I thought it was rather peculiar myself. Looks as if

the police know something. Whoever had the guts to fix
O'Callaghan I reckon was a national hero. I don't care
who knows it, either," said Nigel defiantly.

"You're right," cried Banks, "you're right. You can't
heal a dog-bite without a cautery." She produced this
professional analogy so slickly that Nigel guessed it was
a standardised argument. "All the same," added Banks
with a slight change of voice, "I don't believe anyone
could, if they would, claim the honour of striking this
blow for freedom. It was an accident—a glorious
accident."

Her hands trembled and the knitting-needles chat-
tered together. Her eyes were wide open and the pupils
dilated.

"Why, she's demented," thought Angela in alarm.

"Hyoscine," murmured Nigel. "Wasn't that the
drug Crippen used?"

"I believe it was," said Angela. "Isn't that the same
as Twilight Sleep?"

She paused hopefully. Banks made no answer. A
young man came and sat in front of them. He looked
intelligent and would have been rather a handsome
fellow if his blond curls had been shorter and his teeth
less aggressively false.

"I don't know," said Nigel; "I'm no chemist. Oh!
Talking of chemists, we must see if we can find that
chap Harold Sage here. I'd like to meet him."

"Well, it's so difficult. They never said what he was
like. Perhaps—er——" Angela turned towards Miss
Banks. "Perhaps you could help us. There's a gentleman here who knows a friend of ours." She wondered
if this was risky. "His name's Harold Sage. He's a
chemist, and we thought if we could see him——"

The young man with the blond curls turned round
and flashed a golden smile at her.

"Pardon," he fluted throatily. "That won't be very
difficult. May neem's Hawrold Seege."

CHAPTER XIII

SURPRISING ANTICS OF A CHEMIST

Tuesday to Wednesday. The small hours.

To say that Nigel and Angela were flabbergasted by this announcement is to give not the slightest indication of their derangement. Their mouths fell open and their eyes protruded. Their stomachs, as the saying is, turned over. Mr. Sage continued the while to smile falsely upon them. It seemed as if they took at least three minutes to recover. Actually about five seconds elapsed before Angela, in a small voice that she did not recognise, said:

"Oh—fancy! What fun!"

"Oh," echoed Nigel, "fancy! What luck! Yes."

"Yes," said Angela.

"I thought I heard someone taking my name in vain," continued Mr. Sage playfully. It would be tedious to attempt a phonetic reproduction of Mr. Sage's utterances. Enough to say that they were genteel to a fantastic degree. "Aye thot Aye heeard somewon teeking may neem in veen," may give some idea of his rendering of the above sentence. Let it go at that.

"I was just going to make you known to each other," said Nurse Banks. So great was their dilemma they had actually forgotten Nurse Banks.

Mr. Sage cast a peculiar reluctant glance upon her

and then turned to his quarry. "And who," he asked gaily, "is the mutual friend?"

Frantic alternatives chased each other through Angela's and Nigel's brain. Suppose they risked naming Marcus Barker again—he of the vermilion pamphlet. He had a shop. He was in prison. That was all they knew of Comrade Barker. Suppose——

Nigel drew a deep breath and leant forward.

"It is——" he began.

"Comrades!" shouted a terrific voice. "We will commence by singing the Internationale."

They turned, startled, to the platform. A gigantic bearded man, wearing a Russian blouse, confronted the audience. Comrade Kakaroff had arrived.

The comrades, led by the platform, instantly burst into a deafening rumpus. Nigel and Angela, pink with relief, made grimaces indicative of thwarted communication at Mr. Sage, who made a suitable face in return and then stood to attention and, with a piercing headnote, cut into the Internationale.

When they talked the affair over afterwards with Inspector Alleyn they could not remember one utterance of Comrade Kakaroff during the first half of his speech. He was a large Slav with a beautiful voice and upright hair. That was all they took in. When the beautiful voice and upright hair. That was all they took in. When the beautiful voice rose to an emotional bellow they managed to exchange a panicky whisper.

"Shall we slip away?"

"We *can't*. Not now."

"Afterwards?"

"Yes—perhaps too fishy."

"What do you mean?"

"Ssh! I'm going to——"

"Ssh!"

They glared at each other. To his horror, Nigel saw that Angela was about to get the giggles. He frowned at her majestically and then folded his arms and stared, with an air of interest, at Comrade Kakaroff. This unfortunately struck Angela, who was no doubt hysterical, as being intolerably funny. Her blood ran cold, her heart sank, she was panic-stricken, but she felt she must laugh.

"Shut up," breathed Nigel out of the corner of his mouth. He was foolish enough to kick her. Her chair quivered. She looked round wildly to the four corners of the room. In the fourth corner, between a diagonal vista of rapt faces, she saw someone who watched her. It was the man to whom Alleyn had spoken when they first arrived. Her throat quivered no longer. It went dry. Suddenly nothing seemed funny. Perhaps no one had noticed her. Banks, uttering an occasional "Hear! hear!" in a tone of magisterial approval, gazed only at Nicholas Kakaroff. Mr. Sage's back was towards them. Angela was herself again and greatly ashamed. She began to think coherently and presently she formed a plan. Alleyn had talked at some length about Ruth O'Callaghan. He had a vivid trick of description and Angela felt she knew exactly what Miss O'Callaghan was like. Suppose——? She stared like an attentive angel at Comrade Kakaroff and as she stared she made up her mind. As if in echo of her thoughts, she suddenly became aware of his utterances.

"The death of the late Home Secretary—Derek O'Callaghan," boomed Comrade Kakaroff. Jerked out of their unhappy meditation, they began to listen with a will.

"——not for us the sickly sentiment of an effete and decadent civilisation. Not for us the disgusting tears of the wage-slave hypocrite. It was in a good hour that man died. Had he lived he would have worked us great evil. He was struck down with the words of tyranny on his lips. I say it was in a good hour he died. We know it. Let us boldly declare it. He was the enemy of the people, a festering sore that drained the vitality of the proletariat. Listen to me, all of you. If he was deliberately exterminated and I knew the man who had done it, I would greet that man with the outstretched hand of brotherhood. I would hail that man as—Comrade."

He sat down amidst loud noises of encouragement. Mr. Sage had sprung excitedly to his feet.

"Comrade!" he shouted excitedly. It was as if he had touched a spring. The age-old yeast of mob-hysteria was at work. Half of them were on their feet yelling. Miss Banks cast down her knitting and made curious staccato gestures with her hands. "Up, the anarchists!" someone screamed behind them. The uproar lasted for some minutes while Kakaroff gazed intently at his work. Then Comrade Robinson walked to the edge of the platform and held up his hands. It was not until the Russian, half contemptuously, had joined him that the din died away.

"Friends," said Kakaroff, "have patience. It will not be for long. In the meantime—be patient. It is with difficulty we manage to hold these meetings. Let us not arouse too much suspicion in the brilliant brains of those uniformed automatons who guard the interests of the capitalist—our wonderful police."

The comrades made merry. Angela distinctly heard the rare laugh of Inspector Alleyn. The meeting broke up after a brief word from Comrade Robinson about standing subscriptions. Mr. Sage, a winning smile upon his face, turned eagerly towards them.

"Magnificent, wasn't it?" he cried.

"Marvellous!"

"Wonderful!"

"And now," continued Mr. Sage, looking admiringly upon Angela, "please tell me—who is our mutual friend?"

"Well, she's not exactly a *close* friend," said Angela,

"although we both like her ever so much." She glanced round her and leant forward. Mr. Sage gallantly inclined his curls towards her.

"Miss Ruth O'Callaghan," said Angela, just loud enough for Nigel to hear. He instantly supposed she had gone crazy.

Mr. Sage must have tilted his chair too far backwards, for he suddenly clutched at the air in a very singular manner. His feet shot upwards and the next instant he was decanted over their feet.

"Murder!" ejaculated Nigel, and hurriedly bent over him. Mr. Sage fought him off with great violence, and after a galvanic struggle, regained his feet.

"I say," said Angela, remembering her new voice, "I do hope you haven't hurt yourself. I'm ever so sorry."

Mr. Sage gazed at Nigel in silence for some moments. At last he drew in his breath and said: "No, thanks. Aye'm quate O.K."

"But you've gone pale. It was an awful bump you came. Sit down for a moment."

"Thanks," he said, and sank into a chair. "Dear me, that was a very silly thing to do."

"Very painful, I should say," remarked Nigel solemnly.

Suddenly Angela began to laugh.

"Oh," she said, "I'm awfully sorry. It's just horrid of me, but I can't help it."

"Really, An—Pippin!" scolded Nigel.

"The instinct to laugh at bodily injury," said Mr. Sage, who had recovered his colour, "is a very old one. Possibly it goes back to the snarl of the animal about to engage an adversary. You can't help yourself."

"It's nice of you to take it like that," said Angela through her tears. "It was rather a funny introduction."

"Yes."

"I'd better explain," continued Angela. Nigel, who

had regarded the upsetting of Mr. Sage as a dispensation of Providence, listened in horror. "We come from Clearminster-Storton in Dorset, near the holy ancestral home of the O'Callaghan. We've no time for the others and let it be known frankly. But she's different, isn't she, Claude?"

"Quite different."

"Yes. We've seen her in London and tried to make her look at things in the enlightened way, and although she's hidebound by the tradition of her class, she doesn't refuse to listen. She told us about you, Mr. Sage. She thinks you're awfully clever, doesn't she, Claude?"

"That's right," said poor Nigel.

"So that is the way of it?" said Mr. Sage. "I, too, have attempted to make Miss O'Callaghan think, to open her eyes. She is a customer of mine and is interested in my work. I accept patronage from nobody, mind. She has not offered patronage, but comradeship. I don't really know her well, and——" He paused and then, looking straight at Nigel, he added: "To be frank with you, I have not seen much of her since O'Callaghan introduced his infamous Bill. I felt the situation would be too severe a strain on our friendship. We have never discussed her brother. She knows my views and would understand. Er—quite."

"Oh, quite," murmured Angela.

"Just so," said Nigel.

"As a matter of fact," continued Mr. Sage, "I must own I don't go as far as Comrade Kakaroff in the matter of O'Callaghan's death. Undoubtedly it is well he is gone. I realise that theoretically there is such a thing as justifiable extermination, but murder—as this may have been—no."

"This *was* justifiable extermination," said Nigel fiercely.

"Then it should have been done openly for the Cause."

"No one fancies the rope."

"Claude, you are awful. I agree with Mr. Sage."

"Thank you Miss—er. Pardon, I'm afraid I don't know——"

"Pippin!" exclaimed Nigel suddenly. "We're keeping our pal waiting. He's hanging round outside the door there. Murder! It's half-past one and we swore we'd meet those other chaps before then."

"Ow, gracious, how awful!" said Angela. They grasped Mr. Sage's hand, said hurriedly they hoped they'd meet again, and scuttled away.

The comrades had broken up into groups. Many of them had gone. Nigel and Angela saw Alleyn at the door with his gloomy friend. A short, well-dressed man followed them out, passed them, walked quickly to the outer door, and ran noisily down the iron stairs. Alleyn stood and stared after him. He and the truculent man exchanged a glance.

"Come on," said Alleyn.

As they all walked out Nigel and Angela kept up a rather feverish conversation in their assumed voices. Alleyn was completely silent and so was his friend. Angela felt rather frightened. Did this man suspect them?

"I thought it was a perfectly marvellous meeting," she said loudly as they walked down the empty street.

"Stimulating—that's what it was, stimulating," gushed Nigel.

The man grunted. Alleyn was silent.

"I was so pleased to meet Comrade Sage," continued Angela with an air of the greatest enthusiasm.

"He's all right," conceded Nigel, "but I wouldn't say he was quite sound."

"You mean about O'Callaghan? Oh, I don't know. What did you think about O'Callaghan, comrade?" Angela turned desperately to Alleyn.

"Oh, I'm all for bloodshed," said Alleyn dryly. "Aren't you, comrade?" He turned to his friend.

The man uttered a short sinister laugh. Angela took Nigel's hand. "He was an ulcer," she said confusedly, but with energy. "When we find an ulcer we—we——"

"Poultice it?" suggested Alleyn.

"We cut it out."

"Paw ongcourager les autres," said the man in diabolical French.

"Oh," said Nigel, "not exactly that, comrade—er——?"

"Fox," said Alleyn. "You've met before."

"?!!"

"It's all right, sir," said Inspector Fox soothingly. "It's the removal of my dentures that did it. Rather confusing. You were getting on very nicely. It was quite a treat to listen to you."

"Stimulating—that's what it was, stimulating," added Alleyn.

"Inspector Alleyn," said Angela furiously, "I'll never forgive you for this—never."

"Hist!" said Alleyn. "The very walls have ears."

"Oh!" stormed Angela. "Oh! Oooo! Oh!"

"Murder!" said Nigel very quietly.

They walked on in silence until they came out by the river. A taxi drew up alongside them and they got in. Inspector Fox took a cardboard box from his pocket, turned delicately aside, and inserted his plates.

"Begging your pardon, miss," he said, "but it's pleasanter to have them."

"And now," said Alleyn, "just exactly what have you been up to?"

"I won't tell you."

"Won't you, Miss Angela? That's going to make it rather difficult."

"Oh, come on, Angela," said Nigel resignedly. "He'll have to know. Let's come clean."

They came clean. The two policemen listened in silence.

"Yes," said Alleyn when they had finished. "That's all very interesting. It's informative too. Let me get it straight. You say that when you quoted Miss O'Callaghan as your friend—a very dangerous trick, Miss Angela—Sage fell over backwards. Do you think he did this accidentally or deliberately? Do you think he got such a shock he overbalanced and crashed, or did you feel he used this painful ruse to distract your attention? Or were you both acting your socks off so enthusiastically that you did not notice?"

"Certainly not. At least——"

"I think he got a shock," said Nigel.

"Well, yes," agreed Angela, "so do I. But he seemed more upset, oddly enough, afterwards, when he was lying there. His face went pea-green. Oh dear, he *did* look dreadfully funny."

"No doubt. What did you say—did you say anything that would account for this diverting phenomenon?"

"I—no. Nigel said something. We both exclaimed, you know."

"I grabbed hold of him and he fairly fought me off."

"And then, you know, he got up and we asked if he was hurt and he said he was 'quate O.K.' and seemed to get better."

"What was it you said, Bathgate?"

"I dunno. 'Gosh!' or 'Help!' or 'Oh Fie!' Something."

"Subsequently he said that he did not altogether respond to Comrade Kakaroff's wave of brotherly love for O'Callaghan's murderer—that it?"

"He seemed to think that was going a bit far."

"And yet"—Alleyn went on—"and yet I seem to remember that at the conclusion of Kakaroff's jolly little talk, Comrade Sage leapt to his feet and yelled 'Comrade.' "

"Yes—he did," Nigel agreed, "but he may have

been all carried away. He's not a bad little tick really, I should say, once you've got past his frightful refinement."

"He spoke quite decently about Miss O'Callaghan," added Angela.

"So it appears. Did he and my girl-friend Banks have anything to say to each other?"

"Not a word."

"Well, Fox?"

"Well, sir?"

"I suppose I visit Mr. Sage at his shop to-morrow—oh, Lard, it's to-day, isn't it? What's the time?"

Inspector Fox drew his watch from the inside pocket of the threadbare coat he was wearing. He held it up in a large and filthy paw. "Just on two, I make it," he said. "Listen."

He lowered the window of the taxi. The lost, woebegone voice of a siren sounded out on the river. Then Big Ben, up in the cold night air, tolled two.

Inspector Fox regarded his watch with grave approval, put it away, and laid his hands on his knees.

"Longing for your bed, Fox?" asked Alleyn.

"I am for mine," said Angela.

"Suppose we let Bathgate take the taxi on, and turn into the office for half an hour?"

"Right ho, sir."

"Here we are."

He tapped on the window and the taxi stopped. The two detectives got out. Their breath hung mistily on the frosty air. Alleyn spoke for a moment to the driver and then looked inside.

"Thank you so much for your help, both of you," he said.

"I say, Alleyn, I hope you don't think we've made awful mugs of ourselves?" said Nigel lugubriously.

Alleyn thought for a moment.

"It was a very spirited effort, I consider," he said at last.

"We shall have to get you both in the Force, sir," added Fox. His matter-of-fact voice sounded oddly remote out there in the cold.

"Ah, Inspector Fox," said Nigel suspiciously, "I've heard you say that before."

"Good night, Comrade Angela," said Alleyn, "sleep well."

"Good night, inspector; I don't grudge you your joke."

"Bless you," answered Alleyn gently and slammed the door.

The taxi drove off. Farther along the Embankment men were hosing down the street surface. A great fan of water curved out and made all the sound there was except for the siren and the distant toot of the taxi. The two men stared at one another.

"I wonder just how much harm they've done," said Alleyn.

"None at all, sir, I should say."

"I hope you're right. My fault if they have. Come on, let's have a smoke."

In Alleyn's room they lit their pipes. Alleyn wrote at his desk for some time. Fox stared gravely at the opposite wall. They looked a queer couple with their dreadful clothes, grimy faces and blackened hands.

"She seems a very nice young lady," Fox said presently. "Is she Mr. Bathgate's fiancée, sir, if I may ask?"

"She is."

"A very pleasant young couple."

Alleyn looked at him affectionately.

"You're a quaint old bag of nonsense." He laid down his pen. "I don't think, really, I took too big a risk with them. The little man was nowhere near them. You recognised him, of course?"

"Oh, yes—from the inquest. I didn't see who it was

till he passed us in the doorway, but I'd noticed him earlier in the evening. He had his back towards us."

"Yes. I saw him, too. His clothes were good enough to shine out in that assembly. No attempt made to dress down to comrade level."

"No," said Fox. "Funny—that."

"It's altogether very rum. Passing strange. He walked straight past Sage and Nurse Banks. None of them batted an eyelash."

"That's so. If they are in collusion, it might be deliberate."

"You know, Fox, I can't think this Communist stuff is at the root of it. They're a bogus lot, holding their little meetings, printing little pamphlets, making their spot of trouble. A nuisance from our point of view, but not the stuff that assassins are made of. Of course, given one fanatic——" He stopped and shook his head.

"Well," said Fox, "that's so. They don't amount to much. Perhaps he's different, though. Perhaps he's the fanatic."

"Not that sort, I'd have through. I'll go and see him again. To-morrow. To-day. I rather like the bloke. We'll have to get hold of the expert who's doing the Kakaroff bunch and find out if he's deep in. It's been a field day, this. It seems an age since we sat here and waited for the report on the post-mortem. Damn. I feel we are as one about to be had. I feel we are about to give tongue and run off on a false scent. I feel we are about to put two and two together and make a mess."

"That's a pity," said Fox.

"What's the time? Half-past two. Perhaps Bathgate will be back in his own flat by now, having dropped Miss Angela, who looked tired, at her uncle's house. I think I shall send him to bed happy."

He dialled a number on his telephone and waited.

"Hullo, Bathgate. How much are you betting on your funny little man?"

"Roberts?" quacked Nigel's voice clearly.

"Yes, Roberts."

"Two to one, wasn't it? Why? What's up?"

"Did you notice he was at the meeting to-night?"

"Roberts!"

"Yes, Roberts. Good night."

He hung up the receiver.

"Come on," he said wearily. "Let's put two and two together and make a mess."

CHAPTER XIV

"FULVITAVOLTS"

Wednesday, the seventeenth. Morning and afternoon.

THE following morning Chief Inspector Alleyn and Inspector Fox reviewed their discussion.

"The Lenin Hall theory looks even shoddier by the light of day," said Alleyn.

"Well, sir," said Fox, "I won't say it isn't weak in places, but we can't ignore the thing, can we?"

"No. I suppose not. No."

"If there's nothing in it, it's a peculiar coincidence. Here's this lady, deceased's sister——"

"Oh yes, Fox, and by the way, I'm expecting the family solicitor. Mr. Rattisbon, of Knightley, Knightley and Rattisbon, an uncle of Lady O'Callaghan's, I believe. Unusually come-toish advance—rang up and suggested the visit himself. He mentioned Miss O'Callaghan so guardedly that I can't help feeling she plays a star part in the will. You were saying?"

"I was going to say here's this lady, deceased's sister, giving him patent medicines. Here's the Sage affair, the chemist, a member of the advanced party that threatened deceased, supplying them. Here's the doctor that gave the anæsthetic turning up at the same meeting as the chemist and the nurse that gave the injection. The nurse knows the chemist; the chemist, so Mr. Bathgate says, isn't so keen to know the nurse. The doctor, seemingly, knows neither of them. Well now, that may be bluff on the doctor's part. Suppose they were all working in collusion? Sage wouldn't be very keen on associating himself with Nurse Banks. Dr. Roberts might think it better to know neither of them. Suppose Sage had supplied Miss O'Callaghan with a drug containing a certain amount of hyoscine, Nurse Banks had injected a bit more, and Dr. Roberts had made a job of it by injecting the rest?"

"All of them instructed by Comrade Kakaroff?"

"Well—yes."

"But why? Why involve three people when one might do the trick? And anyway, none of them knew O'Callaghan was going to throw a fit and lie-for-dead in the House of Commons and then be taken to Sir John Phillips's nursing-home."

"That's so, certainly, but Sage would know, through Miss O'Callaghan, that her brother intended having Sir John to look at him as soon as the Bill was read. It seems they knew it was appendix. Mightn't they even have said he'd better go to the hospital and have it out? The lady tells Mr. Sage about this. He reports. He and Nurse Banks and Dr. Roberts think they'll form a plan of action."

"And, lo and behold, it all comes to pass even as they had said. I don't like it, Fox. And anyway, my old one, how did Dr. Roberts give the injection with no syringe? Why didn't he take the golden opportunity of exercising his obvious right of giving the hypodermic? To establish his innocence, you will say. He gave it on the sly, all unbeknown. But how? You can't carry a syringe all ready for use, complete with lethal dose, in your trouser pocket. And anyway, his trousers like all the rest of him, were covered with a white nightie. And he was never alone with the patient."

"That's so, and I admit it's a bit of a facer. Well—

perhaps he simply arranged the matter with Miss Banks and she gave the injection, using hyoscine instead of camphor."

"Subsequently letting everyone know how delighted she was at the death. Do you think that was sublety or stupidity?"

Fox shook his head solemnly.

"I don't say I support the theory, chief, but it *is* a theory."

"Oh yes. There's another point about the hyoscine. It's kept in a bottle, which Thoms tells me is very out of date—it should be in an ampoule. Phillips, I suppose, doesn't object, as he always uses his own tablets. Now Jane Harden says that the bottle was full and that one injection has since been used. I've checked that. When I saw the bottle it was almost full. Thoms brought it to me."

"Thoms did?" repeated Fox in his slow way.

"Yes. I got a sample and am having it analysed. If anyone has added water, the solution will be below strength."

"Yes—but they might have managed to add more solution."

"I don't see how. Where would they get it from? It would have to be done there and then."

Alleyn got up and walked about the room.

"You've never told me your views on intuition," he said.

"I can't say I've got any. No views, I mean—and no intuition either, for a matter of that. Very unimaginative I've always been. I recollect at school I was a poor hand at writing compositions, as they called them. Still I wouldn't say," said Fox cautiously, "that there is no such thing as intuition. I've known you come out rather strong in that line yourself."

"Thank you, Fox. Well, the weird is upon me now, if that's the expression. By the pricking of my thumbs, something wicked this way comes. I've got a hunch that the Bolshie lot is not one of the principal factors. It's a secondary theme in the bloody cantata. And yet, blast it, we'll have to follow it up."

"Oh well," Fox rose to his feet. "What's my job of work for to-day, sir?"

"Get hold of Boys or whoever has been watching the comrades and see if Roberts's connection with them can be traced. If there's anything in this we'll have to try and get evidence of collusion. Since the Krasinky-Tokareff affair Sumiloff has had to fade out, but there's Comrade Robinson. He seems to have wormed his way into the foreground. You'd better call him in. We pay the brute enough; let him earn it. Call him in, Fox, and tell him to ferret. He might tell the comrades we've been asking questions and see how they respond. And, talking about ferreting, I've been going through the reports on the medical gentlemen. It's the devil's own game beating it all up and there's a lot more to be done. So far there's nothing very much to excite us." He pulled forward a sheaf of papers. "Here you are. Phillips—Educated at Winchester and Cambridge. Medical training at Thomas's. Brilliant record. Distinguished war service. You can read it. Inspector Allison has spent days on this stuff. Thomas's was full of enthusiasm for one of its brightest boys. No bad marks anywhere. Here's Detective-Sergeant Bailey on Roberts. Educated at home. Delicate child. Medical training at Edinburgh and abroad, in Vienna. After qualifying went to Canada, Australia, and New Zealand, returning to England after war. Red Cross work, during war, in Belgium. Books on heredity—he lent me one and it seems damn' good. I suppose we'll have to go into the history abroad. I'll ring up Toronto to-night. We'll have to check up on that story about the overdose. Talk about routine! How long, O Lord, how long! Thoms—Educated St. Bardolph's, Essex, and Guy's. I rang up a friend of mine at Guy's who was his contemporary. Very good assistant surgeon and never likely to get much further than that. Undistinguished but blameless career, punctuated by mild scandals about women. Little devil! My friend was rather uncomplimentary about Thoms. He called him a 'lecherous little blight.' That's as far as we've got."

The telephone rang and Alleyn answered it.

"It's Mr. Rattisbon. Go down and make much of him, Fox. Bring him up tenderly, treat him with care. If he's anything like the rest of his family, he'll need warming. Use your celebrated charm."

"O.K." said Fox. *"Toojoor la politesse.* I'm on to the third record now, chief, but their peculiar ways of pronunciation give me a lot of trouble. Still, it's a sort of hobby, as you might say."

He sighed and went out, returning to usher in Mr. James Rattisbon, of Knightley, Knightley and Rattisbon, uncle to Lady O'Callaghan and solicitor to the deceased and his family. Mr. Rattisbon was one of those elderly solicitors whose appearance explains why the expression "dried-up" is so inevitably applied by novelists to men of law. He was desiccated. He was dressed in clothes of a dated type that looked rather shabby, but were actually in good repair. He wore a winged collar, rather high, and a dark tie, rather narrow. He was discreetly bald, somewhat blind, and a little tremulous. He had a kind of quick stuttering utterance, and a curious trick of thrusting out his pointed tongue and rattling it exceedingly rapidly between his thin lips. This may have served as an antidote to the stutter or it may have signified a kind of professional relish. His hands were bird-like claws with very large purplish veins. It was impossible to picture him in any sort of domestic surroundings.

As soon as the door had been closed behind him he

came forward very nimbly and said with incredible speed:

"Chief Detective-Inspector Alleyn?"

"Good morning, sir," said Alleyn. He advanced a chair towards Mr. Rattisbon and offered to take his hat.

"Good morning, good morning," said Mr. Rattisbon. "Thank-yer, thank-yer. No, thank-yer. Thank-yer."

He clung to his hat and took the chair.

"It's good of you to call. I would have been delighted to save you the trouble by coming to your office. I believe you want to see me about the O'Callaghan business?"

"That is the business—that is the reason—it is in connection with that matter that I have waited upon you, yes," rattled Mr. Rattisbon. He stopped short, darted a glance at Alleyn, and beat a finicky tatoo on the crown of his hat.

"Oh yes," said Alleyn.

"As no doubt you are aware, Inspector Alleyn, I was the late Sir Derek O'Callaghan's solicitor. I am also his sister's, Miss Catherine Ruth O'Callaghan's, solicitor, and of course his wife's—his wife's—ah, solicitor."

Alleyn waited.

"I understand from my clients that certain representations made by Lady O'Callaghan were instrumental in prompting you to take the course you have subsequently adopted."

"Yes."

"Yes. I understand that is the case. Inspector Alleyn, this is not, strictly speaking, a professional call. Lady O'Callaghan is my niece. Naturally I have a personal as well as a professional interest in the matter."

He looked, thought Alleyn, as though he was incapable of any interest that was not professional.

"Of course, sir," said Alleyn.

"My niece did not consult me before she took this

step. I must confess that had she done so I should—
I should have entertained grave doubts as to the ad-
visability of her action. However, as matters have turned
out, she was fully justified. I was, of course, present at
the inquest. Since then I have had several interviews
with both these ladies. The last took place yesterday
afternoon and was—was of a somewhat disquieting
nature."

"Really, sir?"

"Yes. It is a matter of some delicacy. I have hesitated
—I have hesitated for some time before making this
appointment. I learn that since the inquest Miss O'Callaghan has visited you and has—has suggested that you
go no further with your investigation."

"Miss O'Callaghan," said Alleyn, "was extremely
distressed at the idea of the post-mortem."

"Quite. Quite so. It is at her request that I have
come to see you myself."

"Is it, by Jove!" thought Alleyn.

"Miss O'Callaghan," continued Mr. Rattisbon, "fears
that in her distress she spoke foolishly. I found it difficult to get from her the actual gist of her conversation,
but it seems that she mentioned a young protégé of hers,
a Mr. Harold Sage, a promising chemist, she tells me."

"She did speak of a Mr. Sage."

"Yes." Mr. Rattisbon suddenly rubbed his nose very
hard and then agitated his tongue. "She appears to think
she used somewhat ambiguous phrasing as regards the
young man, and she—in short, inspector, the lady has
got it into her head that she may have presented him
in a doubtful light. Now I assured her that the police
are not to be misled by casual words spoken at a time
of emotional stress, but she implored me to come and
see you, and though I was disinclined to do so, I could
scarcely refuse."

"You were in a difficult position, Mr. Rattisbon."

"I *am* in a difficult position. Inspector Alleyn, I

feel it my duty to warn you that Miss Ruth O'Callaghan, though by no means *non compos mentis,* is at the same time subject to what I can only call periods of hysterical enthusiasm and equally hysterical depression. She is a person of singularly naïve intelligence. This is not the first occasion on which she has raised an alarm about a matter which subsequently proved to be of no importance whatever. Her imagination is apt to run riot. I think it would not be improper to attribute this idiosyncrasy to an unfortunate strain in her heredity."

"I quite appreciate that," Alleyn assured him. "I know something of this family trait. I believe her father——"

"Quite so. Quite," said Mr. Rattisbon, shooting a shrewd glance at him. "I see you take my point. Now, Inspector Alleyn, the only aspect of the matter that causes me disquietude is the possibility of her calling upon you again, actuated by further rather wild and, I'm afraid, foolish motives. I did think that perhaps it would be well to——"

"To put me wise, sir? I'm grateful to you for having done so. I should in any case have called on you, as I shall be obliged to make certain inquiries as regards the deceased's affairs."

Mr. Rattisbon appeared to tighten all over. He darted another glance at the inspector, took off his glasses, polished them, and in an exceedingly dry voice said:

"Oh, yes."

"We may as well get it over now. We have not yet got the terms of Sir Derek's will. Of course, sir, we shall have to know them."

"Oh, yes."

"Perhaps you will give me this information now. Just the round terms, you know."

It is perfectly true that people more often conform to type than depart from it. Mr. Rattisbon now completed his incredibly classical portrait of the family lawyer by placing together the tips of his fingers. He did this over the top of his bowler. He then regarded Alleyn steadily for about six seconds and said:

"There are four legacies of one thousand pounds each and two of five hundred. The residue is divided between his wife and his sister in the proportion of two-thirds to Lady O'Callaghan and one-third to Miss Catherine Ruth O'Callaghan."

"And the amount of the entire estate? Again in round terms?"

"Eighty-five thousand pounds."

"Thank you so much, Mr. Rattisbon. Perhaps later on I may see the will, but at the moment that is all we want. To whom do the legacies go?"

"To the funds of the Conservative Party, to the London Hospital, to his godchild, Henry Derek Samond, and to the Dorset Benevolent Fund, one thousand in each instance. To Mr. Ronald Jameson, his secretary, five hundred pounds. To be divided among his servants in equal portions of one hundred each, the sum of five hundred pounds."

Alleyn produced his notebook and took this down. Mr. Rattisbon got up.

"I must keep you no longer, Inspector Alleyn. This is an extremely distressing affair. I trust that the police may ultimately—um——"

"I trust so, sir," said Alleyn. He rose and opened the door.

"Oh, thank-yer, thank-yer," ejaculated Mr. Rattisbon. He shot across the room, paused, and darted a final look at Alleyn.

"My nephew tells me you were at school together," he said. "Henry Rattisbon, Lady O'Callaghan's brother."

"I believe we were," answered Alleyn politely.

"Yes. Interesting work here? Like it?"

"It's not a bad job."

"Um? Oh, quite. Well, wish you success," said Mr. Rattisbon, who had suddenly become startlingly human. "And don't let poor Miss Ruth mislead you."

"I'll try not to. Thank you so much, sir."

"Um? Not at all, not at all. Quite the reverse. Good morning. Good morning."

Alleyn closed the door and stood in a sort of trance for some minutes. Then he screwed his face up sideways, as though in doubt, appeared to come to a decision, consulted the telephone directory, and went to call upon Mr. Harold Sage.

Mr. Sage had a chemist's shop in Knightsbridge. Inspector Alleyn walked to Hyde Park Corner and then took a bus. Mr. Sage, behind his counter, served an elderly lady with dog powders, designed, no doubt, for a dyspeptic pug which sat and groaned after the manner of his kind at her feet.

"These are our own, madam," said Mr. Sage. "I think you will find they give the little fellow immediate relief."

"I *hope* so," breathed the elderly lady. "And you *really* think there's no need to worry?"

The pug uttered a lamentable groan. Mr. Sage made reassuring noises and tenderly watched them out.

"Yes, sir?" he said briskly, turning to Alleyn.

"Mr. Harold Sage?" asked the inspector.

"Yes," agreed Mr. Sage, a little surprised.

"I'm from Scotland Yard. Inspector Alleyn."

Mr. Sage opened his eyes very wide, but said nothing. He was naturally a pale young man.

"There are one or two questions I should like to ask you, Mr. Sage," continued Alleyn. "Perhaps we could go somewhere a little more private? I shan't keep you more than a minute or two."

"Mr. Brayght," said Mr. Sage loudly.

A sleek youth darted out from behind a pharmaceutical display.

"Serve, please," said Mr. Sage. "Will you just walk this way?" he asked Alleyn and led him down a flight of dark steps into a store-room which smelt of chemicals. He moved some packages off the only two chairs and stacked them up, very methodically, in a dark corner of the room. Then he turned to Alleyn.

"Will you take a chair?" he asked.

"Thank you. I've called to check up one or two points that have arisen in my department. I think you may be able to help us."

"In what connection?"

"Oh, minor details," said Alleyn vaguely. "Nothing very exciting, I'm afraid. I don't want to take up too much of your time. It's in connection with certain medicines at present on the market. I believe you sell a number of remedies made up from your own prescriptions—such as the pug's powders, for instance?" He smiled genially.

"Oh—quayte," said Mr. Sage.

"You do? Right. Now with reference to a certain prescription which you have made up for a Miss Ruth O'Callaghan."

"Pardon?"

"With reference to a certain prescription you made up for a Miss Ruth O'Callaghan."

"I know the lady you mean. She has been a customer for quite a while."

"Yes. This was one of your own prescriptions?"

"Speaking from memory, I think she has had several of my little lines—from tayme to tayme."

"Yes. Do you remember a drug you supplied three weeks ago?"

"I'm afraid I don't remember off-hand———"

"This is the one that contained hyoscine," said Alleyn. In the long silence that followed Alleyn heard the shop-door buzzer go, heard footsteps and voices above his head, heard the sound of the Brompton Road train down beneath them and felt its vibration. He watched Harold Sage. If there was no hyoscine in any of the drugs, the chemist would say so, would protest, would be bewildered. If there was hyoscine, an innocuous amount, he might or might not be flustered. If there was hyoscine, a fatal amount—what would he say?

"Yes," said Mr. Sage.

"What was the name of this medicine?"

"'Fulvitavolts.'"

"Ah, yes. Do you know if she used it herself or bought it for anyone else?"

"I reely can't say. For herself, I think."

"She did not tell you if she wanted it for her brother?"

"I reely don't remember, not for certain. I think she said something about her brother."

"May I see a packet of this medicine?"

Mr. Sage turned to his shelves, ferreted for some time and finally produced an oblong package. Alleyn looked at the spirited picture of a nude gentleman against an electric shock.

"Oh, this is not the one, Mr. Sage," he said brightly. "I mean the stuff in the round box—so big—that you supplied afterwards. This has hyoscine in it as well, has it? What was the other?"

"It was simply a prescription. I—I made it up for Miss O'Callaghan."

"From a doctor's prescription, do you mean?"

"Yes."

"Who was the doctor?"

"I reely forget. The prescription was returned with the powder."

"Have you kept a record?"

"No."

"But surely you have a prescription-book or whatever it is called?"

"I—yes—but—er—an oversight—it should have been entered."

"How much hyoscine was there in this prescription?"

"May I ask," said Mr. Sage, "why you think it contained hyoscine at all?"

"You have made that quite clear yourself. How much?"

"I—think—about one two-hundredth—something very small."

"And in 'Fulvitavolts' ?"

"Less. One two-hundred-and-fiftieth."

"Do you know that Sir Derek O'Callaghan was probably murdered?"

"My Gawd, yes."

"Yes. . . . With hyoscine."

"My Gawd, yes."

"Yes. So you see we want to be sure of our facts."

"He 'ad no hoverdose of 'yoscine from 'ere," said Mr. Sage, incontinently casting his aitches all over the place.

"So it seems. But, you see, if he had taken hyoscine in the minutest quantity before the operation we want to trace it as closely as possible. If Miss O'Callaghan gave him 'Fulvitavolts' and this other medicine, that would account for some of the hyoscine found at the post-mortem. Hyoscine was also injected at the operation. That would account for more."

"You passed the remark that he was murdered," said Mr. Sage more collectedly.

"The coroner did," corrected Alleyn. "Still, we've got to explore the possibility of accident. If you could give me the name of the doctor who prescribed the powder, it would be a great help."

"I can't remember. I make up hundreds of prescriptions every week."

"Do you often forget to enter them?"

Mr. Sage was silent.

Alleyn took out a pencil and an envelope. On the envelope he wrote three names.

"Was it any of those?" he asked.

"No."

"Will you swear to that?"

"Yes. Yes, I would."

"Look here, Mr. Sage, are you sure it wasn't your own prescription that you gave Miss O'Callaghan?"

" 'Fulvitavolts' is my own invention. I told you that."

"But the other?"

"No, I tell you—no."

"Very well. Are you in sympathy with Comrade Kakaroff over the death of Sir Derek O'Callaghan?"

Mr. Sage opened his mouth and shut it again. He put his hands behind him and leaned against a shelf.

"To what do you refer?" he said.

"You were at the meeting last night."

"I don't hold with the remarks passed at the meeting. I never 'ave. I've said so. I said so last night."

"Right. I don't think there's anything else."

Alleyn put the packet of 'Fulvitavolts' in his pocket.

"How much are these?"

"Three and nine."

Alleyn produced two half-crowns and handed them to Mr. Sage, who, without another word, walked out of the room and upstairs to the shop. Alleyn followed. Mr. Sage punched the cash register and conjured up the change. The sleek young man leant with an encouraging smile towards an incoming customer.

"Thank you very much, sir," said Mr. Sage, handing Alleyn one and threepence.

"Thank you. Good morning."

"Good morning, sir."

Alleyn went to the nearest telephone-booth and rang up the Yard.

"Anything come in for me?"

"Just a moment, sir . . . Yes. Sir John Phillips is here and wants to see you."

"Oh. Is he in my room?"

"Yes."

"Ask him to speak to me, will you?"

A pause.

"Hullo."

"Hullo. Is that Sir John Phillips?"

"Yes. Inspector Alleyn—I want to see you. I want to make a clean breast of it."

"I'll be there in ten minutes," said Alleyn.

CHAPTER XV

OF SIR JOHN PHILLIPS
THE "CLEAN BREAST"

Wednesday to Thursday.

PHILLIPS stared at Chief Inspector Alleyn's locked desk, at his chair, at the pattern of thick yellow sunlight on the floor of his room. He looked again at his watch. Ten minutes since Alleyn had rung up. He had said he would be there in ten minutes. Phillips knew what he was going to say. There was no need to go over that again. He went over it again. A light footstep in the passage outside. The door handle turned. Alleyn came in.

"Good morning, sir," he said. "I'm afraid I've kept you waiting." He hung up his hat, pulled off his gloves and sat down at his desk. Phillips watched him without speaking. Alleyn unlocked the desk and then turned towards his visitor.

"What is it you want to tell me, Sir John?"

"I've come to make a statement. I'll write it down afterwards if you like. Sign it. That's what you have to do, isn't it?"

"Suppose I hear what it's all about first," suggested Alleyn.

"Ever since you went away yesterday I've been thinking about this case. It seems to me I must be suspected of the murder. It seems to me things look very black for me. You know what I wrote to O'Callaghan. You know I injected a lethal drug. I showed you the tablets—analysis will prove they only contain the normal dosage, but I can't prove the one I gave was the same as the ones you analysed. I can't prove I only gave one tablet. Can I?"

"So far as I know, you can't."

"I've thought of all that. I didn't kill O'Callaghan. I threatened to kill him. You've seen Thoms. Thoms is a decent little ass, but I can see he thinks you suspect me. He's probably told you I used a lot of water for the injection and then bit his head off because he said so. So I did. He drove me nearly crazy with his bloody facetiousness. Jane—Nurse Harden—told me what you'd said to her. You know a hell of a lot—I can see that. You possibly know what I'm going to tell you. I want her to marry me. She won't, because of the other business with O'Callaghan. I think she believes I killed him. I think she was afraid at the time. That's why she was so upset, why she hesitated over the serum, why she fainted. She was afraid I'd kill O'Callaghan. She heard Thoms tell me about that play. D'you know about the play?"

"Thoms mentioned that you discussed it."

"Silly ass. He's an intelligent surgeon, but in other matters he's got as much *savoir-faire* as a child. He'd swear his soul away I didn't do it and then blurt out something like that. What I want to make clear to you is this. Jane Harden's distress in the theatre was on my account. She thinks I murdered O'Callaghan. I know she does, because she won't ask me. Don't, for God's sake, put any other interpretation on it. She's got a preposterous idea that she's ruined my life. Her nerves are all to blazes. She's anæmic and she's hysterical. If you arrest me, she may come forward with some damn' statement calculated to drag a red herring across my trail. She's an idealist. It's a type I don't pretend to understand. She did nothing to the syringe containing the serum. When Thoms cursed her for delaying, I turned and looked at her. She simply stood there dazed and half fainting. She's as innocent as—I was going to say as I am, but that may not carry much weight. She's completely innocent."

He stopped abruptly. To Alleyn it had seemed a most remarkable little scene. The change in Phillips's manner alone was extraordinary. The smooth, guarded courtesy which had characterised it during their former interview had vanished completely. He had spoken rapidly, as if urged by some appalling necessity. He now sat glaring at Alleyn with a hint of resigned ferociousness.

"Is that all you came to tell me, Sir John?" asked Alleyn in his most non-committal voice.

"All? What do you mean?"

"Well, you see, you prepared me for a bombshell. I wondered what on earth was coming. You talked of making a clean breast of it, but, forgive me, you've told me little that we did not already know."

Phillips took his time over answering this. At last he said:

"I suppose that's true. Look here, Alleyn. Can you give me your assurance that you entertain no suspicions as regards Jane Harden?"

"I'm afraid I can't. I shall consider everything you have told me very carefully, but I cannot, as this stage, make any definite announcement of that sort. Miss Harden is in a very equivocal position. I hope she may be cleared, but I cannot put her aside simply because, to put it baldly, you tell me she's innocent."

Phillips was silent. After a moment he clasped his well-shaped, well-kept hands together, and looking at them attentively, began to speak again.

"There's something more. Has Thoms told you that

I opened a new tube of tablets for the hyoscine injection?"

Alleyn did not move, but he seemed to come to attention.

"Oh yes," he said quietly.

"He has! Lord, what an ingenuous little creature it is! Did you attach any significance to this second tube?"

"I remembered it."

"Then listen. During the week before the operation I'd been pretty well at the end of my tether. I suppose when a man of my age gets it, he gets it badly —the psychologists say so—and—well, I could think of nothing but the ghastly position we were in—Jane and I. That Friday when I went to see O'Callaghan I was nearly driven crazy by his damned insufferable complacence. I *could* have murdered him then. I wasn't sleeping. I tried alcohol and I tried hypnotics. I was in a bad way, Alleyn. Then on top of it he came in, a sick man, and I had to operate. Thoms rubbed it in with his damn-fool story of some play or other. I scarcely knew what I did. I seemed to behave like an automaton." He stopped short and raised his eyes from the contemplation of his hands. "It's possible," he said, "that I may have made a mistake over the first tube. It may not have been empty."

"Even if the tube had been full," suggested Alleyn, "would that explain how the tablets got into the measure-glass?"

"I . . . what do you say?"

"You say that the first tube may not have been empty, and you wish me to infer from this that you are responsible for Sir Derek's death?"

"I . . . I . . . That is my suggestion," stammered Phillips.

"Deliberately responsible or accidentally?"

"I am not a murderer," said Phillips angrily.

"Then how did the tablets get into the measure-glass?"

Phillips was silent.

The inspector waited for a moment and then, with an unsual inflexion in his deep voice, he said:

"So you don't understand the idealistic type?"

"What? No!"

"I don't believe you."

Phillips stared at him, flushed painfully and then shrugged his shoulders. "Do you want a written statement of all this?" he asked.

"I don't think so. Later, if it's necessary. You have been very frank. I appreciate both the honesty and the motive. Look here—what can you tell me to help yourself? It's an unusual question from a police officer, but—there it is."

"I don't know. I suppose the case against me, apart from the suggestion I have just made, is that I had threatened O'Callaghan, and that when the opportunity came I gave him an overdose of hyoscine. It looks fishy, my giving the injection at all, but it is my usual practice, especially when Roberts is the anæsthetist, as he dislikes the business. It looks still more suspicious using a lot of water. That, again, is my usual practice. I can prove it. I can prove that I suggested another surgeon to Lady O'Callaghan and that she urged me to operate. That's all. Except that I don't think—— No, that's all."

"Have you any theories about other people?"

"Who did it, you mean? None. I imagine it was political. How it was done, I've no idea. I can't possibly suspect any of the people who worked with me. It's unthinkable. Besides—why? You said something about patent medicines. Is there anything there?"

"We're on that tack now. I don't know if there's anything in it. By the way, why does Dr. Roberts object to giving injections?"

"A private reason. Nothing that can have any bearing on the case."

"Is it because he once gave an overdose?"

"If you knew that, why did you ask me? Testing my veracity?"

"Put it like that. He was never alone with the patient?"

"No. No, never."

"Was any one of the nurses alone in the theatre before the operation?"

"The nurses? I don't know. I wouldn't notice what they did. They'd been preparing for some time before we came on the scene."

"We?"

"Thoms, Roberts and myself."

"What about Mr. Thoms?"

"I can't remember. He may have dodged in to have a look round."

"Yes. I think I must have a reconstruction. Can you spare the time to-day or to-morrow?"

"You mean you want to go through the whole business in pantomime?"

"If I may. We can hardly do it actually, unless I discover a P.C. suffering from an acute abscess of the appendix."

Phillips smiled sardonically.

"I might give him too much hyoscine if you did," he said. "Do you want the whole pack of them?"

"If it's possible."

"Unless there's an urgent case, nothing happens in the afternoon. I hardly think there will be an urgent case. Business," added Phillips grimly, "will probably fall off. My last major operation is enjoying somewhat unfavourable publicity."

"Well—will you get the others for me for to-morrow afternoon?"

"I'll try. It'll be very unpleasant. Nurse Banks has left us, but she can be found."

"She's at the Nurses' Club in Chelsea."

Phillips glanced quickly at him.

"Is she?" he said shortly. "Very well. Will five o'clock suit you?"

"Admirably. Can we have it all as closely reproduced as possible—same impedimenta and so on?"

"I think it can be arranged. I'll let you know."

Phillips went to the door.

"Good-bye for the moment," he said. "I've no idea whether or not you think I killed O'Callaghan, but you've been very polite."

"We are taught manners at the same time as point-duty," said Alleyn. Phillips went away and Alleyn sought out Detective-Inspector Fox, to whom he related the events of the morning. When he came to Phillips's visit Fox thrust out his under lip and looked at his boots.

"That's your disillusioned expression, Fox," said Alleyn. "What's it in aid of?"

"Well, sir, I must say I have my doubts about this self-sacrifice business. It sounds very nice, but it isn't the stuff people hand out when they think it may be returned to them tied up with rope."

"I can't believe you were no good at composition. Do you mean you mistrust Phillips's motive in coming here, or Nurse Harden's hypothetical attempt to decoy my attention?"

"Both, but more particularly number one. To my way of thinking, we've got a better case against Sir John Phillips than any of the others. I believe you're right about the political side—it's not worth a great deal. Now Sir John knows how black it looks against him. What's he do? He comes here, says he wants to make a clean breast of it, and tells you nothing you don't know already. When you point this out to him he says he may have made a slip over the two tubes. Do you believe that, chief?"

"No—to do the job he'd have had to dissolve the contents of a full tube. However dopey he felt he couldn't do that by mistake."

"Just so. And he knows you'll think of that. You ask me, sir," said Fox oratorically: " 'What's the man's motive?' "

"What's the man's motive?" repeated Alleyn obediently.

"Spoof's his motive. He knows it's going to be a tricky business bringing it home to him and he wants to create a good impression. The young lady may or may not have been in collusion with him. She may or may not come forward with the same kind of tale. 'Oh, please don't arrest him; arrest me. I never did it, but spare the boy-friend,' " said Fox in a very singular falsetto and with dreadful scorn.

Alleyn's mouth twitched. Rather hurriedly he lit a cigarette.

"You seem very determined all of a sudden," he observed mildly. "This morning you seduced me with tales of Sage, Banks, and Roberts."

"So I did, sir. It was an avenue that had to be explored. Boys is exploring, and as far as he's got it's a wash-out."

"Alack, what news are these! Discover them."

"Boys got hold of Robinson, and Robinson says it's all my eye. He says he's dead certain the Bolshie push hasn't an idea who killed O'Callaghan. He says if they'd had anything to do with it he'd have heard something. It was Kakaroff who told him about it and Kakaroff was knocked sideways at the news. Robinson says if there had been any organization from that quarter they'd have kept quiet and we'd have had no rejoicing. They're as pleased as punch and as innocent as angels."

"Charming! All clapping their hands in childish glee. How about Dr. Roberts?"

"I asked him about the doctor. It seems they don't know anything much about him and look upon him as a bit of an outsider. They've even suspected him of being what they call 'unsound.' Robinson wondered if he was one of our men. You recollect Marcus Barker sent out a lot of pamphlets on the Sterilization Bill. They took it up for a time. Well, the doctor is interested in the Bill."

"Yes, of course," agreed Alleyn thoughtfully. "It's in his territory."

"From the look of some of the sons of the Soviet," said Fox, "I'd say they'd be the first to suffer. The doctor saw one of these pamphlets and went to a meeting. He joined the Lenin Hall lot because he thought they'd push it. Robinson says he's always nagging at them to take it up again."

"So that's that. It sounds reasonable enough, Fox, and certainly consistent with Roberts's character. With his views on eugenics he'd be sure to support sterilization. You don't need to be a Bolshie to see the sense of it, either. It looks as though Roberts had merely been thrown in to make it more difficult."

Fox looked profound.

"What about Miss Banks and little Harold?" asked Alleyn.

"Nothing much. The Banks party has been chucking her weight about ever since the operation, but she doesn't say anything useful. You might call it reflected glory."

"How like Banks. And Sage?"

"Robinson hasn't heard anything. Sage is not a prominent member."

"He was lying about the second dose Miss O'Callaghan gave O'Callaghan. He admitted he had provided it, that it was from a doctor's prescription, and that he had not noted it in his book. All my eye. We can sift that out easily enough by finding out her doctor, but of course Sage may simply be scared and as innocent as a babe. Well, there we are. Back again face to face with the clean breast of Sir John Phillips."

"Not so clean, if you ask me."

"I wonder. I'm doing a reconstruction to-morrow afternoon. Phillips is arranging it for me. Would you say he was a great loss to the stage?"

"How d'you mean, chief?"

"If he's our man, he's one of the best actors I've ever met. You come along to-morrow to the hospital, Fox, and see what you shall see. Five o'clock. And now I'm going to lunch. I want to see Lady O'Callaghan before the show, and Roberts too, if possible. I may as well get his version of the Lenin Hall lot. *Au revoir*, Fox."

"Do you mind repeating that, sir?"

"*Au revoir.*"

"*Au revoir*, monsieur," said Fox carefully.

"I'm coming to hear those records of yours one of these nights, if I may."

Fox became plum-coloured with suppressed pleasure.

"I'd take it very kindly," he said stiffly and went out.

Alleyn rang up the house in Catherine Street and learnt that Lady O'Callaghan would be pleased to receive him at ten to three the following afternoon. He spent half an hour on his file of the case. The analyst's report on Phillips's tablets and the hyoscine solution had come in. Both contained the usual dosage. He sent off the "Fulvitavolts" and the scrap of paper that had enclosed Ruth O'Callaghan's second remedy. It was possible, but extremely unlikely, that there might be a trace of the drug spilt on the wrapper. At one o'clock he went home and lunched. At two o'clock he rang up the Yard and found there was a message from Sir John Phillips to the effect that the reconstruction could be held the following afternoon at the time suggested. He asked them to tell Fox and then rang Phillips up and thanked him.

Alleyn spent the rest of the day adding to the file on the case and in writing a sort of résumé for his own instruction. He sat over it until ten o'clock and then deliberately put it aside, read the second act of *Hamlet,* and wondered, not for the first time, what sort of a hash the Prince of Denmark would have made of a job at the Yard. Then, being very weary, he went to bed.

The next morning he reviewed his notes, particularly that part of them which referred to hyoscine.

"Possible sources of hyoscine," he had written:
"1.   *The bottle of stock solution.*

"Probably Banks, Marigold, Harden, Thoms, Phillips, all had opportunity to get at this. All in theatre before operation. Each could have filled anti-gas syringe with hyoscine. If this was done, someone had since filled up bottle with 10 c.c.'s of the correct solution. No one could have done this during the operation. Could it have been done later? No good looking for prints.
"2.   *The tablets.*

"Phillips could have given an overdose when he prepared the syringe. May have to trace his purchases of h.
"3.   *The patent medicines.*

"(a) *"Fulvitavolts."* Negligible quantity unless Sage had doctored packet supplied to Ruth. Check up.

"(b) *The second p.m.* (more p.m.'s!) supplied to Ruth. May have been lethal dose concocted by Sage, hoping to do in O'Callaghan, marry Ruth and the money, and strike a blow for Lenin, Love, and Liberty."

After contemplating these remarks with some disgust Alleyn went to the hospital, made further arrangements for the reconstruction at five and after a good deal of trouble succeeded in getting no further with the matter of the stock solution. He then visited the firm that supplied Sir John Phillips with drugs and learnt nothing that was of the remotest help. He then lunched and went to call on Lady O'Callaghan. Nash received him with that particular nuance of condescension that hitherto he had reserved for politicians. He was shown into the drawing-room, an apartment of great elegance and no character. Above the mantelpiece hung a portrait in pastel of Cicely O'Callaghan. The artist had dealt competently with the shining texture of the dress and hair, and had made a conscientious map of the face. Alleyn felt he would get about as much change from the original as he would from the picture. She came in, gave him a colourless greeting, and asked him to sit down.

"I'm so sorry to worry you again," Alleyn began. "It's a small matter, one of those loose ends that probably mean nothing, but have to be tidied up."

"Yes. I shall be pleased to give you any help. I hope everything is quite satisfactory?" she said. She might have been talking about a new hot-water system.

"I hope it will be," rejoined Alleyn. "At the moment we are investigating any possible sources of hyoscine. Lady O'Callaghan, can you tell me if Sir Derek had taken any drugs of any sort at all before the operation?" As she did not answer immediately, he added quickly: "You see, if he had taken any medicine containing hyoscine, it would be necessary to try and arrive at the amount in order to allow for it."

"Yes," she said, "I see."

"Had he, do you know, taken any medicine? Perhaps when the pain was very bad?"

"My husband disliked drugs of all kinds."

"Then Miss Ruth O'Callaghan's suggestion about a remedy she was interested in would not appeal to him?"

"No. He thought it rather a foolish suggestion."

"I'm sorry to hammer away at it like this, but do you

think there's a remote possibility that he did take a dose? I believe Miss O'Callaghan did actually leave some medicine here—something called 'Fulvitavolts,' I think she said it was?"

"Yes. She left a packet here."

"Was it lying about where he might see it?"

"I'm afraid I don't remember. The servants, perhaps——" Her voice trailed away. "If it's at all important——" she said vaguely.

"It is rather."

"I am afraid I don't quite understand why. Obviously my husband was killed at the hospital."

"That," said Alleyn, "is one of the theories. The 'Fulvitavolts, are of some importance because they contain a small amount of hyoscine. You will understand that we must account for any hyoscine—even the smallest amount—that was given?"

"Yes," said Lady O'Callaghan. She looked serenely over his head for a few seconds and then added: "I'm afraid I cannot help you. I hope my sister-in-law, who is already upset by what has happened, will not be unnecessarily distressed by suggestions that she was responsible in any way."

"I hope not," echoed Alleyn blandly. "Probably, as you say, he did not touch the 'Fulvitavolts.' When did Miss O'Callaghan bring them?"

"I believe one night before the operation."

"Was it the night Sir John Phillips called?"

"That was on the Friday."

"Yes—was it then, do you remember?"

"I think perhaps it was."

"Can you tell me exactly what happened?"

"About Sir John Phillips?"

"No, about Miss O'Callaghan."

She took a cigarette from a box by her chair. Alleyn jumped up and lit it for her. It rather surprised him to find that she smoked. It gave her an uncanny resemblance to something human.

"Can you remember at all?" he said.

"My sister-in-law often came in after dinner. At times my husband found these visits a little trying. He liked to be quiet in the evenings. I believe on that night he suggested that she should be told he was out. However, she came in. We were in the study."

"You both saw her, then?"

"Yes."

"What happened?"

"She urged him to try his medicine. He put her off. I told her he expected Sir John Phillips and that we ought to leave them alone. I remember she and I met Sir John in the hall. I thought his manner very odd, as I believe I told you."

"So you went out, leaving the medicine in the study?"

"I suppose so—yes."

"Did you come across it again?"

"I don't think so."

"May I speak to your butler—Nash, isn't it?"

"If you think it is any help." She rang the bell.

Nash came in and waited.

"Mr. Alleyn wants to speak to you, Nash," said Lady O'Callaghan. Nash turned a respectful eye towards him.

"I want you to think back to the Friday evening before Sir Derek's operation," Alleyn began. "Do you remember that evening?"

"Yes, sir."

"There were visitors?"

"Yes, sir. Miss O'Callaghan and Sir John Phillips."

"Exactly. Do you remember noticing a chemist's parcel anywhere in the study?"

"Yes, sir. Miss O'Callaghan brought it with her, I believe."

"That's the one. What happened to it?"

"I had it removed to a cupboard in Sir Derek's bathroom the following morning, sir."

"I see. Had it been opened?"

"Oh, yes, sir."

"Can you find it now, Nash, do you think?"

"I will ascertain, sir."

"Do you mind, Lady O'Callaghan?" asked Alleyn apologetically.

"Of course not."

Nash inclined his head solemnly and left the room. While he was away there was a rather uncomfortable silence. Alleyn, looking very remote and polite, made no effort to break it. Nash returned after a few minutes with the now familiar carton, on a silver salver. Alleyn took it and thanked him. Nash departed.

"Here it is," said the inspector cheerfully. "Oh, yes, Nash was quite right; it has been opened and—let me see—one powder has been taken. That doesn't amount to much." He put the carton in his pocket and turned to Lady O'Callaghan. "It seems ridiculous, I know, to worry about so small a matter, but it's part of our job to pick up every thread, however unimportant. This, I suppose, was the last effort Miss O'Callaghan made to interest Sir Derek in any remedy?"

Again she waited for a few seconds.

"Yes," she murmured at last, "I believe so."

"She did not mention another remedy to you after he had been taken to the hospital?"

"Really, Inspector Alleyn, I cannot possibly remember. My sister-in-law talks a great deal about patent medicines. She tries to persuade everyone she knows to take them. I believe my uncle, Mr. James Rattisbon, has already explained this to you. He tells me that he made it quite clear that we did not wish this matter to be pursued."

"I am afraid I cannot help pursuing it."

"But Mr. Rattisbon definitely instructed you."

"Please forgive me," said Alleyn very quietly, "if I seem to be unduly officious." He paused. She looked at him with a kind of cold huffiness. After a moment he went on. "I wonder if you have ever seen or read a play called *Justice,* by Galsworthy? It is no doubt very dated, but there is an idea in it that I think explains far better than I can the position of people who become involved, whether voluntarily or involuntarily, with the Law. Galsworthy made one of his characters—a lawyer, I think—say that once you have set in motion the chariot wheels of Justice, you can do nothing at all to arrest or deflect their progress. Lady O'Callaghan, that is the exact truth. You, very properly, decided to place this tragic case in the hands of the police. In doing so you switched on a piece of complicated and automatic machinery which, once started, you cannot switch off. As the police officer in charge of this case I am simply a wheel in the machine. I must complete my revolutions. Please do not think I am impertinent if I say that neither you nor any other lay person, however much involved, has the power to stop the machine of justice or indeed to influence it in any way whatever." He stopped abruptly. "I am afraid you *will* think me impertinent—I have no business to talk like this. If you will excuse me——"

He bowed and turned away.

"Yes," said Lady O'Callaghan, "I quite understand. Good afternoon."

"There's one other thing," said Alleyn. "I had nearly forgotten it. It's something that you can do, if you will, to help us as regards the hospital side of the problem."

She listened, apparently without any particular surprise or agitation, to his request, and agreed at once to do as he suggested.

"Thank you very much indeed, Lady O'Callaghan. You understand that we should like Miss O'Callaghan to be with you?"

"Yes," she said after a long pause.

"Shall I see her, or—perhaps you would rather ask her yourself?"

"Perhaps that would be better. I would much prefer her to be spared this unnecessary ordeal."

"I assure you," said Alleyn dryly, "that it may save her a more unpleasant one."

"I'm afraid I do not understand you. However, I shall ask her."

In the hall he walked straight into Miss Ruth O'Callaghan. When she saw him she uttered a noise that was something between a whoop of alarm and a cry of supplication, and bolted incontinently into the drawing-room. Nash, who had evidently just admitted her, looked scandalised.

"Is Mr. Jameson in, Nash?" asked Alleyn.

"Mr. Jameson has left us, sir."

"Really?"

"Yes, sir. His duties, as you might say, have drawn to a close."

"Yes," said Alleyn, unconsciously echoing Lady O'Callaghan. "I quite understand. Good afternoon."

CHAPTER XVI

RECONSTRUCTION BEGUN

Thursday, the eighteenth. Afternoon.

ALLEYN found he still had over an hour to wait before
the reconstruction. He had tea and then rang up Dr.
Roberts, found he was at home, and made his way once
more to the little house in Wigmore Street. He wanted,
if possible, to surprise Roberts with an unexpected reference to the Lenin Hall meeting. The diminutive man-
servant admitted him and showed him into the pleasant
sitting-room, where he found Roberts awaiting him.

"I hope I'm not a great nuisance," said Alleyn. "You
did ask me to come back some time, you know."

"Certainly," said Roberts, shaking hands. "I am
delighted to see you. Have you read my book?" He
swept a sheaf of papers off a chair and pulled it forward. Alleyn sat down.

"I've dipped into it—no time really to tackle it yet,
but I'm enormously interested. At Lord knows what
hour this morning I read the chapter in which you refer
to the Sterilization Bill. You put the case for sterilization better than any other sponsor I have heard."

"You think so?" said Roberts acidly. "Then you will
be surprised to hear that although I have urged that
matter with all the force and determination I could
command, I have made not one inch of headway—not

an inch! I am forced to the conclusion that most of the people who attempt to administer the government of this country are themselves certifiable." He gave a short falsetto laugh and glared indignantly at Alleyn, who contented himself with making an incredulous and sympathetic noise.

"I have done everything—everything," continued Roberts. "I joined a group of people professing enlightened views on the matter. They assured me they would stick at nothing to force this Bill through Parliament. They professed the greatest enthusiasm. *Have* they done anything?" He paused oratorically and then in a voice of indescribable disgust he said: "They merely asked me to wait in patience till the Dawn of the Proletariat Day in Britain."

Chief Inspector Alleyn felt himself to be in the foolish position of one who sets a match to the dead stick of a rocket. Dr. Roberts had most effectively stolen his fireworks. He had a private laugh at himself. Roberts continued angrily:

"They call themselves Communists. They have no interest in the welfare of the community—none. Last night I attended one of their meetings and I was disgusted. All they did was to rejoice for no constructive or intelligent reason over the death of the late Home Secretary."

He stopped abruptly, glanced at Alleyn, and then with that curious return to nervousness which the inspector had noticed before he said: "But, of course, I had forgotten. That is very much your business. Thoms rang me up just now to ask me if I could attend at the hospital this afternoon."

"*Thoms* rang you up?"

"Yes. Sir John had asked him to, I believe. I don't know why," said Dr. Roberts, suddenly looking surprised and rather bewildered, "but I sometimes find Thoms's manner rather aggravating."

"Do you?" murmured Alleyn, smiling. "He is rather facetious."

"Facetious! Exactly. And this afternoon I found his facetiousness in bad taste."

"What did he say?"

"He said something to the effect that if I wished to make my get-away he would be pleased to lend me a pair of ginger-coloured whiskers and a false nose. I thought it in bad taste."

"Certainly," said Alleyn, hurriedly blowing his own nose.

"Of course," continued Dr. Roberts, "Mr. Thoms knows himself to be in an impregnable position, since he could not have given any injection without being observed, and had no hand in preparing the injection which he did give. I felt inclined to point out to him that I myself am somewhat similarly situated, but do not feel, on that account, free to indulge in buffoonery."

"I suppose Mr. Thoms was in the anteroom all the time until you went into the theatre?"

"I've no idea," said Roberts stiffly. "I myself merely went to the anteroom with Sir John, said what was necessary, and joined my patient in the anæsthetic-room."

"Ah, well—we shall get a better idea of all your movements from the reconstruction."

"I suppose so," agreed Roberts, looking perturbed. "It will be a distressing experience for all of us. Except, no doubt, Mr. Thoms."

He waited a moment and then said nervously:

"Perhaps this is a question that I should not ask, Inspector Alleyn, but I cannot help wondering if the police have a definite theory as regards this crime?"

Alleyn was used to this question.

"We've got several theories, Dr. Roberts, and all of them more or less fit. That's the devil of it."

"Have you explored the possibility of suicide?" asked Roberts wistfully.

"I have considered it."

"Remember his heredity."

"I have remembered it. After he had the attack in the House his physical condition would have rendered suicide impossible, and he could hardly have taken hyoscine while making his speech."

"Again remember his heredity. He might have carried hyoscine tablets with him for some time and under the emotional stimulus of the occasion suffered a sudden ungovernable impulse. In the study of suicidal psychology one comes across many such cases. Did his hand go to his mouth while he was speaking? I see you look incredulous, Inspector Alleyn. Perhaps you even think it suspicious that I should urge the point. I—I—*have* a reason for hoping you find that O'Callaghan killed himself, but it does not spring from a sense of guilt."

A strangely exalted look came into the little doctor's eyes as he spoke. Alleyn regarded him intently.

"Dr. Roberts," he said as last, "why not tell me what is in your mind?"

"No," said Roberts emphatically, "no—not unless —unless the worst happens."

"Well," said Alleyn, "as you know, I can't force you to give me your theory, but it's a dangerous business, withholding information in a capital charge."

"It may not be a capital charge," cried Roberts in a hurry.

"Even suppose your suicide theory is possible, it seems to me that a man of Sir Derek's stamp would not have done it in such a way as to cast suspicion upon other people."

"No," agreed Roberts. "No. That is undoubtedly a strong argument—and yet inherited suicidal mania sometimes manifests itself very abruptly and strangely. I have known instances . . ."

He went to his bookcase and took down several volumes, from which he read in a rapid, dry and didactic manner, rather as though Alleyn was a collection of students. This went on for some time. The servant brought in tea, and with an air of patient benevolence, poured it out himself. He placed Roberts's cup on a table under his nose, waited until the doctor closed the book with which he was at the moment engaged, took it firmly from him and directed his attention to the tea. He then moved the table between the two men and left the room.

"Thank you," said Roberts vaguely some time after he had gone.

Roberts, still delivering himself of his learning, completely forgot to drink his tea or to offer some to Alleyn, but occasionally stretched out a hand towards the toast. The time passed rapidly. Alleyn looked at his watch.

"Good Lord!" he exclaimed, "it's half-past four. We'll have to collect ourselves, I'm afraid."

"Tch!" said Roberts crossly.

"I'll call a taxi."

"No, no. I'll drive you there, inspector. Wait a moment." He darted out into the hall and gave flurried orders to the little servant, who silently insinuated him into his coat and gave him his hat. Roberts shot back into the sitting-room and fetched his stethoscope.

"What about your anæsthetising apparatus?" ventured Alleyn.

"Eh?" asked Roberts, squinting round at him.

"Your anæsthetising apparatus."

"D'you want that?"

"Please—if it's not a great bore. Didn't Sir John tell you?"

"I'll get it," said Roberts. He darted off across the little hall.

"Can I assist you, sir?" asked the servant.

"No, no. Bring out the car."

He reappeared presently, wheeling the cruet-like apparatus with its enormous cylinders.

"You can't carry that down the steps by yourself," said Alleyn. "Let me help."

"Thank you, thank you," said Roberts. He bent down and examined the nuts that fastened the frame at the bottom. "Wouldn't do for these nuts to come loose," he said. "You take the top, will you? Gently. Ease it down the steps."

With a good deal of bother they got the thing into Roberts's car and drove off to Brook Street, the little doctor talking most of the time.

As they drew near the hospital, however, he grew quieter, seemed to get nervous, and kept catching Alleyn's eye and hurriedly looking away again. After this had happened some three or four times Roberts laughed uncomfortably.

"I—I'm not looking forward to this experiment," he said. "One gets moderately case-hardened in our profession, I suppose, but there's something about this affair" —he blinked hard twice—"something profoundly disquieting. Perhaps it is the element of uncertainty."

"But you have got a theory, Dr. Roberts?"

"I? No. No. I did hope it might be suicide. No— I've no specific theory."

"Oh, well. If you won't tell me, you won't," rejoined Alleyn.

Roberts looked at him in alarm, but said no more.

At Brook Street they found Fox placidly contemplating the marble woman in the waiting-room. He was accompanied by Inspector Boys, a large red-faced officer with a fruity voice and hands like hams. Boys kept a benevolent but shrewd eye on the activities of communistic societies, on near-treasonable propagandists, and on Soviet-minded booksellers. He was in the habit of alluding to such persons who came into these categories as though they were tiresome but harmless children.

"Hullo," said Alleyn. "Where are the star turns?"

"The nurses are getting the operating theatre ready," Fox told him. "Sir John Phillips asked me to let him know when we are ready. The other ladies are upstairs."

"Right. Mr. Thoms here?"

"Is that the funny gentleman, sir?" asked Boys.

"It is."

"He's here."

"Then in that case we're complete. Dr. Roberts has gone up to the theatre. Let us follow him. Fox, let Sir John know, will you?"

Fox went away and Alleyn and Boys took the lift up to the theatre landing, where they found the rest of the dramatis personæ awaited them. Mr. Thoms broke off in the middle of some anecdote with which he was apparently regaling the company.

"Hullo, 'ullo, 'ullo!" he shouted. "Here's the Big Noise itself. Now we shan't be long."

"Good evening, Mr. Thoms," said Alleyn. "Good evening, matron. I hope I haven't kept you all waiting."

"Not at all," said Sister Marigold.

Fox appeared with Sir John Phillips. Alleyn spoke a word to him and then turned and surveyed the group. They eyed him uneasily and perhaps inimically. It was a little as though they drew together, moved by a common impulse of self-preservation. He thought they looked rather like sheep, bunched together, their heads turned watchfully towards their protective enemy, the sheep-dog.

"I'd better give a warning bark or two," thought Alleyn and addressed them collectively.

"I'm quite sure," he began, "that you all realise why we have asked you to meet us here. It is, of course, in order to enlist your help. We are faced with a difficult problem in this case and feel that a reconstruction of the operation may go far towards clearing any suspicion of guilt from innocent individuals. As you know, Sir Derek O'Callaghan died from hyoscine poisoning. He was a man with many political enemies, and from the outset the affair has been a complicated and bewildering problem. The fact that he, in the course of the operation, was given a legitimate injection of hyoscine has added to the complications. I am sure you are all as anxious as we are to clear up this aspect of the case. I ask you to look upon the reconstruction as an opportunity to free yourselves of any imputation of guilt. As a medium in detection the reconstruction has much to commend it. The chief argument against it is that sometimes innocent persons are moved, through nervousness or other motives, to defeat the whole object of the thing by changing the original circumstances. Under the shadow of tragedy it is not unusual for innocent individuals to imagine that the police suspect them. I am sure that you are not likely to do anything so foolish as this. I am sure you realise that this is an opportunity, not a trap. Let me beg you to repeat as closely as you can your actions during the operation on the deceased. If you do this, there is not the faintest cause for alarm." He looked at his watch.

"Now then," he said. "You are to imagine that time has gone back seven days. It is twenty-five minutes to four on the afternoon of Thursday, February 4th. Sir Derek O'Callaghan is upstairs in his room, awaiting his operation. Matron, when you get word will you and the nurses who are to help you begin your preparations in the anteroom and the theatre? Any dialogue you remember you will please repeat. Inspector Fox will be in the anteroom and Inspector Boys in the theatre. Please treat them as pieces of sterile machinery." He allowed himself a faint smile and turned to Phillips and Nurse Graham, the special.

"We'll go upstairs."

They went up to the next landing. Outside the door of the first room Alleyn turned to the others. Phillips was very white, but quite composed. Little Nurse Graham looked unhappy, but sensibly determined.

"Now, nurse, we'll go in. If you'll just wait a moment, sir. Actually you are just coming upstairs."

"I see," said Phillips.

Alleyn swung open the door and followed Nurse Graham into the bedroom.

Cicely and Ruth O'Callaghan were at the window. He got the impression that Ruth had been sitting there, perhaps crouched in that arm-chair, and had sprung up when the door opened. Cicely O'Callaghan stood erect, very *grande dame* and statuesque, a gloved hand resting lightly on the window-sill.

"Good evening, Inspector Alleyn," she said. Ruth gave a loud sob and gasped "Good evening."

Alleyn felt that his only hope of avoiding a scene was to hurry things along at a business-like canter.

"It was extremely kind of you both to come," he said briskly. "I shan't keep you more than a few minutes. As you know, we are to go óver the events of the operation, and I thought it better to start from here." He glanced cheerfully at Ruth.

"Certainly," said Lady O'Callaghan.

"Now." Alleyn turned towards the bed, immaculate with his smooth linen and tower of rounded pillows. "Now, Nurse Graham has brought you here. When you come in you sit—where? On each side of the bed? Is that how it was, nurse?"

"Yes. Lady O'Callaghan was here," answered the special quietly.

"Then if you wouldn't mind taking up those positions——"

With an air of stooping to the level of a rather vulgar farce, Lady O'Callaghan sat in the chair on the right-hand side of the bed.

"Come along, Ruth," she said tranquilly.

"But why? Inspector Alleyn—it's so dreadful—so horribly cold-blooded—unnecessary. I don't understand . . . You were so kind . . ." She boggled over her words, turned her head towards him with a gesture of complete wretchedness. Alleyn walked quickly towards her.

"I'm so sorry," he said. "I know it's beastly. Take courage—your brother would understand, I think."

She gazed miserably at him. With her large unlovely face blotched with tears, and her pale eyes staring doubtfully up into his, she seemed dreadfully vulnerable. Something in his manner may have given her a little help. Like an obedient and unwieldly animal she got up and blundered across to the other chair.

"What now, nurse?"

"The patient half regained consciousness soon after we came in. I heard Sir John and went out."

"Will you do that, please?"

She went away quietly.

"And now," Alleyn went on, "what happened? Did the patient speak?"

"I believe he said the pain was severe. Nothing else," murmured Lady O'Callaghan.

"What did you say to each other?"

"I—I told him it was his appendix and that the doctor would soon be here—something of that sort. He seemed to lose consciousness again, I thought."

"Did you speak to each other?"

"I don't remember."

Alleyn made a shot in the dark.

"Did you discuss his pain?"

"I do not think so," she said composedly.

Ruth turned her head and gazed with a sort of damp surprise at her sister-in-law.

"You remember doing so, do you, Miss O'Callaghan?" said Alleyn.

"I think—yes—oh, Cicely!"

"What is it?" asked Alleyn gently.

"I said something—about—how I wished—oh, Cicely!"

The door opened and Nurse Graham came in again.

"I think I came back about now to say Sir John would like to see Lady O'Callaghan," she said with a troubled glance at Ruth.

"Very well. Will you go out with her, please, Lady O'Callaghan?" They went out and Ruth and the inspector looked at each other across the smug little bed. Suddenly Ruth uttered a veritable howl and flung herself face-down among the appliqué-work on the counterpane.

"Listen," said Alleyn, "and tell me if I'm wrong. Mr. Sage had given you a little box of powders that he said would relieve the pain. Now the others have left the room, you feel you must give your brother one of these powders. There is the water and the glass on that table by your side. You unwrap the box, drop the paper on the floor, shake out one of the powders and give it to him in a glass of water. It seems to relieve the pain and when they return he's easier? Am I right?"

"Oh," wailed Ruth, raising her head. "Oh, how did you know? Cicely said I'd better not say. I told her. Oh, what shall I do?"

"Have you kept the box with the other powders?"

"Yes. He—they told me not to, but—but I thought if they were poison and I'd killed him——" Her voice rose with a shrill note of horror. "I thought I'd take them—myself. Kill myself. Lots of us do, you know. Great-Uncle Eustace did, and Cousin Olive Casbeck, and——"

"You're not going to do anything so cowardly. What would he have thought of you? You're going to do the brave thing and help us to find the truth. Come along," said Alleyn, for all the world as if she were a child, "come along. Where are these terrible powders? In that bag still, I don't mind betting."

"Yes," whispered Ruth, opening her eyes very wide. "They are in that bag. You're quite right. You're very clever to think of that. I thought if you arrested me——" She made a very strange gesture with her clenched hand, jerking it up across her mouth.

"Give them to me," said Alleyn.

She began obediently to scuffle in the vast bag. All sorts of things came shooting out. He was in a fever of impatience lest the others should return, and moved to the door. At last the round cardboard box appeared. He gathered up the rest of Ruth's junk and bundled it back as the door opened. Nurse Graham stood aside to let Phillips in.

"I think it was about now," she said.

"Right," said Alleyn. "Now, Sir John, I believe Miss O'Callaghan left the room while you examined the patient, diagnosed the trouble, and decided on an immediate operation."

"Yes. When Lady O'Callaghan returned I suggested that Somerset Black should operate."

"Quite so. Lady O'Callaghan urged you to do it yourself. Everyone agree to that?"

"Yes," said Nurse Graham quietly. Ruth merely sat and gaped. Lady O'Callaghan turned with an unusual abruptness and walked to the window.

"Then you, Sir John, went away to prepare for the operation?"

"Yes."

"That finishes this part of the business, then."

"No!"

Cicely O'Callaghan's voice rang out so fiercely that they all jumped. She had faced round and stood with her eyes fixed on Phillips. She looked magnificent. It was as if a colourless façade had been floot-lit.

"No! Why do you deliberately ignore what we all

heard, what I myself have told you? Ask Sir John what my husband said when he saw who it was we had brought here to help him." She turned deliberately to Phillips. "What did Derek say to you—what did he say?"

Phillips looked at her as though he saw her for the first time. His face expressed nothing but a profound astonishment. When he answered it was with a kind of reasonableness and with no suggestion of heroics.

"He was frightened," he said.

"He cried out to us: 'Don't let——' You remember" —she appealed with assurance to Nurse Graham—"you remember what he looked like—you understood what he meant?"

"I said then," said Nurse Graham with spirit, "and I say now, that Sir Derek did not know what he was saying."

"Well," remarked Alleyn mildly, "as we all know about it, I think you and I, Sir John, will go downstairs." He turned to the O'Callaghans.

"Actually, I believe, you both stayed on in the hospital during the operation, but, of course, there is no need for you to do so now. Lady O'Callaghan, shall I ask for your car to take you back to Catherine Street? If you will forgive me, I must go to the theatre."

Suddenly he realised that she was in such a fury that she could not answer. He took Phillips by the elbow and propelled him through the door.

"We will leave Nurse Graham," he said, "alone with her patient."

CHAPTER XVII

RECONSTRUCTION CONCLUDED

Thursday, the eighteenth. Late afternoon.

THE "theatre party" appeared to have entered heartily into the spirit of the thing. A most convincing activity was displayed in the anteroom, where Sister Marigold, Jane Harden and a very glum-faced Banks washed and clattered while Inspector Fox, his massive form wedged into a corner, looked on with an expressionless countenance and a general air of benignity. A faint bass drone from beyond the swing-door informed Alleyn of the presence in the theatre of Inspector Boys.

"All ready, matron?" asked Alleyn.

"Quite ready, inspector."

"Well, here we all are." He stood aside and Phillips, Thoms and Roberts walked in.

"Are you at about the same stage as you were when the doctors came in?"

"At exactly the same stage."

"Good. What happens now?" He turned to the men. No one spoke for a moment. Roberts turned deferentially towards Phillips, who had moved across to Jane Harden. Jane and Phillips did not look at each other. Phillips appeared not to have heard Alleyn's question. Thoms cleared his throat importantly.

"Well now, let's see. If I'm not speaking out of my

turn, I should say we got down to the job straight away. Roberts said he'd go along to the anæsthetic-room and Sir John, I believe, went into the theatre? That correct, sir?"

"Did you go into the theatre imediately, Sir John?" asked Alleyn.

"What? I? Yes, I believe so."

"Before you washed?"

"Naturally."

"Well, let's start, shall we? Dr. Roberts, did you go alone to the anæsthetic-room?"

"No. Nurse—er——?" Roberts blinked at Banks. "Nurse Banks went with me. I looked at the anæsthetising apparatus and asked Nurse Banks to let Sir Derek's nurse know when we were ready."

"Will you go along, then? Fox, you take over with Dr. Roberts. Now, please, Sir John."

Phillips at once went through into the theatre, followed by Alleyn. Boys broke off his subterranean humming and at a word from Alleyn took his place in the anteroom. Phillips, without speaking, crossed to the side table, which was set out as before with the three syringes in dishes of water. The surgeon took his hypodermic case from his pocket, looked at the first tube, appeared to find it empty, took out the second, and having squirted a syringeful of water into a measure-glass, dropped in a single tablet.

"That is what—what I believe I did," he said.

"And then? You returned to the anteroom? No. What about Mr. Thoms?"

"Yes. Thoms should be here now."

"Mr. Thoms, please!" shouted Alleyn.

The door swung open and Thoms came in.

"Hullo, hullo. Want me?"

"I understood you watched Sir John take up the hyoscine solution into the syringe."

"Oh! Yes, b'lieve I did," said Thoms, rather less boisterously.

"You commented on the amount of water."

"Yes, I know, but—look here, you don't want to go thinking——"

"I simply want a reconstruction without comment, Mr. Thoms."

"Oh, quite, quite."

Phillips stood with the syringe in his hand. He looked gravely and rather abstractedly at his assistant. At a nod from Alleyn he filled the syringe.

"It is now that Thoms remarks on the quantity of water," he said quietly. "I snub him and go back into the anæsthetic-room, where I give the injection. The patient is there with the special nurse."

He took up the syringe and walked away. Thoms moved away with a grimace at Alleyn, who said abruptly:

"Just a moment, Mr. Thoms. I think you stayed behind in the theatre for a minute or two."

"No, I didn't—beg your pardon, inspector. I thought I went out to the anteroom before Sir John moved."

"Sir John thought not, and the nurses had the impression you came in a little later."

"Maybe," said Thoms. "I really can't remember."

"Have you no idea what you did during the two or three minutes?"

"None."

"Oh. In that case I'll leave you. Boys!"

Inspector Boys returned to the theatre and Alleyn went out. In about a minute Thoms joined him.

Sir John appeared in the anteroom and washed up, assisted by Jane Harden and the matron, who afterwards helped the surgeons to dress up.

"I feel rather an ass," said Thoms brightly. Nobody answered him.

"It is now, said Phillips in the same grave, detached

manner, "that Mr. Thoms tells me about the play at the Palladium."

"All agreed?" Alleyn asked the others. The women murmured an assent.

"Now what happens?"

"Pardon me, but I remember Mr. Thoms went into the theatre and then called me in to him," murmured Sister Marigold.

"Thank you, matron. Away you go, then." Alleyn waited until the doors had swung to and then turned to where Phillips, now wearing his gown and mask, stood silently beside Jane Harden.

"So you were left alone together at this juncture?" he said, without stressing it.

"Yes," said Phillips.

"Do you mind telling me what was said?"

"Oh, please," whispered Jane. "Please, please!" It was the first time she had spoken.

"Can't you let her off this?" said Phillips. There was a sort of urgency in his voice now.

"I'm sorry—I would if I could."

"I'll tell him, Jane. We said it was a strange situation. I again asked her to marry me. She said no—that she felt she belonged to O'Callaghan. Something to that effect. She tried to explain her point of view."

"You've left something out—you're not thinking of yourself." She stood in front of him, for all the world as though she was prepared to keep Alleyn off. "He said then that he didn't want to operate and that he'd give anything to be out of it. His very words. He told me he'd tried to persuade—her—*his* wife—to get another surgeon. He hated the idea of operating. Does that look as though he meant any harm? Does it? Does it? He never thinks of himself—he only wants to help me, and I'm not worth it. I've told him so a hundred times——"

"Jane, my dear, don't."

There was a tap on the outer door and Roberts looked in.

"I think it's time I came and washed up," he said.

"Come in, Dr. Roberts."

Roberts glanced at the others.

"Forgive me, Sir John," he began with the deference that he always used when he spoke to Phillips, "but as I remember it, Mr. Thoms came in with me at this juncture."

"You're quite right, Roberts," agreed Phillips courteously.

"Mr. Thoms, please," called Alleyn again.

Thoms shot back into the room.

"Late again, am I?" he remarked. "Truth of the matter is I can't for the life of me remember all the ins and outs of it. I suppose I wash up now? What?"

"If you please," said Alleyn sedately.

At last they were ready and Roberts returned to Inspector Fox and the anæsthetic-room. The others, accompanied by Alleyn, went to the theatre.

The cluster of lights above the table had been turned up and Alleyn again felt that sense of expectancy in the theatre. Phillips went immediately to the window end of the table and waited with his gloved hands held out in front of him. Thoms stood at the foot of the table. Sister Marigold and Jane were farther away.

There was a slight vibratory, rattling noise. The door into the anæsthetic-room opened and a trolley appeared, propelled by Banks. Dr. Roberts and Nurse Graham walked behind it. His hands were stretched out over the head of the trolley. On it was a sort of elongated bundle made of pillows and blankets. He and Banks lifted this on the table and Banks put a screen, about two feet high, across the place that represented the patient's chest. The others drew nearer. Banks pushed the trolley away.

Now that they had all closed round the table the

illusion was complete. The conical glare poured itself down between the white figures, bathing their masked faces and the fronts of their gowns in a violence of light, and leaving their backs in sharp shadow, so that between shadow and light there was a kind of shimmering border that ran round their outlines. Boys and Fox had come in from their posts and stood impassive in the doorways. Alleyn walked round the theatre to a position about two yards behind the head of the table.

Roberts wheeled forward the anæsthetising apparatus. Suddenly, entirely without warning, one of the white figures gave a sharp exclamation, something between a cry and a protest.

"It's too horrible—really—I can't——!"

It was the matron, the impeccable Sister Marigold. She had raised her hands in front of her face as if shutting off some shocking spectacle. Now she backed away from the table and collided with the anæsthetising apparatus. She stumbled, kicked it so that it moved, and half fell, clutching at it as she did so.

There was a moment's silence and then a portly little figure in white suddenly screamed out an oath.

"What the bloody hell are you doing? Do you want to kill——"

"What's the matter?" said Alleyn sharply. His voice had an incisive edge that made all the white heads turn. "What is it, Mr. Thoms?"

Thoms was down on his knees, an absurd figure, frantically reaching out to the apparatus. Roberts, who had stooped down to the lower framework of the cruet-like stand and had rapidly inspected it, thrust the little fat man aside. He tested the nuts that held the frame together. His hands shook a little and his face, the only one unmasked, was very pale.

"It's perfectly secure, Thoms," he said. "None of the nuts are loose. Matron, please stand away."

"I didn't mean—I'm sorry," began Sister Marigold.

"Do you realise—" said Thoms in a voice that was scarcely recognisable—" do you realise that if one of those cylinders had fallen out and burst, we'd none of us be alive. Do you know that?"

"Nonsense, Thoms," said Roberts in an unsteady voice. "It's most unlikely that anything of the sort could occur. It would take more than that to burst a cylinder, I assure you."

"I'm sure I'm very sorry, Mr. Thoms," said matron sulkily. "Accidents will happen."

"Accidents mustn't happen," barked Thoms. He squatted down and tested the nuts.

"Please leave it alone, Mr. Thoms," said Roberts crisply. "I assure you it's perfectly safe."

Thoms did not answer. He got to his feet and turned back to the table.

"And now what happens?" asked Alleyn. His deep voice sounded like a tonic note. Phillips spoke quietly.

"I made the incision and carried on with the operation. I found peritonitis and a ruptured abscess of the appendix. I proceeded in the usual way. At this stage, I think, Dr. Roberts began to be uneasy about the pulse and the general condition. Am I right, Roberts?"

"Quite right, sir. I asked for an injection of camphor."

Without waiting to be told, Nurse Banks went to the side table, took up the ampoule of camphor, went through the pantomime of filling a syringe and returned to the patient.

"I injected it," she said concisely.

Through Alleyn's head ran the old jingle: "A made an apple pie, B bit it, C cut it—I injected it," he added mentally.

"And then?" he asked.

"After completing the operation I asked for the anti-gas serum."

"I got it," said Jane bravely.

She walked to the table.

"I stood, hesitating. I felt faint. I—I couldn't focus things properly."

"Did anybody notice this?"

"I looked round and saw something was wrong," said Phillips. "She simply stood there swaying a little."

"You notice this, Mr. Thoms?"

"Well, I'm afraid, inspector, I rather disgraced myself by kicking up a rumpus. What, nurse? Bit hard on you, what? Didn't know how the land lay. Too bad, wasn't it?"

"When you had finished, Nurse Harden brought the large syringe?"

"Yes."

Jane came back with the syringe on a tray. "Thoms took it," went the jingle in Alleyn's head.

"I injected it," said Thoms.

"Mr. Thoms then asked about the condition," added Roberts. "I said it was disquieting. I remember Sir John remarked that although he knew the patient personally he had had no idea he was ill. Nurse Banks and I lifted the patient on to the trolley and he was taken away."

They did this with the dummy.

"Then I fainted," said Jane.

"A dramatic finish—what?" shouted Thoms, who seemed to have quite recovered his equilibrium.

"The end," said Alleyn, "came later. The patient was then taken back to his room, where you attended him, Dr. Roberts. Was anyone with you?"

"Nurse Graham was there throughout. I left her in the room when I returned here to report on the general condition, which I considered markedly worse."

"And in the meantime Sir John and Mr. Thoms washed up in the anteroom?"

"Yes," said Phillips.

"What did you talk about?"

"I don't remember."

"Oh yes, sir, you do, surely," said Thoms. "We talked about Nurse Harden doing a faint, and I said I could see the operation had upset you, and you—" he grinned —"you first said it hadn't, you know, and then said it had. Very natural, really," he explained to Alleyn, who raised one eyebrow and turned to the nurses.

"And you cleaned up the theatre, and Miss Banks gave one of her well-known talks on the Dawn of the Proletariat Day?"

"I did," said Banks with a snap.

"Meanwhile Dr. Roberts came down and reported, and you and Mr. Thoms, Sir John, went up to the patient?"

"Yes. The matron, Sister Marigold, joined us. We found the patient's condition markedly worse. As you know, he died about half an hour later, without regaining consciousness."

"Thank you. That covers the ground. I am extremely grateful to all of you for helping us with this rather unpleasant business. I won't keep you any longer." He turned to Phillips. "You would like to get out of your uniforms, I'm sure."

"If you're finished," agreed Phillips. Fox opened the swing-door and he went through, followed by Thoms, Sister Marigold, Jane Harden, and Banks. Dr. Roberts crossed to the anæsthetising apparatus.

"I'll get this out of the way," he said.

"Oh—do you mind leaving it while you change?" said Alleyn. "I just want to make a plan of the floor."

"Certainly," said Roberts.

"Would you be very kind and see if you can beat me up a sheet of paper and a pencil, Dr. Roberts? Sorry to bother you, but I hardly like to send one of my own people hunting for it."

"Shall I ask?" suggested Roberts.

He put his head round the door into the anteroom and spoke to someone on the other side.

"Inspector Alleyn would like——"

Fox walked heavily across from the other end of the theatre.

"I can hear a telephone ringing its head off out there, sir," he said, looking fixedly at Alleyn.

"Really? I wonder if it's that call from the Yard? Go and see, will you, Fox? Sister Marigold won't mind, I'm sure."

Fox went out.

"Inspector Alleyn," ventured Roberts, "I do hope that the reconstruction has been satisfactory——" He broke off. Phillips's resonant voice could be heard in the anteroom. With a glance towards it Roberts ended wistfully: "—from every point of view."

Alleyn smiled at him, following his glance.

"From *that* point of view, Dr. Roberts, most satisfactory."

"I'm extremely glad."

Jane Harden came in with a sheet of paper and pencil, which she gave Alleyn. She went out. Roberts watched Alleyn lay the paper on the side table and take out his steel tape measure. Fox returned.

"Telephone for Dr. Roberts, I believe, sir," he announced.

"Oh—for you, is it?" said Alleyn.

Roberts went out through the anæsthetic-room.

"Shut that door, quick," said Alleyn urgently.

Evidently he had changed his mind about making a plan. He darted like a cat across the room and bent over the frame of the anæsthetic apparatus. His fingers were busy with the nuts.

Boys stood in front of one door, Fox by the other.

"Hell's teeth, it's stiff," muttered Alleyn.

The double doors from the anteroom opened suddenly, banging Inspector Boys in the broad of his extensive back.

"Just a minute, sir, just a minute," he rumbled.

Under his extended arm appeared the face of Mr. Thoms. His eyes were fixed on Alleyn.

"What are you doing?" he said. "What are you doing?"

"Just a minute, if *you* please, sir," repeated Boys, and with an enormous but moderate paw he thrust Thoms back and closed the doors.

"Look at this!" whispered Alleyn.

Fox and Boys, for a split second, glimpsed what he held in his hand. Then he bent down again and worked feverishly.

"What'll we do?" asked Fox quietly. "Go right into it—now?"

For an instant Alleyn hesitated. Then he said:

"No—not here. Wait! Work it this way."

He had given his instructions when Roberts returned from the telephone.

"Nobody there," he told them. "I rang up my house, but there's no message. Whoever it was must have been cut off."

"Bore for you," said Alleyn.

Sister Marigold came in, followed by Thoms. Marigold saw the Yard men still in possession, and hesitated.

"Hullo, 'ullo," shouted Thoms, "what's all this. Caught Roberts in the act?"

"Really, Mr. Thoms," said Roberts in a rage and went over to his apparatus.

"All right, matron," said Alleyn, "I'm done. You want to clear up, I expect."

"Oh, well—yes."

"Go ahead. We'll make ourselves scarce. Fox, you and Boys give Dr. Roberts a hand out with that cruet-stand."

"Thank you," said Roberts, "I'll manage."

"No trouble at all, sir," Fox assured him.

Alleyn left them there. He ran downstairs and out into Brook Street, where he hailed a taxi.

In forty minutes the same taxi put him down in Wigmore Street. This time he had two plain-clothes sergeants with him. Dr. Roberts's little butler opened the door. His face was terribly white. He looked at Alleyn without speaking and then stood aside. Alleyn, followed by his men, walked into the drawing-room. Roberts stood in front of the fireplace. Above him the picture of the little lake and the Christmas trees shone cheerfully in the lamplight. Fox stood inside the door and Boys near the window. The anæsthetic apparatus had been wheeled over by the desk.

When Roberts saw Alleyn he tried to speak, but at first could not. His lips moved as though he was speaking, but there were no words. Then at last they came.

"Inspector Alleyn—why—have you sent these men —after me?"

For a moment they looked at each other.

"I had to," said Alleyn. "Dr. Roberts, I have a warrant here for your arrest. I must warn you——"

"What do you mean?" screamed Roberts. "You've no grounds—no proof—you fool—what are you doing?"

Alleyn walked over to the thing like a cruet. He stooped down, unscrewed something that looked like a nut and drew it out. With it came a hypodermic syringe. The "nut" was the top of the piston.

"Grounds enough," said Alleyn.

It took the four men to hold Roberts and they had to put handcuffs on him. The insane are sometimes physically very strong.

CHAPTER XVIII

RETROSPECTIVE

Saturday, the twentieth. Evening.

Two evenings after the arrest Alleyn dined with Nigel
and Angela. The inspector had already been badgered
by Nigel for copy and had thrown him a few bones to
gnaw. Angela, however, pined for first-hand information. During dinner the inspector was rather silent and
withdrawn. Something prompted Angela to kick Nigel
smartly on the shin when he broached the subject of
the arrest. Nigel suppressed a cry of pain and glared at
her. She shook her head slightly.

"Was it very painful, Bathgate?" asked Alleyn.

"Er—oh—yes," said Nigel sheepishly.

"How did you know I kicked him?" Angela inquired.
"You must be a detective."

"Not so that you would notice it, but perhaps I am
about to strike form again."

"Hullo—all bitter, are you? Aren't you pleased with
yourself over this case, Mr. Alleyn?" Angela ventured.

"One never gets a great deal of gratification from a
fluke."

"A fluke!" exclaimed Nigel.

"Just that."

He held his glass of port under his nose, glanced
significantly at Niget and sipped it.

"Go on," he said resignedly. "Go on. Ask me. I know perfectly well why I'm here and you don't produce a wine like this every evening. Bribery. Subtle corruption. Isn't it, now?"

"Yes," said Nigel simply.

"I won't have Mr. Alleyn bullied," said Angela.

"You would if *he* could," rejoined Alleyn cryptically. "I know your tricks and your manners."

The others were silent.

"As a matter of fact," Alleyn continued, "I have every intention of talking for hours."

They beamed.

"What an angel you are, to be sure," said Angela. "Bring that decanter next door. Don't dare sit over it in here. The ladies are about to leave the diningroom."

She got up; Alleyn opened the door for her, and she went through into Nigel's little sitting-room, where she hastily cast four logs on the fire, pulled up a low table between two arm-chairs, and sat down on the hearthrug.

"Come on!" she called sternly.

They came in. Alleyn put the decanter down reverently on the table, and in a moment they were all settled.

"Now," said Angela, "I do call this fun."

She looked from Nigel to Alleyn. Each had the contented air of the well-fed male. The fire blazed up with a roar and a crackle, lighting the inspector's dark head and his admirable hands. He settled himself back and, easing his chin, turned and smiled at her.

"You may begin," said Angela.

"But—where from?"

"From the beginning—well, from the operating theatre."

"Oh. The remark I invariably make about the theatre is that it afforded the ideal setting for a murder. The whole place was cleaned up scientifically—hygienically

—completely—as soon as the body of the victim was removed. No chance of a fingerprint, no significant bits and pieces left on the floor. Nothing. As a matter of fact, of course, had it been left exactly as it was, we should have found nothing that pointed to Roberts." Alleyn fell silent again.

"Begin from where you first suspected Roberts," suggested Nigel.

"From where *you* suspected him, rather. The funny little man, you know."

"By gum, yes. So I did."

"Did *you*?" Angela asked.

"I had no definite theory about him," said Alleyn. "That's why I talked about a fluke. I was uneasy about him. I had a hunch, and I hate hunches. The first day I saw him in his house I began to feel jumpy about him, and fantastic ideas kept dodging about at the back of my mind. He was, it seemed, a fanatic. That long, hectic harangue about hereditary taints—somehow it was too vehement. He was obviously nervous about the case and yet he couldn't keep off it. He very delicately urged the suicide theory and backet it up with a lecture on eugenics. He was certainly sincere, too sincere, terribly earnest. The whole atmosphere was unbalanced. I recognised the man with an *idèe fixe*. Then he told me a long story about how he'd once given an overdose, and that was why he never gave injections. That made me uncomfortable, because it was such a handy proof of innocence. '*He* can't have done the job, because he never gives an injection.' Then I saw his stethoscope with rows of notches on the stem, and again there was a perfect explanation. He said it was a sort of tally for every anæsthetic he gave successfully to patients with heart disease. I was reminded of Indian tomahawks and Edward S. Ellis, and more particularly of a catapult I had as a boy and the notches I cut in the handle for every bird I killed. The fantastic notion that the stetho-

scope was *that* sort of tally-stick nagged and nagged at
me. When we found he was one of the Lenin Hall lot I
wondered if he could possibly be their agent, and yet I
didn't somehow think there was anything in the Lenin
Hall lot. When we discovered he had hoped to egg
them on over the Sterilization Bill I felt that accounted
perfectly for his association with them. Next time I
saw him I meant to surprise him with a sudden question about them. He completely defeated me by talking
about them of his own accord. That might have been a
subtle move, but I didn't think so. He lent me his book
and here again I found the fanatic. I don't know why
it is that pursuit of any branch of scientific thought
which is greatly concerned with sex so often leads to
morbid obsession. Not always, by any means—but very
often. I've met it over and over again. It's an interesting
point and I'd like to know the explanation. Roberts's
book is a sound, a well-written plea for rational breed-
ing. It is not in the least hysterical, and yet, behind it,
in the personality of the writer, I smelt hysteria. There
was one chapter where he said that a future civilization
might avoid the expense and trouble of supporting its
a-ments and de-ments, by eliminating them altogether.
'Sterilization,' he wrote, 'might in time be replaced by
extermination.' After reading that I forced myself to
face up to that uneasy idea that had worried me ever
since I first spoke to him. O'Callaghan came of what
Roberts would regard as tainted stock. Suppose—suppose, thought I, blushing at my own credulity, suppose
Roberts had got the bright idea of starting the good
work by destroying such people every time he got the
opportunity? Suppose he had brought it off several
times before, and that every time he'd had a success he
ticked it up on his stethoscope?"

"Oh, murder!" Nigel apostrophised.

"You may say so."

"Have some port."

"Thank you. It sounded so incredibly far-fetched that I simply hadn't the nerve to confide in Fox. I carried on with all the others—Mr. Sage and his remedies, Phillips and his girl, Banks and the Bolshies. Well, the patent medicine Sage provided through Miss O'Callaghan—'Fulvitavolts,' he calls it—has an infinitesimal amount of hyoscine. The second lot that Miss O'Callaghan administered in the hospital was an unknown quantity until I got the remnant from her. Of course, the fact that he had been responsible for O'Callaghan taking any hyoscine at all threw our Harold into a fearful terror, especially as he was one of the Lenin Hall lot. He tried to get me to believe the second concoction was a doctor's prescription, and very nearly led himself into real trouble. We have since found that this drug, too, only contained a very small amount of hyoscine. Exit Mr. Sage. Banks might have substituted hyoscine for camphor when she prepared the syringe, but I found that the stock solution of hyoscine contained the full amount minus one dose that was accounted for. She might have smuggled in another somehow, or she might have filled up the jar afterwards, but it didn't seem likely. Phillips remained and Phillips worried me terribly. He loomed so large with his threats, his opportunity, his motive. Roberts paled beside him. I caught myself continually opposing these two men. After all, as far as one could see, Roberts had had no chance of giving a hypodermic injection, whereas Phillips, poor devil, had had every opportunity. I staged the reconstruction partly to see if there *was* any way in which Roberts could have done it. I called for him at his house. Now, although I had asked Phillips specifically to have the anæsthetic appliance, Roberts was coming away without it. When I reminded him, he went and got it. I noticed that he wasn't keen on my handling it, and that several times he touched the nuts. It was perfectly reasonable, but it made me look at them and kept them in my mind. Remember I was by no means wedded to my fantastic idea—rather the reverse. I was ashamed of it and I still reasoned, though I did not feel, that Phillips was the principal suspect. We watched them all closely. Then came the fluke—the amazing, the incredible fluke. Old Marigold lost her nerve and did a trip over the cruet-thing that holds the gasometers, Thoms helped Roberts, in a way, by a spirited rendering of the jack-in-office. Thoms is a bit of a funk and he was scared. He made a rumpus. If it hadn't been for my 'idea,' I shouldn't have watched Roberts. As it was, he gave a magnificent performance. But he went green round the gills and he was most careful to let no one touch the nuts. As a matter of fact, I believe Thoms's funk was entirely superfluous—it is most unlikely that the cylinder would blow up. Think what a shock it must have been to Roberts. Suppose the syringe had fallen out! Practically an impossibility— but in the panic of the moment his imagination, his 'guilty knowledge' if you like, would play tricks with his reason. I rather felt I had allowed mine to do the same. My dears, my head was in a whirl, I promise you."

"But when," asked Angela, "did Dr. Roberts inject the hyoscine?"

"I think soon after the patient was put on the table. The screen over the chest would hide his hands."

"I see."

"After the reconstruction Roberts wouldn't leave us alone. He hung about in the theatre, intent, of course, on keeping me away from the cruet. Fox, bless his heart, rumbled this ruse and staged a bogus telephone call. He saw I wanted to be rid of Roberts. As soon as we were alone I fell on the cruet, and, after a nerve-racking fumble, unearthed the syringe. Eureka! Denouement! Fox nearly had a fit of the vapours."

"So you arrested him there and then!" cried Angela.

"No. No, I didn't. For one thing I hadn't a warrant and for another—oh, well——"

Alleyn rested his nose on his clasped hands.

"Now what's coming?" asked Angela.

"I rather liked the little creature. It would have been an unpleasant business pulling him in there. Anyway, I went off and got a warrant, and Fox and Boys accompanied him home. They watched him carefully in case he tried to give himself the *coup de grâce,* but he didn't. When I arrested him he had, I believe, a sudden and an appalling shock, a kind of dreadful moment of lucidity. He fought us so violently that he seemed like a sane man gone mad, but I believe he was a madman gone sane. It only lasted a few minutes. Now I don't think he cares at all. He has made a complete confession. He's batty. He'll have to stand his trial, but I think they'll find that the nut in the cruet-stand is not the only one loose. It may even be that Roberts, recognizing the taint of madness in himself, felt the eugenic urge the more strongly and the need for eliminating the unfit. In that point of view there is precisely the kind of mad logic one would expect to find in such a case."

"If it hadn't been for the matron's trip, would you never have got him?" asked Nigel.

"I think we should—in the end. We should have got his history from Canada and Australasia. It's coming through now. When it's complete I am pretty certain we shall find a series of deaths after anæsthetics given by Roberts. They will all prove to be cases where there were signs of hereditary insanity. I shouldn't mind betting they correspond with the notches on the stethoscope—minus one."

"Minus one?" asked Nigel.

"He added a fresh notch, no doubt, on Thursday, the eleventh. The last one does look more recent, although he'd rubbed a bit of dirt into it. You may think, as judges say when they mean you ought to think, that it was an extremely rum thing for him to leave the syringe in the cruet after the job was done. Not so rum. It was really the safest place imaginable. Away from there it would have been a suspicious-looking object, with a nut, instead of the ordinary top, to the piston. I believe that extraordinary little man filled it up with hyoscine whenever he was called out to give an anæsthetic to someone he did not know, just on the off-chance the patient should turn out to be what I understand sheep-farmers call a 'cull.' It's a striking example of the logic of the lunatic."

"Oh," cried Angela, "I do hope they find him insane."

"Do you?"

"Don't you?"

"I hardly know. That means a criminal lunatic asylum. It's a pity we are not allowed to hand him one of his own hypodermics."

There was a short silence.

"Have some port?" said Nigel.

"Thank you," said Alleyn. He did not pour it out, however, but sat looking abstractedly into the fire.

"You see," he murmured at last, "he's done his job. From his point of view it's all a howling success. He does nothing but tell us how clever he's been. His one anxiety is lest he may not be appreciated. He's busy writing a monograph for which all your gods of Fleet Street, Bathgate, will offer fabulous prices. At least he is assured of competent defence."

"What about Sir John Phillips and Jane Harden?" asked Angela.

"What about them, Miss Angela?"

"Is she going to mary him now?"

"How should I know?"

"She'll be a fool if she doesn't," said Angela emphatically.

"I'm afraid you've got the movie-mind. You want a

final close-up. 'John—I want you to know that—that——' Ecstatic glare at short distance into each other's faces. Sir John utters an amorous growl: 'You damned little fool,' and snatches her to his bosom. Slow fade-out."

"That's the stuff," said Angela. "I like a happy ending."

"We don't often see it in the Force," said Alleyn. "Have some port?"

"Thank you."

"SHE WRITES BETTER THAN CHRISTIE."
—THE NEW YORK TIMES BOOK REVIEW—

NGAIO MARSH

BESTSELLING PAPERBACKS BY A
"GRAND MASTER" OF THE MYSTERY WRITERS OF AMERICA.

_____	06341-X ARTISTS IN CRIME	$2.50
_____	05871-8 BLACK AS HE'S PAINTED	$2.25
_____	06013-5 CLUTCH OF CONSTABLES	$2.25
_____	05997-8 DEATH AND THE DANCING FOOTMAN	$2.25
_____	05998-6 DEATH AT THE BAR	$2.25
_____	06224-3 DEATH IN A WHITE TIE	$2.50
_____	06166-2 DEATH IN ECSTASY	$2.50
_____	06177-8 DEATH OF A FOOL	$2.50
_____	06091-7 DEATH OF A PEER	$2.25
_____	05943-9 ENTER A MURDERER	$2.25
_____	06118-2 FINAL CURTAIN	$2.25
_____	06178-6 GRAVE MISTAKE	$2.50
_____	06309-6 HAND IN GLOVE	$2.50
_____	06071-2 KILLER DOLPHIN	$2.25
_____	05966-8 LAST DITCH	$2.25
_____	06490-3 A MAN LAY DEAD	$2.50
_____	06477-1 SCALES OF JUSTICE	$2.50
_____	06185-9 SINGING IN THE SHROUDS	$2.25
_____	06179-4 SPINSTERS IN JEOPARDY	$2.50
_____	06164-6 VINTAGE MURDER	$2.25
_____	06180-8 WHEN IN ROME	$2.50

Available at your local bookstore or return this form to:

J JOVE/BOOK MAILING SERVICE
P.O. Box 690, Rockville Center, N.Y. 11570

Please enclose 50¢ for postage and handling for one book, 25¢
each add'l book ($1.25 max.). No cash, CODs or stamps. Total
amount enclosed: $_____ in check or money order.

NAME_____

ADDRESS_____

CITY_____STATE/ZIP_____

Allow six weeks for delivery.   SK-7

NGAIO MARSH

_____	06014-3	COLOUR SCHEME	$2.50
_____	06019-4	DIED IN THE WOOL	$2.50
_____	06007-0	FALSE SCENT	$2.50
_____	05967-6	THE NURSING HOME MURDER	$2.50
_____	06011-9	OVERTURE TO DEATH	$2.25
_____	05995-1	PHOTO FINISH	$2.50
_____	06285-5	TIED UP IN TINSEL	$2.25

"Why can't you leave me alone?"

Jassy cried desperately, her mind seeming to split in two. "I hate you!"

She wanted to believe that was true, but the truth was she no longer knew what she felt.

"Do you?" Leigh inquired, unmoved. "Or do you just hate me for saying what you don't want to hear?"

Those tiger's eyes seemed to burn into Jassy's gray ones, challenging and mesmerizing all at once so that Jassy was unable to drag her gaze away.

"Why don't you face up to the truth," he continued. "I don't mind admitting I want to make love to you. You're a very lovely girl. But it's more than that—you're something special. I knew from the first moment I saw you that I wanted you. I still do."

Kate Walker chose the Brontë sisters, the development of their writing from childhood to maturity, as the topic for her master's thesis. It is little wonder, then, that she should go on to write romance fiction. She lives in the United Kingdom with her husband and son, and when she isn't writing, she tries to keep up with her hobbies of embroidery, knitting, antiques and, of course, reading.

Books by Kate Walker

HARLEQUIN ROMANCE

2783—GAME OF HAZARD
2826—ROUGH DIAMOND
2910—CAPTIVE LOVER
2920—MAN OF SHADOWS
2957—THE CINDERELLA TRAP
3078—JESTER'S GIRL

HARLEQUIN PRESENTS

1053—BROKEN SILENCE
1196—CHASE THE DAWN
1269—LEAP IN THE DARK

THE GOLDEN THIEF

Kate Walker

Harlequin Books

TORONTO • NEW YORK • LONDON
AMSTERDAM • PARIS • SYDNEY • HAMBURG
STOCKHOLM • ATHENS • TOKYO • MILAN

Original hardcover edition published in 1990
by Mills & Boon Limited

ISBN 0-373-03107-6

Harlequin Romance first edition February 1991

For Noelle

CHAPTER ONE

'I WON'T do it!'

Jassy's tone was adamant, her wide grey eyes stony with rejection of the suggestion that had just been put to her.

'No, Sarah,' she continued emphatically. 'You can say what you like, but I will *not* work for that man.'

'Jassy, you can't mean it!' Her flatmate's tone was sharp with disbelief. 'You can't be thinking of turning this down.'

'I'm not thinking—I'm doing it. I'd have to be totally desperate even to consider it.'

'But a job like this comes up once in a blue moon. And correct me if I'm wrong, but I got the impression that you *were* desperate.'

And that was something she couldn't deny, Jassy admitted privately, pushing a disturbed hand through her long ash-blonde hair before picking up the knife she had dropped when her flatmate had made her announcement, and turning her attention to slicing tomatoes for the salad she was preparing for their evening meal, the unnecessary force of her actions revealing her inner turmoil only too clearly.

She *was* desperate, that was the problem. Her formerly thriving career as an actress had come to an abrupt halt when the play she had been appearing in had turned out to be a complete flop, closing after only three weeks, and for the past two months she had been what was euphemistically known as 'resting'—in other words, unemployed—and the situation showed no sign of righting itself.

She had been to several auditions, but had been unsuccessful, the parts going to other, more experienced actresses, and nothing else seemed to be forthcoming.

7

As a result, she was stony-broke and bored out of her head, which was why she had turned to Sarah's older sister for help. Francesca Templeton ran a secretarial agency, and as Jassy had taken a shorthand and typing course at her parents' insistence she had hoped that the older woman would be able to find a temporary job to tide her over this difficult patch. She would take any job, she had said, but she hadn't anticipated *this* one.

A frown crossed Jassy's forehead as she thought back over the evening from the moment the phone had rung and Sarah had gone to answer it. She had come back into the kitchen with a smugly triumphant grin on her face.

'I told you Cheska would sort things out!' she declared brightly, helping herself to a stick of raw carrot and crunching it between firm white teeth.

'She's found me a job?' Jassy asked, and Sarah nodded, her eyes gleaming.

'And what a job! You've struck lucky this time, mate!'

'What is it? Sarah!' Jassy exclaimed protestingly as her friend smiled mysteriously. 'Tell me!'

'Leigh Benedict!' Sarah announced, rolling her eyes dramatically, then she broke into a wide grin at the look of bewilderment on Jassy's face.

'Leigh Benedict?' she echoed blankly. 'What——?'

'Oh, come on, Jassy! You're the actress——'

'I know of *the* Leigh Benedict, of course!' Jassy declared in exasperation. 'You don't have to be an actress to know about him—but you can't mean——'

'Oh, but I do,' Sarah put in firmly, her response leaving her friend at a loss for words. For a moment Jassy simply stared, her thoughts whirling.

'*The* Leigh Benedict,' she repeated at last, her voice shaking slightly as memories she had thought buried rushed into her mind.

'The Golden Thief himself. You lucky thing! What I wouldn't give for a chance to meet him—and you walk straight into a job as his secretary.'

'I haven't got it yet!' Jassy protested automatically, admitting to herself that, even if she was offered the job, she was unlikely to want to take it. 'What does he want a secretary for anyway?' she added, curiosity getting the better of her.

'To sort out his fan mail,' Sarah told her with a laugh. 'No—honest—it's true. His current secretary's in hospital—appendicitis—and he needs someone to deal with all the letters and generally keep things in order until she gets back. Of course, there'll be other work too. From what Cheska said he's pretty busy with negotiations for this new film he plans to direct, but the fan mail will be more interesting, don't you think? All those love-letters from adoring women, telling him their most secret fantasies.'

'What an awful thought!'

Jassy's face twisted into a grimace of distaste at the idea, and at the thought of the Leigh Benedict hysteria that seemed to have afflicted almost all the female population of Great Britain and America for the past five years. She distrusted such adulation instinctively, mainly because it concentrated on the actor's looks and lifestyle, rather than any critical appreciation of his work. Leigh Benedict was devastatingly handsome, there was no denying that. The blond good looks that had, in part, earned him the nickname of the Golden Thief in the popular Press would always make him stand out in a crowd, even in the film world, and, having seen him in person, Jassy knew that his physical attraction had in no way been exaggerated. But looks weren't everything and she had her own private reasons for believing that Leigh Benedict was not the sort of man she would like in the least. However tempting the idea of gaining inside knowledge of his projected film might be, the thought of working for him was positively distasteful.

Benedict's nickname of the Golden Thief had been acquired early on in his career when he had starred in a film with Anna Golden, a beautiful and well-established actress some years older than himself, who was married, for the second time, to another actor, David Carrington. Even while filming was still going on, rumours of a romance were rife, and a few months later Carrington had sued for divorce on the grounds of his wife's adultery with Leigh Benedict.

Jassy remembered those events vividly because they had occurred at a time when, knowing that acting was the only thing she wanted to do, she had devoured absolutely anything she could find on the subject in books, magazines and newspapers. Having seen Leigh Benedict in several television plays and his first film, she had been stunned by the power of his acting, and so had been delighted when he had won his first Oscar for the film in which he had appeared with Anna Golden.

The next morning the newspapers had been full of photographs of him, his blond hair gleaming in the spotlight, the gold statuette in one hand, and the actress clinging possessively to his other arm. One of the more popular papers, playing on the fact that David Carrington had also been strongly tipped for that year's Best Actor award, had added the caption, 'The Man Who Stole the Limelight—and Anna Golden', but in a later edition, with a fanciful play on words, that had been changed to 'The Golden Thief', and the name had stuck, in spite of the fact that the affair between Leigh Benedict and Anna Golden had never come to the marriage everyone had anticipated.

But it was not of Anna Golden that Jassy was thinking when she frowned uneasily and turned to Sarah again.

'Couldn't Cheska find something else?' she said slowly, her heart sinking as her flatmate shook her head firmly.

'It's this or nothing. There's very little on the books, and she has her regular girls to consider. She said you should count yourself lucky she was even offering it to you. She's only doing it because your background knowledge of the acting world gives you that extra edge on anyone else. They'd kill her if they knew she'd given you first chance of such a job.'

They were welcome to the job, Jassy reflected, admitting to herself that anyone else would probably jump at the chance of working for the man who had been described as the sex symbol of the century. But then anyone else would be able to face Leigh Benedict quite easily, and not always be remembering...

Almost three years before, when she had been nearing the end of her course at drama school, Jassy had been totally involved in a production of *Romeo and Juliet* which the final year students had been working on under the guidance of their tutor, Benjamin Carstairs, affectionately known as Benjy. Jassy, who, to her delight, had been given the role of Juliet, had thrown herself into the part with an intensity and commitment that had been given an added impetus when the news broke that a guest at one performance was to be Leigh Benedict himself. She had seen all the actor's films and some of his stage performances since she had come to London, and had always admired his brilliant acting even if she'd shied away from the mass adulation his fame brought him.

All the stories of his wealth, his jet-set lifestyle, the string of beautiful women whose names had been linked with his could in no way detract from the fact that Leigh Benedict was currently number one on any critic's list for best actor of the year—and deservedly so. He had a reputation for being savagely critical, and Jassy had felt that if she could win one word of praise, however small, for her performance, then she would know she really could act, and the fight she had had to get to drama school in the face of her parents' opposition would all have been worthwhile. To have the approval of such a master of his craft as Leigh Benedict would be like a dream come true.

On the day of the performance she had been sick with nerves, her hands fumbling with the heavy dark wig she was to wear, as she dressed and made up in the crowded dressing-room. But she knew that once she got on stage those nerves would vanish as they always did. She felt like this before every performance, only coming alive under the heat of the stage lights when she became the other person, the part she was to play, but tonight she felt so much worse because she desperately wanted everything to go right. She was keyed-up to give the per-

formance of her life before Leigh Benedict, so much so
that it hit her like a slap in the face when one of her
friends who had taken a surreptitious peep through the
curtains came back into the dressing-room looking
decidedly glum.

'Don't get your hopes up, girls,' Louisa announced in
response to a buzz of excited questions. 'It looks as if
the great man isn't coming. Anna Golden's there, sitting
in state beside Benjy as if she were the superstar and not
the old has-been that she is, but I'm afraid lover-boy's
not with her.'

'He's not coming?' Jassy exclaimed, and Louisa shot
her a sympathetic glance.

''Fraid not. I suppose he thinks we lesser mortals aren't
worthy of his attention now he's got his second Oscar.
It's rotten luck for you though. This was going to be
your big night, wasn't it? Your chance to catch the
Golden Thief's eye and maybe win a name for yourself.'

'I wanted to know what he thought of me as an actress,' Jassy responded fervently, and heard Louisa's
amused laughter.

'You're always so intense about things, Jassy! We all
want to act, but success is the name of the game in this
business—and Leigh Benedict is success personified. He's
not just a star, he's the sun and the moon and the planets
all rolled into one. No director's going to argue with him
if he wants a particular co-star in one of his films, so
he can make or break beginners like us with one word
from that sexy mouth of his. Get him hooked, and there's
no looking back.'

'I'm here to play Juliet, not get myself a lover.'

Jassy's laugh was a little uneven. She wasn't alone in
her hostility towards the casting-couch phenomenon, her
strong objections to the idea of success gained by
knowing someone with influence, but, perhaps because
she had had to fight so hard to get where she was, because she was determined to convince her parents that
her desire to act was a serious conviction, her chosen
career one she was determined to work at with all the
dedication and ability of which she was capable, she had

found that she took the matter much more seriously than many of her fellow students.

'I want to impress the actor, not the man.'

'Why stint yourself, kiddo, when you can do both? And looking like that you would have had a fair chance of doing just that.'

Louisa's gesture took in the long, dark blue velvet dress whose flowing lines made the most of Jassy's tall, slender figure, the low-cut, tightly laced bodice enhancing the soft curves of her breasts, giving her a cleavage for the first time in her life. The black wig added a touch of drama to the widely spaced soft grey eyes which Jassy sometimes felt were a little insipid when teamed with her own ash-blonde hair and naturally pale complexion. Heavy stage make-up had darkened her long, thick lashes, emphasising her fine cheekbones, and making her mouth look even fuller and softer so that she hardly recognised herself.

At that moment, a voice in the corridor outside warned them that the performance was about to begin. Louisa held up her hand, fingers firmly crossed.

'Knock 'em dead, kid! Who knows, perhaps your luck's in and the Golden Thief's turned up after all?'

But the first thing Jassy noticed when she went on stage was the empty seat in the front row, next to Benjy. It remained empty during the performance, but, after that first moment of bitter disappointment, she was too caught up in the world of the play to notice. But when the final words had been spoken and Jassy and the rest of the cast were taking their bows, that empty space struck her once more as silent evidence of Leigh Benedict's arrogant lack of interest in their efforts, and she felt a strong surge of anger rush through her.

Only when the costumes had been put away and almost everyone had gone home did the actor put in an appearance. Jassy was the only one of the students to see him arrive, and that was only because she was waiting for Sarah and her current boyfriend who had promised her a lift home and who were, as always, very late.

She didn't particularly mind waiting, feeling the need to be alone while she was still in the throes of the let-down she always experienced after a performance, something which was especially difficult to cope with on this particular occasion, and so, because of her mood, she shrank back into the shadow of a wall as a sleek, powerful car drew up outside the main entrance to the college.

From her hiding-place she watched unobserved as Leigh Benedict sauntered up the steps as if he owned the place, meeting Benjy and Anna Golden at the door. His skin glowed from the early summer sun, his bright hair was bleached almost white at the front, and his strong body was very casually dressed in well-worn denim jeans and a black T-shirt with a light cotton jacket slung care-lessly over one shoulder, the casual clothes seeming to imply that he had been doing nothing very important that night, but had simply not bothered to turn up. Jassy watched, her resentment growing by the minute, as he took Anna Golden's hand, pressing a kiss against the back of her fingers with elaborate courtesy, and mur-mured an easy greeting to Benjy, his words drifting easily to where she stood, biting her lip in frustration and anger.

'So how was your day on the beach?' Anna asked, the faint tartness of her tone belied by the way she slid her hand under Leigh's arm and pressed herself close up against him. Jassy heard the actor's contented sigh.

'It was idyllic. Sun, sand and sea, what more could you ask? I suppose I missed the production of the year?' he added, addressing his remark to Benjy without a hint of embarrassment or apology.

'I thought it went very well,' Benjy responded affably, not appearing to mind the lack of penitence in Leigh Benedict's tone.

'Mercutio had the most wonderful legs in those tights,' Anna put in, her clear, carrying voice sounding sharply in the silent street. 'And you wouldn't have been com-pletely bored, darling. Juliet was a pretty little thing; she'd have kept you from falling asleep.'

Unable to suppress her feelings of annoyance and resentment, Jassy had been about to move away and wait for her friends at the far corner of the street, but the mention of Juliet stilled her and she listened to the rest of the conversation unashamedly. The old saying that eavesdroppers never heard any good of themselves slid into her mind, but she pushed it away firmly, curiosity getting the better of her.

'Actually, Juliet's rather special,' Benjy was saying. 'I would have liked you to meet her, Leigh.'

'Heaven, spare me, Benjy!' Leigh Benedict groaned. 'The last time you introduced me to one of your leading ladies it took me three months to disentangle myself from her clutches! I've had my fill of seductive little sirens who are so desperate to get on that they've practically got their clothes off before they say hello.'

'That sounds like my Gemma,' Benjy agreed with a rueful laugh. 'But this girl's different. She's got talent—and, unlike Gemma Morgan and her type, she's quiet, hard-working, and really rather shy.'

'She sounds painfully naïve.' Anna gave her words a harsh mocking intonation that grated on Jassy's raw nerves. 'And you were going to let Leigh loose on the poor creature! Benjy, you're too cruel—he eats children like that for breakfast! She'll not last long if she's really the innocent you make her out to be—will she, darling?' She turned an intimate, smiling glance on Leigh.

'Don't be so cynical, Anna,' Benjy remonstrated. 'You saw her; she can act—and I find her innocence, as you call it, refreshing. There are too many Gemma Morgans in this world already.'

The three of them had come down the steps and on to the pavement, Anna still curved seductively against Leigh's side, his arm resting around her waist, and as Jassy moved even further back against the wall she could not miss the cynical twist to the actor's mouth as he spoke again.

'Your little innocent will learn, Benjy,' he drawled lazily. 'Heaven help her, she'll have to. The acting world is a jungle full of preying animals, and the ones who

start out with stars in their eyes sell their souls soon
enough when they discover the truth—either that or they
go under. When she finds out she's getting nowhere, your
sweet Juliet will resort to Gemma Morgan tactics like
the rest; they always do.'

In spite of her determination to remain hidden, Jassy
was unable to control an involuntary angry movement,
her hand itching to come up and wipe that sardonically
knowing smile from Leigh Benedict's face. She suppressed it almost immediately, but the tiny gesture had
caught Benjy's eye.

'Jassy!' he exclaimed as she tried to shrink even further
into the shadows, cursing the way she had betrayed
herself as he came towards her. 'I didn't know you were
still here. You must come and meet Leigh and Anna.'

Meet Leigh and Anna! Jassy almost exploded at the
thought. She didn't want to meet either of them, couldn't
have found a word to say to Leigh Benedict even if he
were God himself—which he clearly thought he was, she
told herself bitterly, unwillingly acknowledging that part
of her inner fury came from disillusionment at seeing
the truth about this man whom she had so much
admired—as an actor, at least.

'No, Benjy,' she protested faintly. 'I——'

'But why not, honeybun——?' Benjy was clearly taken
aback.

'This is a first, isn't it, Leigh?' Anna's amused tones
broke in. 'Someone's actually *reluctant* to meet you—
usually the reaction is quite the opposite. This little Juliet
must be a very rare bird.'

'A very rare bird indeed.'

Leigh Benedict's sardonically drawled agreement was
the last straw, setting a spark to the smouldering resentment in Jassy's mind and making it flare into a raging
flame. Benjy's bulky frame and the shadows that surrounded her hid her from Leigh and Anna, and that fact
gave her a glorious sense of freedom that loosed her precarious grip on her tongue.

'I don't want to meet your *friends*,' she declared, her
voice high and tight, a cynical emphasis on the last word.

'I thought Mr Benedict came here as an actor, to offer constructive criticism and advice, but as he hasn't even seen my performance there's nothing he can say that I could possibly want to hear—and I can think of no other reason why I should want to talk to him. Leigh Benedict is not my type at all,' she rushed on thoughtlessly. 'I think his appeal is distinctly overrated! His publicity agents may claim that every woman in the country would put him at the very top of any list of the ten most sexually attractive men in the world, but he'd come way down on my personal rating—in fact, I doubt if he'd even be on it!'

The sudden silence that greeted her outburst brought her down to earth with a jarring bump. Benjy was staring at her as if she had suddenly gone completely mad before his eyes—which, in his opinion, she supposed she had, she reflected wryly. Leigh Benedict was a very powerful force in the film and theatre world; to antagonise him like this was a distinctly unwise move, possibly professional suicide, but she didn't care. The memory of the way he had implied that any young actress would willingly sell herself in order to achieve success made her blood feel as if it were boiling in her veins.

'And for your information, Mr Benedict——' she raised her voice, using all her training to project it clearly to where he stood '—here is one actress who isn't prepared to use her body to get the parts she wants. I intend to make a success of my career—but by my own efforts and ability, not by any other means!'

Luckily at that moment Sarah's car drew up beside her and Jassy hurriedly opened the door and clambered in, suddenly finding herself shaking all over in reaction to what had happened as the realisation of just what she'd said hit home. The last thing she heard through the car's open window was Leigh Benedict's voice, indolently cynical and with a thread of amused disbelief running through it.

'A *very* rare bird indeed.'

All the way home Jassy raged inwardly at the thought of the arrogance and selfishness of a man who had spent

the day lazing on a beach somewhere without a thought
for the effort, energy and time that had gone into the
performance he had so callously not condescended to
honour with his presence. Probably, as Louisa had said,
he regarded such occasions as being beneath him now
that he was a star. Her hurt pride eased slightly as she
recalled Benjy's comment on her own part in the play,
but any pleasure she might have taken in his words was
tainted by the recollection of Leigh Benedict's cynical
reaction.

The man was insufferable! He had implied that any
girl who wanted to make her way in the acting world
would be only too willing to sell herself to the highest
bidder—and by that he probably meant himself. Jassy
was suddenly intensely grateful for the fact that Leigh
Benedict had not arrived in time to watch her performance. To have acted Juliet in all the glory and agony
of her young love before this cynical, jaded man would,
she felt, have been an act of sacrilege. Love would be
just a word to him, something he had no understanding
of, just as he had no understanding of idealism and
integrity.

Well, she'd show him! Even if he wasn't aware of it—
because the likelihood of their ever meeting again was
slim, to say the least—she was even more determined
than ever before to stick to her principles. She would
sink or swim by her own efforts and never, ever resort
to the sort of tactics Leigh Benedict seemed to expect.

And now, over two years later, she was still sticking
rigidly to the vow she had made, though at times she
had reluctantly had to admit that experience had taught
her that there had been more than just cynicism and a
prejudiced view of the world behind Leigh Benedict's
comments; there had been some degree of truth as well.
In her brief experience of the acting world, as opposed
to drama school, she had come up against more than
one director who seemed to believe that the casting-couch
system was alive and well, and who became openly hostile
when she made it plain that she had no intention of going
along with their suggestion of providing 'a small favour'

in order to win the part she had auditioned for. Only the previous week she had lost a part which she had believed was hers when another actress, a girl who had been in her year at drama school, had snatched it from under her nose because, as she had scornfully declared afterwards, she 'hadn't behaved like some Victorian virgin' when the director had suggested they mix business with pleasure.

But admitting that there had been some truth in what Leigh Benedict had said and agreeing to work for him for two months were two very different things. What would happen if he recognised her, remembered her impetuous words which, with hindsight, Jassy admitted had been foolhardy and rash to say the least? Sarah, who knew the whole story of course, was distinctly sceptical on that point.

'Don't be a complete moron, Jasmine!' she exclaimed, using the full version of Jassy's name which she knew her friend detested to emphasise her point. 'So you stung his pride a bit, but it was years ago. He'd probably forgotten all about it by the next morning. Besides, he never even saw you. I didn't realise you were there at first, you were so well hidden behind Benjy. He won't know you from Adam—sorry, Eve,' she corrected herself with a grin. 'You've got to be practical—this job's well paid, and you need the money. You can't muddle through on a pittance from Social Security much longer. You'd be a fool to turn this down.'

All sorts of a fool, Jassy admitted. What other temporary secretarial job would still give her some contact with the world she loved? And she had to admit that being involved, even if only on the most mundane level, with *Valley of Destiny*, Leigh Benedict's latest film, his first as director, was an opportunity she found it hard to resist. If rumour spoke true, the film was destined to be one of the greatest popular and critical successes of the year, and it was already one of the most talked-about productions, creating excitement and speculation whenever it was mentioned.

'I'll go for the interview anyway,' she said, reluctant to commit herself further. At least the interview wasn't with Leigh Benedict himself, but with a Steve Carter, the actor's personal assistant, so it would give her an opportunity to test the ground, find out just what her position would be. Perhaps she wouldn't have to have much contact with Leigh Benedict after all.

By the time the interview took place the next morning, Jassy knew that, if it was offered, she was going to take the job. It was too valuable an opportunity to miss, and a quick check with Francesca confirmed that the likelihood of anything as interesting—indeed, anything at all—turning up was just about non-existent, as she was already stretched to the limit to find work for her regular girls.

Jassy's half-formed decision was reinforced by the fact that Steve Carter turned out to be the sort of person whose friendly manner put her at her ease at once. He was an attractive man too, in his early thirties, tall, with light brown hair, blue eyes, and an open, pleasant face. He had none of Leigh Benedict's dramatic good looks, but Jassy privately felt that she infinitely preferred his easy approachability to the condescending arrogance that came with the actor's rugged sexuality.

The interview itself was routine enough, Steve Carter checking Jassy's certificates and references and detailing her duties, which were much as Sarah had already described. But Jassy's interest quickened as he went on, 'And of course there'll be a fair bit of work involved with this film Leigh's planning to direct—if we ever find a female lead.'

'Is there some difficulty over that?' Jassy tried hard to keep her voice even. Steve knew that the secretarial work was only a second string to her bow, she'd had to admit that to explain why she hadn't worked in that field over the past couple of years, but she didn't want him to think that she was trying to use her present position as a stepping-stone to greater things. She needed this job—only that morning, a postal delivery consisting of the electricity and telephone bills had brought home to her how much she needed it—and she didn't want to make any false moves that might ruin her chances.

'You could say so.' Steve's tone was dry. 'It's turning into a repeat of the search for someone to play Scarlett in *Gone With the Wind*. Leigh has very definite ideas about the sort of woman he wants to play Clara and so far no one's suited him. *Valley of Destiny* is very important to him. He's been involved in every part of it— the idea's his, the script's his. He's put a great deal of himself into the project and I'm afraid that doesn't make him exactly easy to work with. Your only consolation is that if he drives you hard he'll drive himself ten times harder. Of course, you won't be seeing much of him at first. You'll mainly be working with me—Leigh's in Scotland, filming at the moment, and he'll be there at least till the end of the month.'

The wave of release that washed over Jassy was so intense that she barely caught herself in time to hold back a sigh of relief. As she and Steve had talked she had become more and more convinced that she wanted this job in spite of its obvious drawback in the shape of the man who was to be her employer, but now it seemed that even that was not going to be the problem she had anticipated. Leigh Benedict's absence was an unexpected bonus, and one that left her able to respond to Steve's next words with unconstrained enthusiasm.

'I'm used to Leigh, I've known him since we were kids, and he's always been a workaholic, but it's only fair to warn you. Just don't take it to heart if he roars at you— it isn't personal. If you learn to shrug it off, you'll manage fine—that is, if you still want the job.'

'When do I start?' Jassy said quickly.

'Tomorrow, if possible. Your office and mine are on the ground floor of Leigh's house.' Steve scribbled something on a piece of paper and held it out to her. 'This address, nine o'clock.'

The first few days of Jassy's new job passed in a flurry of learning the ropes, finding where everything was kept, and forcing her mind and fingers to remember their long unused skills of shorthand and typing, but after that the work itself proved no problem, other than conquering her distaste for some of the letters she had to answer.

The amount and content of Leigh Benedict's fan mail frankly amazed her. To some of his fans it seemed that Leigh was not just a man but a god, his films the only bright spark in their otherwise depressingly routine lives, and some of them poured out their heart to him in a way that was almost unbelievable. The prying personal questions in some of the letters shocked Jassy, giving her a disturbing insight into the invasion of privacy that resulted from her employer's superstar status, and replying to them took a particular sort of tact in order to avoid their becoming a positive nuisance. She was well aware of the fact that it was just this sort of public exposure that had been one of her parents' major objections to her own desire to take up acting. So often, they had seen the private lives of popular stars plastered across the front pages of newspapers, and they had dreaded anything similar happening to her—something which would have caused waves of shock to reverberate round the small village where her father was the local GP.

How did Leigh Benedict cope with living in the glare of the spotlight as he did? she wondered, privately doubting that he would have any trouble adapting to the insatiable curiosity about his every movement. In every interview she had seen he had exuded an aura of total self-confidence, handling reporters and photographers with an easy, relaxed charm, accepting their attentions with the air of a man who had never known a moment's insecurity in his life.

The fan mail was the bulk of the correspondence, but there were other, official letters on matters of business that Jassy consulted Steve about, and a few personal ones that she put on one side for forwarding to Leigh in Scotland, but she was unsure how to proceed when, sorting through one morning's batch of post, she came across a letter addressed to Leigh with the name of a children's home stamped on the back.

'What do I do with this?' she asked Steve. 'Is it business or personal?'

Steve held out his hand for the letter, glancing briefly at the address on the back. 'Oh, Pinehurst again,' he said, clearly familiar with the name. 'Leave it with me and I'll see that Leigh gets it.'

He pocketed the letter and Jassy heard no more about it. When a second letter arrived from the same address she passed it on to Steve without comment, though deep inside she couldn't suppress a feeling of intrigued curiosity, wondering just what the connection between her employer and a suburban local authority children's home might be.

All this time Leigh Benedict himself was still away in Scotland and was expected to stay there for another two weeks; after that, he would be back in London to continue the search for an actress to play the role of Clara in *Valley of Destiny*. But, in spite of his physical absence, Jassy very soon came to realise that Steve had been telling the truth when he had said that the actor was not an easy man to work for.

Even though he was working day and night on one film, an endless stream of instructions about his next project were relayed to her through Steve, and from the first week she learned that the standards he set were very high indeed. But by the end of that week she was caught up in the job herself; the insights she gained into the production side of film work were rewarding enough to compensate for the demands her employer put on her time and energy, and she found an intense personal satisfaction in meeting every new command as swiftly and efficiently as possible. She rarely had time to think about her clash with Leigh Benedict two years before, but sometimes, when her mind wandered for a minute from the task in hand, she would remember those moments outside the drama college and a cold, apprehensive shiver would run through her at the thought that one day, before very long, she would have to come face to face with her employer.

When that happened she refused to allow herself to dwell on it, telling herself that what would be would be.

Probably, as Sarah had said, he wouldn't even recognise her, and if he did—well, she'd handle that when it came.

Jassy and Steve soon fell into an easy routine in which she was the one who made the mid-morning cup of coffee, so she was in the streamlined, ultra-modern kitchen one morning almost three weeks after she had started work when she heard the sound of a car drawing up outside, and a few minutes later the kitchen door opened abruptly and a tall, masculine figure strode into the room, halting abruptly as he registered her presence.

For a few confused seconds Jassy did not recognise him, her overall impression one of forceful vitality and an overpowering aura of physical strength. Then her gaze focused on a tangled mane of black hair, a heavy beard and moustache, and a pair of golden brown eyes that held her own so completely that for a moment she stood as if transfixed. But then the man spoke and the whole scene shifted, changed and took on a whole new meaning.

'Who the hell are you?' he demanded harshly, his tone making it only too plain that, whoever she was, she was not welcome.

From the first word Jassy's confusion vanished to be replaced by a shivering sense of apprehension as her stomach coiled into painful knots of near-panic. There was no mistaking that glorious voice, the one that had earned him the title of the new Richard Burton. Earlier than she had thought, her time had run out, the peace and quiet she had enjoyed was over, she acknowledged as, looking into those dark, hostile eyes, she saw past the misleading disguise of the dyed hair and beard and realised that she was face to face with Leigh Benedict.

CHAPTER TWO

'I SAID—who the hell are you?'

In spite of the warm summer sun streaming through the window, Jassy felt as if she had slipped back in time to a cool spring evening outside the college, as if she were twenty-one again, hearing that voice with its coolly cynical drawl from her hiding-place in the shadows, and the memory revived the angry feelings she had experienced then so that her own voice was cold and proud as she answered him.

'My name is Jassy Richardson,' she declared, feeling it was best to have that fact out in the open at once, her heart jolting inside her as she saw the slight flicker of response that crossed his face. Was that because Steve had told him her name as his new temporary secretary, or was he recalling where he had heard it over two years before, in a very different situation? Not for the first time she wished she had been called Mary or Anne, or anything that was more commonly used. 'I'm Mrs Eldon's replacement—from the Jobs Galore Agency.'

And right now she wished that Francesca *had* had jobs galore to offer her, so that she could have been anywhere but here.

'Ah, yes, the little secretary bird.' Leigh's indolent drawl had Jassy stiffening in indignation, warm colour washing her cheeks as she saw the blatantly assessing way his eyes roved over her face.

Her colour grew deeper as Leigh Benedict's gaze slid down over her tall, slender body, seeming to linger on the curves at breast and hip. Jassy felt naked under his obvious appraisal, as if he had stripped the clothes from her body with the intensity of his scrutiny. When he finally lifted his eyes to hers again she felt a tingling sense of shock and awareness shoot through her with

the force of a powerful electric current as she saw the
warmly sensual glow in those dark eyes, the slight, appreciative smile that curved the corners of an otherwise
hard mouth.

Perhaps for many other women that smile would have
seemed like the fulfilment of a dream, but, recalling his
contemptuous dismissal of women in general, and actresses in particular, Jassy found that the only feelings
it aroused in her were disgust and outrage, so that instead of looking away she stared right back, taking in
his appearance fully for the first time without the shock
of his sudden arrival clouding her eyes.

Leigh Benedict might give an impression of rugged
sensuality in his films, but in fact he was not as broad
and powerful as he appeared on the screen. In fact, his
body was leanly built, that impression of strength coming
from the firmly muscled lines of his chest and a pair of
wide, straight shoulders around which a supple cream
leather jacket clung like a second skin.

The black hair and beard were explained by the be-
lated recollection that, as Steve had told her, Leigh's
current role was that of a gypsy horse thief which had
necessitated his growing and dyeing his blond hair. His
fans were going to be bitterly disappointed, she reflected
with a touch of irony. There was no sign of the golden
mane or the strong-boned jaw that drove so many of
them into ecstasies—but his eyes, of course, remained
the same. Even in someone of only average good looks,
those eyes would be stunning enough to cause a few
female hearts to flutter. Clear and wide-set, their rich
deep brown flecked with startling gold, and fringed with
long, thick lashes, they were what drew and held her
unwilling gaze.

Leigh Benedict was a spectacularly handsome creature,
Jassy admitted reluctantly. There was nothing in the least
boyish about him; he was a mature, virile character with
an air of assurance that spoke of a worldly experience
that would show in the lines etched around his nose and
mouth if the heavy beard hadn't hidden them. The fan
mail she had read had told her that few women felt that

those lines in any way spoilt his looks—in fact, for most of them they enhanced his appearance. All in all, Leigh Benedict was a rugged devil of a man with a hard, lithe body whose firmly muscled lines were set off to advantage by the cream leather jacket, worn with a tan-coloured shirt and dark brown trousers which seemed moulded on to long, lean legs.

If she had hoped to disconcert him by returning his scrutiny stare for stare, then she had failed, Jassy admitted when the actor appeared not in the least disturbed by her defiant silence. But then, of course, Leigh Benedict was used to being the centre of attention. He thrived on it; in fact, he would probably be shocked if he was deprived of it. He had probably assumed that her own reaction had been one of the open adoration he was so accustomed to receiving.

Anxious to have that impression erased from his mind, Jassy rushed into unguarded speech. 'Could I have my body back now?' she enquired coolly. 'If you've finished with it, that is.'

That made his mouth twitch in a response that could have been anger, but then again might simply have been amusement, and Jassy was forced to regret her deliberately provocative remark as he responded silkily, 'As a matter of fact, no, I haven't finished. I'd like to take matters very much further.'

Once more those topaz eyes slid down her body, the curl at the corners of his mouth growing deeper as he caught Jassy's indignantly indrawn breath.

'You have a singularly attractive body, Miss Richardson, as I'm sure you're well aware, so I have to admit to being somewhat at a loss to understand why you seem determined to conceal its appeal under those appalling clothes.'

Leigh's description of himself as being at a loss was so blatantly untrue—he looked anything but, totally at ease and infuriatingly sure of himself—that his carefully assumed self-deprecatory tone added fuel to the fires of Jassy's anger so that she drew herself up stiffly, her grey eyes black with anger.

The role of secretary had taxed her limited wardrobe severely, the jeans and casual shirts that were perfectly suitable for rehearsals in huge, dusty, and often unheated theatres being completely inappropriate to her current position, so that she had been hard-pressed to find the right sort of things to wear. The problem had been compounded by the fact that she had wanted to choose clothes that, should she and Leigh Benedict ever meet, would project a mature, responsible and very conventional image to her employer, and so, hopefully, avoid awakening any memories of a casually dressed drama student he had once encountered.

It now seemed that she had succeeded in her aim. In fact, it appeared that she had succeeded only too well, she reflected rather ruefully, seeing the contemptuous distaste in those golden eyes as they flicked over her slightly old-fashioned grey cotton suit and neat white blouse. But then, of course, his taste inclined towards a rather more flamboyantly sexual style of female dressing, she acknowledged, recalling Anna Golden's dramatic appearance. *That* was not Jassy's style at all, though it was impossible to suppress a prick of very feminine pique at the way Leigh's mouth had twisted when he'd looked at her.

'I dress to please myself, Mr Benedict!' she snapped. 'I hardly think my appearance is any concern of yours. Did you object to the clothes Mrs Eldon wore, too?'

Her tartness was a mistake. She knew that as she saw his head go back slightly in response to her sharp tone. It might remind him of her outburst outside the college. So far he had shown no sign of connecting her with that incident, but if she didn't get a grip on herself she might revive memories which she would do better to try and leave buried.

Leigh's shake of his head sent his dark mane flying and a sudden, wicked grin made his teeth flash whitely against his tanned skin. 'No,' he murmured, so softly that instinctively Jassy tensed, suspecting strongly that he wasn't going to leave it at that, 'but then, of course, Mrs Eldon is nearing retirement age, and is very much the strait-laced schoolmistress type—she doesn't just dress as if she was.'

Without warning he reached out a hand and touched her hair, tugging one pale strand of it free from the neat chignon in which she wore it, and letting it curl around one long finger, his eyes glinting with a disturbing fire. Jassy froze, stunned by the total unexpectedness of the gesture.

'Pale hair, pale eyes.' Leigh's voice was a disturbingly husky whisper, one that made Jassy's nerves twist in instinctive response even as she tried to tell herself that this was just the tone he had used in the sensual love scenes in his last film. 'You look like some ice maiden in a fairy-story. What a terrible crime to have hair this beautiful and then drag it back in that unflattering style.'

'I . . .' Jassy began, but the words died in her throat as, with one hand behind her head, the pressure of his strong fingers at the nape of her neck gentle but irresistible, Leigh drew her face slowly and inexorably towards his.

His kiss was warm and slow, sensually exploring her lips with an expertise that she had never experienced before. Part of Jassy's mind wanted desperately to break free, get away, but another, less rational side to her brain seemed to be controlling her body, so instead she found herself doing quite the opposite, instinctively leaning nearer, the warm scent of Leigh Benedict's body filling her nostrils and a drowsy, glowing sensation flooding her veins, drugging her senses so that she couldn't think straight.

'Not so much of the ice maiden, after all,' Leigh murmured against her mouth, and his words were like the shock of cold water in Jassy's face, jolting her mind back into action so that she wrenched herself free, one hand flying up to her flushed face.

'How dare you?' she exclaimed furiously, struggling to meet those tawny eyes which were regarding her with a mixture of cynical amusement and frank disbelief. 'You had no right to do that!'

'You didn't exactly pull away,' Leigh pointed out with infuriating reasonableness.

'That doesn't mean I was enjoying it!'

Leigh's mouth twisted again, this time in a way that sent a *frisson* of cold discomfort through Jassy's body. 'Don't kid yourself, sweetheart. I hate to sound like some clichéd film script, but I do know when a woman's responding and when she's not—and you were definitely not fighting me off.'

'That's not true! I—I . . .'

The words died on Jassy's lips as the amusement in Leigh's eyes changed swiftly to dark contempt. She shook her head dazedly, unable to understand why she had been so disturbed by one kiss. It wasn't as if she'd never been kissed before! And it wasn't the fact that Leigh Benedict was a stranger to her, a man she despised and disliked, that had worried her. During her training, and on stage, she had had to kiss complete strangers and men she didn't like often enough not to let that bother her. But that had been acting, playing the part of someone else, not as herself.

Nor had it been the way Leigh's kiss had been deliberately calculated to arouse, holding a sensual invitation unknown in all the light-hearted romantic attachments she had experienced that had made her turn on him in this way. The real shock had come from the realisation that his cold calculation had worked only too well. She had been aroused in a way she had never known before and, if she admitted the truth to herself, until she had heard him speak she had thoroughly enjoyed the experience. It had been exactly what she wanted, so much so that the sardonically murmured comment, its cool tones indicating painfully clearly that Leigh had felt none of the heady response that had surged through her, had brought her down to earth with a shattering bump.

Leigh Benedict was watching her closely; Jassy sensed his tawny eyes on her face as she drew herself up stiffly.

'If you wanted to see Steve, he's in his office,' she said coldly, exerting every ounce of control she possessed over her voice so that it came out clipped and curt.

'Heaven help us, the ice maiden act again,' Leigh drawled mockingly. 'But it doesn't have quite the same effect any more,' he added as he turned towards the door. 'We both know you're not really Mrs Eldon's type, even if you try very hard to pretend to be.'

Believing him to be on his way out of the room, Jassy brought her teeth down hard on her lower lip to bite back the angry retort she was strongly tempted to flash at him. Just another minute, she told herself. Just sixty seconds and he would be gone...

But then, to her consternation, Leigh Benedict paused in the doorway and swung round to face her once more. 'Some other time, when I'm not quite so busy, we must continue this interesting—conversation,' he said in a voice that was laced with satirical mockery. 'I'd be intrigued to know what you're really like—to discover the woman like underneath all that ice.'

Left alone, Jassy drew a long, tremulous breath, too stunned by that final comment to be able to think. Automatically she reached for the kettle, but found that her hands were shaking too much to be able to turn on the taps to fill it, and slammed it down again on the worktop, her fingers clenching tightly over the handle as she struggled with the whirling, conflicting emotions in her mind.

Why did she feel like this? How could she have let Leigh Benedict get to her so badly? She didn't even like the man, and yet from the moment he had walked into the room every nerve in her body had become hyper-sensitive to his very physical presence. His objectionable, arrogant behaviour had alienated her from the start, but at the same time there was something indefinable about him that excited as much as it unnerved her.

Jassy felt hot and then cold as she thought of the way Leigh had kissed her, recalling the heady sensations the touch of his lips had awoken—which was crazy, because she hadn't wanted him to kiss her. Rationally, she would have said that that was the last thing she wanted from

him. But he had kissed her, and her reaction had been
so very far from rational.

Shaking her head at her own foolishness, Jassy took
another deep breath, feeling her racing pulse calm as she
regained control. She had been caught off balance,
disconcerted by Leigh Benedict's sudden appearance,
particularly because she had been dreading this meeting
ever since she had taken on the job. As a result, she had
acted completely out of character. She would be better
prepared the next time, and at least she had one thing
to be thankful for—her employer had shown no sign of
recognising her or remembering the incident on the night
of the production of *Romeo and Juliet*.

The sound of Leigh Benedict's car driving away a short
time later told Jassy that the unwelcome visitor had gone,
so it was with an easy mind that she carried the mugs
of coffee into Steve's office, knowing she would not have
to face her employer again that morning. It was as they
chatted casually over their drinks that Steve surprised
her by asking suddenly, 'Are you doing anything tonight?
If not, I wondered if you'd like to have dinner with me.'

Jassy considered. She liked Steve and it was some time
since she had had an evening out. There was no man in
her life at the moment, and her strained finances had
made it impossible even to go along with Sarah and her
current boyfriend when they went for a drink at the local
pub. And perhaps a night spent in Steve's pleasant,
undemanding company would restore her sense of
balance, erase the memory of a pair of mocking gold-
flecked eyes, a cynically taunting voice.

'What a lovely idea! I'd like that very much.'

'I'm afraid I have a confession to make,' Steve said as
Jassy finished her meal and leaned back with a sigh of
contentment. 'This evening wasn't purely for pleasure—
though I've enjoyed your company very much. I have
to admit to having an ulterior motive.'

'Oh?' Jassy was intrigued. 'What was that?'

'I wanted to ask if you'd mind putting in a bit of
overtime this weekend.'

'Overtime?' Jassy echoed the word because it was so unexpected. 'But of course I will! You didn't have to take me out to dinner just to ask that.'

'Ah, well——' to Jassy's astonishment Steve looked vaguely embarrassed '—this isn't exactly routine overtime—it would involve your staying at Leigh's house overnight. Look, let me explain. Leigh's due back this weekend—for once, filming's finished earlier than expected—and, knowing him, he's going to go hell for leather into work on *Valley of Destiny*—there are some script changes he's planning, for one thing. He's rewritten the damn thing three times, but he's still not satisfied. He'll want to get down to it straight away, so we'll need you on Saturday morning if that's possible.'

'I can manage that easily. But I don't quite understand. Why can't I just come in on Saturday? I don't see why I have to stay the night.'

'That's another complication. Leigh's driving down from Scotland on Friday night. Now usually there's a housekeeper who comes in when he's been away and gets the house ready, cooks a meal, that sort of thing. But I didn't expect Leigh back until next week so I gave her some time off. She's gone to see her daughter in Cornwall and won't be back until Monday. So——'

'You want me to take the housekeeper's place,' Jassy finished for him, and Steve nodded.

'I can't be around myself. I have to go to Jersey on Friday to check on a house we plan to use for filming, and I'll be gone all weekend. I can't say what time Leigh will arrive, he's not sure when he'll get away himself, but I don't expect it will be till late. That's why I suggested you stay at the house overnight.'

'Won't Mr Benedict object to my staying there?' Jassy asked, trying to gain time in which to think.

After her confrontation with her employer that afternoon she had been forced to reconsider her position and had come to the conclusion that her earlier inclination to refuse this job had, after all, been the right one—but not for the reasons she had originally believed. Earlier she had simply detested Leigh Benedict's cynical attitude towards up-and-coming young actresses, believing it was just actresses who were the object of his contempt. From the way he had behaved earlier she was now coming to the conclusion that it was women in general that he felt that way about.

'Oh, no. As a matter of fact, Leigh was the one who first came up with the idea.'

Jassy's eyes widened until they were soft grey pools of shock. *That* she hadn't expected. Just what had been in Leigh Benedict's mind when he had made that suggestion? The memory of his final declaration, 'I'd be intrigued to know what you're really like—to discover the woman like underneath all that ice,' had her opening her mouth in a rush to declare that the office overtime on Saturday she could manage, but the rest of Steve's request was impossible.

But Steve forestalled her.

'Leigh's perfectly capable of driving all that way after a day's filming and launching straight into work without any break, even for food, so I need someone who'll keep him on the straight and narrow, make him see sense, rest—eat.' His eyes had darkened with the sort of appeal that anyone would have found hard to resist. 'This really would be the most tremendous help to me, Jassy.'

The rain lashed against the window-pane with a fury that seemed to threaten to shatter the glass, and Jassy shivered slightly, feeling the chill in the air after the heavy heat of the day. The storm had broken early in the evening, not long after Steve had driven away on his trip to Jersey, leaving Jassy alone in the house—to wait for Leigh Benedict.

She still didn't know quite why she had overcome her misgivings and agreed to this when it was the last thing she wanted to be doing. She was being handsomely paid for her time, of course, and the money would be very welcome, but she would willingly trade that extra cash for a quiet night in her flat—preferably with a script to study.

But that was a forlorn hope. Only that morning she had phoned her agent, praying that some chance of an audition had turned up, only to have her hopes dashed.

'Nothing doing, I'm afraid, Jassy. Try again next week. If anything crops up in the meantime I'll let you know.'

So now she was here, completely at a loose end, with only the prospect of a meeting with her employer—something she was not looking forward to at all—ahead of her. She had unpacked her overnight bag, prepared a meal that would not spoil no matter what time Leigh put in an appearance, and had no idea what to do with herself next.

She had never been in this part of the house before, and the luxury of the room in which she was sitting, so unlike her own small, shabby flat or her parents' comfortable, rather old-fashioned home, made her feel distinctly ill at ease. She felt thoroughly out of place in the well-worn denim jeans and bright pink shirt she had changed into earlier. She wasn't here as Leigh Benedict's secretary, she had told herself. She was doing him, or rather, Steve, a favour, so she might as well be comfortable.

But comfortable was the last thing she felt. Everything around her was ultra-modern and undeniably expensive, but the long room with its stark white walls, thick grey carpet and black leather settee and armchairs seemed unlived in somehow, soulless, more like a showroom than a home. It had none of the personal touches that stamped a place with the personality of its owner, as if Leigh simply used the house as somewhere to eat and sleep—and work—and the rest of his life was lived elsewhere. Steve had told her that the entire place had been put in the hands of a currently fashionable interior designer, and, while she recognised Max Allen's style in the sleek, uncluttered lines of every room, there was nothing there to give her any clue about Leigh Benedict himself, nothing to help her.

Because she needed some help, Jassy admitted to herself. She had to talk to the wretched man about something. She couldn't just serve up the meal and spend the rest of the evening in stony silence, even if she would personally find that the easiest way out, knowing that she would have to keep a strong grip on herself in order not to let her personal feelings slip out. Acting, of course, was forbidden ground if she wanted to avoid sparking off a volcanic explosion when he remembered her foolhardy, impetuous comments over two years before—so what *could* she talk about?

There was little enough to go on in the publicity material she had worked on with Steve. All that told her was that both Leigh's parents were dead, when or how she didn't know, and he had no other family. He had trained at the same drama school Jassy herself had attended, but that was hardly something she would want to risk mentioning. Other than that there was nothing, just a list of productions he had appeared in and, of course, the seemingly endless array of awards.

The sound of a car door slamming outside interrupted Jassy's thoughts, bringing her hastily to her feet. It was such a dreadful night—he would welcome a hot drink straight away.

As she reached for the milk to pour it into a jug the kitchen door swung open and Jassy's hand jerked involuntarily as unconsciously she stiffened in apprehension. She couldn't look round yet, she thought, struggling against the memories of their previous meeting in exactly the same place that flooded into her mind. She couldn't face those tawny eyes until she was calmer, so she sensed rather than saw how Leigh paused just inside the room.

'Do you spend all your time making coffee?' The softly drawled mockery in his voice set Jassy's teeth on edge. 'Or do you just have a knack for knowing when I'm due to arrive?'

Or have you been sitting on tenterhooks just waiting for me to turn up? The implication was clear to Jassy, infuriating her, all the more so because that was exactly what she *had* been doing, if not quite for the reasons he believed. Exasperated, she swung round on him.

'Don't be ridiculous! I——'

The words died on her lips as her breath exploded in a shocked gasp. She knew she was staring, but she couldn't help it, couldn't drag her eyes away from the man before her.

She had expected the dark gypsy who had confronted her a few days before, but this man was so very different. The height and strong build were the same, he even wore the same cream leather jacket, now heavily spattered with rain, the white shirt underneath it soaked through and clinging to his chest where he had left the jacket carelessly unzipped. But he was clean-shaven and the firm mouth, no longer half hidden by the heavy black beard, looked harder, faintly cruel, the muscles in his jaw tense as if he was imposing a strong control over his uncertain temper.

Above that uncompromising mouth the tawny eyes were watching Jassy intently, noting every fleeting expression that crossed her face. She hadn't forgotten those eyes—their arrogantly appraising expression under heavy lids was one she remembered only too clearly. But the thick hair, slightly flattened against his forehead by the driving rain, no longer hung in an overlong mane almost to his shoulders. Even the effects of the wind and the rain could not disguise the fact that it had been carefully and expertly styled, and, although darkened by its drenching during the walk across the courtyard, it was very definitely not black but the bright golden blond that had helped earn Leigh Benedict his nickname.

Jassy had a sudden vivid image of all the newspaper and magazine photographs she had ever seen of this man, photographs that she now realised had, like the brief glimpse of him she had had over two years before, given only the vaguest impression of the full physical impact of Leigh Benedict's stunning good looks.

'The Golden Thief!'

Without meaning to, she had spoken the words out loud, and as soon as she heard her own voice she wished them back again, knowing they were a mistake as Leigh

Benedict's face darkened, a ferocious scowl distorting his handsome features.

'So you read the gossip columns,' he commented savagely. 'Well, why stop there? What about "The Man Who Stole Anna Golden"? Surely you know that one too? Or have the gutter Press coined a new name—one I haven't heard yet?'

The cold, hard voice penetrated the haze in Jassy's mind, bringing her back to an awareness of herself and where she was.

'I'm—sorry,' she stammered. 'But I didn't expect—your hair——'

Leigh Benedict gave a short, harsh laugh, raking one hand roughly through his wet hair so that drops of rain-water from it spattered Jassy's face.

'Perhaps I should have left it black—you seemed to be able to find plenty to say to me then,' he muttered, the sardonic inflection in his voice making Jassy draw herself up hastily.

'I'm not taking back anything I said then,' she said stiffly. 'You——'

She broke off abruptly as Leigh sighed his exasperation.

'Heaven spare me! Not the ice maiden act again! Why do you pretend to be someone you're not? I know there's a real woman underneath it all, remember?'

Jassy's heart seemed to lurch inside her. She didn't want to be reminded of that particular incident. Since the time he had kissed her, here, in the kitchen, she had tried to erase the scene from her mind—unsuccessfully, she had to admit, remembering how thoughts of that kiss and the feelings it had aroused had crept insidiously into her mind no matter how hard she'd tried to force them away. More especially, she didn't want to recall those feelings now, when she had to be alone with him in his house for the rest of the night.

'I don't choose to remember that,' she said tightly, her inner turmoil making the words come out in a cold, hard voice that was quite unlike her own.

'You don't choose to remember,' Leigh echoed with such an uncannily accurate mimicry of her tone that, in spite of herself, Jassy admitted privately to a swift rush of admiration. 'But I do. I remember it very clearly. It's not something I'm likely to forget in a hurry.' Those gold-flecked eyes warmed suddenly, disturbingly. 'In fact, it's something I'd like to repeat.'

The gleam in his eyes warned Jassy, and as he took a step towards her she swung away sharply, moving swiftly across the kitchen.

'Well, I certainly wouldn't,' she said as coolly as she could from the comparative safety of the other side of the room, cursing the unevenness in her tone that gave too much away.

Leigh's movement, bringing him so much closer to her, had brought home to her forcefully that, for all his lean build, he still possessed a whipcord strength that was unnervingly imposing. Her sensitivity to his physical presence disturbed her, making her feel small and strangely fragile in a way she was not at all used to. Under normal circumstances she was well able to handle any man she met; five years in London had taught her the knack of putting down unwanted advances without any trouble, but this man was different, and from the look in his eyes she strongly suspected that he was not one to take no for an answer easily.

But to her surprise Leigh simply smiled and then quite deliberately let his gaze wander over her face and body, giving a small, silent nod of satisfaction as he did so.

'I hardly recognised you—I never realised that a change of hairstyle could have so much effect,' he murmured softly, and with a small exclamation of shock Jassy lifted a hand to her hair, feeling the loose, pale blonde strands of it falling softly about her shoulders.

She had meant to pin it up earlier, but had completely forgotten, and anger flared in her mind as the look on Leigh's face told her just what interpretation he had put on that one small fact. His next words confirmed her suspicions.

'What happened to the schoolmistress image? I must admit I prefer the current look—*much* sexier. What brought about the change, I wonder?'

Jassy faced those mocking topaz eyes, her own grey ones flashing a fiery denial of his arrogant assumption.

'I told you before—I dress to please myself and no one else! Your meal's ready whenever you want it,' she added hastily, taking refuge in practical matters to avoid any further confrontation. 'Don't you think you should get out of those wet things before you eat?'

Leigh glanced down at his clothes as if only just becoming aware of the way the rain had soaked them, plastering his shirt against the firm lines of his chest. Even his brown cord trousers were wet, clinging damply to his long legs in a way that Jassy found very disturbing. Her suggestion that he change out of his damp clothes was not purely a practical one. Once she had noticed the hard, lean shape of his body, emphasised by the soaking material, she found she could not look away. She had never been so forcefully aware of the potent attraction of a man's body before, and she just wanted him out of the room for a few minutes to give her the chance to come to terms with these new and unwanted feelings.

'Perhaps you're right,' Leigh said slowly, one hand going to his golden hair, brushing back the heavy, damp strands that had fallen over his forehead. His hand came away wet and he regarded it with a rueful expression that was disconcertingly appealing, tugging at something deep inside Jassy.

'If you get changed, I'll have the food ready by the time you come down,' Jassy said briskly, moving to take cutlery from a drawer, feeling the need of action to defuse the sudden and inexplicable tension that had gripped her. 'Well—go on!' she added when he seemed to hesitate.

'Yes, ma'am!' Leigh responded with a swift and disturbingly boyish grin.

Jassy was shocked to find herself suddenly filled with a longing to grab a towel and rub that glorious blond hair dry herself, feeling the softness of it beneath her fingers. The sensation was so strong, so unexpected that it took her breath away, leaving her incapable of thought. Unconsciously she half turned back towards Leigh, but he had already gone, and with a strange mixture of intense relief and something worryingly close to regret she heard his footsteps mounting the stairs to his room.

The rain had ceased, the thunder dimmed to a low growling in the distance, by the time Jassy joined Leigh in the living-room after clearing away the remains of the meal, but the restless, unsettled feeling she had experienced earlier had her in its grip again, making her feel very ill at ease. It was something like the feeling she had experienced before her first day at drama college, but then she had been on the verge of something very important and exciting, something that had been going to change the course of her whole life. In her present situation, such feelings seemed totally inappropriate.

She found Leigh sprawled in one of the huge leather armchairs, the black sweatshirt and jeans he had changed into blending with its darkness and providing a sharp contrast to the bright colour of his hair which was highlighted by the glow of a table-lamp he had switched on nearby. A tumbler of whisky stood on the coffee-table at his side, and he had a file of papers open on his knee which he was studying closely, occasionally making some note in the margin of a page. A workaholic all right, Jassy reflected, remembering Steve's comments. It was almost eleven and yet Leigh seemed set for a long night's work. It seemed she need not have worried about how to talk to him after all, she told herself with a touch of irony. He hadn't even noticed her come into the room.

Leigh's long legs were stretched out in front of him so that she had to step over them as she moved to sit on the settee. Her movement disturbed him and he glanced up, frowning slightly as if, totally absorbed in what he was doing, he had forgotten her presence and was trying to remember who she was. Then his expression cleared.

'Would you like a drink?' he asked affably enough, getting to his feet. 'I'm sure you could do with one after all your efforts.'

'A Martini would be nice—with lemonade.'

Jassy thankfully accepted the glass he held out to her, relieved to see that the rigidly controlled aggression she had always sensed in him before seemed to have eased and he appeared relaxed and much more approachable. She sipped her drink slowly, the ice clinking against the side of the glass. Perhaps the alcohol would help to relax her too. She would welcome anything that would ease the prickling, jittery sensation that felt like pins and needles all over her body.

Leigh returned to his chair, stretching his arms lazily, drawing the dark sweatshirt taut over his straight shoulders, and sighed deeply, tiredly. 'I must thank you for helping out like this. That was an excellent meal.'

'It was no trouble,' Jassy said carefully. She had suddenly remembered that Leigh himself had suggested that she come here tonight, and that thought intensified the pins and needles almost unbearably. 'Cooking in your kitchen is heaven after the conditions in our flat. You have a beautiful home,' she went on hurriedly in an effort to maintain the conversation.

Leigh lifted his shoulders in an offhand shrug. 'It'll do,' he said dismissively. 'It suits the so-called image, anyway. I hope being here hasn't upset any plans you had for the weekend. I'm sure there must be someone you'd rather be with tonight.'

Jassy wished he would look away. That remark about his image had awoken disturbing echoes of her own outburst over two years before, and his tone had altered perceptibly on his last comments, becoming strangely intent in a way that, combined with the direct, probing force of those golden eyes, scrambled her thoughts in the most worrying way.

'Well, Steve's out of town.' She blurted out the first thing that came into her head, even if the relationship she was implying did not actually exist. Although he had told her several times how much he had enjoyed their evening together, Steve had not actually suggested another date.

Her words seemed to change Leigh's mood suddenly. The heavy lids hooded his eyes, hiding their expression, as he leaned forward and replaced his glass on the table with meticulous care.

'I had forgotten about Steve,' he said cryptically.

He turned his attention back to the papers in his lap once again, and Jassy's curiosity got the better of her.

'Is that the script of *Valley of Destiny*?' she asked diffidently, and at Leigh's silent nod of agreement a flame of interest lit up inside her. Over the past few weeks she had learned a lot about the business side of the actor's work, but this was the first time that she had had a chance to touch on the creative aspect that most concerned her. 'Steve said you've already rewritten it three times.'

Again came that silent nod. Damn the man! He was being infuriatingly unforthcoming!

'Why?' she persisted, then stumbled over her words as his eyes lifted from the page to rest speculatively on her face once more. 'I mean—why is this film so important to you?'

The expression that crossed Leigh's face was neither a smile nor a frown, but a disconcerting mixture of the two.

'I want it to be a success.'

'But surely that's inevitable?' Jassy couldn't erase the shock and surprise from her voice. Anything Leigh Benedict touched turned to gold, and his name on the credits of a film guaranteed that it would be a surefire box-office hit.

'That depends on what you define as success.'

For a moment Jassy stared at him in blank confusion, then, recalling the letters she had had to deal with, she suddenly felt she was beginning to understand what he meant.

'The Golden Thief,' she murmured, her intonation very different from the one she had used earlier.

Leigh nodded agreement, the muscles of his face taut, drawing his skin tightly across his cheekbones.

'The feminist movement is swift to condemn any hint of a woman being treated as a sex object. Quite rightly, they see it as humiliating and degrading, but what they don't appear to have considered is that a man might find the experience every bit as distasteful. I'm an actor; I've served my apprenticeship and I'm on my way to becoming a craftsman. I've been lucky—I'm successful—but success can be a two-edged sword.'

'Don't you enjoy your work?' Jassy's voice was uneven as she tried to adjust to these new and unexpected developments. Was this man who described himself in such modest terms the same person she had dismissed as arrogant and self-centred?

'Enjoy it?' Leigh repeated thoughtfully. 'The work, yes, and I try to give the best damn performance I can— but whatever I do I can't shake off that sex-symbol label.' His mouth twisted wryly. 'Being flavour of the month every month can get a bit stale. Look, before I left Scotland I had an interview with a journalist from one of the major women's magazines——'

'It didn't go very well?' Jassy questioned, alerted by his tone.

'Well enough—in her opinion. I shall reserve judgement until I read what she writes about me. That's the trouble with reporters, they listen to every word you say— "Oh, yes, Mr Benedict, or may I call you Leigh? I'm sure our readers will find this fascinating."'

As he spoke Leigh unconsciously assumed a soft, breathless voice, making Jassy smile in delight, secretly enchanted by the way he slipped into a role without thinking, and envying the skill that made her believe, just for a moment, that even a man so blatantly masculine as Leigh Benedict had become that woman reporter. She could learn so much from this man!

'But then what they write bears no relation to anything I've said. They've got an image in their mind and that's what they feed the public, ignoring anything that doesn't fit—and heaven help you if you don't live up to it. This woman didn't want to know about my *work*—she was more interested in my love life, which is nobody's damn business but my own! You're a woman,' he went on abruptly, startling Jassy with his sudden change of tone. 'Is that really what interests you?'

Caught off guard, Jassy shook her head vehemently.

'It would bore me silly!' she declared. 'I'd want to know why you choose the roles you do, how you prepare for them, how much of yourself you put into them . . .'

Her voice faltered uncertainly as she saw the way Leigh's eyes were fixed on her face, making her suddenly aware that she was treading on very thin ice indeed.

'I've never been terribly interested in what the stars eat for breakfast, what music they like, what car they drive,' she added hastily, and with what she hoped was a convincing degree of airiness.

'Well, that's what they ask me about,' Leigh said with a grimace of distaste. 'Personally, I'd like to hope that what I do is much more interesting than who I am. That's why I'm taking a back seat on this new project—letting someone else be the star. I'm doing this for my personal satisfaction—and to prove a point.'

'But surely you've proved yourself to be more than just a sex symbol already?'

Honesty forced the comment from Jassy. Whatever she thought of this man—and the things he had said had thrown her opinions into confusion—she could never deny that he was a brilliant actor who deserved every bit of the critical acclaim he had had heaped on him.

'Have I?' The question came with disturbing speed and force.

'Well—yes—you've won an Oscar.'

'Two, to be precise,' Leigh amended expressionlessly.

He wasn't boasting, there was something in his tone that told Jassy that without any room for doubt. He sounded more as if he was dismissing his achievement, reducing it to something totally negligible. Jassy couldn't believe it. If she had won any award she felt sure it would delight her for the rest of her life.

'But didn't that give you personal satisfaction?'

'You're an actress, you tell me. Would it be the *awards* that brought you satisfaction?'

'I see what you mean.'

Jassy's own experience gave her the answer. Wasn't that how she felt, sometimes seeming only really to come alive on stage. Awards, success, even the applause at the end of a play were somehow extraneous to the act itself.

'It's the *acting* that counts, giving the very best performance you're capable of.' Unconsciously she echoed Leigh's own words. 'What matters is getting across what the author means—expanding on the words on the page, enhancing them. Sometimes when a performance ends it's like dying a little...'

His question had touched a spark in her, firing her enthusiasm, and she had answered it without hesitation, but it was only now, when the first rush of excitement had died, that his quietly spoken first sentence hit her with the force of an explosion so that she froze, gaping like a stranded fish.

'You're an actress,' he had said!

'You—you know!'

Leigh didn't bother to pretend he didn't know what she meant, but merely nodded, those bronze eyes dark and expressionless, unfathomable.

'I knew from the moment I saw you—or at least from the second I heard you speak. I caught only the briefest glimpse of your face that night, but voices are my stock in trade, after all.' A faintly ironic smile touched his beautifully shaped mouth. 'I could never forget you.'

Or the things she had said, Jassy reflected uneasily, colour flooding her cheeks at the memory. 'Then why did you let me stay? Why didn't you dismiss me on the spot?'

That was what she would have expected. Surely he wouldn't want her to work for him when she had been so deliberately insulting, had scorned him so openly in front of his friends? But then, from what he had said tonight, the reputation she had shown such contempt for meant little or nothing to him.

'I needed a secretary.' Leigh's tone was bland, no trace of emotion ruffling its smooth surface. 'And Steve assured me that you were very efficient. I'd seen that for myself too, in the speed and accuracy with which you dealt with everything I sent from Scotland. And...'

'And?' Jassy prompted when he paused.

Those tawny eyes regarded her steadily and something deep in them made her heart lurch nervously and wish her question unsaid.

'You intrigued me,' Leigh said softly.

Jassy expected him to continue, elaborate on his enigmatic comment, but instead he picked up his pen again, turning his attention back to the script he was working on, his attitude telling her only too clearly that as far as he was concerned the conversation was at an end and he wouldn't welcome any attempt to start it again.

But Jassy had plenty to think about, her mind full of conflicting feelings, uppermost of which was the fact that she had not expected this degree of integrity from Leigh. She had assumed—quite wrongly, it seemed—that he enjoyed the adulation and attention his fame brought him. Clearly there were facets of his character that he took care to keep hidden from the Press and the public, and she wondered how many more she had yet to discover.

He had answered her questions frankly and openly, which was not at all how she might have expected him to behave when she considered how she had insulted him to his face on the night of *Romeo and Juliet*. And that was something she now had to reconsider in the light of all Leigh had said. Her hasty assumptions had to be brought out and looked at in this new light, like clothes that had once been an especial favourite but now, examined more closely, could be seen to be outdated and ill-fitting.

'You intrigued me.' That cryptic remark sounded in her thoughts, the tone in which it had been spoken reminding her of the last, cynically drawled words she had heard Leigh Benedict speak over two years before when he had described her as a very rare bird indeed. Just what did Leigh think of her? And, more complicated, what did she now think of him?

Absorbed in her thoughts, Jassy had almost forgotten Leigh sitting silently in the chair opposite, but gradually she became aware that even the faint rustle of a page being turned had ceased. Curiously she turned her head and found that he had fallen asleep, his head slightly to one side with his cheek against the soft leather of the chair, his blond hair falling over his face.

What did she do now? Jassy simply sat and watched him for a moment, frozen by her own indecision. She couldn't make up her mind whether to let him sleep or try to wake him so that he could go to bed and rest properly. If the truth were told, she felt distinctly nervous at the prospect of disturbing him. With those fierce bronze eyes hidden under heavy lids, and his face relaxed, he did not look at all dangerous. Sleep had softened the harsh lines of his face, smoothing away the hard, cynical expression he wore when awake, and, looking at him now, Jassy admitted that if she had never seen him before she would have to acknowledge a strong pull of attraction, drawing her almost to the point of wanting to like him.

Asleep, Leigh Benedict was just a man, never an ordinary one, for his looks defied any such description, but a very human man whose tiredness had caught up with him so that he had drifted asleep with the ease of an exhausted child. But underneath this disturbingly defenceless creature asleep in the chair lay the other man, the one she had seen outside the drama college, and, recalling the indolent arrogance of that man, the jaded tone in which he had drawled the cynical comments that had so angered and disgusted her, Jassy knew that this more youthful, vulnerable appearance was just an illusion. If she were to wake him then the real Leigh, the man she had so detested, would be back, and right now she was glad of a respite from having to be always on her guard against letting her true feelings show.

Leigh stirred slightly, murmuring softly in his sleep, and the file of papers on his knee slipped, threatening to fall and send a cascade of pages over the floor. Hastily Jassy got to her feet and eased the file from under his limp hand. Straightening the papers carefully, she put them on the coffee-table and then, to her complete consternation, found herself unable to move away again.

She was so near to Leigh that she could hear the soft sound of his breathing in the silent room, see the way his chest rose and fell, the occasional flicker of the long, thick eyelashes that lay like dark crescents against his skin. The rich golden hair glowed in the light of the lamp, reminding her of that incomprehensible longing to touch it that she had felt earlier. As if of its own volition her hand reached out tentatively until it rested lightly on Leigh's head, feeling the soft strands of hair slide under her fingertips. The slight contact was intoxicating, making her shiver involuntarily.

As if sensing her touch, Leigh stirred again, sighing faintly as he shifted position, and Jassy snatched her hand away as if she had been burned. Perversely, in spite of the fact that only minutes before she had been glad that Leigh was asleep, she now wanted him to wake. His deceptively vulnerable appearance, combined with her own alien urge to touch him, made her feel that she would be much safer if he were awake. Then his face would resume its hard, aloof expression, she would see the cold light in those gold-flecked eyes, and know her present mood for the fancy it was.

'Leigh,' she said slowly, her voice soft and hesitant.

There was no response from the silent figure in the chair; he was too deeply asleep to hear her. Impulsively Jassy sank down on the arm of the chair, moving nearer to him so that she could rouse him carefully, not daring to contemplate his possible reaction if he was startled into wakefulness.

'Leigh,' she tried again. 'Mr Benedict.'

The long lashes fluttered slightly, but Leigh did not open his eyes. Leaning forward, Jassy touched his shoulder, meaning only to shake him gently, but the feel

of the hard muscle beneath the soft cotton of his sweatshirt affected her as swiftly and shockingly as the moment
she had touched the silkiness of his hair, and to her
horror her fingers tightened convulsively, exploring the
strength beneath them.

Leigh Benedict's eyes snapped open, looking straight
into Jassy's face with a wary, questioning expression,
and Jassy froze, the force of that tawny gaze holding
her as if mesmerised, still leaning half across him, her
hand still on his shoulder. A moment later the wariness
faded from his eyes to be replaced by a warmly sensual
look that was almost a physical caress and his mouth
curved into an unexpected smile.

'Well,' he murmured softly. 'What have we here?'

One long-fingered hand moved to Jassy's face, tracing
the line of her cheekbone with infinite gentleness, then
slid slowly down to her neck, holding her without the
slightest effort when she made a small, half-hearted
attempt to move away.

'This is a most unexpected pleasure,' Leigh drawled,
still in that low, seductive voice, as he drew her face
gently but irresistibly towards his.

Jassy's throat was painfully dry. She wanted desperately to speak, but no words would form in her mind.
She knew that she should move away and stop this now,
before he got the wrong idea entirely—if he hadn't
already—but she couldn't find the strength to break free
from that light but inexorable grip on the back of her
neck, and, if she was strictly honest with herself, she
wasn't at all sure she wanted to.

Leigh's lips brushed hers in a tantalisingly brief caress
and she felt all trace of resistance seep from her, to be
replaced by a warm, glowing sensation that flowed
through her veins like the effect of some potent wine.
She scarcely noticed as Leigh's free arm slid round her
waist, gently pulling her down from her perch on the
chair arm so that she was half sitting, half lying across
him, her head against his chest. When Leigh's mouth
touched hers for the second time in a slow, lingering
exploration of her lips Jassy closed her eyes with a faint

sigh, oblivious of anything beyond this moment of total abandonment to the exquisitely pleasurable sensations his kiss was awakening in her. Deep inside she felt as if she had never truly been kissed before, as if, like some modern Sleeping Beauty, this was the one caress she had been waiting for all her life.

Sensing her surrender, Leigh tightened his grip around her waist, pulling her even closer, and her arms crept up around his neck, a small, wordless sound of disappointment escaping her when his mouth left hers for a moment. She heard his soft laughter then her lips were captured again, this time in a fierce, bruising kiss that forced her mouth open beneath his, sending shock-waves of reaction burning through her as if the blood in her veins were on fire. Leigh's hands were against her back; Jassy could feel the warmth of his touch through the thin cotton of her blouse, and her own fingers clenched in his hair in response.

'Hell!'

Leigh's exclamation came huskily against Jassy's lips as she moved in his arms, pressing herself closer still, her hands shaking as they tangled in the thick silkiness of his hair. Still keeping one strong arm tight around her, Leigh's other hand moved to the front of her blouse, dealing swiftly with the small pearly buttons that fastened it, until his hand closed firm and warm over the creamy breast his impatient fingers had exposed.

A fiery sensation of pleasure such as she had never experienced in her life before shot through Jassy, a pleasure so sharply powerful that it was almost like a shaft of pain, making her gasp aloud. The very intensity of it left her mind suddenly very clear so that she heard Leigh's voice with a stunning clarity.

'I know what *I* want, my lovely secretary, so, tell me— what is it you're after?'

At once all those memories, so close to the surface of her mind because she had been reviewing them earlier, came flooding into Jassy's thoughts as inside her head she heard that same rich-toned voice saying with dark cynicism, 'When she finds out she's getting nowhere, your sweet Juliet will resort to Gemma Morgan tactics like the rest; they always do.'

She started violently, twisting in Leigh's grasp. She didn't want this, she thought wildly, not with this man, and, finding that his grip on her had loosened slightly, she pushed violently away so that the force of her movement carried her, stumbling, halfway across the room to stand, her heart pounding painfully, with her back to him.

Behind her she could hear Leigh's uneven breathing, could almost feel those fierce tawny eyes burning into her as she pressed her fist up against her mouth, trying to crush down the anger and disgust that rose up inside her.

'I'd be intrigued to know what you're really like—to discover the woman like underneath all that ice,' he had said, and he had done just that. She could have no doubt that what had happened had meant anything to him beyond a purely sensual experience, a deliberate experiment, but she had succumbed to an assault on her senses every bit as calculated and unfeeling as the way in which he had kissed her a few days before. And what made matters far worse was the fact that he probably believed that she had responded to him because of who he was; he probably saw her as just another like the Gemma Morgan he had described so scathingly.

A harshly indrawn breath warned her that Leigh had recovered from his surprise enough to speak, and instinctively she tensed, nerving herself for his anger.

'You teasing bitch!'

The words were spoken in a low, controlled voice that was all the more frightening for the lack of violence in it. Anger she had expected, but not this icy coldness. Fearfully she kept her back towards him, struggling for some degree of control.

'No!' Jassy's response was tremulous, her voice just a shaken whisper as reaction set in. She couldn't believe the way she had behaved, anger and disgust warring in her at the way she had let this happen, the way she had

responded to him, making her head spin. 'I *wasn't*
teasing! I——'

'No?' the hard voice behind her questioned savagely.
'Then what do *you* call it? I wake up to find you
practically in my lap, and when I respond as any normal
man would under the circumstances you freeze up like
some frigid little virgin. You were making all the moves,
lady. Surely you're not going to claim I was forcing you?'

'No.' Jassy's voice was very low. There was no way
she could claim he had used force, but violence could
have been no more devastating than the cold-hearted
expertise with which he had deliberately set out to arouse
her.

Suddenly she swung round to him, her dishevelled hair
tumbling around her pale face in which her eyes seemed
huge and dark.

'But it wasn't what you think! I was only trying to
wake you.'

The cynical lifting of one eyebrow almost destroyed
what was left of her shattered self-control. She was
painfully aware of the fact that she wasn't handling this
at all well, which was strange. After all, it wasn't that
long since she'd been in a slightly similar situation,
having to explain to Andy, the man she'd been seeing,
that she had no intention of going to bed with him, and
then she had had no trouble getting her message across
calmly and easily. But then Andy was not Leigh Benedict.
He was everything this man was not, warm, considerate,
and he openly admired and respected the women he
worked with, his attitude light-years away from Leigh's
cynical degrading opinion of 'seductive little sirens'.

When her mind threw at her the irrefutable fact that
Andy had also never been able to arouse her, make her
forget herself in the way Leigh had done with just one
touch of his lips, her throat dried painfully so that she
had to swallow hard before she could go on.

'You didn't look very comfortable,' she said awkwardly. 'I thought you'd be better off in bed.'

'With you?'

Jassy stared at the fine-boned face before her, seeing arrogance and contempt stamped clearly on the hard mouth, glittering in the golden eyes, and a hot wave of anger swept through her, driving away any thought of caution from her mind.

'You're so bloody conceited!' she stormed, shocking herself with her ferocity. She was over-reacting again, but this time she didn't care. Even the swift, ominous narrowing of Leigh's eyes was ignored as she gave vent to the feelings that had been stored up inside her since the night of *Romeo and Juliet*. 'You really think that just because you're Leigh Benedict—the damn Golden Thief—every woman you meet must be longing to get into your bed—that they'll lie down and let you trample all over them if you'll just spare them a minute of your precious time! Well, you've misjudged things completely this time! Here's one woman who's totally indifferent to your much-vaunted charms. In fact, Mr Superstar Benedict, you make me sick!'

She had been right, Jassy told herself ruefully as the sound of her voice died away—right to have such strong doubts about taking this job, right to think that her anger and resentment at the things she had heard him say could not be kept in check when she and this man came face to face. There was a bitter taste in her mouth as she recalled how, such a short time earlier, she had come close to revising her opinion of Leigh Benedict, had admitted to some sympathy, even some admiration for him. The swift destruction of that fragile understanding had added fuel to the bitterness that had caused her final outburst.

She opened her mouth to speak again, though not really knowing what more she could say, but the slow, sardonic curl of Leigh's lips closed her throat.

'Is that so?' he said softly, his eyes mocking her piti-lessly. 'Well, you'll have to forgive me if I don't exactly believe you. If that was indifference—or more—you have the damnedest way of showing it.'

The silkily spoken taunt brought a shaky gasp to Jassy's lips. Her anger deserted her just when she needed it most, and it took all her fast-dwindling reserves of strength to say anything.

'You took me by surprise. If I'd had time to think . . .'

Jassy's tightly controlled voice faltered beneath Leigh's steely gaze. That wasn't true—and he knew it, damn him! She squared her shoulders and, drawing herself up proudly, forced herself to look him straight in the face.

'But it won't happen again, do you understand? *Never!* I'm not available—certainly not to you!'

'Don't flatter yourself,' was the swift, uncomplimentary response. 'I'm not so desperate for female company that I'd choose to spend my time on some immature schoolgirl who doesn't know her own mind.'

Insulting as his words were, they were infinitely welcome to Jassy. If that was how he felt then surely she was safe from any repetition of what had happened? She felt the tension in her body ease, leaving her drained and exhausted.

But she had relaxed too soon. With a sudden lithe movement Leigh was out of his chair and had caught her arm in a painful grip, his other hand wrenching her chin up, forcing her eyes to meet the cold blaze of anger in his.

'But I warn you, I don't take too kindly to some juvenile Lolita using me to practise her wiles on. I reckon I owe you one, and I don't forget easily, so you remember that. Meanwhile, here's a little something on account——'

Before Jassy quite realised what Leigh intended she was pulled into his arms and he kissed her hard, a harsh, savage kiss that was more a bruising assault than any form of caress. He controlled her struggles with an easy indolence that belied the strength of his grasp, forcing her tight up against his body and holding her for just as long as he wanted before he released her so abruptly that she staggered backwards, one hand going automatically to her bruised mouth.

'I think that evens the score a little,' Leigh declared grimly.

He surveyed her dishevelled appearance coldly, his eyes, like chips of golden ice, lingering for a moment on the soft swell of her breasts still clearly visible beneath her unfastened blouse, before they flicked back up to her flushed face.

'Fasten yourself up,' he ordered brutally. 'I've seen quite enough of you for one night.'

And the appalling thing was that, even as the door swung to behind him, Jassy had to admit to herself that although that last kiss had been given in anger, meaning only to punish her and nothing more, it had stirred those unwanted longings deep within her just as surely as any of his earlier, more gentle caresses had done.

CHAPTER THREE

IF IT had been at all possible, Jassy would have left Leigh's house then and there and never come back, and to hell with her job, no matter how much she needed it. But it was well after midnight, she didn't have enough money in her purse for a taxi fare, and it would be the height of foolishness to risk making the long journey back to her flat alone at this time of night. So she had no alternative but to go to the room Steve had shown her, where she got into bed, but not to sleep.

Instead, she tossed and turned restlessly as her mind replayed over and over again the events of the evening like a film projected on a screen, never coming any nearer to a rational explanation for her own behaviour.

The response Leigh Benedict's coldly calculated caresses had awoken in her had had something of the same effect as being thrown into a swimming-pool at the deep end with only the vaguest idea of how to swim. Since she had come to London to study, and in the years since she had left drama college, her dedication to the idea of becoming an actress had been all that had motivated her, and the time and commitment that had been demanded had left her with little energy or inclination for any serious romantic attachments. Casual sexual relationships were not for her, the risks were too high, and besides, she had always believed that true physical fulfilment could only come from loving someone and knowing that they loved you. So she had always said no—and meant it—but there had never been any panic, any recrimination. She was able to call a halt with a word and a smile, ensuring there was no ill-feeling on either side.

But with Leigh Benedict her carefully thought-out approach had deserted her. As an actor, he commanded

her respect and admiration, but as a man the feelings he
aroused in her were exactly the opposite, and yet, in a
few brief minutes, he had taught her more of what it
really meant to be a woman than any other man she had
ever met. He had brought her to a point at which she
had had no thought of principles, or even the way she
had decided was the best, she would have said the *only*,
one for her. Leigh had somehow found the key that
opened the door to her own personal sexuality, and,
having had that door opened, Jassy knew she had to go
through it. There was no way she could simply close it
again and pretend she didn't know what lay on the other
side.

But she would not go through it with Leigh. What had
happened between them had meant nothing to him; he
saw her only as one of the actresses he had described,
believing her to be attracted by the aura of fame, power
and influence he carried with him, and had treated her
accordingly. The thought repelled her and in the cold
light of dawn she came to a decision.

She would have to leave; there was no way she could
work for Leigh now. She was not prepared to work for
a man who despised her, however unjustly. She did not
allow herself to consider how she might feel if she never
saw Leigh again.

Fired with resolve, she made her way to her office the
next morning. Her office no longer, she thought on a
pang of regret. She had enjoyed her job, and in any other
circumstances would have been happy to keep it—not
least because the pay was good and she desperately
needed the money. But Leigh gave her no chance to
declare her intention of leaving, glancing up from the
pile of papers on his own desk to wave a hand at a bundle
of letters.

'See to those, will you?' he said with a casualness that
astounded Jassy. 'I shall want to dictate some letters to
you later.'

Jassy could only stand still and stare at him. This was
not how she had expected the morning to go! A carefully formal speech of resignation was clear in her head,

but somehow she couldn't bring herself to form the words she had practised over and over again.

Just to see Leigh had brought memories of the previous night rushing back into Jassy's mind, but he was behaving as if that night had never been, as if she had just arrived for work on an ordinary morning. Then her mind cleared. She had forgotten what a consummate actor Leigh was. He was a man who could turn on any emotion, or the lack of it, at the word of a director or, as he was doing now, for his own private reasons.

Well, she was an actress too, wasn't she? If she treated her position here simply as a part, a role she had to play, then perhaps she could hide last night's turmoil behind a mask as distant as his own and play the scene as Leigh directed.

'I take it you still want me to work for you?'

She recognised that voice; it came from her last part but one, when she had played a haughty French aristocrat during the Revolution—all that was missing was the accent.

'I expect you to work *with* me——' Leigh returned imperiously. 'We're going to be snowed under with paperwork for the next couple of weeks and I need someone I can rely on to work efficiently under pressure.'

Glancing up, he caught the slight change in her expression that she was unable to hide.

'I need a *secretary* more than ever.'

The emphasis on the single word couldn't be clearer, and it revived the feelings of outrage that had held her in their grip through the long, dark hours of the night. Now was the time to tell him just what he could do with his job.

'But . . .'

Her voice failed her as a smile tugged at the corners of that firm mouth. The smile told her everything and pulled out from under her feet her conviction that leaving was her only way out of this situation with her self-respect intact.

Leigh *expected* her to leave! If she walked out now it would confirm his cynical suspicions, his belief that the only reason she had come to work for him was because she had hoped to seduce him into using his influence in the acting world to help her a few steps up the career ladder. Handing in her resignation would only make him assume that he had been right in his interpretation of her behaviour last night and that, finding that her sexual tactics hadn't worked, she was leaving because there was nothing to be gained by staying.

She was caught in a cleft stick. She didn't want to stay, couldn't bear to think of working for this arrogant, self-centred devil, but her self-respect mattered more. She had declared to his face that she was one actress who wouldn't sell herself in order to get on, and if she was to convince Leigh of that—and suddenly convincing him of the truth had become much more important than anything else—then she had to stay.

'I'll get on with the post then,' she said crisply, every inch the perfect secretary—something which clearly had not escaped Leigh, as that lop-sided and singularly attractive smile, an infuriatingly irrational part of her brain acknowledged, tugged at his mobile mouth again.

'Do that,' he said drily.

The routine of opening, sorting, and answering the letters was by now so familiar to Jassy that the procedure soothed her jangled nerves and she was soon absorbed in the task, able to forget Leigh's disturbing silent presence temporarily at least. When Leigh did speak to her, his tone was strictly businesslike, with no hint of anything beyond the matter in hand to worry her. His behaviour was purely that of employer to employee, polite but uninvolved, and if he was to keep it that way she felt she might be able to cope with working for him after all.

Halfway through the morning the phone rang and Leigh answered it, firing questions swiftly at the person on the other end of the line and making brief notes on a pad in front of him.

'That was Steve,' he said a short time later when he had put the receiver down. 'He asked me to tell you he'll be back tomorrow.'

Leigh was watching her, waiting for her reaction in a way that made Jassy feel vaguely uneasy, and that feeling, combined with a sudden strong sense of relief at the thought that when Steve returned his cheerful personality would act as a buffer between herself and Leigh, made her over-react, putting more enthusiasm than was strictly necessary into her reply.

'That's great. I'll look forward to that,' she said brightly, then deliberately followed Leigh's own example and turned her attention firmly to her work, not waiting to see how he reacted.

There, she thought with a small sense of triumph, let him make what he wanted of that! With any luck he would think that she and Steve were rather more than just friends and, hopefully, that would make him keep his distance. Surely even Leigh Benedict would have the decency not to try anything with his friend's girl? When an inner, coldly realistic part of her mind reminded her that Leigh had made it plain that he had no intention of trying anything, that, on the contrary, he believed that *she* was the one who might make any move, she pushed the thought away hastily, forcing herself to concentrate on her work instead.

After lunch, when Leigh insisted that Jassy took the full hour she was entitled to though he spared himself only ten minutes away from his desk, the silence in the room began to feel oppressive. Jassy was used to having no one to talk to, having spent so many days alone in this room in the past few weeks, but this silence was constrained and unnatural and she longed for something to break it, so that when the telephone rang again she snatched at it swiftly, grateful for the interruption.

'Mrs Eldon?' The distinctively husky female voice at the other end of the line was instantly recognisable, especially as Jassy had heard it again so very recently, and her mind went back to the evening Steve had taken her out to dinner.

Anna Golden had been seated at another table in the restaurant, surrounded by a group of friends, the dramatic mane of red-gold hair falling halfway down her back instantly revealing her identity to Jassy. Glancing up, the actress had recognised Steve and had immediately got to her feet, heading towards their table.

Jassy had watched her come, her mind full of the last time she had seen the older woman, over two years before. Anna Golden was deeply tanned, her bronzed skin in strong contrast to the soft beige suede of the sleeveless trouser suit that plunged to a deep V over her voluptuously curved breasts. Gold chains glinted at her throat, a wide gold belt encircled her narrow waist and her already impressive height was emphasised by a pair of ridiculously high-heeled sandals. Jassy knew that the actress must be around forty, but she could have claimed to be ten years younger and got away with it. Her acting career might have been eclipsed by that of her younger, more successful lover, but as she swayed seductively across the room Anna Golden still clearly thought of herself as a star.

'Steve, darling!'

Her smile was obviously insincere, and Steve's in response was equally forced. Instinctively Jassy stiffened, feeling vibrations of dislike and distrust reach her as if on the air she breathed.

'Have you heard from Leigh when he's coming back from Scotland? Poor darling, he must be terribly lonely up there in the wilds. There's no civilisation for miles. But I'll make it up to him when he gets back. I'm planning a very special reunion—just the two of us, a quiet meal, and some excellent champagne.'

Steve gave a non-commital murmur, but Anna did not appear to need any reply.

'Give Leigh a message for me when you see him. Just tell him I'll be waiting for him—he'll understand.'

That purring voice was beginning to grate on Jassy's nerves, the breathy, caressing intonation making her feel positively sick. It seemed there was little difference between Anna Golden and all those adoring women whose letters she had been dealing with for weeks. But perhaps that was the way Leigh Benedict liked it.

'I know how strung up he is when he's finished filming, but I have my own special ways of making him unwind.'

'He'll be working hard when he gets back.'

Jassy was distracted from her private reflections on Anna's comment that Leigh would be 'strung up', something she personally understood only too well, by the evident constraint in Steve's voice.

'We're auditioning for the female lead in *Valley of Destiny* very soon.'

'Ah, yes, Leigh's precious film.' Anna's tone was tart. 'I should have thought he'd be desperately tired of dealing with young hopefuls by now. He'll be ready for some more—sophisticated company to take his mind off things.'

The actress stretched luxuriously like a contented cat, a sensual smile curling her lips as if at some private memory, her green eyes lighting with a lascivious gleam that was almost indecent in a public place. That smile was in Jassy's mind now, making her voice cool and distant as she spoke into the telephone receiver.

'Mrs Eldon's on sick leave, Miss Golden. I'm acting as secretary temporarily.'

'Oh, yes, Steve's little friend.' Anna Golden's tone implied that Jassy she had found all too easy to forget.

Out of the corner of her eye Jassy saw the way Leigh's head had lifted on hearing the caller's name, and now he was quite obviously listening to every word she said. A sudden wave of hot anger washed over her at the thought that, last night, Leigh had made his unjustified contempt of her so plain when his own slate wasn't exactly clean in such matters. His affair with Anna Golden had been responsible for the break-up of the actress's marriage, and yet he had had the nerve to be so contemptuous of her own behaviour and the motive he had ascribed to it.

'Anyway, it's Leigh I want to speak to. He is there, isn't he?'

Automatically Jassy glanced across at Leigh, questioning expression on her face as she held the telephone slightly towards him. She was frankly surprised by the

moment's hesitation before he nodded in response to her
unspoken enquiry.

'Yes, he's here,' she said to Anna. 'Just one moment.'
She held out the receiver to Leigh as he came to take it
from her.

'Anna——' Leigh's voice was urbane and good-
humoured, the momentary hesitation apparently
forgotten so that Jassy wondered if in fact she had
imagined it '—when did you get back from Greece?'

With an effort Jassy directed her attention back to her
work, struggling to ignore the lean body resting against
her desk, one long-fingered hand lying casually on its
top, very close to her typewriter. She didn't like Leigh,
she told herself firmly. In fact, she positively detested
him—but that thought did nothing to calm her pulse
which had quickened in the most disconcerting way
simply because of his nearness.

'Tonight?' Leigh was saying. 'That could be difficult.
Oh, I see—well, I suppose I could manage that. I've a
couple of things to sort out here, but I could be free
later. After seven OK?'

Clearly the actress had planned that tonight would be
the time for that 'very special reunion' Jassy reflected
cynically. Though, strangely, Leigh did not appear as
enthusiastic about the scheme as Anna's words had led
her to expect. She supposed that that was because he
resented anyone, even his mistress, interrupting the work
on the film that he had made plain was so very important
to him. She couldn't resist a small smile at the thought
of Anna Golden's reaction to having to take second place
to Leigh's work.

A moment later Leigh was laughing, a warm, relaxed
sound that Jassy had not heard from him before.
Involuntarily she glanced up to catch the smile on his
face, that sudden, swift smile that changed him so dramatically, transforming his hard features, and an unexpected sharp pang shot through her at the thought that
last night he had smiled at her like that, just once—but
never again.

'Anna, you are incorrigible! That remark was definitely slanderous. Restrain your lurid imagination, you'll offend my new secretary's delicate sensibilities.'

Jassy started slightly at his reference to herself, and at that moment the tawny eyes swung round to her face. She was held transfixed by Leigh's mocking gaze, unable to look away when he spoke again.

'You've met her? When?'

As he listened to Anna's reply another smile curved Leigh's beautifully shaped mouth, but, unnervingly, Jassy noticed that this one did not reach his eyes. Deliberately he paused and let his gaze sweep over her, insolent and assessing in a way that brought hot colour rushing into her cheeks.

'No,' he drawled slowly, 'nothing like Mrs Eldon.'

Jassy's embarrassment fled before a wave of fiery anger at his words. How dared he discuss her with Anna Golden like this as if she weren't in the room? Biting her lower lip hard to keep back the furious outburst that almost escaped her, she reached for the letters in front of her and began sorting through them aimlessly. There was nothing more to be done with them, they were all finished and waiting for Leigh's signature, but she needed something—*anything*—to occupy her so that she didn't have to meet Leigh's eyes again.

Mercifully he put the phone down a few seconds later and silently held out his hand for the letters, glancing through them swiftly before he signed his name at the bottom of each page. Then, to Jassy's surprise, he read them all again, frowning thoughtfully as he did so.

'How did you learn to do this?' he asked suddenly. 'Mrs Eldon's been answering these things for years so she knows what I want, but you've hit exactly the right note straight away.'

Jassy did not know how to answer him. She had replied to the fan letters as she would have wanted them answered if she were in Leigh's position, trying to avoid obvious formula letters and yet, while showing appreciation of their interest, always being aware of the need for reticence in order to preserve some personal privacy.

'It's not always easy,' she said diffidently.

'I'm aware of that.' Leigh turned that disturbingly direct gaze on her once more. 'But they're part of the job. The people who write those letters helped to put me where I am, so the least I can do is answer them—but I'll not let myself be eaten alive because of that. Publicity's a fact of life in this business, but publicity for my work, Leigh Benedict the actor—everything else is quite irrelevant. You show an unusual understanding of that fact, and I couldn't have done better myself.'

'I tried to put myself in your place when I answered them,' Jassy murmured, torn between a desire to keep her distance as much as possible and a need to give in to the unexpected glow of pleasure his appreciative comments had sparked off inside her.

'That can't have been easy,' Leigh flashed back, reverting to his usual satirical character. 'You must have had to work damned hard to suppress your true feelings.'

Abruptly his expression changed, those bright eyes suddenly intent on Jassy's face so that instinctively she flinched away from the probing force of his gaze. She felt as if he was searching deep into her mind, trying to draw out her innermost thoughts.

'What sort of actress are you?' he demanded, throwing Jassy completely off balance mentally at this unexpected turn of the conversation into an area that felt perilously like a minefield.

'I——'

'Are you any good?'

How did she answer that? Professional pride gave her the confidence to meet his eyes. 'I had a couple of decent reviews, but I'm only just starting out.'

'What have you done?'

'Cecily in *The Importance Of Being Earnest*; Viola in *Twelfth Night*——' when compared with his own achievements it sounded so very little, so insignificant 'and I was Rosalie in *Moonrise*, but——' her smile was wry '—that didn't last very long.'

Leigh nodded slowly. 'I saw that—the play was appalling.'

Jassy felt as if someone had just punched her in the stomach, leaving her gasping for breath. *Leigh* had seen her performance as Rosalie! Irrationally, she felt that it was impossible that he had been in the audience and she hadn't known. Even disliking him as much as she did, she couldn't deny the forceful impact of his physical presence. Surely some sixth sense should have alerted her to the fact that he'd been in the theatre?

Then the memory of how much she had wanted his critical opinion of her abilities over two years before crept into her mind and it was impossible not to dwell on that cryptic 'the play was appalling' and wonder what he had thought of her performance. The question burned on her lips, but pride and a sudden strong sense of self-preservation forced it back.

She was here as Leigh's secretary, nothing more. He had made that only too plain. To ask his opinion of her performance could be interpreted as another attempt to use her position here to her own advantage, something she had vowed she would never let him do. But all the same, she wouldn't be human if she didn't wonder. *Had* there been the slightest emphasis on 'the *play*'? Could Leigh have meant to imply that *she* hadn't been as bad as the production?

But as her eyes went to Leigh's face in an attempt to try to read in it if there had been something else behind his words he moved away towards his desk to pick up a thick folder which he dumped unceremoniously down in front of her.

'That's the final draft. I've done all the alterations, now it just needs typing up—but I need it done quickly. Can you come in tomorrow?'

Jassy opened her mouth to speak, then hesitated. At the back of her mind warning bells were sounding faintly, woken as a result of Leigh's disturbing and unexpected questions. Could she really continue to work for him, knowing what he thought of her, or wouldn't it be wiser, safer, to tell him now that she was leaving and get out with some shred of pride left intact?

'Double time.' Leigh's voice sounded tautly in her ears.

But Jassy really wasn't listening. Still wrestling with her inability to make a decision, she had lifted the cover of the folder on the desk and what she saw underneath it made her draw in her breath sharply.

This was the script of *Valley of Destiny*, the production that had had the whole film world talking and speculating for months. Was she really going to turn down the chance to be a part, however lowly, of the team that worked on that film? Already there were rumours that it would be one of the biggest films of the year, if not the decade. This might be the only opportunity she would ever have to work on something so important.

'I can come in any time you want.' Jassy heard her own voice with something of a shock. She had spoken from the heart; rationally she still had not decided.

But the words had been said, there was no taking them back, and if she was honest she did not want to retract her agreement. Even typing out the script would add to her knowledge of the process of filming and she couldn't afford to pass up such a valuable chance. After today she would be well settled in to her role as Leigh's secretary, and if he continued to be as distant and aloof as he had been all day then she could put last night's events behind her and play that part as long as was necessary. Feeling more confident, she lifted her eyes to Leigh's.

'I'll do as much overtime as you need,' she said firmly.

'Fine.' Leigh's tone was crisp. 'I'd appreciate that.'

Unexpectedly he leaned towards her, resting his hands on the desktop, his nearness infinitely disturbing to her peace of mind.

'I really would appreciate it,' he said with a new and very different note in his voice. 'I realise what I'm asking. You've already given up more than half of your weekend to help me out. If you think I'm pushing you too hard you've only got to say.'

Jassy could hardly believe her ears. Such consideration was the last thing she had expected! But then she had forgotten that Leigh was playing the part of the perfect boss. It was a role he played particularly well too, she reflected satirically, recalling the bouquets of flowers she had sent, on Leigh's instructions, to the indisposed Mrs Eldon. He knew all he moves, all the gestures.

'No, it's all right, I can cope,' she said awkwardly as Leigh straightened up.

'Thanks,' Leigh said briefly, but the single word was accompanied by a smile so unforced and so unexpected that it took her breath away.

Even when he was back at his own desk she found that it still affected her, making her hands suddenly clumsy so that they hit all the wrong keys, making a terrible mess until she tore the paper from her typewriter in a fury of exasperation at the chaos she had made of a perfectly simple task.

Damn him, she thought to herself, flinging the crumpled sheet in the vague direction of the waste-paper basket, not caring that she missed it completely. Just when she thought she'd got things all sorted out and knew exactly where she stood with him, something like that had to happen, setting her pulse racing, bringing every nerve alive in the most unsettling way, and she was right back where she had started, thoroughly confused by her own reactions, and not at all sure that she liked what was happening to her.

With the typical unreliability of an English summer, the rain began to fall late in the afternoon, lightly at first, spattering the window with fine drops, then steadily increasing until it was a savage, torrential downpour. Jassy sighed faintly, thinking of her journey home, and Leigh glanced up, frowning as he looked out at the sodden garden.

'You can't go home in this,' he said, almost as if he had read her thoughts. 'If you can hang on till six-thirty I'll drive you home.'

'It doesn't matter,' Jassy answered hastily. 'I can get a bus.'

'You'd drown before you reached the bus-stop,' Leigh told her in a tone that brooked no further argument. 'I'll take you—I have to go out anyway.'

Yes, and she knew just where he was going. Jassy couldn't help wondering if he would have bothered to offer her a lift if he had not been going out already. Another gesture.

Just after six Leigh stretched lazily and got to his feet.

'You can pack up now,' he told Jassy. 'And get your things from upstairs. I'm just going to get changed—I won't be long.'

It took only a few minutes to straighten her desk and put the cover on her typewriter; then, picking up the script of *Valley of Destiny* ready to put it in a drawer, Jassy hesitated. From the start, the power of the script had caught her up in its imaginary world. Thinking as an actress, she had been able to visualise the scenes vividly, and the pages she had typed had only whetted her appetite to read more. No one would know if she took it home. She could read it overnight and return it the next day with no one any the wiser. Impulsively she slipped the folder into the roomy shoulder-bag that lay beside her desk.

The next task was to collect her few belongings from the bedroom, but once she had packed everything into her overnight bag Jassy found herself lingering inexplicably, recalling with painful clarity the thoughts and feelings that had assailed her in this room in the early hours of the morning.

Leigh might as well have made love to her, she reflected, because she would never be able to go back to the way she had been before. She had been smugly convinced of her ability to handle her sexual feelings, when the truth of the matter was that she had never felt anything approaching real sexual desire before. All her emotional energy had been directed towards her acting, the need to prove herself to herself and to her parents uppermost in her mind so that she had never wanted any more than the kisses and mild caresses she had shared with her boyfriends.

But now, when a man she did not like, let alone love, a man so cynical and arrogant that under normal circumstances she would have avoided him like the plague, could so easily make her forget all her convictions, could bring her to the point where she had desperately wanted him to make love to her without any thought of the consequences, she was forced to look at things in a very different light. The shock of realising that she was capable of experiencing such intense physical passion had stripped away the self-confidence she had built up over the years and reduced her once more to the gauche, uncertain girl she had been when she had first left home. Deep inside, Jassy sensed intuitively that she would never be able to respond to a man, any man, in quite the same way again. After knowing that sense of heightened awareness and need that she had felt in Leigh's arms, would she ever again be satisfied with the light-hearted lovemaking she had enjoyed in the past?

Leigh was waiting for her when she went back downstairs. He had discarded his casual shirt and jeans in favour of a lightweight beige suit and a bronze-coloured shirt that picked up the colour of his eyes so that they reminded Jassy of the watchful, golden gaze of a tiger. Seeing him, she immediately wished she had insisted on catching the bus. Dressed like this, Leigh was no longer the man she had worked with all day, the polite if somewhat distant boss. With the change of clothes he had once more assumed the public image of Leigh Benedict, the film star, and the sheer force of his rugged sexual magnetism awoke memories of the previous night that almost overwhelmed her, making her feel shaky and ill at ease.

'Ready?' Leigh asked, glancing at his watch. He seemed impatient to be off, with no sign now of the reluctance he had appeared to feel earlier, so that Jassy was convinced that she must have misread his reaction.

Recalling the lascivious way Anna Golden had spoken of her plans to help Leigh unwind, her voice, her eyes, even her movements implying a sensual pleasure in simply anticipating the time they would spend together, she could not wonder at Leigh's impatience. No doubt the worldly actress would more than compensate him for the frustrations of the previous night, she told herself bitterly, and felt a slow, cold shiver slide down her spine at the thought of how she might have been feeling now if she had let Leigh make love to her, only to see him return to his mistress the very next day.

Leigh's car was as sleekly powerful as Jassy remembered it from the night of *Romeo and Juliet*, the sight of it reviving the feelings of anger and disgust she had felt then, so that she sat stiffly in her seat, holding her bag tightly in her lap, as Leigh swung the car out of the gate. She could only pray that the journey to her flat would not take long. The confined space of the car's interior had forced her into an intimate proximity to Leigh that was infinitely disturbing. She was shiveringly aware of the warmth of the lean body beside her, abnormally sensitive to the movements of his hands on the wheel as she stared fixedly ahead of her, unable to relax.

'What made you decide to take a secretarial course?' Leigh's quietly spoken question broke into Jassy's thoughts, so that she rushed into her answer without pausing to reflect whether she wanted to reveal anything so very personal to him.

'My parents hated the thought of my becoming an actress. They thought it was an unstable, insecure, and somehow very trivial sort of occupation. They wanted me to get a "real job", like my brothers and sister who are all highly respectable professional people. Acting, in their opinion, was better kept as an interesting hobby.'

She was unaware of the note of unhappiness that had crept into her voice at the recollection of her parents' opposition and scorn for her private dreams.

'It's certainly not a regular nine-to-five job,' Leigh put in drily. 'But, in my opinion at least, the rewards outweigh the disadvantages. I know that feeling of wanting—*needing*—to act, but I can also understand your parents' point of view. How did you get them to change their minds?'

'When I got a place at drama school, I was dependent on Mum and Dad for my living expenses—I only got a minimum grant. They still refused to let me go—until I came up with a compromise. I would do a secretarial course at an evening class, and then, if I couldn't get work as an actress, I would always have something to fall back on.'

'That sounds like an eminently sensible idea.' To Jassy's surprise there was a strong note of admiration in Leigh's quiet voice. 'There have been times when I've wished I had a second string to my bow; "resting" has to be the most inappropriate term ever. To an actor, it's more like living death.'

Jassy's attempt at laughter was shaken, uneven. She had never expected to find this degree of empathy between them.

'That's just how I feel. At times like this, I'm beginning to see what my parents meant.'

'You do keep in touch with your agent?' Leigh's tone was stern, very much the established professional advising a beginner in his field.

'Oh, yes, I ring her every day—but nothing's available. It's been three months now,' Jassy said on a sigh.

'Three months isn't so long. I was out of work for over a year at the beginning, and as I didn't have your practical forethought I ended up working behind a bar, hating every minute of it and convinced that I'd be there for the rest of my life. I was sure that my acting career was jinxed—finished before it had even begun.'

Jassy couldn't suppress a faint start of surprise. Success and acclaim seemed so intrinsically linked with Leigh's name that she found it hard to imagine him without them, as a beginner like herself, struggling to find a foothold on the rocky slopes of their profession. To her consternation, she found the image he had given her intensely appealing. It made him appear so very much more human than the godlike figure the newspapers and magazines had created.

'What broke the jinx?'

The question came a little breathlessly because something had made her heart kick painfully at the thought of Leigh at twenty or so, struggling to make his mark, younger, more innocent, without those cynical opinions that had so alienated her. Or had he always felt that way?

A brief grin flashed over Leigh's face, lighting it brilliantly for a moment.

'Would you believe pantomime?'

He glanced swiftly at Jassy's dumbfounded expression and the grin widened devastatingly.

'It's true,' he assured her. 'I played Wishee Washee in *Aladdin* in some ropey little provincial theatre. I sang, I danced, told appalling jokes—I even did a little magic.'

Jassy's heart jerked again, but this time it was not the past that had affected her but her instinctive response to that wide, unconstrained smile. This was a side to Leigh she had never seen before, and it was one she found herself liking very much. Encouraged by his more open, approachable mood, she found herself responding with enthusiasm.

'Funnily enough, it was a pantomime that got me hooked. I was seven years old and Mum and Dad took me to see *Cinderella*. It was the first time I'd ever been inside a theatre and from the moment the show started I knew that this was what I wanted to do. I pestered my parents to let me join a children's theatre club on Saturday mornings, and then, later, I joined the local amateur dramatic group.'

'Your parents didn't object to that?'

'Not when it was just a hobby. It was only when I wanted to make a *career* out of it that they objected. I knew that it would be very hard work, that if I made any sort of living out of acting I'd be incredibly lucky, but I never expected instant stardom.'

Would he let her get away with another question? She was going to risk it anyway; there was so much she wanted to ask him.

'When did you know that acting was what you wanted to do?'

'I don't remember ever making that decision. I spent so much of my early childhood in and around theatres that I thought that was the only way to exist. It was only later that I learned that not everyone lived that way, and then—people—tried to dissuade me.'

'Your parents?'

The words slipped out before Jassy had time to consider whether they were wise or not, and she knew immediately that they had been a mistake as Leigh's face changed dramatically, setting in hard, distant lines, the atmosphere in the car turning from springlike warmth to icy winter in an instant.

'My father was never around to comment,' Leigh said curtly. 'And as my mother had been dead for years by the time I decided on what I wanted to do, her opinion was irrelevant—though I doubt if she'd have encouraged me to follow in her footsteps.'

'Your mother was an actress?'

Curiosity overcame Jassy's repugnance at the darkly sardonic way Leigh had spoken of his parents. 'I spent so much of my early childhood in and around theatres,' he had said; that was something she hadn't known. There had been no mention of it in the brief biography that was used for publicity purposes.

'Who——?'

'She didn't act under her real name,' Leigh snapped, clearly anticipating her question, and equally obviously not liking it. 'We're here.'

And if they hadn't arrived outside her flat at that point, Jassy thought, he wouldn't have answered any more questions—that much was evident from the tautness of every muscle in his face, the way his mouth was drawn into a thin, hard line. That part of Leigh's life was definitely not for public consumption, his expression said—and who could blame him? she acknowledged, considering privately how she would feel if the Press began poking around into her own family background.

As the car came to a halt Jassy hastily gathered her belongings together and got out, feeling suddenly supremely conscious of the contrast between the shabby, run-down street where she lived and Leigh's elegant town house.

'What time do you want me to come in tomorrow?' she asked jerkily, anxious for him to be gone and yet strangely reluctant to be the one who moved away first, the loss of that unexpected openness and sharing nagging at her like an aching bruise in her mind.

'After ten will do.' Leigh's response was abstracted, his thoughts seeming to be elsewhere—probably already on his evening with Anna Golden, Jassy told herself, and was shocked to find how much that fact stung.

The slight movement of a curtain at an upper window caught her eye and she groaned inwardly. Sarah must have heard the car and had come to see who had brought her home. Suddenly she became painfully aware of how foolish she must look, lingering in the rain when any sensible person would have hurried inside.

'I'll see you tomorrow——' she began, but Leigh had already started the engine. Without so much as a glance at her he steered the car away from the kerb and a few seconds later it had turned the corner and was out of sight.

Jassy had barely reached the top of the stairs before the door to the flat opened and Sarah appeared, fairly bubbling with excitement and curiosity.

'Was that who I think it was? What's been going on? Jassy, you've got to tell me *everything*!'

'There's nothing to tell.'

Wearily Jassy followed her friend into the flat, dropped her bags on the floor, and sank down into a chair. Leaning her head back against it, she rubbed her temples hard, trying to soothe the ache that had started as she had watched Leigh drive away.

'Nothing to tell?' Sarah echoed incredulously. 'That wasn't Steve's car, so it must have been the man himself. It *was* Leigh Benedict, wasn't it?'

'Yes, it was,' Jassy admitted tiredly. She didn't want to talk about Leigh, didn't want to *think* about him again tonight. Never before had any man raised such ambiguous feelings in her; she seemed to have been veering between attraction and repulsion with exhausting frequency all day long as if she were on some crazy emotional roller-coaster.

She glanced thoughtfully round the room, half expecting to find that it had changed in the time she had been away. She hardly felt like the same person as the girl who had left for work the morning before. But the flat was reassuringly the same, though it looked shabbier than ever after the luxury of Leigh's home.

It had looked worse than this, she reflected, remembering the dark, drab little rooms before she and Sarah had put up posters, added cushions, but at least it was homely and she was fond of it. She frowned slightly at the memory of Leigh's indifference to his luxurious surroundings. From the things he had let slip about his early struggle for success, she would have thought that he would take a great delight in the material wealth his fame had brought him—but then, on several occasions, Leigh had proved himself to be very different from what she had expected.

Becoming aware of Sarah's curious gaze, Jassy forced a smile.

'Sorry,' she said hastily. 'It's been a long day and Mr Benedict's not a man to let grass grow under his feet.'

She saw her friend's eyebrows lift at the formal 'Mr Benedict' and admitted to herself that she had used the words deliberately in an attempt to distance herself from the man who, in her private thoughts, she had thought of as Leigh all day.

'He works non-stop and expects everyone else to do the same. I've got to go in tomorrow too.'

'Is that all you're going to tell me?' Sarah put in plaintively. 'Why did he bring you——?'

'Sarah, it was raining. He gave me a lift home because he was coming this way anyway. He was going to see Anna—his...' she couldn't understand why she was having trouble getting the word out '...his mistress,' she finished baldly.

'Anna Golden? I didn't know she was still in favour. I thought he'd moved on to pastures new—and younger. But tell me, is he really as gorgeous as he seems on film? Oh, those eyes!'

Sarah rolled her own eyes and sighed dramatically, making Jassy laugh naturally for the first time.

'He's just as good-looking in the flesh, in fact more so, but——' Jassy sobered abruptly '—he knows it. He's an arrogant devil—just because producers are down on their knees begging him to appear in their latest film, it doesn't give him the right to treat the rest of us mere mortals as less than the dirt beneath his feet!'

The uneasy awareness of the fact that she was speaking considerably less than the truth, the memory of Leigh's genuine concern and consideration for her—as his employee, at least—gave Jassy's words an unusual ferocity that Sarah noticed at once.

'He has put your back up, hasn't he? This can't be just because he didn't see your brilliant Juliet—I didn't either, and you haven't murdered me yet. What *did* he do?'

'He——' Jassy began and then stopped.

What *had* Leigh done? He had kissed her, had tried to make love to her, something other men had done without making her feel like this. Jassy could just imagine Sarah's reaction if she told her that.

Because, looking back, she was disturbed to find that she now saw the scene in Leigh's living-room with very different eyes and, to her mental discomfort, she found it hard to condemn Leigh himself as totally as she had done then. *She* had behaved totally inexplicably, completely out of character, rational thought washed away on that crazy tide of need to touch Leigh, and, seen through his eyes, the situation could have had a very different interpretation.

What was it Leigh had said? He had responded as any normal man would when he'd found her practically in his lap, and for that she hated him? Those other, detestable words, 'What is it you're after?' burned in her mind, but, strangely, she couldn't bring herself to speak them to Sarah, even though to do so would easily explain her antipathy towards Leigh Benedict.

'He——' she tried again, not really knowing what she was going to say, but at that moment the sound of the doorbell announcing the arrival of Sarah's boyfriend diverted her friend's attention.

Jamie's appearance turned the conversation on to more general topics, and a short time later he and Sarah departed for their night out, much to Jassy's relief. If her friend had persisted with the subject of Leigh Benedict, she had no idea how she would have answered. The man she hated was one side of him, but the man she had found so easy to talk to, both last night and again in the car, was a very different matter.

That particular quandary wasn't one she felt ready to cope with, so she made a determined effort to push it to the back of her mind as she prepared and ate a light meal then ran a warm, perfumed bath, feeling the tension in her neck and shoulders that had plagued her all day begin to ease as she relaxed lazily. A while later, dried and dressed in a light cotton robe, she gave in to the temptation that had been tormenting her all evening and allowed herself to open her bag and take out the script, curling up on the old, battered settee to read.

Time slipped away as she instantly became absorbed, the scenes coming vividly alive in her mind so that once or twice she spoke the heroine's words out loud, knowing instinctively how they should be delivered. Every page was evidence of the fine, intelligent mind she had seen at work earlier in the day, the part of Leigh that she could respect without constraint, ignoring other, less attractive aspects of his character. If he saw this film as a way of proving that intelligence to the world, then she could have no doubt that he would succeed.

All the time she was reading, a small, insistent voice at the back of Jassy's mind was saying over and over again, 'I *want* this part.' It was the part of a lifetime; the sort of role that any actress would give everything she possessed to be able to play, and she felt she was beginning to understand just why Leigh was having so

much trouble casting it. Clara had to age over fifteen
years in the course of the film, appearing first as a child
of fourteen then maturing into a sophisticated woman,
yet still retaining an essential innocence. There was no
thought now of proving herself or winning acclaim in
Jassy's mind—it was *Clara* she wanted to play.

But she had promised herself that she would never use
her position to her own advantage, that she would never
take anything at all from Leigh. That thought had her
closing the script hurriedly, knowing that to continue
reading it was just a masochistic form of self-torture
when her private vow meant that, even if Leigh were to
offer her a chance of auditioning for the role, she would
have to refuse.

But there was no way she could leave Clara's story
unfinished—and, anyway, there was no chance at all of
Leigh offering her an audition. It was more likely that
her eyes would turn green, knowing how he felt about
her, she admitted with painful realism, a deep sigh
escaping her as she opened the file again.

A short time later, deeply involved in a passionate
scene between Clara and the male lead, Francis, Jassy
imagined herself and Leigh speaking the words, trying
to picture the intensity of the moment enhanced by the
performance she knew Leigh to be capable of giving.
The realisation of what she was doing brought her head
up sharply and she found herself staring blankly at the
wall, her mind whirling.

What was she thinking of? There wasn't the slightest
chance of her ever being considered for the role of Clara,
but even if there were, could she possibly act such a scene
with *Leigh*? She had little doubt that he would be able
to put aside any personal feelings and concentrate solely
on the character he was playing, but could she? Would
her training, the techniques she had learned so rigor-
ously, be any defence against the feelings he could arouse
in her simply by existing? She knew that Leigh had told
her that he was concentrating on directing *Valley of
Destiny*, but that was no comfort; it did nothing to ease
the uneven thud of her heart that had started simply as

a result of just *thinking* of those moments in Leigh's arms.

From the time Leigh had appeared in the kitchen of his home, the atmosphere between them had been highly charged, like the growing tension before a storm finally broke, as it had done last night. Never before had she felt so totally out of control. For the first time in her life she knew what it really meant to want a man physically, and she had been fool enough to pick on, as the object of that newly awakened desire, a man who felt nothing but contempt for her.

Sarah had a phrase for it, 'Falling into lust,' she called it, and the words came home to Jassy with a new and disturbing force because they described exactly how she felt about Leigh Benedict. But what made matters so much worse was the fact that if he should even suspect how she was feeling he would simply rank her with the women who were attracted to the sex-symbol image he so detested, or the actresses who would sell themselves to anyone with the influence that could be used to help them.

Jassy hated the idea of being thought of in that way, every ounce of self-respect she possessed cried out against it, but she didn't know how long she could continue to work for Leigh and manage to hold out against what she was feeling without giving herself away completely. She had the frightening feeling that she was sitting on a keg of gunpowder and someone had lighted a slow-burning fuse. She could only pray that the fuse was long enough to allow her to get through the rest of her time as Leigh's secretary before the gunpowder exploded right in her face, scarring her for life.

CHAPTER FOUR

THEY were all still at the breakfast table when the doorbell rang suddenly, shattering the lazy Sunday morning atmosphere.

'Who can that be?' Sarah asked, puzzled. 'No one we know is ever out and about before midday on a Sunday—and it's only just nine now.'

'Well, you'd better go and answer it,' Jamie said with a grin. 'You're the only one who's respectable.'

Glancing down at herself, and then at Jamie, Jassy had to agree that he was right. For some time now, Jamie had been a permanent fixture in the flat at weekends, and Jassy was well accustomed to his appearing at the breakfast table in his scruffy old dressing-gown. She liked Jamie—he and Sarah were clearly crazy about each other, and were saving hard to be able to turn their relationship into a permanent one—and she had fallen into the way of treating him like one of her brothers, keeping to her old habit of enjoying a lingering Sunday morning breakfast while still in her nightclothes. This particular morning, it was Sarah's turn to make the regular weekly trip to the launderette, so she was the only one fully dressed.

'They're getting impatient,' Jamie added as the doorbell rang again, more loudly this time.

'Who do you think it could be?' Jassy wondered aloud as Sarah left the kitchen.

'No idea.' Jamie was concentrating on spreading marmalade thickly on his toast.

'Perhaps it's Sarah's mother,' Jassy suggested wickedly, knowing how very much in awe of Mrs Templeton Jamie was.

Jamie's look of dismay was so comical that she couldn't help laughing at his discomfiture, and a few moments later Jamie joined in. They were both still chuckling when Sarah returned.

'A visitor for you, Jassy,' she announced.

'For me?'

The look on her friend's face should have warned her; Sarah's eyes were glowing with barely suppressed excitement. As Jassy glanced towards the door every trace of laughter faded from her own face as she recognised the tall, golden-haired figure that now appeared behind her flatmate.

Her first coherent thought was that Leigh was wearing the same clothes that he had had on the night before, when he had been on his way to visit Anna Golden. The logical conclusion to be drawn from that was that he had not been home at all, but had spent the night with Anna—which was exactly what Jassy would have expected, so she was stunned to find that the thought brought a sudden, stabbing pain that was thoroughly disconcerting. Why should she care where Leigh had spent the night—and with whom?

Suddenly she became embarrassingly aware of the way she was staring, gaping bemusedly at Leigh, who was obviously waiting for her to speak.

'Good morning,' she managed, her voice infuriatingly breathless and uneven, revealing too much of the disturbed state of her thoughts.

Leigh's only response was a slight inclination of his blond head in acknowledgement of her greeting. He too looked slightly less composed than she would have expected, almost as if it had been as much of a shock to find himself here as his arrival had been to her. Jassy wished he would say something, anything to break the silence that seemed to be stretching out her nerves to snapping point. Luckily, at that moment, Sarah took charge.

'Won't you sit down, Mr Benedict?' she said, pulling out a chair. 'Would you like some coffee?'

'I'd love some.' Leigh spoke at last, lowering himself into the chair and stretching his long legs out in front of him. 'And, please, not Mr Benedict—Leigh will do.'

Still struggling for composure, Jassy suddenly thought that she had never fully realised just how attractive Leigh's voice was; it was as if she were hearing it for the first time. In fact, seeing him here in her flat, away from his usual surroundings, she felt as if she were seeing him for the first time. Even sitting down, the tall, lithe body seemed to dominate the small room. The golden hair was almost too bright in the morning sunlight, the tawny eyes incredibly clear and mesmerising, and Leigh's immaculate appearance, the superb cut of his clothes were in stark contrast to Jamie's ancient dressing-gown and unshaven face.

The thought of Jamie, sitting silently beside her, jolted Jassy back to reality. 'I'm sorry,' she said hastily, 'I should have introduced you. Sarah's my flatmate—and this is Jamie.'

As Jassy's slight gesture drew Leigh's attention to the man at her side she was stunned by the swift change in the actor's face. She could not miss the way the bronze eyes narrowed sharply as they rested on Jamie then swung back to her own face, darkened by a look of such scathing contempt that it almost seemed to scorch her skin.

For a moment she was bewildered, unable to see any reason for Leigh's reaction, then it came home to her that Jamie's dishevelled appearance and the way she was dressed, wearing only a pink cotton nightshirt, could make it appear that they, and not Jamie and Sarah, had just got out of the same bed—which was obviously the conclusion Leigh had come to. Anger flared at the thought that he might actually believe she was capable of trying to seduce him when she was already sleeping with someone else, putting a defiant note in her voice when she spoke.

'Was there something you wanted, Mr Benedict?' she asked, meeting his eyes deliberately, refusing to let that direct tawny gaze disconcert her, and carefully emphasising the formal 'Mr Benedict' so that it was obvious she was ignoring his instructions to use the more familiar 'Leigh'.

'Yes—you,' Leigh answered softly, the tiniest flicker of a smile showing that he'd registered her involuntary start of surprise. 'I thought you might want a lift into work,' he continued evenly. 'So as I was coming this way I called in.'

It was all perfectly reasonable and considerate of him, Jassy told herself; he was being the perfect boss again. So why did she feel so hostile, prickling all over like a cat faced with an intruder into its territory? It couldn't be just because he had so obviously come here straight from Anna.

'But you said after ten!' she protested, voicing her only real grievance. 'I'm not ready!'

She regretted the words as she saw the way Leigh's eyes dropped from her face to survey her body in a swift, appraising glance that made her feel hot and then shiveringly cold as she became intensely aware of just how little she had on. All the mornings Jamie had been there, he had never once made her feel like this. Leigh's glance seemed to strip away the delicate pink cotton, revealing her nakedness beneath it.

Jassy shifted uneasily on her chair, trying to tuck her long, slender legs further under the table to hide them from Leigh's probing eyes. She was deeply grateful for the fact that Jamie and Sarah had started a conversation of their own and seemed oblivious of her embarrassment.

'I am rather early, I admit.' The blandness of Leigh's tone was almost shocking in contrast to the burning light in his eyes. 'But there's no rush. I can wait.'

He lounged back in his chair, reaching for his coffee, totally at his ease. Damn the man! Jassy thought angrily. This was her flat, yet he looked so completely at home, somehow managing to make *her* feel as if she were in alien territory.

'I'd better get dressed, then,' she declared tautly, getting to her feet.

'Don't hurry on my account,' was the silkily murmured response. 'I'm perfectly happy to wait.'

The warmly sensual light in his eyes, the way his gaze went deliberately to the length of her legs beneath the short nightshirt made Jassy's cheeks burn hotly, and she had to bite her tongue to keep back the angry retort that sprang to her lips.

What had brought about this sudden change in attitude? In contrast to the man who only the day before had made it painfully clear that he had no interest in her as a woman, it now seemed that he was openly flirting with her, encouraging the sort of attention he had repulsed so violently, and for the life of her she couldn't understand why.

'I wouldn't want to waste your time, Mr Benedict,' she said tartly, smiling slightly to herself as she saw that the double-edged comment was not lost on him. 'I realise that you must be anxious to get to work.'

Leigh smiled lazily over the top of his coffee-mug. 'Not at all,' he drawled, then, taking the ground from beneath her feet, added softly, 'Right now, work is the last thing on my mind.'

Her face bright scarlet, Jassy fled from the room. Once, just once, she would like to get the better of him, but somehow he was always one step ahead of her.

She had just finished dressing when a brisk tap at the door announced Sarah's arrival in search of Jassy's contribution to the washing bundle.

'You're not going like that!'

'Why not?' Jassy asked defensively, considering her reflection in the mirror. The navy skirt and yellow short-sleeved shirt might not be brand-new, but they looked perfectly respectable. 'I wore this outfit last week and you didn't make any comment then.'

'But there was only Steve there last week—Leigh's quite different. You ought to dress up a bit—impress him.'

'I don't want to impress him!' Jassy declared, reaching for a brush and pulling it through the long, pale curtain of her hair, avoiding her friend's eyes as she did so, afraid her discomposure would be only too clear in her face.

'Oh, come off it, Jassy! He's Leigh Benedict!'

'So? He's just a man—and *not* the sort of man *I* want to impress. I don't like him, Sarah.'

'I can't see why.' Sarah looked genuinely puzzled. 'I think he's a real charmer—and gorgeous with it. But, like him or not, wouldn't it do your career prospects some good if he were to notice you?'

It's likely to do just the opposite, Jassy was tempted to retort, but, conscious of the awkward questions that remark might lead to, she hastily bit the words back.

'You know that's not the way I want to do things, Sarah. If someone offers me a part, I want it to be because I can *act*, not because of who I know.'

'But surely it wouldn't hurt to be specially nice to him—just in case?'

'It would hurt my self-respect.' The knowledge of all she was holding back made Jassy's voice sharp. 'Besides, I couldn't use anyone in that way.'

'Well, it's up to you. If you want to miss out on the best chance of getting your foot in the door of the film world you're ever likely to get, that's your business—but I think you're crazy—especially when he seems to fancy you.'

'What?' Jassy's brush stilled abruptly and she stared at Sarah's reflection in the mirror, her own eyes wide grey pools of shock. 'What are you talking about, Sarah? Leigh doesn't *fancy* me!'

'I wouldn't be so sure about that,' Sarah declared archly. 'I saw the way he looked at you—and he didn't have to come and collect you this morning, did he?'

'No...'

Jassy allowed herself half a minute to consider the possibility that what Sarah had said might conceivably be true. How would she feel then? It would be flattering, to say the least, to know that a man who could have his pick of the most beautiful women available should even think her attractive. Jassy considered her own face in the mirror and was thoroughly disconcerted to see a new and unexpected glow in her soft grey eyes, a softness round her mouth, colour flaring high on her cheekbones. Then reason prevailed and, with an effort, she drove such fanciful thoughts from her mind.

'Don't be daft!' The words were addressed to herself as much as to Sarah. 'Why should he even look twice at me when there are women like Anna Golden around? And, as for coming to collect me—well, you heard the man. He was coming this way so he called in. If I know him, he's only here because he wants to make sure I get in a full day on that precious script of his.'

That comment reminded her that Leigh's 'precious script' was still on her bedside table. Picking up the folder, she pushed it deep inside her bag, zipping the bag up firmly as a protection against Leigh's probing eyes.

'All right, have it your own way!' Sarah sighed her exasperation. 'So he's not interested—but I still think you could get him to be.'

'No, thanks!' Jassy said swiftly. The brief experience she had had of Leigh being 'interested' had disturbed her enough already.

'Why not? Jassy, what is this with you and Leigh? I've never known you react like this before. What happened between you two?'

'I told you last night.'

'You told me nothing last night! All you gave me was a load of guff about his being arrogant and unpleasant—none of which fits with the man I've just been talking to.'

'We just didn't hit it off. It happens, Sarah.'

'But not with you—you're one of the most tolerant people I know, and you've never taken such an instant dislike to anyone.'

Jassy couldn't cope with any more. How could she answer Sarah's questions when she couldn't even answer her own?

'Leave it, will you, Sarah? I have to go. Leigh will be sick and tired of waiting.'

In fact, Leigh looked anything but impatient at being kept waiting. His jacket discarded and slung carelessly over the back of a chair, he was deep in conversation with Jamie, and Jassy's heart lurched treacherously as she registered once more how vital and attractive a man he was. It seemed impossible that any one man could have so much: looks, talent, money, and—yes, charm. Jassy had to admit that. Catching him unawares like this, seeing his hard face suddenly animated and smiling, she could see why Sarah found it so hard to understand her own dislike of him. And then, unwanted, her flatmate's other comment slid insidiously into her mind.

Could this devastating man really be attracted to her? At that moment Leigh glanced up, that smile still lingering on his face, making her heart jolt painfully in her chest so that she had to catch her breath before she could speak.

'I'm ready—I hope I didn't keep you waiting too long.'

'Not at all. I was just thinking that it's a pity we have to work at all today. I'd be quite happy to stay here all morning.'

Jassy couldn't think of the right way to react. She was not at all sure just what role Leigh was playing now; she only knew that it was not the remote, distant boss of the day before. Awkwardly she fumbled with her jacket, avoiding the 'I told you so' look she knew must be on Sarah's face. Leigh got to his feet, taking the jacket from her and holding it out for her.

'Thank you.'

Jassy's voice was very low, just a murmur, as she slid her arms into the sleeves, her heart seeming to beat high up in her throat in response to his closeness. As Leigh adjusted the jacket over her shoulders, gently freeing a long strand of fair hair that had caught under the collar, the tips of his fingers brushed the delicate skin of her neck in a brief, tantalising touch that was almost a caress, sending a *frisson* of reaction running down her spine. For a moment his hands seemed to linger on her shoulders as if he was reluctant to release her, but so fleetingly that Jassy couldn't be sure that she hadn't imagined it, because a second later he had moved away and was shrugging himself into his own jacket, thanking Sarah for the coffee as he did so.

'You must come again,' Sarah told him, blithely ignoring the furious glare Jassy shot at her. 'Perhaps you'd like to come round for a meal some time.'

'I'd like that.' Leigh's eyes slid to Jassy's face and she saw the challenging light in them. 'Will you be there or is there someone who might object?'

The look he slanted in Jamie's direction told Jassy all she needed to know. So no one had enlightened him about Jamie's true position! She didn't even try to hide the triumph in her eyes as she answered him.

'This is Sarah's flat as much as mine,' she told Leigh sweetly. 'She's entitled to invite anyone she likes for a meal, and if Jamie doesn't mind your visiting his girl-friend, then I can see no reason why anyone else might object.'

Her sense of triumph grew as she saw anger darken Leigh's eyes as he realised his mistake and the way she had turned it back on him. Intoxicated by the knowledge that at last she had got the better of him, Jassy could not resist adding, 'And I doubt if Steve would object if I joined you. He would understand that sometimes a secretary has to have dinner with her boss, even if it's more of a duty than a pleasure.'

And that was probably the best exit line she was going to get! Not even looking at Leigh to see how he had reacted to her final dart, she tossed her hair back in a defiant gesture and left the room, running lightly down the stairs without a backward glance.

Leigh caught up with her at the front door. Before she could slam it shut behind her, his hand closed over her wrist, strong fingers digging into her skin so that she winced with pain as he swung her round to face him, his topaz eyes glittering with cold anger.

'What the hell do you think you're playing at?' he demanded in a low, furious voice and Jassy flung up her head to meet his savage gaze.

'I'm not playing at anything, Mr Benedict,' she declared, her own voice cold and tight. 'This is no game, I can assure you; I meant what I said. Now would you please let go of my wrist? You're hurting me.'

'And have you try to run away again?' Leigh shook his head adamantly. 'No chance. We have some talking to do.'

'I have nothing to say to you,' Jassy declared, turning her face away from him and staring determinedly out across the street. Leigh sighed his exasperation.

'Well, I've got plenty to say to you, sweetheart. I'm not at all sure what's going through that pretty head of yours, but I think it's time I found out—so we talk. It's your choice—we can have this conversation here or at my place.'

That brought Jassy's head swinging round to him again.

'Are you suggesting that I'm ever going to set foot in your house again?' she demanded furiously. 'Because if so, you'd better think again. I don't want to go anywhere with you!'

'You have some work to do, remember?' Leigh reminded her almost gently and, tormented by thoughts that constantly swung from one extreme to another without any sort of resolution, Jassy felt she'd had more than enough of this situation and threw caution to the winds.

'I have no intention of working for you ever again!' she stormed, not caring that her voice sounded unnaturally loud in the quiet street. 'Get yourself another secretary—I'm leaving!'

'But I don't want another secretary.' Leigh's softly spoken words were shaded with a touch of menace that sent a shiver down Jassy's spine. 'You suit me fine; I have no complaints about your work. So why don't we get into the car and go back to the house so that we can talk this out like two rational adults? People are starting to notice us,' he added in an infuriatingly reasonable voice.

'I'm not going anywhere with you!'

Jassy felt as if she were banging her head against a wall; Leigh's immovable calm only seemed to aggravate the incoherence of her own whirling thoughts. How had she got herself into this situation? In desperation she fought to free herself from Leigh's restraining hand, but in vain. Her struggles merely drew the attention of an elderly couple who were passing and who frowned reprovingly at such a disturbance on a peaceful Sunday morning.

'See?' Leigh's amused voice sounded very close to Jassy's ear, his breath stirring her hair, brushing over her skin where her nerves were so hypersensitive to his nearness that the its soft touch seared through her, making her shudder in reaction. 'Why don't you stop making an exhibition of yourself?'

Jassy wanted to scream. Leigh clearly had no intention of releasing her unless she did as he said, but the thought of being alone with him—and her own unpredictable, inexplicable reactions—was more than she could bear.

'I don't give a damn if people stare!' she hissed at Leigh. 'I'm not the one with an image to keep up! Is that what's worrying you?' she demanded vindictively. 'Will it damage your bright public image to be seen like this? Leigh Benedict, superstar, idol of millions, caught with the one woman who can't stand the sight of him— it's not quite what the papers like to print, is it?'

She flung the words at Leigh's face, fully expecting to see the hard, set mask darken in anger, but, amazingly, Leigh smiled. Jassy didn't like that smile one little bit; it was slow, cynical, curling his lips, but never reaching his eyes, not lighting his face at all.

'On the contrary,' he told her silkily, 'that's just the sort of story the papers would love—and it's a story they'll get too if you don't see sense and get away from here before someone recognises me. I've told you, I don't give a damn about my image. The papers have printed what they like about me for years now, but it could make things difficult for *you*. So unless you want your face plastered all over the gossip columns tomorrow morning you'd better stop behaving like some three-year-old having a tantrum and get in the car.'

Still Jassy hesitated. She knew that what Leigh said was true, and was horrified at the thought of the disruption of her life that would follow any such publicity, but to obey Leigh was to admit defeat, something she was determined not to do. Leigh's grip on her arm tightened painfully.

'You have precisely ten seconds in which to make up your mind and come quietly,' he said in a low, dangerous voice. 'Because if you don't, I will pick you up and put you in the car myself—and to hell with the publicity if we're seen. I don't intend to wait around here all day—I have a script to work on and I've wasted enough time as it is.'

As Leigh's words reminded her of something that her anger had driven from her mind, the angry colour faded swiftly from Jassy's face, leaving her looking white and strained. A cold fear filled her mind and her fingers clenched tightly over the bulk of the script inside her shoulder-bag. She would have to go with Leigh now, if only to return the folder to her desk. Leigh's reaction if he discovered that it was missing was too terrifying to contemplate because she could imagine only too well just what interpretation he would put on that discovery. He would assume that her declaration of wanting nothing from him was a lie, that, when her seductive tactics had failed, she had taken the script to study in order to be able to impress him with her understanding of the part. No matter what she said, he would believe that she meant to use him for her own advantage.

'Your time's up.'

Jassy's shoulders slumped dejectedly. She felt suddenly exhausted; there was no fight left in her.

'I'll come,' she said dully.

If Leigh felt any surprise at her sudden surrender, no sign of it showed on his face as, with his hand still on her arm, he steered her down the steps and into the car, where she sat hunched in her seat, staring gloomily out into the sunlit street. As Leigh slid into his place beside her and leaned forward to insert his key in the ignition, his arm brushed against Jassy's in an unwelcome reminder of the way she had felt in this car the night before, reawakening that overwhelming sense of the nerves in her body coming tinglingly awake. The sensation was intolerable in her present mood, and without thinking

she moved as far away from him as possible, pressing
up close against the door in an effort to avoid any further
contact.

Out of the corner of her eye she saw the way Leigh's
hands tightened on the steering-wheel until his knuckles
showed white, and nerved herself for the inevitable
explosion. Surprisingly, it didn't come; instead, Leigh's
jaw clamped tightly shut as if he was holding back some
furious response. His frightening silence lasted the length
of the time it took him to drive down the street, then as
they turned the corner he expelled his breath suddenly
in a sigh.

'Just what is bugging you?' he demanded. 'I can't
make you out. I've only got to look at you the wrong
way and you explode. Just what is it that makes you so
hostile?'

'You!'

And me, she added more honestly in the privacy of
her thoughts, because, deep down, she knew that her
own behaviour was disturbing her far more than any of
his. As Sarah had said, she wasn't usually the sort to
take an instant dislike to anyone—and if dislike was all
she felt, how much easier things would be.

'Me?'

Those tawny eyes swung round to her face, and for a
moment Jassy almost believed that the perplexity in them
was genuine—until she remembered just how well he
could act.

'You don't like it, do you?' Something worryingly like
disappointment made her voice coldly spiteful. 'You
really can't believe that I might not like you. You claim
you don't like your sex-symbol image, but you're so used
to having every woman fall at your feet just because
you're Leigh Benedict that you can't accept that there
might be one woman who isn't susceptible to your looks
and your money. Well, for your information, there is
such a woman—me!'

In the silence that followed her outburst, the car
careered around a corner with a violence that jolted Jassy
roughly in her seat. Glancing hastily at Leigh, she

shivered involuntarily as she saw the way his mouth was tightly compressed, his lips just a thin, hard line. For a few minutes more he drove the car in silence, manoeuvring the powerful vehicle at a speed that was positively dangerous, even in the comparative quiet of the Sunday morning traffic. Then, just as Jassy was beginning to feel distinctly panicky, he slowed gradually.

'No,' he said at last. 'That's not it. There's more to it than that.'

'Isn't that enough?' Jassy retorted, but some of the sting had gone from her voice. It had started out as mere dislike, but somewhere along the line it had got much, much more complicated.

'No,' Leigh said again. 'I don't think it is enough. If you're going to treat me as if I'm some appalling monster that's just crawled out of the primeval slime, then I reckon you owe me a bit more than, "I don't like you."'

On the last words his voice took on almost exactly the same intonation as Jassy's, so that she could not suppress an involuntary gasp of admiration—but one that was mixed with shame and embarrassment at hearing just how childish and petty her words had sounded.

'If you'll just let me explain...' she began hesitantly.

'I'm listening,' Leigh said quietly.

His stern, unrelenting profile offered no encouragement, but this might be the only chance she would ever get to convince him that, in her case at least, his cynical opinion of women was totally unjustified. Jassy didn't know why it was so very important, over and above the need to let him know she was not just a 'seductive little siren', she only knew that, at this moment, it mattered intensely to her that somehow they might just have come to some sort of turning-point, and that thought made her swallow hard before she spoke.

'I don't know why you have such a low opinion of women—and actresses in particular—but I object to being tried and condemned by you without any evidence or a chance to speak in my own defence. For your information, I have never offered any sort of "favours" to *anyone* to win any part, and I have no intention of

ever doing so. I told my parents I was serious about
acting, that if I had any talent I'd succeed, and I meant
it. If I'm any good I'll succeed, but my *acting* is what
matters. There's no satisfaction in winning any other
way. Perhaps there are people who wouldn't think twice
about jumping into bed with someone to further their
career, but that's not the way I want to do it. It would
destroy my self-respect.'

She paused, waiting for Leigh's reaction, but he kept
his eyes on the road, no flicker of emotion crossing his
face.

'Go on,' he commanded after a moment, and to
Jassy's intense relief his voice seemed to have lost some
of the acidic bite of moments before.

The next bit was more difficult.

'You seem to have assumed that just because you're
Leigh Benedict and I'm female, the rest is automatic.
When we first met you forced yourself—your kisses on
me when it must have been clear that your attentions
were repellent to me, and on Friday—— '

'On Friday?' Leigh echoed dangerously.

'You know what happened then! You took advantage
of the fact that I was alone with you and tried to seduce
me. I realise now that you must have thought I only
took this job because I'd be working for the Golden
Thief, but you couldn't be more wrong—— '

Leigh's laugh broke in on her, a harsh, cynical sound
that seemed to splinter the air inside the car.

'*I* tried to seduce *you*?' he declared sardonically. 'Well,
that's an interesting twist, I must say. Let's get one thing
straight, lady—you were the one doing the seducing. You
were practically begging me to take you.'

Something seemed to explode inside Jassy's mind as
Leigh's cold voice echoed over and over in her head.
The fact that she couldn't deny her own part in Friday's
events was swept away under a wave of fury, as was the
memory of the other Leigh, the one she had actually
found herself liking. All she could see was this arrogant
devil of a man who was determined to think the worst
of her. Her temper flared and, heedless of her own safety,

she lashed out, striking Leigh hard on the temple with her clenched fist, jarring his head to one side.

For a moment the car veered dangerously across the road, narrowly avoiding crashing into a van parked on the opposite side, but Leigh's reactions were incredibly swift. His left hand shot out to push Jassy firmly back in her seat and hold her there while he controlled the car with the other. Seconds later, they had turned into a quiet side-street where he pulled up and sat silently for a moment, gripping the steering-wheel tightly as if he could not trust himself if he let go. The rigidly controlled violence in him terrified Jassy, so that she shrank back in her seat as Leigh rounded on her, his golden eyes blazing.

'Now *you'll* listen to me,' he told her in that low, dangerous voice Jassy had come to dread, his hands gripping her shoulders as if he wanted to shake her hard. 'You've been flinging accusations at me—now it's my turn, and you're going to listen if we have to stay here all day.'

Jassy knew she had no choice. The strength of Leigh's grip on her shoulders brought home to her forcefully just how little chance she had of getting away from him if she tried to struggle.

'All right,' she said flatly, 'I'm listening.'

Leigh released her immediately, his hands moving once more to the steering-wheel, his long fingers tapping restlessly on it, then stilling suddenly as he began to speak.

'Let me tell you a story.' The darkly sardonic tone was back, colouring his beautiful voice in a way that made Jassy's breath catch in her throat. 'It's about a young actress, a girl who'd just left drama college—the same one that you went to, as a matter of fact.'

Gemma Morgan. Jassy stiffened in her seat, remembering the exchange between Leigh and Benjy.

'I met her at a party given by one of her tutors. She seemed a nice enough kid, and I quite enjoyed talking to her, but that was all—on my part, at least. It wasn't enough for her, however. She spun me some tale about her car being out of commission and not being able to

afford a taxi fare home, so, naturally, I offered her a
lift. We'd barely got halfway down the street before she
threw herself at me, blouse unbuttoned down to her
navel, and her skirt somewhere around her waist—and,
just in case I couldn't take a hint, she was extremely
explicit as to what she wanted me to do.'

Leigh's mouth twisted bitterly at the memory and Jassy
wasn't surprised. If the positions had been reversed, any
woman would have been screaming accusations of assault, or at the very least sexual harassment, under those
circumstances.

'I declined the offer,' Leigh continued laconically, 'and
thought that was that—I couldn't have been more wrong.
For the next few weeks I couldn't go anywhere without
that young lady——' his intonation gave the word a
meaning that was the exact opposite of its real one
'—appearing in what she considered to be provocative
and enticing outfits and trying to get me into bed with
her. She even managed to persuade my housekeeper to
let her into the house, and when I got home I found her
waiting for me in my bed—stark naked. And all this was
because she wanted to play the female lead in my latest
film—and she was prepared to do anything to get the
part. When she realised she was getting nowhere with
me, she turned her attention to the director, using the
same tactics.'

Jassy flinched inside at the searing contempt in Leigh's
tone. It was no wonder he had been anxious to avoid
meeting another one of Benjy's protégées after his experiences with Gemma.

'And she wasn't the only one—just the latest in a long
line of young hopefuls who'd try any trick in the book
to get what they want.'

There was a sour taste in Jassy's mouth, and a sense
of nausea had invaded her as she listened to this sordid
story. If Leigh had often been subjected to this sort of
harassment then it was no wonder that he should feel
so contemptuous of the Gemma Morgan type, especially
if, according to what he had just told her, and much to
her surprise, he had not, as many others would have

done in his place, simply taken advantage of what was being offered without giving anything in return.

But all actresses weren't like that—the majority of them felt as she did, she was sure. She might understand Leigh's cynicism better now, but she still deeply resented the way he had lumped her in with Gemma Morgan without any concrete evidence—well, on only the flimsiest of evidence, she forced herself to amend with uncomfortable honesty.

'That still——' she began, but a flash of anger in Leigh's eyes silenced her. Suddenly she felt intuitively that there was more behind Leigh's attitude than he was admitting, but she didn't dare ask him anything further. She was still too frighteningly aware of his physical strength to risk adding fuel to the burning anger that seemed to have died down to a smouldering ember, recognisable only in the hard light in Leigh's eyes, the tautness of the muscles in his jaw.

'Now we come to Friday, when, as you so quaintly put it, I forced myself on you——'

'Why?' Jassy broke in, unable to stop herself.

'*Why?*' Leigh repeated the word as if he didn't quite understand it. 'Why did I kiss you?'

With a sudden, violent movement that made her start in panic he hit the steering-wheel hard with the edge of his hand.

'Dammit, woman, because I wanted to! I told you at the time—you're damnably attractive when you're angry. I kissed you because I wanted to more than anything else—as I want to kiss you now,' he added with disconcerting softness.

Shock made Jassy's eyes very wide and dark. Her throat was painfully dry and she swallowed hard to relieve it as Leigh reached out a hand to touch her cheek. Although the brush of his fingertips was as light as a butterfly's wing she couldn't stop herself from flinching away, her heart sinking as she saw the way his face hardened at her reaction, and he snatched his hand back swiftly as if he had been burned.

'But I won't,' he said in a flat, emotionless voice. 'Because you find my kisses repellent—or so you say.'

The momentary pause had brought about a dramatic change of mood. Those tiger's eyes seemed to burn into Jassy's grey ones, challenging and mesmerising all at once so that Jassy found herself unable to drag her gaze away.

'But don't kid yourself, sweetheart. I didn't imagine your response that first time—or again on Friday. You wanted what I was offering, wanted it every bit as much as I did—if not more. You were the one who did the seducing that night. What did you expect me to do when I woke up and found you draped across me—tell you a bedtime story? Tell me——' he demanded, his voice hardening sharply '—did you really panic, or did you plan to lead me on and then leave me cold like that?'

The taunting words showed painfully clearly that he hadn't believed a word Jassy had said. She had thought she might clear the air, but instead she was still torn between anger and an inexplicable, deep, aching hurt at the realisation that he still put her in the same category as Gemma Morgan and her type. And the real trouble was that, in all honesty, she could not deny that, if she had been in Leigh's place, that was how she would have interpreted her own actions too—but admitting that was far too dangerous.

'Stop it!' she cried desperately, her mind seeming to split in two. 'Why can't you leave me alone? I hate you!'

She wanted to believe that was true, but couldn't any longer. The truth was she didn't know what she felt.

'Do you?' Leigh enquired, unmoved. 'Or do you just hate me for saying what you don't want to hear? Why don't you face up to the truth? I don't mind admitting I want to make love to you—I'd be a fool if I didn't, you're a very lovely girl. But it's more than that—you're something special. I knew it from the moment I first saw you, even in that appalling matronly suit, with your hair scraped back into that unflattering bun. I knew then that I wanted you—I still do.'

Leigh's eyes were very deep and dark as he spoke, and Jassy felt as if she could lose herself completely in them. She couldn't believe what she had heard, and yet Leigh's words repeated over and over in her head. Such a short time before, she had flirted with the idea that this disturbingly attractive man might actually be interested in her, not really considering the matter seriously. Now he had declared quite openly that he thought her not only attractive but very desirable—and she was quite unable to cope with such a declaration, taken unawares by the warm glow that flooded through her at his words. She felt strangely breathless as if his words had struck her like a physical blow, and her blood was pounding in her veins, making her temples throb so that she felt giddy and filled with a strange, nervous desire to laugh. But there was no laughter in Leigh's face; he was deadly serious. Never before had Jassy felt so helpless, so very vulnerable.

'I—don't want you,' she managed with difficulty, the words sounding hopelessly unconvincing, even to her own ears.

'No?' Leigh questioned softly. 'Forgive me for doubting you, but I think that right now I'm a better judge of what you do want than you are yourself. Try admitting it,' he encouraged gently. 'We could have something very good, if only you'd stop fighting me.'

But Jassy was incapable of forming any coherent thoughts, let alone voicing them, as Leigh's arm slid around her shoulders, drawing her slowly towards him. As if in a dream she felt the warmth of his mouth on her forehead, her closed eyelids, and then, heartbreakingly briefly, on her lips.

'See?' Leigh whispered against her hair. 'There's nothing to be afraid of.'

Slowly he drew away from her again. Jassy's eyes felt heavy, as if she had just woken from a very deep sleep, and when she opened them Leigh's face was blurred, as if her eyes would not focus on him properly. When her vision cleared it was as if she were looking at some other man who was Leigh and yet somehow very different, and she knew that the change was not in him but in her mind, in the way she saw him. The long, silent moment was broken at last when Leigh moved to start the car again.

'I think we'd better get going,' he said quietly.

As he turned his head to check the street before pulling out he winced slightly as the movement jarred his bruised temple. Acting purely instinctively, Jassy reached out to touch the place where her fist had struck him, shame flooding through her at the thought of her own mindless violence as she felt the slight swelling just over the bone. What was it about this man that made her behave in such totally uncharacteristic ways?

'I'm sorry,' she said, her voice very low. 'I didn't mean to hurt you.'

'Yes, you did,' Leigh told her drily. 'But maybe I asked for it.'

With gentle fingers Jassy traced the shape of the bruise and heard Leigh's sharply indrawn breath.

'Does it hurt if I touch it?'

'A bit—but I reckon I can stand it. It's not the pain that's bothering me,' he added with a look that was so blatantly sensual and inviting that Jassy snatched her hand away again in a flurry of confusion.

Leigh laughed, this time in genuine amusement.

'As I said, I think we'd better get going. I don't think I could be answerable for the consequences if we stayed here.'

CHAPTER FIVE

IT WAS not until she saw the familiar bright red sports car parked in the courtyard that Jassy remembered that Steve was due back that morning, the realisation sending her thoughts into completely new channels. She had been grateful for Leigh's silence during what remained of the journey, needing a breathing-space, both mentally and physically, to absorb the new and bewildering developments and consider her own feelings about them. Suddenly the Jassy who had applied for the job as Leigh's secretary seemed like someone she had known a long time ago, almost a stranger, with none of the thoughts and feelings she was now experiencing.

Only hours before, she had been convinced that she actively disliked Leigh, had declared to his face that she hated him. Now she longed for the clarity of that emotion, but knew that the peace of such clear-cut feelings had gone for good. She only knew that with Leigh she felt fully alive as never before, seeing everything in a completely new way as if every sense had been heightened by his presence; yet at the same time she felt very much afraid. The nearest she had come to anything like this before had been in the moments standing in the wings, waiting for the cue for her first appearance, with a new performance ahead of her. In the short time it took to reach Leigh's house she had swung from exhilarating joy to overwhelming despair and back again with frightening rapidity, and finally got out of the car with nothing resolved.

It was strange, Jassy thought as she walked towards the house, how only the day before she had clung to the thought of Steve's return as a welcome protection from being alone with Leigh, but now she vaguely resented the fact that he would be there. She felt she needed more time to explore the change in her relationship with Leigh, to consider just what it meant for her future, because she had no doubt that her immediate future at least was intimately entwined with Leigh's. There was no going back, and, whatever happened, nothing would ever be the same again.

Steve was in the kitchen, the inevitable mug of coffee in his hand, and he waved it cheerfully at Leigh and Jassy as they came in.

'You timed that just right. Want some?'

'Just what I need,' Leigh said, pulling off his jacket and slinging it carelessly over a chair. 'Then I must have a shower and change before I start work.'

'You are a trifle overdressed for a day in the office,' commented Steve. 'I suspect you've only just got in from a night on the tiles.'

'Guilty, milord.' Leigh accepted his coffee with a grateful smile. 'I spent the night at Anna's—and you needn't look so disapproving. I'm a big boy now; I can take care of myself.'

'Hmm.' Steve looked unconvinced. 'I still think——'

'Lay off it, Steve,' Leigh said abruptly, but without anger, as if this was an argument they had had many times before. 'We agreed to differ over Anna, so less of the big-brother act.'

'Have it your own way.' Steve was handing the second mug of coffee to Jassy. 'But I see she's been up to her old tricks again.'

He indicated the bruise on Leigh's face which had now darkened to a dull red, and Jassy tensed, waiting for his friend's reply.

'Oh, that.' Leigh touched the mark carelessly. 'No, that was my own fault—I—walked right into something.'

Jassy's initial rush of relief was swiftly replaced by another, far less comfortable concern. She had been fool enough to forget about Anna Golden. How could Leigh tell her that he wanted her, only an hour or two after he had left the actress's flat after having spent the night there?

But then, yesterday, Leigh had hesitated perceptibly before he'd spoken to Anna on the phone, and Steve had assumed that it had been the older woman who had bruised Leigh's face during a quarrel, his tone implying that such behaviour was commonplace, so perhaps the relationship between Anna and Leigh was not the thriving affair Anna had led her to believe. Jassy was stunned by the immediate lifting of her spirits at the thought.

'Sit down, Jassy.' It was Leigh who spoke. 'Enjoy your coffee. I know we have plenty to do, but I'm not such a slave-driver that I expect you to launch into it straight away.'

There was a new note of warmth in his voice, one so unmistakable that Jassy wondered if Steve noticed it too and what he made of it. But then Steve had never seen the two of them together before. He knew nothing about Friday night—was it really only two days ago? Jassy felt as if the events of that night were so firmly etched on to her brain that it seemed impossible that they had not sent reverberations out into the atmosphere, affecting even those who had not been involved.

'Did you get that damn script finished?' Steve asked, and Leigh nodded his response.

'Jassy started the typing yesterday, that's why I asked her to come in this morning. What about the house? Is it what we're looking for?'

'Perfect! And there was no trouble getting permission to use it—it's all signed and sealed.'

'Thank heaven for that! At least something's going right. Now, if we can just have some better luck with these wretched auditions we might actually be able to start work.'

Leigh was prowling restlessly about the room, his actions making Jassy think of the pacing of a caged tiger, reminding her irresistibly of that intangible, dangerous streak in his character, a controlled power that set him apart from all the other men she knew.

'For heaven's sake, man, ease up!' Steve protested. 'You only finished filming on Friday; can't you give yourself a day off once in a while? Jassy and I are only human, even if you're not—and, quite frankly, I could do with a break.'

'Soon—maybe—when we've found our Clara—but today I'll want details of that house. I'll have to see it myself as soon as possible.'

'OK, boss,' Steve sighed good-humouredly. 'I suppose I'd better get down to it.'

He drained the last of his coffee and went to put his mug in the sink, moving close to Leigh as he did so, and, watching them, Jassy was stunned by her own response. No one could ever have denied that Steve was a good-looking man—she had been very attracted to him herself, the first time they had met—and yet now it seemed that his appeal was completely overshadowed by the vibrant power of the man at his side, a power she had once foolishly dismissed as too showy.

If only she could have stayed attracted to Steve, how much easier things would have been. With Steve there would never have been the fear that her feelings might be misinterpreted, no memory of those past, cynical words to sour the present. But it wasn't Steve who had turned her world upside-down—it was Leigh.

Absorbed in her thoughts, Jassy was only vaguely aware of Steve's leaving the room. As she heard the door close behind him Leigh came to stand opposite her, on the other side of the table, his fingertips resting lightly on the polished surface.

'Don't look so worried, Jassy,' he said softly, clearly misinterpreting the reasons for her disturbed frown. 'Is it such a dreadful thing to know that I want to make love to you?' he added with gentle derision.

Jassy wished she could say yes, that that was the last thing she wanted, so would he please leave her alone, but she knew that would not be the truth. She was only just beginning to realise how much it *could* mean to her, how much she wanted Leigh to desire her in this way. The fuse on the powder keg was burning faster than she had ever expected, her memory of the man she had seen outside the college, the man who had so angered and alienated her, growing cloudy and dim, and as it faded so did her instincts for self-preservation. The fury and disgust she had felt then were not enough to overcome the new feelings she did not yet know how to handle.

'No,' she managed, her voice little more than a whisper. 'I'm flattered——'

'*Flattered?*' Leigh's laugh was harsh. 'I'd hoped for something more than that!'

Suddenly his expression changed, his eyes darkening as he reached out a hand to touch her hair, twining a pale, silky strand around his finger.

'But don't worry; it will come. I can wait. When I make love to you it will be because you want it every bit as much as I do—and you will. You do now, only you're too scared to admit it. But one day you won't be afraid any more, and I'll be waiting. I reckon you'll be well worth waiting for.'

Jassy kept her eyes fixed on the table-top, unable to meet that searching tawny gaze. Even the light touch of Leigh's hand on her hair had her whole body crying out for more, and she was afraid that he would read her feelings in her eyes if she looked at him.

'One other thing,' Leigh went on, his voice hardening abruptly. 'Whatever there is between you and Steve will have to be sorted out. I don't share my women; even with my best friend.'

'There's nothing to sort out.'

The words slipped out before Jassy quite realised she had spoken. Looking back, she couldn't say whether she had exaggerated her friendship with Steve as a defence against Leigh's attentions or her own disturbing feelings, but either way it hadn't worked.

And what about you and Anna? Isn't that something that needs 'sorting out', she wanted to ask, but didn't dare. Behind her, the kitchen clock struck the half hour, and she grasped thankfully at the chance of escape offered by more practical concerns.

'I'll get started on that typing now,' she said hastily, getting to her feet in a rush that betrayed more of her inner feelings than any words could ever do.

As she moved past him Leigh caught her shoulders and swung her round to face him. From the look in his eyes she guessed at his intention and her heart lurched painfully. Not yet! She wasn't ready for things to move on a stage just yet!

Leigh's kiss was brief, warm, and sweet, and with a supreme effort Jassy managed to remain passive in his arms, neither responding to nor fighting against his embrace. Then he released her and turned her towards the door.

'Off you go,' he said lightly. 'If I can't have the lover just yet, I suppose I'll have to make do with the secretary.'

The trouble was, Jassy thought as she crossed the hall, that she was no longer sure which role she was playing any more—the secretary or the lover—she didn't even know which one she *wanted* to play.

Steve was in her office, looking flushed and rather annoyed, his hair slightly ruffled as if he had been pushing at it impatiently. Several drawers had been pulled out of her desk, and he was searching through one of them as Jassy opened the door.

'Just the person I need!' he exclaimed. 'Jassy, love, where have you put that damned script? Leigh said you had it yesterday, but I can't find the wretched thing anywhere.'

Jassy froze, her fingers tightening on her bag. 'The script?' she asked rather breathlessly, though she knew only too well what he meant.

'*The* script. The one and only final, revised version in existence—and worth several times its own weight in Oscars—hopefully. Where have you hidden it?'

The smile that accompanied his words calmed Jassy's racing heart. This was Steve she was dealing with, not Leigh.

'Don't panic,' she told him laughingly. 'I've got it here.' Unzipping her shoulder-bag, she pulled out the folder. 'It's quite safe. I took it home with me last night.'

'You did *what*?'

The steely voice exploded from the doorway behind her, coming with the force of a physical blow on Jassy's back so that she took an involuntary step forward before whirling round to face Leigh, quailing inside at the sight of the black fury that darkened his face.

'You did what?' Leigh repeated with icy menace.

'I took it home with me!' Jassy blurted the words out desperately. 'It's so much easier to type something if you know what's coming so I—I took it home,' she finished lamely, bitterly conscious of the half-truths she was telling, and the interpretation Leigh must inevitably put on her actions.

'You took it home.' Leigh repeated her words with cynical disbelief. 'You took it home to read—to make sure you could type it up correctly. Do you really expect me to believe that? Of course you had no other motive whatsoever.'

'Leigh, don't be ridiculous!'

'No!' Jassy and Steve spoke together. 'No! No! No!' Jassy went on despairingly as, looking into Leigh's eyes, she saw how the warmth and desire of only minutes before had vanished, leaving his face a mask of coldly savage anger, pain stabbing deep into her heart at the knowledge of what he must be thinking.

She had anticipated just such a reaction if Leigh had ever discovered that the script was missing, but that made it no easier to bear now—in fact, recent developments made the situation far, far worse. It seemed a bitterly ironic twist of fate that she and Leigh should have reached, if not a peace, then at least a sort of truce such a short time before, only to return to open hostilities almost immediately.

'It wasn't anything like that!' she declared vehemently. 'I wouldn't do that—I couldn't!'

Jassy almost choked on the words. She felt bruised and sore, hurting physically from the accusation blazing in Leigh's eyes.

An uncomfortable silence descended on the room as Leigh regarded Jassy's pale face and over-bright eyes, his tawny gaze coldly hostile. For one dreadful moment

Jassy wondered if he could see into her mind, read her whirling thoughts, and know that she was not telling the whole truth. Because it wasn't the truth. Deep inside, she knew how much she desperately wanted to play Clara, but knew that that could never happen. Even if by some miracle that chance were to come her way, she would have to deny it to herself because of what had happened between herself and Leigh.

'For goodness sake, Leigh!' Steve exclaimed reproachfully. 'She's telling the truth—surely you can see that?'

Still Leigh was silent, every taut muscle in his body revealing the ruthless control with which he was holding his temper in check. The terrifying silence seemed to drag on endlessly, and in that time Jassy saw Leigh with a sudden sharp clarity as never before. She saw his face, bleak, hard and implacable, the golden chips of ice that were his eyes, and had to bite back the cry of pain that almost escaped her, feeling as if a knife were being slowly twisted in her heart. In that moment she felt as if she had lost something infinitely valuable, something as essential to her life as the air she breathed.

At last Leigh moved, shrugging indifferently.

'Maybe,' he said slowly, addressing his words to Steve, but then his eyes swung back to Jassy's face. 'But I'm warning you, one more trick like that...'

He left the rest of the sentence unspoken, but there was no need for him to say any more, and, as he turned on his heel and strode out of the room, the door slamming shut behind him, Jassy found that her legs would no longer support her and sank into a chair with a tiny, shocked gasp. Steve stared after Leigh, a stunned expression on his face.

'What the hell got into him?'

Jassy shook her head helplessly. 'Forget it, Steve,' she said in a low, shaken voice. 'You don't understand.'

Steve could never understand, not fully, because he had no idea of all that had passed between her and Leigh. There was no way he could know that Leigh had reacted as he had because less than an hour before he had

admitted that he was not objective where she was
concerned. Would she be a fool to hope that Leigh had
turned on her in this way because, after all, he *had* believed her when she had told him that she wanted to
succeed by her ability alone?

But then the truth hit home with the realisation that,
even if he had come anywhere near believing her, that
tiny link between them had now been broken and, once
again, Leigh believed only the very worst of her motives.

'You're damn right, I don't understand!' Steve said
grimly. 'But Leigh's not going to get away with this.'

He was moving towards the door as he spoke and, as
she watched him, a cold panic filled Jassy's mind. The
mood Leigh was in, he would probably believe that *she*
had persuaded Steve to talk to him.

'No, Steve—please——'

But she was too late; Steve had gone.

Left alone, Jassy sat as if frozen in her chair. Only
her hands moved, twisting tightly together in her lap,
but her mind was racing. Even the memory of Leigh's
anger had faded to a dull blur, all but driven from her
thoughts by the recollection of the moment when she
had looked into Leigh's hard, set face and felt that
terrible sense of loss. In that moment she had found
herself a prey to a host of totally new feelings.

Or, rather, not new, because now that she was calm
enough to think Jassy had to admit that those feelings
had been there from the moment Leigh had arrived back
from Scotland, when she had seen him as if for the first
time, but she hadn't recognised them for what they were.
If she had, she would have fled from him then, abandoning her job, everything, mindful only of the foolishness of getting involved with a man as dangerous to
her peace of mind as Leigh Benedict.

Because she *was* involved, there was no way she could
deny that. With a sigh, Jassy acknowledged what she
had been trying to hide from herself since the moment
Leigh had first kissed her. It was as if in some strange
way the whole of her life had been leading up to that
moment, but she had tried to deny her instincts, had

blurred the issue by dwelling on his arrogant behaviour, deceiving herself into believing that she positively disliked him. She couldn't have been more wrong.

Like or dislike didn't come into it; she *wanted* this man. He made her come alive, so fully alive that she wondered if she had been blind, deaf and dumb before now. He had only to touch her for her to know that she was truly a woman, with all the hopes, dreams and passions that had been buried for so long—buried under her ambition, her need to prove herself.

For the first time Jassy recognised that underneath her reluctance to commit herself to anything deeper than friendship with other men lay a fear, unacknowledged until now, that such commitment would drain the energy and dedication she devoted to her acting. With Leigh she hadn't even thought of that. It seemed that he possessed the key to the Pandora's box of feeling and desire that lay inside her, and he had used it to devastating effect. He wasn't right for her in the way she had dreamed of finding a man who would love her for the rest of her life, but she had fed too long on dreams. There would be no forever with Leigh; if she wanted him, she had to take the man he was.

But, after what had just happened, would Leigh ever let her near him again? He was even more convinced than before that all that attracted her to him was, as he had suspected all along, the power and influence he possessed, the public image of the Golden Thief. Jassy flinched away from the irony of the fact that, just as her behaviour seemed to have proved that fact, *she* had realised that the change in her feelings towards Leigh had come about when he had appeared in the kitchen wet and dishevelled, and, even more so, when he had seemed so boyishly vulnerable in sleep. In his own home he had cast aside the image he so hated and appeared as just a man; and it was *that* man whom Jassy wanted.

Upstairs a door banged shut and Jassy heard the sound of footsteps descending the stairs. Hastily she pulled her typewriter towards her, snatched off the cover and inserted a sheet of paper into the machine. Steve was coming back, and she didn't want him to find her sitting here like this. If he did, he would inevitably ask questions—questions she wouldn't know how to answer.

Acting purely automatically, Jassy adjusted the paper in the typewriter and opened the folder that contained the film script. She even managed to type a line or two before the door opened, and did not look up as quiet footsteps crossed the room and a tall figure came between her and the light from the window, throwing a long shadow over the page.

'Steve informs me that I'm a heartless swine,' a quiet, ruthlessly controlled voice said. 'In fact, from what he told me, I'm surprised to find you're still here. He had me convinced that you would be unable to tolerate my hateful presence any longer.'

Jassy's fingers froze over the typewriter keys and she kept her eyes fixed on the sheet of paper in front of her until the words on it blurred into each other. She should have known it was Leigh! Some sixth sense should have warned her as soon as he opened the door.

That stiffly polite voice seemed to drain all the warmth from her blood as she listened to it. Was this the same man who had kissed her with such passion just two days before, and again, with gentle tenderness, only that morning? There was no trace of passion in his tone now, and as for tenderness—such an emotion seemed totally alien to the man before her. Keeping her head lowered, Jassy said nothing and waited for Leigh to speak again.

'I apologise if you think I treated you unfairly.' Leigh sounded as if the words had had to be dragged from him. 'Steve has convinced me that my suspicions were unfounded.'

'Steve has convinced me'! For a moment Jassy closed her eyes against the pain that ripped through her. If this was an apology, then she would infinitely have preferred it if Leigh had stayed angry. At least then he was being honest!

Drawing on all her strength, Jassy folded her hands on top of her typewriter. Still not looking at Leigh, knowing it would destroy her composure to do so, she stared at a patch of carpet some yards from her desk and said in a cold, proud voice that matched Leigh's own, 'If that is the best you can do in the way of an apology, Mr Benedict, then I suppose I shall have to accept it. But I have to tell you that I find it totally inadequate.'

Out of the corner of her eye she saw how Leigh's hands clenched tightly at his sides and she tensed inwardly, waiting for the inevitable explosion, but, surprisingly, it never came. Leigh remained silent, towering over her in a way that made her feel frighteningly vulnerable. Unable to see his face, she could not judge his mood, and she desperately wished that he would say something. But when he did, it was not at all what she had expected.

'You could at least look at me!' Leigh's voice was suddenly inexplicably husky. 'How can I talk to you when I can't even see your face?'

Jassy's control almost deserted her. She was too aware of the new discoveries she had made about herself to be able to see him looking as she knew he must look now, with the black anger darkening his face, cold contempt in his eyes.

'Jassy?' There was a new, questioning note in Leigh's voice, one she had never heard before. 'Jassy, look at me, for heaven's sake!'

Mutely Jassy shook her head, but even as she did so strong fingers caught hold of her chin, stilling the movement and lifting her face to meet his searching gaze.

'What's this? Tears?'

Leigh's finger brushed her cheek where, unknown to her, a single tear had escaped and trailed a glistening path down her cheek. In spite of the gentleness of his touch, Jassy jumped as if she had been burned, and pulled away.

'Yes, tears!' she flung at him. 'Don't tell me you've never made a woman cry before!'

'No more than any other man,' Leigh responded with a flash of his old sardonic humour. 'Even Steve's caused a few tears in his time.' Abruptly his expression sobered again. 'I never meant to hurt you,' he said and his eyes had a strange, stunned expression as if he had just been hit very hard.

'Didn't you? You had me tried and condemned before I could even say a word in my own defence. You thought——'

'Well, what the hell was I supposed to think?' Leigh exploded fiercely, gripping the edge of the desk with such force that Jassy fully expected to see the wood splinter beneath the pressure of his fingers. Suddenly he swung away from her, pushing his hands violently through his hair, ruffling its bright sleekness. 'Dear lord!' he said flatly. 'What are you doing to me?'

Without warning he slumped down in a chair, his head in his hands, looking thoroughly defeated, and at the sight of him suddenly so still, so unlike the Leigh she knew, Jassy's heart twisted inside her, her anger fading swiftly.

'What am *I* doing?' she managed shakily. 'I think it's the other way round. What are *you* doing to me? Why do you always want to believe the worst of me? Why won't you believe me when I tell you that I don't give a damn who you are, that...' Her voice faded as she realised just what she was saying.

Leigh's head came up at her words, and as he tossed a lock of hair out of his eyes Jassy thought she saw a flash of his old fire burning deep in them, but mixed with something else, an intensity of raw emotion that she could not understand at all.

'I want to believe you,' he said huskily. 'I want you so much that I reckon I'll go completely insane if I don't get you. I'm half demented as it is, just being with you——'

At Jassy's sharply indrawn breath he stopped abruptly, his head inclined slightly to one side as if he was listening to his own words over again inside his head.

'Oh, hell,' he groaned, the wry smile tinged with self-derision that accompanied his words dangerously appealing, and Jassy could not help responding to it.

'That wasn't quite what you meant to say?' she teased softly.

'No,' Leigh admitted ruefully. 'I meant to leave that side of things out of this.'

He regarded Jassy with dark, serious eyes, then suddenly the corners of his mouth quirked up and the familiar wicked glint lit his eyes.

'But now that I have said it, I'm damn glad! I couldn't have gone on much longer without saying it. Jassy——' his voice was soft and enticing as he held out his hand to her '—come here.'

Jassy knew it was foolish to give in so quickly, it was possibly even downright dangerous, but she might as well have asked a needle not to be drawn to a magnet. As if in a dream she crossed the room, the narrow stretch of carpet between them suddenly seeming very, very wide. As soon as she was within reach Leigh caught her hands and pulled her down beside him. He took her face between his hands and rested his forehead against hers.

'I'm *sorry*,' he said softly. 'Please forgive me.'

A tiny flame of anger still burned in Jassy's mind as she struggled against the hypnotic spell he was weaving.

'A little better than your last attempt,' she said sharply. 'I suppose you think this makes it all right, wipes out all those accusations!'

'No!' The word was almost a groan, stilling the flow of angry words. 'Jassy, I'm sorry,' Leigh whispered huskily. 'Sorry—sorry—sorry.'

He punctuated the words with gentle kisses and Jassy knew she was lost, all the fight seeping out of her as he pulled her up against him.

'I know my temper's foul, but I wasn't thinking straight—I find it very hard to be rational where you're concerned. I wanted to believe you were different, that you weren't like all the others—I didn't know how much I wanted that until I realised how it felt to think that perhaps, after all, you had been using me. Then I just went completely crazy.'

Leigh stirred slightly, looking down into Jassy's face, and, seeing how his eyes were once more darkly serious, Jassy was reminded of how, earlier, she had wondered if there was more than just his experiences with Gemma Morgan and her type behind his feelings.

'Am I forgiven?'

There was no way Jassy could have said no if she'd wanted to, for, as she lifted her head, his mouth came down on hers in a long, lingering, and yet strangely tentative kiss. As he drew her even closer, his strength lifting her off the floor, Jassy put her arms around him, holding him very tightly, a faint sigh of contentment escaping her. She knew there was no future in it—she would be deluding herself if she asked for any such thing—but she also knew that she no longer cared. She wanted Leigh so much that if he would only hold her like this, kiss her until all rational thought was driven from her mind, then she could be content.

At last, reluctantly, Leigh released her, one hand still lingering in the tumble of pale hair at the back of her neck.

'You, young lady, are a very bad influence,' he said in husky mock reproof. 'I am supposed to be working.'

'So am I,' Jassy reminded him mischievously, relaxing in the warmth of the laughter in his eyes. 'You're paying me overtime, remember?'

'Am I indeed? In that case, you'd better start earning it. Come on——' Leigh got to his feet, pulling Jassy up beside him '—let's have that efficient secretary back again—and I suppose we'd better tell Steve it's safe to come in. I suspect he's staying tactfully out of the way.'

His attention was already drifting away towards his desk, but just as Jassy struggled with the pang of disappointment she felt at his swift change of mood he shot her a dark-eyed sidelong glance.

'But don't bury the lover too deep,' he said in a voice that was a promise and a husky enticement rolled into one. 'I shall want her again later.'

A short time later, it was as Jassy had known it would be. Concentrating on what he was doing, Leigh hardly spared her a second glance, the moments she had spent in his arms apparently wiped from his mind—but this time it was different from the way things had been the day before.

Without being quite sure how it had happened, she realised that the three of them, Leigh, Steve and herself, had become a team, each with their own particular contribution to make to the project that absorbed them all. There was a unique satisfaction in being able to put her hands on any document Leigh wanted, sometimes even before he had asked for it because, in spite of the fact that she was busy typing up the script, she was constantly alert to the discussion between the two men on the other side of the room, and she found she was able to sense the way Leigh's mind was working, knowing instinctively just what he would need. Even the mundane process of typing page after page took on a new dimension because it was an essential part of the process to which she was now as whole-heartedly committed as Leigh himself.

And if occasionally, as she worked, she felt a pang of regret at the thought that the part of Clara could never be hers, she pushed it away ruthlessly. Clara was a wonderful role, but there would be other parts, other plays, perhaps even other films. There was only one Leigh Benedict and, right now, he was all she cared about.

CHAPTER SIX

'LEIGH! I didn't expect to see you tonight.'

'I didn't think I'd be free, either.' Framed in the doorway of Jassy's flat, Leigh looked tired, his tawny eyes shadowed. 'But I got the interview over sooner than I expected, and—can I come in?'

'Of course.'

Released from the surprise of his unexpected late arrival, Jassy held the door open. Moving into the room, Leigh flung himself on to the settee, stretching his legs out in front of him with a sigh.

'Lord, but I'm tired!' he exclaimed. 'And, as you know, interviews are not my favourite occupation.'

Jassy barely heard him, she was still trying to adjust to the fact that he was here, in her flat, for only the second time, something that brought home to her just how short a time she had known him.

It had been a strange week. After the intensity of the previous Sunday there seemed to have been a sort of hiatus, a pause in the development of their relationship. It was as if, having admitted to the desire he felt for her, Leigh had needed time to adjust to what had happened, almost as if he was as stunned by his outburst of three days ago as Jassy herself had been. At work things were very much the same. Leigh was no easier to work for—in fact, it seemed as if the idea of *Valley of Destiny* absorbed him more than ever, and he drove Jassy and Steve—and himself—harder than ever, so that at times it seemed that that passionate declaration had never been made.

But Jassy knew it had, and as a result everything Leigh did, every word he spoke to her was imbued with a new significance. At times she would look up to find his eyes on her, or he would flash his wide, devastating smile and a glowing heat would suffuse her body so that she felt she were in the grip of a raging fever, but he had made no move to take matters any further.

He had simply declared that he wanted her, that he could wait for her, and left it at that. But how long could this waiting time go on? How long would it be before Leigh would press her for a response—a response that she wasn't entirely sure she could give him? Physically, she wanted him as much as he wanted her, but emotionally she still wasn't sure, and that waiting time had given her too many chances to think, to consider the possible repercussions for herself if she embarked on a relationship that she wasn't at all certain she knew how to handle.

'Are you going to stay there all night?' Leigh enquired curiously. 'And why do you look as if you've never seen me before in your life?'

'I'm sorry.' Jassy jerked into life, closing the door hastily.

This was crazy! Ever since Leigh had left the office, heading for yet another interview with a journalist from a women's magazine, she had found herself missing him intolerably, but now that he was here with her she felt restless and unsettled, like a cat on hot bricks. She was also painfully conscious of the fact that the blue cotton robe she had put on after a bath was well past its best. Worn for comfort rather than glamour, the robe was thin from repeated washing, so that in certain lights it was practically transparent—a fact that had clearly not escaped Leigh's notice as his eyes lingered on the soft curves of her body beneath the flimsy covering.

'I thought you were busy tonight,' Jassy said awkwardly, cursing the warm colour that flared in her cheeks.

'I am,' Leigh told her bluntly. 'I really shouldn't be here, but I had to unwind——'

'Then perhaps you'd like a drink.' Nervousness made Jassy break in on him clumsily. Then, remembering the pitiful state of their laughingly labelled 'drinks cabinet', she added ruefully, 'I'm afraid cider's all we've got.'

'Cider will be fine,' Leigh assured her. 'Anything—if you'll just sit down.'

'Did the interview not go very well?' Jassy asked in an attempt to make conversation when, with the drinks poured, she curled up in one of the shabby armchairs, trying to force her racing pulse to slow, her breathing to become more natural.

'We talked about the film, which I suppose has to be an improvement on the usual questions——' Leigh's mouth quirked up suddenly at the corner into an engagingly boyish lop-sided grin '—which is a pity because I was prepared for the old routine—I had my answers all ready.'

'All the important subjects?' Jassy found herself relaxing in the warmth of his smile.

'All of them,' Leigh confirmed with mock gravity. 'And she didn't even want to know.' The grin reappeared, wider this time. 'For your information, I never eat breakfast, I'm hopelessly addicted to old Beatles' records, and you've seen my car—so what else do you want to know?'

His humorous tone dispelled the last of Jassy's tension, washing it away on a rush of delight at the fact that he had remembered their conversation of the previous Friday night, happiness and relief combining in a heady mixture. Leigh was openly flirting with her, and flirting was something she knew how to handle; it was a bit like acting in a way. She heard her voice pitched at just the right level of airy insouciance as she answered him.

'I think that tells me everything about you,' she said, and was rewarded by the warm sound of his laughter.

'And what about you?'

'Oh, I was brought up never to leave the house without a good breakfast inside me, I love folk music, and I don't have a car—I can't even drive.'

'So now we know all about each other and not a point of contact in sight. It makes me wonder what I'm doing here.'

'Drinking rather flat cider,' Jassy said flippantly, and knew from the way his mouth twisted that it was the wrong answer. Her light-hearted mood slipped away from her as she blundered on thoughtlessly. 'I know it's not your usual scene—an exclusive restaurant and vintage champagne must be more your sort of thing.'

As soon as she'd spoken she wished she could cut out her foolish tongue as she remembered Anna Golden's 'very special reunion...a quiet meal, and some excellent champagne.' She saw the flash of anger deep in Leigh's eyes, the way his jaw tightened, and her grip on her glass was unsteady as she waited for the volcano to erupt.

'You've been reading too many magazines,' Leigh said tautly. 'Try again.'

Try again? She didn't know how to! He had snatched the script away from her and she didn't even know the plot of the play!

'You like rather flat cider?' she asked slightly breathlessly, and felt the frantic racing of her heart ease as Leigh answered evenly.

'Steve and I drank nothing else for years.'

'While listening to old Beatles' records?'

'Of course. Only they weren't that old then; it's quite a time since I was eighteen.' For a moment Leigh stared down into his glass, then, when he spoke again, he had unexpectedly changed the subject. 'You said you have brothers and sisters?'

'Two brothers and a sister.'

Jassy's tone was uneasy. Leigh's question had made her think of the conversation she had had with Steve when he have given her a lift home earlier that evening.

'I'm glad you and Leigh have sorted things out,' Steve had said. 'I'd hate to see two people I like—and who obviously like each other——'

His tone had made it evident that 'like' was an understatement, causing Jassy to stiffen in sudden tension. Were her feelings—and Leigh's—so very obvious?

'—torn apart over nothing. I know Leigh was out of order, but I did warn you about his temper—and, let's face it, experience has taught him that it's not wise to trust too easily.'

Gemma Morgan and her type again, Jassy had thought to herself, coming up hard against how little she actually knew about Leigh.

'He's not an easy man to get to know,' she'd said cautiously.

'He's very much the cat who walks by himself,' Steve had agreed. 'But then he's had plenty of practice. He's been on his own all the years I've know him. We met at school—Leigh was at Pinehurst then.'

A memory had floated to the surface of Jassy's mind and she had felt suddenly as if she were on a roundabout spinning out of control.

'There were some letters from there—from a children's home,' she'd said, her voice sliding up and down in the most peculiar way. Steve had nodded slowly.

'Leigh lived there for eight years, and he still keeps in touch. The staff like him to visit—he's living proof that it's possible to make a success of life in spite of a messed-up childhood. His mother——' Steve had caught himself up hastily. 'No, that's Leigh's story—if he wants to tell it.'

Jassy had shifted uncomfortably in her seat, painfully aware of the way she had dismissed Leigh as a man who had never known a moment's insecurity in his life. She couldn't imagine how she would cope without her own close-knit family. She and her parents might disagree over her choice of career, but she knew that if ever she really needed them they would be there. It seemed that Leigh had never known such love and support, but his arrogant self-confidence hid every sign of the boy Steve had been talking about—except once, she had realised, in the car when he had given her a lift home on Saturday night. Then, just the once, the public mask he wore had slipped briefly at the mention of his parents, revealing the more vulnerable inner man.

'He never talks about his past,' she'd said slowly, recalling how swiftly Leigh had clammed up again after that one brief comment about his parents.

'No, that's not his way. The past's irrelevant as far as he's concerned. He's got to the top through a combination of talent and damned hard work, and he's going to make sure he stays there. Leigh's not one to rest on his laurels; there's always one more mountain to climb, each one higher than the last.'

And *Valley of Destiny* was the latest challenge, Jassy had thought, Steve's comments reinforcing a conviction that had already been growing in her mind. The almost obsessive concentration and untiring energy that Leigh put into his work on the new film, together with all she knew about his meteoric career, marked him out as a man to whom success was everything. Perhaps that past wasn't as irrelevant as he claimed, because in his determination to put it behind him he was, as Steve had said, still looking for other mountains to climb.

Leigh's jaded comments, dismissing the awards he had already won as unimportant, showed that nothing satisfied him for very long before he moved on to something new. There was a bitter taste in Jassy's mouth as she was forced to wonder how long the attraction he felt for her would last. How long would it be before he tired of her too, and moved on to fresh conquests?

So now, with the memory of Steve's talk of Leigh's lonely childhood in her mind, Jassy's voice was slow and hesitant as she spoke about her own family.

'There's Philip, Linda, Tony and me. Phil's an architect, and Linda and Tony are both following in Dad's footsteps as doctors—he's as pleased as Punch about that.'

It was impossible to erase the faint thread of wistfulness from her voice. Perhaps one day her father would be as proud of her as he was of the rest of his children.

'And your family wanted you to do something similar.' Leigh's comment, his tone, showed that he had caught the slight unevenness in her voice. 'I can see why you had problems convincing them that acting was worthwhile. I was an only child myself, so there were no comparisons—no favourites.'

Leigh's voice had changed perceptibly on the last comment, a harsh note creeping into it, and Jassy held her breath, waiting to see if he would go on. But he volunteered no further information and, wanting to fill the uneasy silence that had descended, Jassy rushed on, 'The trouble with being the youngest of a big family is that everyone still thinks of you as the baby. I think that's why my parents were so horrified at the thought of their little girl venturing into such a precarious way of life. I'm not sure they've really quite accepted that I've grown up.'

Leigh turned to look at her once more, a smile tugging at the corners of his mouth.

'You *look* like a little girl, curled up like that.'

Jassy was lifting her drink to her lips as he spoke, and at his words she hesitated, eyeing him across the top of her glass in mock indignation.

'Is that how *you* think of me?'

'You know damn well it isn't,' Leigh responded softly, his tone bringing a warm glow to her cheeks. Leaning back in his seat, he frowned briefly and shifted slightly on the battered settee.

'Uncomfortable?' Jassy enquired archly, all her restraint and unease vanishing in the warmth of his tone.

'You bet I am!' Leigh replied feelingly. 'I'd swear this is the most uncomfortable piece of furniture I've ever encountered.'

He moved again and an ancient spring twanged loudly, sending Jassy into a fit of giggles.

'Not quite what you're used to, is it?'

Leigh's eyes were once more disturbingly direct. 'I'm not complaining—or rather——' his voice changed subtly, deepening sensually '—I won't if you come and share this archaic instrument of torture with me. It will take the weight of two people, won't it?'

Jassy nodded, stifling the giggles that were partly due to relief at the way the awkward moment had passed so easily.

'I think so,' she said slightly breathlessly. She had forgotten the effect cider had on her. After only a few mouthfuls she felt light-headed, giddy, and very, very happy—or perhaps it was not just the cider that was going to her head.

She sobered slightly when she saw the look in Leigh's eyes as he held out his hand to her, one finger beckoning her towards him, and suddenly to be with him, to feel his arms around her, was all she wanted in the world, driving all her earlier doubts and uncertainties from her head. Without hesitation she got up and moved to the settee, sitting beside Leigh and pulling her legs up on to the faded cushions. As she leaned her head against Leigh's chest she heard his deep sigh.

'That's much better,' he said contentedly, burying his face in her hair and inhaling deeply. 'You smell delicious. There's something very erotic about freshly washed hair, not to mention that particular glow about a woman who's just got out of a warm, relaxing bath.'

His arms came round Jassy, his hand capturing hers, playing idly with her fingers, his touch setting her skin tingling. His mouth was against her hair, his warm breath stirring it softly as he slid down against the cushions so that Jassy was half lying across him with the powerful muscles of his thighs against her back.

'Tell me,' Leigh said after a moment, 'what happened to that incredible pink garment you were wearing on Sunday?'

'Oh, that.' Jassy leaned her head back so that she could meet his eyes, seeing them glow like polished bronze as she smiled up into them happily. 'Do you like it? If I'd known you were coming I'd have worn it specially.'

She heard Leigh's deep, rich laughter and her heart soared as his arms tightened round her.

'You'll make me spill my drink!' she protested, only half seriously.

'To hell with your drink!' Leigh growled, taking it from her and putting it firmly down on the floor beside his own. Then he lay back against the soft cushions, pulling Jassy down with him. 'I didn't come here to drink cider, and you damn well know it!'

Every trace of laughter fled from Jassy's mind as he pulled her close, curving her body against the hard length of his, one long-fingered hand brushing the hair back from her face. She lay submissive in his arms, knowing that this was what she wanted, that she had only to wait, happy to enjoy the anticipation of his kiss.

She did not have to wait very long. A second later, Leigh's mouth was on hers, moving sensually against her lips, sweeping her away to that dreamlike world where nothing existed but herself and this one man. As his hands slid down her back she could feel their warmth through the thin cotton of her robe, and her flesh seemed to burn as if his gentle touch had scorched a path down her body. With a small, wordless sound she nestled closer, shuddering with pleasure as Leigh's mouth moved down the side of her neck to the opening of her robe, her hands tangling in the golden crispness of his hair as she sighed his name aloud.

'You're beautiful,' Leigh whispered huskily against her throat, and hot tears of happiness pricked at Jassy's eyes so that her lashes were wet when his lips brushed them a moment later.

'Jassy?'

Leigh's voice was softly questioning, his hands still for a moment, but Jassy made a soft murmur of protest, pulling his head down to hers so that their lips met once more.

His hands were more urgent now, pulling impatiently at her robe, but when his fingers closed over her breasts they were suddenly gentle again, caressing the soft flesh with a slow sureness that had Jassy arching against him, murmuring her pleasure incoherently. Seconds later, his lips were where his hands had been and Jassy's voice was silenced, her heart seeming to stand still in delight. She was scarcely breathing, conscious only of the aching need deep inside her that only Leigh could assuage. She wanted him to love her, needed him so desperately that she cried out in pain and disappointment when he moved away from her abruptly, lifting his head, his body suddenly very still.

'Leigh——' she began, but Leigh laid a finger over her lips to silence her.

And then she heard what had alerted him—the faint sound of footsteps in the hall.

'Sarah?' Leigh questioned softly, and Jassy nodded silently, almost weeping with disappointment as Leigh stood up, straightening his shirt and smoothing his ruffled hair.

His actions made Jassy aware of her own dishevelled appearance and she scrambled hastily to her feet, pulling the crumpled, unfastened robe into some semblance of order. Silently Leigh reached for her hairbrush which lay on the coffee-table, and handed it to her.

They were only just in time. While Jassy was still tugging the brush through the worst of the knots in her tangled mane of hair she heard Sarah's key in the door.

'Good evening, Cinderella.' Sarah was alone, evidently Jamie had decided to go back to his own flat that night. 'You should have come with us, we—oh!'

She stopped, startled as she noticed Leigh, who had retrieved his glass from the floor, moved to an armchair, and was calmly drinking cider, looking for all the world as if he had been sitting quietly in the same position all evening.

'Not so much of the Cinderella, I see!' Sarah declared with a knowing glance at Jassy's pink cheeks. 'Hello, Leigh. I didn't expect to see you here tonight. Don't tell me you two have been working this late.'

'Not working, no,' Leigh answered with an easy smile. 'And I was just going.'

How could he look so calm and collected? Jassy wondered. She still felt distinctly shaky after the abrupt change of mood, and the ache of longing that Leigh's interrupted lovemaking had caused would not go away. But, of course, she was forgetting what a consummate actor he was, able to turn on any mood at will. Underneath that controlled exterior he was probably as shaken as she was.

Or was he? Glancing at Leigh's smiling face, Jassy was forced to wonder just which was the role and which was the real Leigh. Had the passionate lover, a part he had played to perfection so many times before, been the truth, or was it just another carefully assumed mask? Or had Leigh simply not felt the intensity of desire that she had experienced herself? Inwardly Jassy sighed. Was she always going to be plagued with these doubts where Leigh was concerned?

'Oh, don't let me drive you away.' Sarah's Cheshire Cat smile jarred painfully on Jassy's hypersensitive nerves. 'I was going to make some supper if you'd like some—I'm starving.'

'Not for me, thanks.' Leigh stood up, setting his glass down on the coffee-table. 'I have a long day ahead of me tomorrow, and I could do with an early night for once. Well, earlyish,' he added with a rueful glance at the clock.

He was turning towards the door as he spoke, and Jassy took a step to follow him, then hesitated, conscious of Sarah's eyes on her.

'Don't bother to see me out,' Leigh told her. 'About tomorrow—I don't expect to be in before five, but if anything urgent crops up Steve will know where to find me.'

He touched Jassy's cheek, very lightly, very briefly.

'See you,' he said softly, then he was gone, and as Jassy heard his swift footsteps descending the stairs she felt that the flat suddenly seemed very cold and empty without him. The light-hearted, giddy mood had gone completely, leaving her with a sense of dissatisfaction and discontent. She felt as flat as her half-finished glass of cider, still standing on the floor where Leigh had placed it, and her body still ached in bitter frustration at the abrupt end to Leigh's lovemaking.

'Well I'm glad to see that you two have buried the hatchet,' Sarah said, dropping her handbag on the settee and shrugging herself out of her jacket. 'You were like a bad-tempered terrier on Sunday, snapping and snarling at Leigh all the time—but you didn't fool me with all that "I don't like him" business. I thought you were only playing hard to get. Have you slept with him?'

Jassy shook her head, reflecting wryly that her friend had never been one for beating about the bush.

'Has he asked you to? Of course he has,' Sarah answered her own question. 'Well, he'll not *ask* again. He's not the asking kind—he's a taking sort of man. I doubt if he'll take no for an answer a second time.'

'I won't be saying no,' Jassy said quietly, bringing Sarah's head round sharply. Her own mind reeled as she heard what she had said, the certainty in her tone. She was stunned to find herself suddenly totally emotionally convinced of something that she couldn't remember ever having made a rational decision about.

'I *see*. He really has bowled you over, hasn't he? And what about your precious hobbyhorse—success by merit and all that? How does that affect your relationship with Leigh?'

'Nothing's changed.' Jassy's tone was a little sharp, because if the truth were told she hadn't stopped to consider that particular aspect of things. 'That won't alter anything,' she went on more quietly. 'My relationship with Leigh is quite separate from my work, and I intend to keep it that way.'

And that was the way Leigh would want it too, she added in the privacy of her own thoughts. He was never likely to offer her *anything* in the way of work—other than as his secretary, of course—because he'd shown himself to be even more opposed to the casting-couch syndrome than she was herself—and with good reason, she acknowledged, thinking of Gemma Morgan.

Even as she accepted that that was the way things would be, for one split second Jassy's ambitions as an actress warred with her belief in personal integrity, but in the end it was no real contest. From the moment she had realised that Leigh felt as strongly as she did about such things, her own convictions had been strongly reinforced, and even if he were to offer the part of a lifetime—and the role of Clara was just that—she knew she would have to refuse it. And deep down inside she also knew that she wouldn't have it any other way. Right now, what she had with Leigh was more important than any career success.

But what about Leigh? What exactly did he feel for her? He had made his desire for her only too plain, but was there anything more than that? He had offered no word of commitment, but then she had never expected that. Leigh's commitment, his dedication, was given to his work—even Anna Golden seemed to have drifted in and out of his life, with Leigh sparing her what little time and energy were left after the demands of his career. The older woman seemed to be able to accept that, or at least had learned to tolerate it, but could Jassy?

And what did Leigh plan to do about Anna? During the past week, the older woman's name had never been mentioned, nor, to Jassy's knowledge, had Leigh contacted her in any way, but, equally, he had never actually said that his affair with the actress was over, and Jassy knew that she would be deceiving herself if she tried to pretend that that didn't matter. She had to face facts, and the fact was that any involvement with Leigh Benedict was probably very unlikely to last, that in the end it would bring as much pain as pleasure.

But another fact was that Jassy was already involved. Leigh was what she needed *now*. Even if it would be safer, less painful in the long run, to stop now, with her heart and her body still intact, she knew she couldn't do it. The one thing she could not deny was the physical passion that flared between herself and Leigh, and if that passion was all that he had to give, then at least she would have had that, and the prospect of even a brief idyll of such delight seemed infinitely preferable to the certainty of emptiness and despair without Leigh in her life at all.

CHAPTER SEVEN

LEIGH'S house seemed strangely deserted when Jassy let herself in the next morning. Even though Steve, already busy at his desk, called out a cheery welcome as Jassy passed his door, his friendly presence did nothing to dispel the sense of emptiness that oppressed her simply because Leigh wasn't there. Throughout the day she was always conscious of the empty desk on the other side of the room, and had to force herself to concentrate on her work. Her abstracted mood was so obvious that Steve commented on it when they shared a snack lunch together.

'Are you sure we haven't been working you too hard? You had no free time at all at the weekend, remember? We must owe you a couple of days off. Why don't you stay at home tomorrow? I'll square it with Leigh. We're going to be tied up all day with these wretched auditions, so there won't be anything going on here. You could go and blow some of the overtime money we're paying you—you've earned it.'

A day off seemed like an excellent idea, Jassy reflected. Perhaps some time on her own, away from Leigh's forceful presence, would give her a chance to think things through, work out just how she really felt about this situation that had blown up like a tropical storm, sweeping her off what she had formerly believed was her steady, well-thought-out path through life. And she would have found it very difficult to cope, being here on her own, knowing that somewhere, at the auditions that Steve and Leigh had organised, other actresses would be testing for the part she so longed to play.

The crawling hands of the clock had finally made their way round to half-past four when the office door opened, making Jassy's heart leap in a way that made a mockery of her earlier belief that she had anything to think through where Leigh was concerned. He was only half an hour early, but her delight at even that tiny reprieve from the emptiness of the day told her how much he had come to mean to her in the short time she had known him.

Her spirits plummeted again violently as she looked up into a pair of cold green eyes, dramatically emphasised by the heavy application of darker green eyeshadow and thick black mascara. Numbly Jassy became aware of the gleaming red hair, the voluptuously curved body in a stunningly simple cream silk dress, as Anna Golden stalked into the room.

'Can I help you, Miss Golden?' Jassy's voice sounded weak and constrained, revealing the effort she was making to sound polite and uninvolved, while her stomach was twisting itself into painful knots of apprehension at the thought of what the actress was doing in Leigh's home. 'I'm afraid Mr Benedict is out at the moment, but——'

She broke off abruptly as Anna raised a heavily ringed hand to silence her in a gesture as imperious as that of some absolute ruler dealing with her lowly subjects.

'Spare me the pleasantries, please. I know exactly where Leigh is—it was you I came to see.'

'*Me?*'

Anna smiled nastily at Jassy's evident astonishment.

'Yes, you, Miss Richardson. I came to see what you were like.' The actress's tone made it plain that, now that she had seen Jassy, she was not at all impressed. A tiny frown crossed her forehead. 'I've seen you before, haven't I?'

'At Julio's.' Recalling that meeting, Jassy wasn't at all surprised that Anna didn't remember her clearly. She had been more concerned with herself and the message she had wanted passing on to Leigh. A feeling like a knife being twisted deep inside made Jassy wince as she remembered the content of that message.

'Now,' Anna clearly wasn't interested in where she had seen Jassy before, or when, 'perhaps you can tell me where Leigh was last night?'

'He had an interview—you must know that—and then——' Jassy broke off abruptly, disturbed by the vindictive flash in Anna's green eyes.

'It's that "and then" that concerns me. I had arranged a dinner party last night, a dinner to which some very special people had been invited, and Leigh had promised to be there, but he didn't turn up. We waited for him for hours, then just after ten he rang to say that something important had cropped up and he wouldn't be coming after all. This morning I discovered what that "something important" really was.' The cat's eyes darkened swiftly in anger. 'He was with you!'

The swift lifting of Jassy's heart at hearing that vital 'something important' restored some of the confidence that Anna's sudden appearance and unexpected attack had drained from her.

'I think you're talking to the wrong person. Naturally, I'm sorry if your dinner party was spoiled, but I had nothing to do with that. If you have any quarrel with anyone, then it must be with Leigh himself.'

Anna's vicious smile surfaced again. 'Oh, I've no quarrel with you—I just came to warn you. I know what's happening to you; I've seen it all before. You think you're in love with Leigh, but you ought to know that he'll never love you back. Leigh isn't capable of love. Don't take my word for it—ask any woman who's been fool enough to get involved with him. Not one of them has ever touched his heart. I've no doubt he makes you feel very special——' This time Anna's smile was one of pure sensual triumph. 'He's a most accomplished lover, as I'm sure you've already discovered—definitely ten out of ten. But the truth is that Leigh has never been faithful to any woman in his life. He's greedy, you see, he can't be content with one when there are so many all ready to fall into his hands like ripe little plums just because of who he is. Oh, I grant you that you might appeal to him just now—you have an uncomplicated attractiveness that would tempt his rather jaded appetite—but when the bloom's worn off he'll discard you like a broken toy and never give you another thought. If you're lucky—and clever—if you don't cling too hard, you might last a few months, but after that——'

'I think you've said quite enough,' Jassy broke in sharply. Anna's tirade had washed over her head like a tidal wave, but one thing the actress had said had struck home, like an arrow hitting a target. All she wanted was to go somewhere quiet and think, but there was no chance of that until the other woman left. 'I'd appreciate it if you left now.'

'Certainly. I've said all I wanted to say—and I think I've made my point. But I'll warn you——' suddenly Anna's voice changed and Jassy had the uneasy feeling that what was coming next was what the older woman had really come to say '—your little idyll with Leigh is going nowhere. If you're wise you'll get out now before you regret it for the rest of your life.'

As the actress stalked from the room Jassy's hands clenched into tight fists, her nails digging into her palms, one phrase Anna had said echoing over and over in her head: 'You think you're in love with Leigh', 'You're in love with Leigh'. *Was* that what had happened? *Had* she been fool enough to fall in love with Leigh? It couldn't be true—could it?

But she was given no time to consider the question for at that moment she heard footsteps in the hall and, before she had a chance to realise what that meant, Leigh was in the room.

'Was that Anna's car I saw leaving?'

Leigh came to an abrupt halt in the middle of the room as he saw Jassy's pallor, her over-bright eyes.

'Jassy?' he said sharply. 'What is it?'

But Jassy could only shake her head. Stunned and bewildered as she was, she only knew that as soon as he had come into the room she had registered once more that glorious sense of excitement that simply seeing him could bring—but was that *love*?

'Jassy, tell me what's wrong. What did Anna say to you? Jassy——' Leigh's voice was quiet, but it had the force of a command '—*tell me!*'

Jassy tried to bring her mind back into focus. It wasn't easy with Leigh's eyes fixed on her face as if he could read deep into her heart, when even she had no idea what he might find there. But she had to say *something*, give Leigh some explanation for her disturbed state.

'She—she said you were her lover,' she faltered, saying the first thing that came into her head. 'That you were—very accomplished—t-ten out of ten.'

'Thank you, Anna!' Leigh muttered sardonically with a bitterly mocking salute in the direction of the door through which the actress had left. 'Would have you preferred it if she'd said I was hopeless?' he went on very softly. 'Jassy, be reasonable. I'm thirty-four; I'm a man, not a monk. You can learn a lot about women in sixteen years—I'd be a pretty insensitive brute if I hadn't picked up one or two "accomplishments" along the way.'

'She——'

'Look——' Leigh broke in sharply '—the world and his wife know that Anna and I had our moment, but let's get one thing straight—she doesn't own me, even if she tries to give that impression. I *was* her lover and I've no intention of denying that, but I've lived with that episode in my life for long enough and I've still got the name to prove it. I've been branded the Golden Thief by the Press and the public and I've learned to live with it, but I will *not* take it from you. Unless you can put Anna, that nickname and the whole bloody image behind you we'll call a halt right now. We're on a long road to nowhere if you don't take me for what I am. I'm making no promises because I don't know if I can keep them—but it has to be just you and me, Jassy. If you're looking for that superstar, then forget him; he doesn't exist. There's just a man called Leigh Benedict—and if you want that then we'll take it from there.'

'I *was* her lover... it has to be just you and me...' Leigh's words dispersed the last of the fog that had been clouding Jassy's mind. She still didn't know if what she felt for Leigh was love or anything close to it, but that didn't matter, just as Anna no longer mattered, or anything in the past. What mattered was right here and now, and Leigh had offered her a new beginning. Her head came up and she looked deep into those tawny eyes, meeting their gaze without fear or hesitation.

'Hello, *Leigh*,' she murmured softly, and knew from the swift darkening of his eyes that he had caught the slight emphasis on his name and knew exactly what she had meant to convey.

'Hello, Jassy,' he said huskily, and was reaching for her when the door opened behind him.

'So this is what you get up to when my back is turned!' Steve declared laughingly. 'Put her down, Benedict, it's time Jassy was on her way home.'

Leigh accepted the interruption good-humouredly, only betraying his disappointment by the faintest rueful glance in Jassy's direction.

'I suppose I'd better let you go, then,' he said lightly. 'Otherwise I'll end up paying you even more time. No——'

The change in Leigh's tone stopped her as she reached automatically for her bag.

'I've got a better idea. Why don't you stay—have dinner with me?'

'I think this is my cue to leave tactfully,' Steve put in with a smile. 'I'll see you both tomorrow.'

Leigh barely noticed his friend's departure; his eyes were on Jassy's face, the intensity of his gaze making her heart miss a beat.

'You will stay, won't you?' he asked, his voice and expression suddenly very serious.

'I'd love to,' Jassy told him, a world of sincerity in her words, and Leigh's delighted smile swept the last bitter memories of Anna's visit from her mind.

'It'll be just the two of us,' he declared. 'We'll shut the door on the whole damn film world just for tonight.'

A sudden harsh light in his eyes, a tightness round his mouth told Jassy that Leigh was not just thinking of the film world in general, but of one female member of that world in particular, and she shivered faintly at the thought of the cold anger that Anna had roused in him. But a moment later Leigh seemed to have shaken off his dark mood as he smilingly led her into the kitchen to begin preparations for the evening ahead of her.

That night Jassy discovered another Leigh, a man who was open, friendly and relaxed, totally without the dangerous, ruthless streak in him that excited and yet frightened her, a man in whose company she found herself relaxing completely and thoroughly enjoying herself. Often, as she helped him prepare their meal, she would find his arm lingering around her waist or her shoulders, his hand touching hers deliberately when he passed her things, and finally, when all was ready and she sank down on the settee with a glass of sherry in her hand, Leigh sprawled beside her with a sigh of contentment, the glow that lit his eyes sending a rush of happiness through her.

'Are you quite comfortable?' he asked softly, with a note in his voice that told her he was not just referring to the way she had kicked off her shoes and curled her legs up underneath her. His arm, lying across the back of the settee, very close to her shoulders, was an open invitation to move closer, one she was strongly tempted to accept, but mischievously she chose to take his question at face-value.

'Perfectly comfortable,' she assured him. 'This is such a contrast to that archaic instrument of torture we have at home,' she added with a flirtatious smile, and saw Leigh's mouth curl slowly, sharing the memory.

He didn't take up the invitation in her eyes, however, but moved suddenly to sit stiffly upright, his position implying a disturbing change of mood.

'I've been thinking,' he said quietly, and Jassy tensed, knowing from his tone that what he was about to say was somehow very important. 'I've been hunting everywhere for an actress to play Clara.'

At the mention of that name Jassy felt every muscle in her body tighten, stretching out her nerves to breaking-point, her stomach twisting painfully in apprehension as the easy, relaxed mood vanished and they moved into territory that was as dangerous as a minefield.

'What about you——?'

'No!'

Jassy's answer came swiftly, sharply. She couldn't begin to guess why Leigh was even suggesting such a thing, unless it was as some sort of test of her integrity; she just knew that there was only one possible answer.

'Not even an audition?'

Leigh sounded genuinely disappointed, and that made it even harder to answer a second time.

'Not even an audition.' The struggle she was having with her own disappointed ambition made it difficult to keep her tone firm and decisive. 'That's not what I want from you, Leigh. Why do you think I left you and Steve to make all the arrangements about tomorrow so that I don't even know where the auditions are going to be held? I don't want anything to do with it—it has to be kept totally separate from you and me.'

Wide and bright, her eyes pleaded with him to believe her, but all the same she didn't know if she felt relief or disappointment when Leigh finally nodded silently.

'I'm not Gemma Morgan!' she declared vehemently, and saw Leigh wince as she reminded him of his own cynical comments.

'Do you think I don't know that?' he growled roughly. 'And it wasn't just Gemma.'

'You told me about——' Jassy began, breaking off hastily when Leigh shook his head violently.

'Not the others—before that—when I was a kid.'

Jassy's heart lurched violently at the realisation that Leigh was close to telling her about that part of his life that he had always kept so very much to himself, that intensely private area into which he allowed only a very few, trusted people.

'Steve told me that you grew up in Pinehurst—the children's home,' she said carefully when he didn't go on, obviously finding the subject extremely difficult to talk about.

The swift, narrow-eyed glance Leigh slanted in her direction made her heart sink in the fear that she had trespassed too far, driving him away from her again. But then Leigh drew in a deep, uneven breath and pushed one hand roughly through the golden silk of his hair.

'I was ten when I went to live there, just after my mother died.'

Leigh's mouth twisted as he caught Jassy's choked exclamation of shock and sympathy.

'I told you that I never knew my father—the truth is that I doubt if even my mother knew who he was. All through my childhood I had a succession of "uncles", none of whom stayed around long, but they all had one thing in common—they all had influence in the film or theatre world, and my mother believed that they would help her up the ladder of success. Next to her, Gemma Morgan and the others were complete innocents. Each new man was the one who was going to make her a star— actors, producers, directors. The irony of it all was that none of it worked. She was never more than a bit-part actress, and in the end not even that. The spells out of work got longer and longer, and that was when she started to drink. When she died, her stomach was awash with booze and sleeping tablets.'

'Leigh!' Jassy couldn't hold back her distress and horror. 'Did she——?'

'I doubt if she meant to kill herself. It was either a complete accident or one last attempt at the big dramatic gesture that would bring the man of the moment to heel. I'm damn sure she thought she'd be found in time, and that when she was he would realise what she meant to him and offer her the part of a lifetime.'

Again came that cynical twist to Leigh's mouth that stabbed straight to Jassy's heart.

'The current "uncle" was a director. But in the end, as usual, that was one more starring role that escaped her.'

The black, sardonic tone was pure adult Leigh, but behind it Jassy could hear the child he had been then.

'And that was how I ended up at Pinehurst.'

Leigh stopped speaking abruptly, and in the silence that followed Jassy felt as if someone had shone a light into a darkened room so that she could see clearly for the first time, Leigh's distrust of actresses was not just the result of the behaviour of people like Gemma Morgan; the seeds of it had been sown long ago, when he was a child, and had been fed by his mother's behaviour, her ultimate despair, and that fact had far-reaching consequences for Jassy herself. Now she felt she was beginning to understand why he concentrated so much of his energies on his work, leaving no time for the personal relationships that seemed to lead only to disillusionment.

'Oh, Leigh, I'm so sorry. I didn't——'

Leigh held up a hand to silence her. 'No apologies, Jassy, and for heaven's sake no sympathy—I don't need either of them.' If he saw the way Jassy winced at his tone, Leigh showed no sign of it. 'I've come a long way since Pinehurst, but the time I spent there taught me one thing—in the end there's just you, no one else. Life's what *you* make of it.'

With an abrupt movement he got to his feet.

'I think it's time we ate.' He was turning towards the door as he spoke, then suddenly swung back to face Jassy. 'What I've told you is all in the past; what matters is now. I meant what I said earlier, Jassy, it's just you and me—I won't have it any other way.'

Jassy could only nod because that was how she wanted it too, but as she watched him walk out of the room she reflected that, even though Leigh had rejected any need of sympathy, the gap between the lonely, ambitious child in the orphanage and the complex, disturbing man who was now the idol of millions was not as great as he made it out to be.

And that made her wonder once again whether the offer of an audition for the part of Clara had been the test she had suspected. Did Leigh still not trust her even now?

A sensation like the touch of tiny, ice-cold footprints trailing over her skin slid down Jassy's back at the thought of how different things could have been if she had answered Leigh's question about the audition any other way, how only a few seconds could have changed everything completely. Even though a tiny part of her still cried out at the loss of such a wonderful opportunity, she was now totally convinced that she had done the right thing. There had been no other possible answer—but now her reasons for that decision were much more complicated. Her pride, her self-respect still mattered intensely, but what was perhaps even more important was that she had to prove to Leigh that not all actresses were like those others, like his mother, Gemma, and even Anna, who Leigh had said thought she owned him.

It was vital that she did convince him because somehow, without being quite sure how it had happened, her doubts and fears had melted away. She didn't know at what point in the evening she had become certain, but when or how didn't matter. The Golden Thief, the newspapers called Leigh, and now, for Jassy, the nickname had a new significance. He was a thief indeed; he had stolen her heart, and no matter what happened it would always belong to him, and to him alone. But she was going to have to tread very carefully until she had finally won his trust. If she made one false move Leigh would walk away from her without a backward glance, rejecting the actress without a thought for the woman.

CHAPTER EIGHT

THE sound of footsteps hurrying down the stairs, the slam of the door, announced Sarah's departure for work, and Jassy, who in spite of the fact that it had been nearly two before her head had touched the pillow had been lying awake for an hour or so, waiting for her friend to leave, flung back the bedclothes, too restless to stay still any longer.

She had not felt able to face Sarah over breakfast; her thoughts were too personal and private for that. Jassy couldn't help wondering if the way she felt right now was the way some girls would feel on the morning of their wedding day—a mixture of happiness, impatient anticipation and sheer blind panic all rolled into one...

She had passed through the rest of the evening at Leigh's in a hazy dream, accepting the knowledge of her love without fear, knowing only a perfect calm as she understood the truth at last. By the time she had joined him in the dining-room, Leigh had thrown off his sombre mood and was soon laughing at some remark she made, pouring wine with a liberal hand as he did so. Throughout the meal, his conversation was as intoxicating as that wine, spiced with a dry wit that was enhanced by the way he unconsciously slipped into the role of the person he was describing and then resumed his normal voice almost without being aware of it. Jassy secretly treasured those moments, the actress in her studying each tiny, vivid performance, watching to see how he captured mannerisms, an accent, a personality without seeming to stop and think.

Often during the meal she glanced up to find Leigh's eyes on her, his gaze warm as a physical caress, and she smiled back at him, their eyes locking together in a suspended moment of perfect unity that excluded the

143

rest of the world. In those moments she wondered if she had ever been truly alive before. Leigh was as essential to her now as the air she breathed, so that she couldn't imagine how she had ever managed to exist without knowing him—and loving him. He had spoken no word of love himself, but she wouldn't ask for that. She had enough for both of them, and she would give him that for as long as she could and then, if that was not enough to hold him, she would let him go, knowing that her love went with him when she no longer had the man himself.

After the meal, they lingered in the living-room, Jassy held tight in Leigh's arms, not moving, rarely even speaking, content just to enjoy the happiness of being together. At last, very reluctantly, Jassy suggested that it was time for her to leave.

'Do you have to go?' Leigh murmured, his cheek against her hair, one hand playing idly with a long, pale strand of it. 'It's early yet.'

'Leigh!' Jassy protested laughingly. 'It's after midnight! I may not have to work in the morning, but you do!'

She saw his eyes darken, felt his hold on her tighten before the golden head bent and his lips captured hers. Drugged by the warmth of his body, the sweetness of his kiss, she almost missed the words he whispered against her mouth.

'Don't go,' he murmured huskily. 'Stay with me tonight, Jassy; let me love you.'

She longed to say yes, wanted it with all her heart, but the memory of everything he had said earlier, the testing offer of an audition, slid insidiously between them.

'It has to be just you and me,' he had said, and until it was truly so, until the issue of who would play Clara was finally decided—until it had been given to some other actress, Jassy admitted on a wrench of pain—she could not give herself to him as freely and openly as he asked. Only when he knew for certain that it was love and not ambition that drew her to him would she really be free to give him that love, knowing he would be able to accept it without any reservations.

But Leigh had sensed her hesitation and he got to his feet with a jarring abruptness, his face shuttered, his eyes hooded and unreadable as, not looking at her, he moved away as if he needed to put some physical distance between them. Feeling lost and bereft without the warm, protective strength of his body beside her, Jassy wanted to reach out, to touch him, but he suddenly seemed very far away from her.

'Leigh—don't——'

'I'm doing this for your own good,' Leigh cut in gruffly. 'If you're going home you go now—before I forget my promise.'

'Your promise?'

'Damn you, Jassy, I said I'd wait until you weren't afraid to say you wanted me!' Leigh declared harshly, shattering the peaceful mood of the evening.

Jassy bit her lip hard, knowing she had blundered very badly. Caught up in her own developing feelings, she had forgotten the promise Leigh had made to her. Slowly she stood up, moving to take his hand very gently, wanting to draw him back to her.

'I just need a little more time, Leigh. Please understand.'

Leigh turned to her, his eyes dark and intense, deep, unfathomable pools in a suddenly drawn face.

'Then when?' he asked urgently. 'Tomorrow? Come to me tomorrow!'

Tomorrow was a new day. Tomorrow the things he had told her about his mother would not be so fresh in her mind—tomorrow someone else would have been chosen to play Clara.

'Tomorrow,' she told Leigh softly, managing a tremulous smile. 'After all, it's really that now—would another few hours be so very long?'

Even as she spoke, the feeling of his hand in hers made her body throb with the need and longing she had felt the night before, and she knew that, were Leigh even to kiss her again, she would be unable to deny him, would yield her body and her heart up to him to cherish or destroy as he willed. But Leigh responded to her gentle teasing, a smile wiping the hard, shuttered expression from his face.

'Right now an hour seems like an eternity,' he said feelingly. 'But I reckon I'll have to be patient a while longer. Come on, woman, let me get you home to your chaste little bed, then maybe I'll even get some sleep myself. At least it'll while away a few hours.'

Peace had been restored, and they were both laughing as they left the house. But a short time later, in the darkness of the car outside her flat, Leigh turned to her and took her hand in his, hard fingers gripping it firmly.

'I want you, Jassy, but you're right—something like this shouldn't be rushed. I want you to know something—that image—the Golden Thief...'

'The sex symbol?' Jassy supplied gently when he seemed to be having difficulty finding the words he wanted.

Leigh nodded silent agreement. 'It isn't real. It's as much a fantasy as the characters I play—just a myth created by the Press and the inevitable publicity that comes with the job.'

'Are you trying to say——?'

'I'm not claiming I'm an innocent, Jassy. I told you, I'm thirty-four, and I have any normal man's appetites and needs—feelings—and in our job there's plenty of temptation, but very little commitment—and one thing I've learned is that the first without the second is a potentially lethal situation. I got caught up in that once, and once was quite enough for me to learn my lesson.'

It was too dark to see Leigh's face, but his voice told Jassy very clearly that the details of that 'lesson' were not something he cared to reveal at this time.

'When I realised what was happening I knew that the whole thing was too damn risky. Quite apart from the dangers to oneself, one plus one making two is fine, but when one and one makes three, then that's trouble with a capital T—and I have no intention of being that irresponsible.'

Jassy's silence was no longer simply because she was listening intently to every word Leigh spoke; now it had an extra dimension of shock in it. She should have thought of this herself, but the truth was that it hadn't even crossed her mind. She knew what Leigh was trying to say. Knowing what she did of his past, the way his mother—and Leigh—had paid the price for his father's irresponsibility, she could understand how he felt.

'I'd never want any child of mine to grow up without a father around, so I determined that there would be no child until I wanted the mother with me for the rest of my life. I know I've rushed you, but I want you to know that I would never let you end up in my mother's situation. You do understand that, don't you?'

Jassy could only nod silently, still too stunned by her own thoughtlessness to frame an answer. That 'until I wanted the mother with me for the rest of my life' reverberated inside her head. Just what had Leigh meant to imply by that? That she could never be that woman—or exactly the opposite? She couldn't tell, and it was too dark to see into his face and read any answer there.

'Now I'm going to let you go,' Leigh said quietly. 'I want you to think about what I've said, and if you decide—well, you know where you can find me. I'll be home around seven tomorrow—tonight,' he amended wryly.

'I'll see you then.' Jassy found her voice at last. It was all she could say, there were too many other thoughts in her mind to allow her to add anything further. But deep inside she knew that there was nothing for her to think about. One thing was certain—tonight she would be with Leigh.

Just as she turned to get out of the car Leigh caught hold of her and pulled her close, crushing her up against him until she felt that her bones might break under the pressure of his hands. He whispered the one word, 'Tonight,' in a low, intense tone that made nonsense of all his carefully rationalised arguments, and Jassy knew that there was no turning back. No matter what happened, she was committed.

* * *

It was early afternoon when Jassy returned to the flat, humming to herself as she dropped the small bundle of carrier bags on to the settee and kicked off her shoes, flinging herself into a chair with a sigh of relief. She had been tramping round the shops for hours, looking for a very special dress, and she had found it—a simple sleeveless design in a sensual silky material in exactly the same shade of pink as the nightshirt Leigh had said he liked. It was the dress she was going to wear tonight.

When the doorbell rang loudly and insistently Jassy was tempted to ignore it. She was tired, and she didn't feel like company. But the caller was clearly not going to give up, and with a sigh she opened the door then stared in astonishment at the dark, heavily built man who stood on the landing.

'Benjy! What are you doing here?'

Her former tutor was the last person she had expected to see. She had become very friendly with Benjy and his wife while she was at college, but just lately she had seen very little of them.

'I've been trying to reach you all day.' Clearly agitated, Benjy wasted no time on polite preliminaries. 'I've rung you every half-hour since nine o'clock.'

'I've been shopping,' Jassy said dazedly. 'I went out early, and I've only just got back.'

'Well, now you're coming with me. My car's outside— we can just make it if we hurry.' He was halfway out of the door as he spoke. Jassy caught hold of his arm before he disappeared completely.

'Hang on, Benjy! We can just make what? Where are we going?'

'To your audition.' Benjy's round face was glowing with excitement. 'The biggest chance you'll ever get, my girl, so stop messing about and let's get going. I'll explain on the way.'

'Now don't get yourself into a frazzle, honeybun,' Benjy soothed as they sped away from the flat. 'I couldn't give you any warning of this because I didn't get any myself—and I can't tell you a great deal because I'm sworn to secrecy about much of it, but all you need to know is that last night I had some friends round to dinner—theatre people—and we started discussing my ex-pupils and what they were doing and, of course, as one of my stars, your name came up. Well, to cut a long story short, one of my friends who has a great deal of influence with a certain producer—mentioning no names, of course—felt you would be perfect for a *very important part*——' Benjy emphasised the last three words dramatically.

'—and would you be interested? Of course, having your best interests at heart, I said you damn well would! A quick telephone call to the right people this morning wangled you an audition, then all I had to do was find you—you didn't exactly make that easy!'

'Benjy, you're an angel!'

Jassy's words came jerkily because of the excitement that seemed to be bubbling like red-hot lava in her veins. 'Theatre people,' Benjy had said, so there must be some new production coming up that even her agent didn't know about yet.

Working for Leigh had been a rewarding experience in more ways than one, but Jassy had missed acting so terribly, and her heart soared with excitement at the thought that she might soon be working at the job she loved—and possibly, to judge from Benjy's hints, in some major new play.

And there was another, secret hope that she hugged tightly to herself as the car sped through the streets. She would go to Leigh tonight, whatever happened. Loving him as she did, she *had* to go, but how much better it would be if she could also tell him that she had won an important role by her own efforts, without his help or even his knowledge. Surely then he would *know* that she loved him for himself and not because of what he could give her as an actress?

'Nearly there,' Benjy warned her, shooting round a corner at breakneck speed. 'I can't tell you anything about the part—I gave my word on that—but I can say one thing: if you get this, then you're *made*, honeybun. Just don't panic, and remember I have faith in you. You

can do it if you don't lose your nerve—so just get in
there and show 'em. We're here,' he added unnecessarily
as the car screeched to a halt.

Not giving Jassy time to get her bearings, Benjy
bundled her out of the car and into the theatre, hurrying
her along a dimly lit corridor until at last they halted
just out of earshot of the stage. The backstage area was
crowded with girls of around Jassy's own age, one or
two of whom she recognised from her years at college.
But she had no time to look around her because someone
had thrust a script into her hands and Benjy was giving
her last-minute instructions in a low, urgent voice.

'Now get your breath and relax. I know you haven't
had time to look at the script, so you'll have to listen
very carefully when they tell you the plot and then take
it from there.' Benjy's smile was positively paternal. 'I
know you're panicking now, but you'll be all right as
soon as you get on that stage—you always are.'

'Miss Richardson,' a voice was calling behind Jassy.
'Miss Richardson, please!'

Benjy gave her a firm push forwards and, her mind
still reeling from the unexpectedness of everything, she
stumbled towards the brightly lit stage where an actor
who she vaguely recalled from a couple of television plays
stood waiting to read the part through with her. In
contrast to the brightness of the stage lights, the theatre
auditorium was very dark. Jassy knew that there must
be several people out there, but blinded by the glare of
the spotlights, she couldn't see a thing.

There was a sudden silence as she appeared on stage;
an inexplicable, paralysing silence that stretched Jassy's
already taut nerves almost to breaking-point, so that she
clutched the pages of her script even tighter as she waited.
If only they would let her begin! She would feel so much
better then. But still the silence went on until at last,
after an unendurable wait, a different voice spoke directly
to her from the darkness.

'OK, Miss Richardson, let me tell you something about
this film . . .'

Film. The word was like a blow to her face, making her head spin sickeningly so that she scarcely heard the brief but comprehensive summary of the plot, the helpful insights into the character of the girl she was to play. She didn't need them anyway; she knew every last detail of the story as well as she knew the voice that had come so shockingly out of the darkness. The script she held in her tightly clenched hands was the script of *Valley of Destiny*, the voice in her ears was Steve Carter's—and if Steve was there then Leigh must be too!

White with panic, Jassy scanned the rows of seats in the auditorium, searching frantically through the blackness until at last she could just make out a gleaming blond head very dimly through the darkness.

Leigh was sitting frighteningly still, his face completely in the shadows, his white shirt in stark contrast to the gloom around him. Jassy could see nothing of his face, but it was his total immobility that terrified her. She had seen that stillness before, when Leigh was very, very angry. She longed to turn and run, go anywhere if she could only escape from the cold, hostile eyes she knew were fixed on her even if they were hidden from her sight, but she knew that if she started running she would never be able to stop. She had to go through with this audition now, though a savage pain seared through her as if her heart were slowly tearing in half.

'I realise that you haven't had time to prepare yourself,' Steve was saying, a strong note of sympathy in his voice. 'We only had your name put forward for the part this morning, so we have rather rushed you through. Would you like a couple of minutes to read over your lines?'

Numbly Jassy shook her head. She just wanted to get on with it, get it over, then she could go away and hide—if there was anywhere she could run to where Leigh would never find her.

'Quite sure? OK—whenever you're ready.'

At last Jassy found the strength to look at the script she held. She had thought that nothing could hurt any more than the pain she already felt, but the first lines that danced in front of her blurred eyes twisted the knife even deeper into her heart.

Of all the scenes in the film, the one chosen for the audition was the very scene Jassy had read aloud to herself on the night she had taken the script home, imagining herself playing Clara opposite Leigh. Now she was being given the chance to act the role she had so longed for, but the man playing Francis was a total stranger, and somewhere in the darkness of the auditorium Leigh's tiger's eyes were watching her.

Jassy could almost feel those golden eyes burning into her as she began to read, stumbling hopelessly over the words. She felt as if she were in the grip of some appalling nightmare from which she couldn't wake, but this was no dream, it was horrifyingly, terrifyingly real, and so there was no way she could even begin to think herself into the part of Clara.

In the privacy of her own flat she had known instinctively how every one of these words should be spoken. She had imagined gestures, movements, intonations, to bring out the character of the woman she was playing, but now all her ideas deserted her. She could remember none of those subtleties, could hardly even focus on the lines on the page before her. She knew that her performance was appalling, her actions wooden, her delivery almost incoherent, but she couldn't bring herself to care. She was ruining the biggest chance of her career, throwing away all hope of being cast in the part she had dreamed of, but the role of Clara, even her own future as an actress, were nothing to her if she lost Leigh—and, knowing how he must inevitably interpret her sudden appearance at the audition, she could have little doubt that after this she had lost him forever.

After what seemed like an eternity the ordeal was over. The last line had been spoken and Jassy stood miserably silent, every ounce of energy drained from her. Glancing at the actor who had read the part of Francis, she could see nothing but pity in his eyes, pity for a young, untalented girl who had made a complete fool of herself.

That was the last straw. Turning awkwardly, Jassy fled blindly from the stage and stumbled into the wings where Benjy was waiting for her.

'Jassy, honeybun, *what* came over you? That wasn't like you at all. You just went to pieces.'

Her tutor put his arm around her waist in a gesture of instinctive comfort, but Jassy didn't even notice. She was beyond comfort, beyond caring.

'Benjy, please,' she pleaded wearily. 'I can't explain, please don't ask me to.' All she wanted to do was go, get away from the theatre, away from Leigh. 'Take me home,' she whispered, her voice dull and lifeless.

Behind her she heard the murmur of voices, a faint commotion further down the corridor, and, looking up, saw the painfully familiar tall, golden-haired figure and knew it was too late. Leigh shouldered his way through the crowded corridor towards her, ruthlessly ignoring all attempts to speak to him, roughly shaking off hands placed on his arm to gain his attention, and Jassy knew she was trapped. There was nowhere for her to run to, and even as she shrank back against the wall brutal fingers closed over her arm and Leigh pulled her roughly round to face him. His face was white with anger, the tawny eyes slitted and pitiless, burning with an icy fury.

'My car's outside,' he said, and it was a command, not a statement.

Without loosening his cruel grip on Jassy's arm, he turned and made his way back down the corridor, dragging her along with him. Jassy had a fleeting glimpse of Benjy staring in shock and bewilderment, she saw the envious faces of the other girls, their envy changing rapidly to doubt as they saw the grim set of Leigh's features, and then they were at the stage door. Leigh paused just long enough to toss a key to the doorman before pushing Jassy out of the door and across the street to where his car stood, unnoticed in the confusion of her arrival less than an hour before. Bundling her unceremoniously into the front passenger seat, Leigh slammed the door shut after her.

It took only a few seconds for him to make his way round to the other side of the car and slide into the driver's seat, but Jassy took her chance and fumbled frantically with the door, trying desperately to open it—but it refused to move. Leigh watched her struggles silently for a moment.

'You're wasting your time. It locks automatically—you can only get out when I let you.'

He reached out a hand to pull her away from the door and, panicking at the thought of having him touch her in cold anger again, Jassy struck out at him blindly. Leigh saw the blow coming and flung up his arm to ward it off so that her fist landed impotently on sinewy muscle. Immediately afterwards, she was slammed back in her seat with a violence that drove all the breath from her body.

'None of that!' Leigh snarled. 'You've done enough damage that way already. Just sit quiet until I get you home, then you can try all the dirty tricks you like. But I warn you, I'll use a few of my own right back, so don't push me. Right now, I'm sorely tempted.'

His grip tightened bruisingly on her arm and Jassy winced in pain.

'You're hateful!' she spat the words into his face in fear and distress, wanting only to hurt him as she was hurting, but Leigh shrugged indifferently.

'We've been through all that before,' he said impassively. 'Personally, I don't give a damn what you think of me—my opinion of you is none too high either. So unless you want to have this out right here and now, where everyone can see us, I suggest you curb that shrewish tongue of yours, for a while at least. It won't take us long to get to my place—if you're wise you'll use the time to think up some new story to tell me this time.'

Abruptly he released her, turning away to start the car, jerking it into gear viciously and swinging away from the kerb at a speed that had the tyres squealing protestingly.

It was a nightmarish journey. Leigh drove with reckless abandon, as if totally oblivious of the early rush-hour traffic and they had several very narrow escapes which had Jassy's stomach contracting in panic before they reached the quiet square where Leigh's house stood. Once released from the car, Jassy stumbled inelegantly across the courtyard, propelled roughly towards the door by Leigh's hand at her back. After unlocking the door, Leigh stood back.

'After you,' he said with a mocking bow.

Defiantly Jassy shook her head. She was not going in there! She couldn't bear to be alone with Leigh here, in this house where such a short time before she had been so very happy.

'Very well,' Leigh declared calmly, and before Jassy quite realised what he had in mind he lifted her bodily from the ground and carried her, struggling frantically, into the house.

Kicking open the first door that led off the hall, Leigh strode into the living-room and deposited Jassy unceremoniously on the floor. Then as she sprawled awkwardly on the thick carpet he moved to the drinks cabinet, splashed a large whisky into a tumbler and gulped down half of it in one go.

Thinking that his attention was off her, Jassy scrambled to her feet and made a desperate dash for the door, but, quick as she was, Leigh's reactions were quicker. He reached the door just before she did and slammed it shut, leaning his broad shoulders against it and effectively preventing any further attempt at escape.

'Sit down!' he ordered, and Jassy knew that she had no alternative but to do as he said.

Leigh watched silently as she sank dejectedly into a chair, painfully and belatedly aware of the fact that her fear had driven her to act in a way that, in his mind, would confirm his belief that she was guilty, that she was afraid of facing him now that he had found out how she had been using him. As she cursed her thoughtless action Leigh reached for his glass, lifting it in a mockery of a toast before he swallowed the rest of his drink.

'Now we can talk,' he said coldly, replacing the glass on the dresser beside him. 'Tell me,' he went on, his tone a grim parody of polite interest, 'do you think you'll get the part?'

'The—the part?' Jassy echoed foolishly, her brain refusing to function properly.

She had expected anger, had nerved herself to face the savage lash of his tongue; instead she was confronted by a coolly civil stranger and she had no idea how to cope with the man Leigh had suddenly become.

'Yes, that very important part.' Leigh smiled cruelly. 'Do you think you'll get to play Clara? After all, you went to a great deal of trouble to make sure the role was yours—a magnificent performance,' he added caustically, and Jassy knew he was not referring to the black farce of her audition. 'So tell me, honestly, how do you rate your chances, Miss Richardson?'

Jassy could find no way to answer him. Every word Leigh spoke seemed to stab straight into her heart like the point of a red-hot knife. Despairingly she covered her face with her hands, but it was no use; she could still see Leigh's darkly taunting face in her mind.

'It was all going so well, wasn't it, my darling? Everything just fell into place for you. You got your hands on a copy of the script so that you could study it before everyone else, and then you went to work on me. You damn nearly succeeded too—you had me just where you wanted me!'

Leigh slammed his fist violently into the wall at his side and Jassy's head jerked up at the sickening thud as his hand hit the paintwork.

'I was crazy over you,' Leigh went on, apparently oblivious of his bruised and reddened knuckles. 'I would have done anything for you, but there was just one thing you wanted. You knew Gemma Morgan's tactics hadn't worked in the past, so you tried another way—so it was, No, Leigh, not tonight; I need more time.'

A small moan of pain escaped Jassy at Leigh's bitter mimicry of her own words. She knew how much he must be hurting inside, but his black cynicism revealed only too clearly how determined he was not to let that pain show. In this mood he would never listen to her, and she could only pray that if she allowed him to give his bitterness free rein he would eventually calm down enough to allow her to explain. Whether he would believe her explanation, she didn't know. She still couldn't believe what had happened herself.

'How far would you have gone, I wonder?' Leigh mused cynically, his head slightly on one side as if he was actually considering the question. 'If I'd been a little more reluctant—not quite so easily enslaved—would you have played your trump card? Would you have let me make love to you, Jassy, if that was what it took to get the part?'

'Leigh, please don't!' Jassy pleaded, her eyes wide dark pools in an ashen face. 'It was never like that! You've got it all wrong! I——'

'Hell, but you must have wanted that part!' Leigh cut in, his voice thick with disgust. 'What wouldn't you have done to get it? Tell me——' his voice altered suddenly, becoming strangely quiet, almost conversational in tone '—do you still want it?'

'What?' Jassy couldn't believe what she was hearing. 'What did you say?' she asked with difficulty, the words clumsy on her tongue.

'I asked if you still wanted the part of Clara.' Leigh's unnerving calmness sent a shiver of fear down Jassy's spine.

He was watching her intently, his narrowed eyes making her think worriedly of a predator watching its prey just before it sprang. In a panic she got to her feet, backing nervously away from him as he moved into the room towards her.

'What if I were to give it to you?' Leigh's question was laced with silky menace. 'What then? What are you offering in return?'

He took a step nearer and Jassy retreated hastily, her mind whirling. He couldn't mean it! He couldn't!

'Leigh...' she faltered, putting out a trembling hand to ward him off. The tiny movement proved her undoing; Leigh's hand snaked out and caught her wrist, pulling her roughly up against him.

'Are you still offering your sexy little body in return for a starring role?' he murmured, one hand sliding down Jassy's back, tracing light, erotic patterns over the thin cotton of her dress. 'Because if you are I might still be open to offers if you're prepared to make it worth my while.'

If Jassy had been scared before, that fear was as nothing when compared with what she felt now. She was terrified, afraid of herself and for herself because she could read what Leigh intended in his eyes and knew only too well what would happen.

'No!' She moaned a protest, but even in her own ears it lacked conviction. Already her traitorous body was betraying her, responding to Leigh's caresses in spite of her frantic efforts to force down the aching sense of longing that filled her as soon as he touched her.

'No?' Leigh questioned softly, subtly increasing the pressure of his hands in a way that made Jassy's pulse race. 'And am I supposed to believe that you mean that?'

One hand moved to Jassy's face, Leigh's thumb slowly tracing the outline of her softly parted mouth. Her throat was painfully dry, but she found she couldn't swallow to relieve it. Why *should* he believe her? She didn't even believe herself, and Leigh had no cause to trust her ever again. She had wanted time, time to convince him that she was not like all the others, but events had caught up with her, her actions seeming to prove exactly the opposite, and now there was no time left.

'I could make you beg me to love you, Jassy,' Leigh whispered, his lips against her forehead as she closed her eyes in despair. 'It would be so easy—you see, I know exactly how to do it.'

Cradling her against the hard warmth of his body, he slid his hand downwards once more to cover one breast, making Jassy catch her breath in a devastating mixture of fear and delight.

'Because there was one thing you hadn't planned on, wasn't there, my sweet? When you set out to make me desire you, you hadn't reckoned on your wanting me every bit as much—and you do, I know you do.'

Jassy could not have denied the truth of Leigh's words if she had wanted to. Her body was acting independently of her mind, pressing close up against Leigh, her heart pounding erratically so that she knew he must be aware of the uneven tenor of her breathing. Her hands were clinging to his shoulders, her fingers clenching over the hard muscles, and unthinkingly she lifted her face to his, blindly offering him her lips.

Leigh swore hoarsely, then his mouth crushed Jassy's in a fierce, punishing kiss that forced her lips apart with its savage pressure. His fingers tightened on her breast, bruising the tender flesh so that she whimpered in pain. But a moment later she was oblivious to the cruel pressure, her mind reeling as if she were delirious. She felt as if she were on fire, the passion Leigh had unleashed in her burning her up, driving all fear or thought of her own safety from her head.

As Leigh sensed her surrender his whole body stiffened, suddenly rigid and unyielding against her. He wrenched his mouth from hers and flung her away from him, the force of his movement sending her halfway across the room.

'You disgust me!' Leigh spat the words into Jassy's white face. 'I could have had you then—you would have let me do anything I liked with you! Even now you have no shame! But you've wasted your time, my lovely Jassy; I wouldn't give you the part if you were the last actress living! How could I work with you when I can't even bear to look at you? I thought you were so different, but you're just like all the rest. How can you be so beautiful and yet so corrupt inside? Get out of here!' For the first time Leigh's voice rose to a shout. 'Get out of here and leave me in peace!'

He made a move as if he would physically throw her from the room, but Jassy had already gone. Tears blurring her eyes, she blundered through the door and out into the hall. For one terrifying moment she thought the front door was locked against her, but at last she managed to wrench it open. Then she was out of the house and running, running from Leigh as she had wanted to run as soon as she had realised his presence in the theatre, fleeing desperately, but with nowhere to go.

CHAPTER NINE

SUMMER turned to autumn and Jassy moved through her life like someone with a permanent dose of concussion, feeling as if the future was a great, dark tunnel stretching endlessly ahead without a hint of light at the end of it. London suddenly did not seem large enough to contain both herself and Leigh; she couldn't settle in her flat when any ring at the doorbell made her stomach cramp in fear that the caller might be him, and even worse was to sit alone in the silent flat, knowing that he would never call, never phone, that she would never see him again.

The one thing that kept her sane was the fact that she was working again. Only three days after the nightmare of that appalling Friday, her agent rang with the news of an audition, and to Jassy's amazement she actually got the part. How she had managed to be successful, she would never know. It seemed she must have been functioning on automatic pilot because at other times she simply went through the motions of living with a listless apathy, not feeling, drained of all energy.

But the new play was a life-saver. Jassy threw herself into the part with an intensity and commitment that drove her to the point of exhaustion, working every waking hour because that way she didn't have time to think. Somehow she got through the days, but at night, alone in her bed, she was no longer able to defend her mind from thoughts of Leigh.

Time after time she lay awake, her body throbbing with a primitive longing that made her moan aloud, afraid to sleep because if she closed her eyes she could see Leigh's face, hear his voice in her mind. Her numbed brain refused to remember that final, shattering time after the audition. It flinched away from recalling the savage anger in Leigh's eyes, the satanic mockery of his words, so that it was always the earlier, more gentle Leigh who haunted her dreams. Jassy could almost feel his touch on her skin, hear the husky intensity of his voice as he whispered, 'Stay with me tonight, Jassy; let me love you.'

Partly because of the demands of her work, but mainly because she had no inclination whatsoever to socialise, Jassy spent all her free time inside the flat in spite of Sarah's urgings that she should go out, pick up the pieces of her life and start again. So when, in late October, Benjy rang with an invitation to a party to celebrate his fiftieth birthday, she was strongly tempted to refuse.

But the party was on a Sunday, when the theatre was closed, and she knew that Benjy would be hurt if she didn't turn up, taking her absence as meaning that she held him personally responsible for the fiasco of an audition with Leigh, and so, reluctantly, she agreed to go.

She planned to arrive early, before the party really got under way, and to stay only a short time, but she knew that Benjy liked his guests to dress up so she chose a black velvet skirt and waistcoat suit worn with a white ruffled blouse, its sombre tones in keeping with her mood. As usual she wore very little make-up and left her hair loose so that it hung in gleaming waves around her face.

Early as she was, the room was already half-full of brightly clothed men and women, and Jassy stood hesitantly in the doorway, searching vainly for a familiar face in the crowd, until she heard someone call her name. Turning, she saw Benjy hurrying towards her.

'Jassy, honeybun, you look wonderful! I love the Puritan look—you make the rest of us look positively overdressed!'

Jassy's mood brightened slightly at Benjy's exuberant welcome.

'Happy birthday, Benjy! You don't look so bad yourself—in fact, you look like an enormous bumble bee in that outfit.'

'Do you like it?' Benjy spun round so that she could get the full effect of the yellow-and-black-striped shirt that did nothing to flatter his heavily built figure. 'Very me, don't you think?'

'Very,' Jassy agreed laughingly as Benjy steered her towards the drinks table and poured her a glass of wine.

'Don't run away tonight, will you, honeybun?' he said. 'I have someone very special I'd like you to meet, and if I know the lady she's bound to be late.'

Jassy's nerves, which had tightened instinctively at that 'someone very special', relaxed again at the realisation that Benjy's friend was a woman. She wouldn't have put it past her tutor to have invited her with the specific intention of trying to make amends for his failure the last time.

'Who's that?'

'Don't be impatient.' Benjy wagged a reproving finger. 'You just wait and see. I still have it in mind to do you a good turn, even if it didn't turn out quite the way I planned it the first time.'

The light faded from Jassy's eyes at his words. She had never explained what had happened at the audition, and Benjy had tactfully never pressed her for any details.

'I'm sorry I let you down, Benjy.'

'Forget it! These things happen—anyone can have an off day. Now come and meet a few people.'

Obediently Jassy followed Benjy into the crowd, acknowledging his introductions automatically with a word and a smile, but hardly registering names and faces. She felt vaguely uneasy, remembering how Benjy's earlier 'good turn' had devastated her life. She couldn't help wondering just what he had in store for her this time.

The room filled up as the evening wore on, and soon the place was packed. The air was almost unbearably warm and smoky, and Jassy felt the beginnings of a headache threaten. If Benjy's friend did not turn up soon she would have to leave, she thought, massaging her temples to ease the tension. She would wait another half-hour, no more.

She was in a quiet corner chatting to Helen Carstairs, Benjy's wife, when the door opened again and a slight commotion announced the arrival of yet another guest. Glancing automatically towards the source of the disturbance, Jassy stiffened, her face paling, her polite words dying on her lips. Anna Golden had paused deliberately in the open doorway, her action nicely calculated to give her entry the fullest possible impact and draw all eyes to her.

Not that she needed any such dramatic tricks, Jassy thought wryly. The white, clinging sheath of her dress with its deeply slashed neckline, the pagan brilliance of the heavy gold necklace around her slender throat, the glorious red hair, all made certain that no one could have missed her arrival.

As Benjy hurried forward to greet Anna, Jassy suddenly found that she was trembling all over. The actress's arrival had stunned her, but now her bemused brain was beginning to work again and her thoughts sent an icy shaft of panic down her spine. In anyone's mind, Anna Golden would always be linked with Leigh Benedict, and Jassy had foolishly forgotten that Leigh had been a student at the same drama school that she had attended. Benjy had been *his* tutor too, so wasn't it more than likely that he would have been invited to this party?

She couldn't stay, Jassy thought in a panic, her unseeing eyes still fixed on the scene in the doorway where Anna was indulgently handing Benjy an enormous parcel gaudily wrapped in shiny gold paper. She couldn't bear the thought that Leigh might arrive, that they might actually come face to face.

But then the crush around Anna and Benjy moved and shifted, a path opened in the crowd, and at the end of that path, just beside Anna, stood the man Jassy so longed and yet dreaded to see.

Leigh looked dreadful, Jassy realised with a shock as the grey haze before her eyes faded and she saw him clearly at last. His face was drawn and haggard, the shadows under his eyes giving them a faintly bruised look. He was superbly dressed as always, in a black silk shirt, black trousers and a grey velvet jacket, but the dark colour of his clothes emphasised the unnatural pallor of his face and the strained lines that were etched into it.

He looked the way she felt, Jassy thought on a pang of distress: like someone who had lost interest in everything that used to matter to him, making her remember the stories she had heard about the production of *Valley of Destiny*. It was well known that hundreds of girls had auditioned for the part of Clara, and that all of them had been rejected by Leigh, often on the slightest pretext. There were even rumours that the film would never be made, that Leigh was thinking of abandoning it or, at the very least, letting someone else direct it. That story had affected Jassy like a physical blow. Knowing how much that particular film meant to Leigh, she couldn't believe that he would willingly hand it over to anyone else.

'That's something of a triumph, isn't it?' a woman beside Jassy murmured to Helen Carstairs. 'I understood Benedict was definitely antisocial these days.'

'Leigh's been too busy to go anywhere.' There was a gently reproving note in Helen's voice. 'These problems with his film take up all his time. But he promised Benjy he'd come tonight, so I knew he'd be here. He's never let us down yet.'

What about the performance of *Romeo and Juliet*? Jassy thought unwillingly. Leigh hadn't kept his promise to Benjy then. To her consternation she found she had spoken her thoughts out loud.

'Well, you can hardly hold that against him! Benjy should have known better than to ask him to come that night—we all knew that was the day Leigh had arranged to take all the kids from Pinehurst to the seaside. It wasn't Leigh's fault if the coach broke down on the way back—and he did ring up and explain and then went straight to the college as soon as he'd got all the children safely home—but by then, of course, it was too late.'

Images were flashing through Jassy's mind like slides projected on to a screen: letters arriving at the office; Steve talking of the children's home where Leigh had lived, saying 'He still keeps in touch. The staff like him to visit'; but most of all, in heartbreaking clarity, Leigh himself, tanned and relaxed, arriving at the college, and the bitter anger she had felt towards him. She had been so swift to condemn him that day, piqued by his non-appearance at her first major performance, so that her hurt pride had blinded her to any possible explanation other than the purely selfish one she had attributed to him.

With a murmured excuse Jassy moved away, trying to blend anonymously with the mass of people in the centre of the room. Her only hope was to try to remain unseen until Leigh was no longer between her and the door and then make her escape. But Leigh showed no sign of moving. He was talking to Helen now, the harsh lines of his face softening as he smiled at her with evident affection.

For a few precious minutes Jassy allowed herself the bitter-sweet luxury of watching him, drinking in the sight of him for what she knew must be the very last time. She knew that she was only torturing herself, that the pain of loving Leigh and knowing he felt only hatred and contempt for her must inevitably be far worse after this masochistic self-indulgence, but she couldn't help herself. Seeing him there, only feet from her and yet emotionally a million miles away, it was impossible not to recall how it had felt to be so very close to him that their bodies seemed to have blended together, becoming like one person instead of two separate beings, and the memory made her blood burn with a heat that had nothing to do with the crowded warmth of the room.

Now, when she was least able to bear it, it seemed that that heat had melted the ice that had held her memories frozen in her mind, and images of that last afternoon with Leigh poured into her thoughts. She remembered his coldly calculated caresses and her own unthinking response. She had yielded to Leigh as she knew she would always yield, a victim of her love for him. The savage intensity of his disgust at her reaction was no less painful because of the passage of time; if anything the pain was far worse because then she had been partially numbed by sheer shock. Now, seeing Leigh talking to Helen with an easy courtesy that hid the streak of explosive violence in his character, anguish seemed to claw at Jassy's heart, tearing it to shreds inside her.

Anna had moved at last and Leigh seemed about to follow her. A weak sigh of relief escaped Jassy's lips. A few more minutes and she would be able to get away. She had to go, even though that crazy masochistic streak in her longed to stay, simply to be in the same room as the man she loved so desperately.

Lost in her thoughts, Jassy was unaware that the crowd around her had thinned as people headed for the supper table, and she was now clearly visible from the door. As Leigh turned he glanced around the room, nodding an abstracted greeting to several people he knew, and too late Jassy realised the vulnerability of her position. Before she had time to move those tawny eyes were on her, narrowing swiftly in shock, and Jassy's stomach clenched in panic as she saw that shock fade to be replaced by a coldly burning fury.

The room seemed to whirl around her, the noise of the party fading to a dull murmur, the faces of the other guests blurring before her eyes while Leigh held her transfixed with that steely golden gaze like a small, terrified rabbit held paralysed by the hypnotic stare of some predatory hunting cat. In spite of the fact that only seconds before she had felt unbearably hot, Jassy's blood had now turned icy cold, so that she felt she would never be warm again.

Then Leigh moved, taking a single step towards her, and abruptly the spell was broken. Turning swiftly, Jassy blundered blindly through the crush of people, heedless of murmurs of protest. She was conscious of nothing beyond the need to put as much distance as possible between herself and Leigh, so that when she reached the patio doors the led out into the garden she didn't hesitate, but fumbled with the catch, breathing a silent prayer of thanks when she found it was not locked. A few seconds later she was outside, taking deep, gulping breaths of the chilly night air in an effort to calm her racing pulse.

Only then did she realise her mistake. The garden was really only a small, square courtyard, enclosed on three sides by a high wall, the fourth side of the square being the house itself. The only way out of it was to go back through the patio doors, back into the brightly lit room where even now Leigh was hunting her like some jungle tiger balked of its prey.

At that moment a slight movement caught Jassy's eyes and she turned towards the house again, freezing in shock as someone stepped out into the garden, the light from the room behind him catching on the brightness of his hair.

'Leigh!' The word was just a whisper, barely stirring the night air as Jassy glanced desperately round for some way of escape. But there was nowhere she could go; she was caught like an animal in a trap. Panic-stricken, she moved even closer to the wall, praying that its shadows would hide her.

The noise she made was very slight, almost imperceptible, but Leigh heard it and his head swung round swiftly, his eyes narrowed against the gloom. He spotted Jassy almost at once, and headed straight towards her, keeping his eyes fixed on her pale face all the time. Without a care for the damage she might be doing to her clothes, Jassy edged nervously away, her back against the wall.

Leigh caught up with her just as she reached the farthest corner. He arrested her attempt at flight by the simple expedient of placing one hand on either side of her shoulders, his long fingers resting on the brickwork, his body directly in front of her, blocking out the light from the house so that he was nothing but a black, threatening shadow that towered over her menacingly. His face was in total darkness, so that Jassy could not make out his features, but the rigidity of his stance told her that his expression would be as hard and unyielding as the rough stones that were digging painfully into her back.

'So this is where you've been hiding.'

Leigh's voice was quiet, but with a cold, cutting edge to it that made Jassy feel sick with dread. She knew this mood and feared it, recognising the signs of that almost unnatural control that was far more dangerous than if he had actually raged at her.

'Well, now,' Leigh continued goadingly, 'and what is the beautiful Miss Richardson doing here, I wonder? Hoping to give the casting couch another try, are you, my sweet?' His tone turned the endearment into an obscenity. 'Don't you ever learn? It didn't work out too well the last time, did it?'

Anger at the injustice of his suspicions drove away Jassy's fear.

'Even *your* mind can't be as warped as that!' She flung the words at Leigh's shadowed face, attacking blindly without a thought for the possible consequences. 'You know perfectly well that Benjy used to be my tutor— you can't possibly imagine that I might be trying anything with him! And for your information, Benjy's wife happens to be a very good friend of mine and I don't go around breaking up my friends' marriages—so don't judge everyone by your own standards, Mr Superstud Benedict!'

The silence that greeted her outburst terrified her, making her wish her rash words back. But it was too late and they seemed to hang on the cold night air, forming an intangible yet powerful barrier between them. Leigh's eyes gleamed dangerously in the moonlight, his very stillness infinitely menacing.

'What a shrewish tongue you have in that pretty head of yours,' Leigh said at last, and the black cynicism of his tone came as almost a relief to Jassy, who had expected a more violent reaction. Her chin lifted as she faced him defiantly.

'What did you expect? Did you think that I was going to let you slander me again and accept it meekly without hitting back? Well, you'd better think again. I have as much right to be here as you have—as Benjy's *friend*, nothing more.'

Leigh's momentary hesitation told her that he had caught that important 'again' and it had made him stop to think. He straightened up slowly, taking his hands from the wall and pushing them deep into the pockets of his trousers, watching her closely all the time. His movement meant that the light from the house fell fully on Jassy's face for the first time, and as it did so she heard Leigh draw in his breath sharply. She couldn't understand why that faint sound should make her feel afraid, but it did. It was not the fear of Leigh's ability to hurt her emotionally that she had felt from the moment she had first seen him, nor was it the purely physical terror she had experienced only moments before, but somehow it combined the two and yet was subtly different from either one.

'I think I'd better go in,' she said hurriedly, her voice shaking with nerves. 'Benjy will be wondering where I've got to. He——'

'No!' Leigh's voice was harsh. His hand caught her arm as she tried to move past him, swinging her round roughly.

'Let me go!' Jassy's high, fear-filled voice sounded sharply in the silence of the night.

'Not yet,' Leigh growled. 'I have things I want to say to you.'

'Well, I have nothing to say to you—and I doubt if you could possibly say anything I would want to hear! I'm going inside. It's late and I'm c-cold.'

Jassy's voice shook noticeably on the last two words. Leigh's hand on her arm seemed to burn through her blouse, scorching the skin beneath the silky material, and in spite of her fear she could feel the familiar, intoxicating sensations creeping through her, warming the blood in her veins so that she was intensely grateful for the darkness that hid the colour in her cheeks. It was hopeless! Leigh had only to touch her like this, even in anger, his grip hard and cruel, and she was lost, ready to fall into his arms without a thought for her own safety.

'Here.'

To her astonishment, Leigh was pulling off his jacket, releasing her arm only for a second as he did so. He draped it over Jassy's shoulders, pulling the lapels closely round her neck. Jassy felt the sensual touch of the velvet, still warm from the heat of Leigh's body, smelt the painfully evocative scent of his aftershave that clung to the soft material, and closed her eyes against the pain of the memories that assailed her.

'Now,' Leigh said softly, his hands still on the lapels of his jacket, effortlessly holding her prisoner, 'I think I'm going to kiss you.'

Jassy's eyes flew open in shock, her face drained of all colour in the moonlight.

'Don't you dare! I mean—Leigh—no!'

She struggled impotently against his restraining hands, twisting her head desperately from side to side, but Leigh simply took one hand from his jacket and caught hold of her chin, turning her face irresistibly towards his. Jassy had one terrifying glimpse of the wild, malevolent glitter in his eyes before the blond head bent and his lips captured hers.

For one stunned second Jassy froze in shock, for Leigh's kiss was not the fierce assault she had anticipated, but soft and sensually teasing, evoking a response deep inside her. Then, drawing on the few shattered remnants that were all that was left of her ability to think clearly, she put out her hands to push Leigh away from her, only to find to her horror that they refused to obey her. The fingers she had intended to flatten against his chest to force him from her curled wantonly around the buttons on Leigh's shirt, tugging at them impatiently until they yielded, and she slid her hands inside the soft silk. She heard Leigh's ragged sigh before his mouth hardened on hers, his kiss no longer gentle but filled with a fierce, demanding passion that forced her lips apart, taking everything she had to give.

The garden, the darkness, the party in the house behind her all faded from Jassy's mind. Even the pavingstones beneath her feet seemed unreal and insubstantial.

The one thing that existed was Leigh, his arms now around her in a grip so powerful that she feared he would crush her completely. After the long, lonely weeks of wanting, longing, dreaming of just such a moment as this, and knowing her dreams to be hopeless, she was overwhelmed by the intensity of her response. She was swept along on a tidal wave of passion, returning Leigh's kisses with an eagerness she did not attempt to conceal, her body arched towards his, pliant against his hardness.

Leigh's hands were moving softly but insistently over her, his fingers closing possessively over the soft swell of her breasts under the white blouse, driving her to a fever-pitch of excitement where there was no room for self-consciousness or shame. She was beyond thought, heedless of the fact that Leigh's jacket had slipped to the ground, conscious only of the wonderful things his lips and hands were doing to her. She was clinging blindly to him, murmuring her need of him in soft, incoherent words when he pulled himself away from her abruptly, removing her clutching hands and holding them in both his own, his body held stiffly away from her. His breathing was slightly uneven, but apart from that he showed no sign of the passion that had been such a tangible force in him only seconds before, and his sudden cold detachment turned Jassy's heated blood to ice.

'Now we're even,' he ground out harshly. 'Now you know what it's like to want someone so much you're aching for them—only to have them freeze you out at the last minute. It isn't pleasant, is it? I should know—I've been there.'

Fear, shock, and bitter frustration deprived Jassy of the ability to speak. She could only stare at Leigh in anguished disbelief, a phrase she had heard him say—a lifetime ago it seemed—repeating over and over in her head. 'I reckon I owe you one, and I don't forget easily.'

'Now perhaps you'll be a little less eager to try your seductive little wiles on some other poor fool.' Leigh's taunting words lashed Jassy like the sting of a whip as he let her hands drop suddenly and began to fasten his shirt with fingers that were only very faintly unsteady.

'You're detestable!' Jassy choked on the words. 'I wish I'd never met you!'

'The feeling's mutual.'

Leigh's sardonic retort was the last straw. 'Oh, why don't you go to hell?' Jassy exploded, driven to the limit of her self-control.

Inexplicably, shockingly, Leigh's mood changed suddenly, the savage, tormenting look fading swiftly from his face.

'I did once,' he said bleakly. 'I reckon I'm still there.'

Jassy's confusion was total, the world tilting crazily around her so that she reeled sickeningly, reaching automatically for Leigh's arm for support. He made no move to help or repulse her, but simply let her hand rest on his arm, regarding her silently with dark, unfathomable eyes. Very slowly the world righted itself again and Jassy swallowed with difficulty, wetting her lips nervously before she could speak.

'I—I don't understand.'

'Don't you?' Leigh questioned harshly, but the fierce, attacking quality had gone from his voice. He shrugged dismissively. 'Why should you understand? I don't even understand myself. What is it about you, Jassy?' he went on with soft intensity. 'Why is it that even now I can't stay away from you? It's like a sickness. I know what you are—a cheap little tramp who'll sell her body to anyone if that's the price of stardom, but when I knew you were here I had to come looking for you. I couldn't settle till I found you. I told you once I was half demented with wanting you; now I think I'm completely, incurably insane.'

The beautiful voice was thick with self-disgust and Leigh shook his head slowly as if in despair at his own foolishness.

'So now you know,' he finished, his tone bitterly derisory. 'I hope you're satisfied.'

Roughly he shook off the hand that still rested on his arm, then bent and snatched his jacket from the ground, slinging it over his shoulder before striding away towards the house without another word. Jassy watched him go, too bewildered by his abrupt change of mood even to try to understand what he had meant by his enigmatic words, until the cold began to impinge on the trance that held her captive and she shivered convulsively. Without Leigh, the garden seemed very dark and threatening, so she followed him hurriedly, suddenly afraid to be alone with her thoughts.

Benjy accosted Jassy as soon as she re-entered the room.

'There you are! I've been looking for you everywhere. I promised you were going to meet someone special, and now I'm going to deliver. This lady is the one who tried to help you before. Yes, I know it didn't work out, but she took a great interest in you from the moment I mentioned your name—because, of course, she'd seen you as Juliet.'

And then, of course, Jassy knew exactly who he meant. She moved as if sleep-walking, every step seeming to be performed in slow motion, one face standing out from the crowd around her, a cold, proud face, crowned with a coil of red hair.

'Anna, darling, I want you to meet a friend of mine. This is Jassy Richardson—my Juliet.'

In the stillness of that moment Jassy sensed someone standing silently at her back and a cold, shivering sensation running down her spine told her exactly who it was without turning to look. Anna did not seem to have noticed Leigh's silent presence, but to Jassy the atmosphere seemed to crackle with a tension that was almost tangible as Benjy continued blithely.

'Jassy, it was Anna who arranged the audition for *Valley of Destiny* at such short notice.' He announced the fact triumphantly, like a gambler producing his trump card, then stared in bewilderment as a nerve-racking silence greeted his words.

'Anna!'

It was Leigh's voice that shattered the silence, and in the second before she spun round Jassy saw how the actress's face paled underneath her make-up, making her look, not like the regal movie queen she had always appeared to be before, but a lost and lonely woman, so that instinctively Jassy felt a pang of sympathy for her. But from the moment she saw Leigh's face all thought of anyone else was driven from her mind. His expression was dark as a storm-cloud, the tawny eyes mere slits in a face that was white with fury. Every muscle in his body was rigid with a tension that communicated itself to the people around him, silencing their animated chatter. Jassy thought that she had seen Leigh angry before, but never, ever like this.

'Is this true?' Leigh demanded ominously.

The few seconds' pause before he had spoken had given Anna time to regain some degree of composure.

'I did it for you, Leigh,' she said, her voice high and sharp. 'It was obvious that she wasn't just the secretary she claimed to be, but one of those little leeches you've always had such trouble with, so I arranged the audition so that you could see just what a scheming little bitch she is!'

'No!' Jassy tried to protest, but Leigh's eyes were fixed on Anna.

'There's more to it than that,' he declared inimically. 'I want the whole truth, Anna.'

Jassy was shaking uncontrollably, this sudden turn of events sending her into a state of shock so that she was only dimly aware of Benjy's arm coming around her protectively.

'Honeybun,' he said quietly, 'I've got the most dreadful feeling I've boobed again. This looks suspiciously like the start of World War Three, and if I know Anna things are going to get very nasty indeed. Let me take you out of here.'

Unresistingly, Jassy let him draw her away towards the door. Neither Leigh nor Anna saw her go, and the image she carried with her as she followed Benjy was of the two of them standing tall and proud in the middle of the room, their eyes locked together and the sparks of anger, like flashes of lightning, almost visible between them.

CHAPTER TEN

JASSY knew she should go to bed. It was almost three in the morning and she was achingly weary, every muscle in her body crying out in protest at being deprived of rest, but she knew that sleep would be impossible when her mind was so agonisingly wide awake.

She had promised Benjy that she would go straight to bed when he had left her at her flat over an hour before, but knowing that she should sleep and being able to do so were two completely different things. She couldn't sleep without knowing what had happened between Leigh and Anna after she had left the party.

Benjy had taken her downstairs to the warm, friendly basement kitchen, and had pressed a drink into her trembling hands.

'You wait here while I go and do my duty as host. I'll have to try and persuade those two crazy people to do their fighting somewhere else. Please don't look so devastated, honeybun. Anyone who knows Leigh has seen this coming a mile off. He's been making it plain that he's sick of Anna's clinging, and I reckon tonight just about finished it. I should have known better than to invite them both on the same night,' he added wryly.

Alone in the kitchen, Jassy had waited tensely, straining her ears for some clue as to what was going on upstairs. Twice she heard the slam of a door and the roar of a car's engine, but that was all, and when Benjy returned he gave her only the briefest outline of events. Anna had stormed out and Leigh had followed her, driving after her 'like a bat out of hell,' Benjy said appreciatively, seeming to have enjoyed the whole experience. Then he had insisted on driving Jassy home.

'It's the least I can do, honeybun. I never meant to get you entangled in Leigh and Anna's private civil war.

And I promise, after this, no more good turns. They don't seem to turn out quite as I plan them.'

Now, sitting in the silent flat, Jassy wished she could break down and weep to ease the aching tension in her heart, but her eyes were painfully dry, burning with the tears she couldn't shed as she forced herself to review her relationship with Leigh though her heart cried out against such self-imposed torture. But she couldn't hide from the truth any more. She had condemned and rejected the women who had seen only the golden public image Leigh projected, but in her hurt pride at his non-appearance at the performance of *Romeo and Juliet* she had made assumptions, blind, foolish assumptions of selfishness and arrogance that had stayed with her, preventing her from really getting to know the man behind the persona of the Golden Thief. Now it was too late. She had seen tonight that the barriers Leigh built around himself, barriers that had started to come down when he was with her, were back in place and stronger than ever.

A sudden sharp knock at the door brought Jassy's head swinging round to stare in the direction of the sound as if she could see through the thick wood. When the knock was repeated, she froze, panic-stricken, her breathing swift and shallow. Who would call at her flat at this time?

'Jassy, I know you're in there, I saw the light.' Leigh's voice coming clearly through the closed door did nothing to soothe Jassy's fear. Irrationally, she felt she might almost have preferred some manic prowler. 'Jassy! Open this door!'

'Go—go away, Leigh!' Jassy forced the words from a throat that was unnaturally tight with tension.

'Not until I've talked to you,' was Leigh's implacable response. 'If you don't open this door I swear I'll break it down—and I don't give a damn who hears me.'

Jassy's apprehensive glance went towards the room in which Sarah lay sleeping. She could have no doubt that Leigh fully intended to carry out his threat, and if he did her friend would be sure to waken.

'All right—just a minute,' she said hastily, hurrying to turn the key, then stumbled back as the door burst open and Leigh strode into the room.

He looked totally dishevelled, the grey velvet jacket discarded somewhere, his face drawn into lines of strain, and his golden hair falling in disorder across his forehead. Seeing him, Jassy's heart twisted and she longed to smooth the tension from his face with gentle hands, but she knew that the time for such displays of tenderness was long gone. Leigh would only interpret any gesture of love as another attempt to seduce him and would repulse her attentions violently.

'What are you doing here, Leigh?' she asked, the tension that gripped her making her voice hard. 'In case you haven't realised, it's nearly three in the morning.'

'I know.' Leigh's voice was strangely quiet, the grim, threatening note gone from it completely. 'I would have been here earlier, but I had to check that you weren't still at Benjy's first—and I had to go home to get this.'

He pulled a thick envelope from his pocket and held it out to Jassy, who stared at it blankly, not moving to take it.

'Take it!' Leigh insisted. 'I brought it for you.'

'What is it?' Jassy asked hesitantly.

Leigh's mouth twisted wryly at the suspicion in her tone.

'The terms of surrender,' he said cryptically. 'Or, to put it another way—a contract.'

Jassy's heart gave a painful lurch and she found that she couldn't breathe properly. None of this could really be happening!

'I—don't understand——' she began, but Leigh broke in on her.

'I'm giving you what you wanted,' he declared harshly. 'The part of Clara—it's yours—that contract says so.'

The pain was white-hot; Jassy couldn't believe that anything could hurt so much.

'I don't want it, Leigh,' she said flatly.

'But you have to take it! It's all I have to give you. It's your part—it always has been. I knew that as soon as I saw you that night outside the drama college, when the film was still only an idea. You were in my mind when I wrote it—why the hell do you think I came to see you in *Moonrise*? It certainly wasn't to see the bloody play!'

Jassy's head was reeling. She had forgotten that Leigh had told her that he had seen her act in that ill-fated production, had forgotten his enigmatic comment that 'the *play* was appalling'.

'I knew then you were my Clara, that no one else would ever do. I've been comparing every actress I've auditioned with you and no one even comes close. If you don't take the part, no one else ever will. I'll scrap the film, forget the whole damn thing.'

The tears that had refused to fall earlier were there now, stinging Jassy's eyes. Leigh was offering her the part she had dreamed of, but the dream had turned into an appalling nightmare. She could never accept it, not like this, because to do so would only reinforce his belief that the part was all she had ever wanted, that she had used him for her own selfish reasons. In despair, Jassy turned away from Leigh, bending her head to hide her tears.

'Don't do that!' Leigh groaned. 'Jassy, don't turn away from me! I know you must hate me, and I don't blame you—I've treated you appallingly. But please let me do something. If you'd prefer it I won't even direct the film—I'll hand it over to someone else. Jassy, please! I know you don't want my love, but at least let me give you this.'

Jassy's eyes were wide open, but she could see nothing. Time seemed to stop, the moment hanging suspended, as she took in what Leigh had said, then, very, very slowly, she came back to reality. Behind her she heard Leigh's despondent sigh as he flung the contract on to the table and she swung round hastily to see him moving towards the door, his head down.

'Wait a minute,' she said, and at first thought he hadn't heard her because shock had weakened her voice. Then he turned back and the empty, defeated expression

in his eyes tore at her heart. There was no sign now of
the Golden Thief, just a man—the man she loved.

'You'll take the part?' Leigh asked, his voice dead,
no hope, nothing in the dull tones.

Jassy's smile was very gentle as she shook her head.
'No, Leigh,' she said quietly, 'I'll not take *that*.'

She emphasised the last word clearly and, bruised as
he was, Leigh noticed and frowned his bewilderment.

'Then what...?' he asked slowly, and Jassy's smile
widened.

'What else were you offering?' she teased softly.

Leigh's hands went to his temples, pressing hard
against them as if to ease some intolerable ache, his eyes
closed.

'I didn't——' he began, then his eyes flew open and
Jassy saw a faint spark in their tawny depths. 'You don't
mean—you can't—Jassy, the only other thing I
mentioned was love!'

The raw emotion in his tone caught at Jassy's heart,
so that her own voice was infinitely tender when she
answered him.

'I know,' she said clearly. 'And that's the only thing
I want from you.'

There was a long, tense pause, then, 'Forgive me if
I've got this wrong,' Leigh said stumblingly, 'but are
you saying you *love* me?'

'Oh, Leigh,' Jassy sighed. 'Did you really not know?
Yes, I love you—I love you with all my heart.'

The stunned expression still hadn't left Leigh's face.
'I don't see how you can,' he said dazedly, 'not after
the way I've treated you, the things I've said. Oh, Jassy,
I never meant to hurt you! I loved you so much—I think
I fell for you the moment I saw you. You looked like a
small, angry kitten spitting at me and I was lost.' A
slightly crooked smile curved Leigh's mouth. 'I couldn't
keep my hands off you, but you made it very clear that
wasn't what you wanted.'

'I didn't know what I wanted,' Jassy put in quickly.
'I'd never felt like that before and I was scared.'

'I know.'

Leigh's tone was very serious. He had taken a step back towards her—just one, but it was a start.

'That Friday night, when I calmed down, I realised that, but then I really thought I'd blown it completely, especially when you were so unflatteringly honest about your opinion of me, and I decided I'd better forget the whole thing. But then on Saturday, when I was at Anna's, all I could talk about was you. I couldn't get you out of my mind, and in the morning I had to see you—I couldn't wait till you got to the office—so I called to offer you a lift. I'd planned to be oh, so polite, to take things very slowly, but you wouldn't let me. First there seemed to be another man with you, and I found I was as jealous as hell, then you fought me every step of the way until I couldn't think straight. The only thing I knew was that I wanted you, so I told you so—hardly the most subtle approach! I know I blew my top over the script, but by the time Steve got to me I'd already had to admit to myself that it wasn't the *script* that was important, and that wasn't something I was exactly prepared for because up until then my work had been my life.'

Leigh paused, frowning slightly as if still reeling from the impact of that realisation, and Jassy waited silently, knowing intuitively that he needed to tell things in his own way.

'I didn't know it then, but that change had been creeping up on me for a while—ever since a small blonde spitfire had let rip at me a couple of years ago.'

The lop-sided smile returned as Leigh caught Jassy's swiftly indrawn breath.

'My mother's experiences—the mess she'd made of her life—had made me wary of any emotional relationships, and I determined that that wasn't going to happen to me. My work I could handle—it was under my control and so I put everything I had into it. Success was the only thing that mattered.'

'I know how that feels,' Jassy murmured. Hadn't she done exactly the same thing in her own way, letting her life be ruled by her determination to prove herself to her parents, not letting other sides of herself, particularly her emotional side, develop?

'Perhaps that's why you got to me so strongly. I must have recognised the same sort of obsession in you, and suddenly everything looked so very different. I thought I had everything I wanted, but somehow it no longer seemed enough—it was a damned empty way to live. I was restless, there was a huge gap in my life, but I couldn't put my finger on where it was. I thought *Valley of Destiny* would fill it—I thought it *had*, because when I came back from Scotland and started work on it again I found a new meaning in everything I did. Then it hit me that it wasn't the film that was doing this to me, but you.'

Leigh's hand reached out to Jassy, his gesture tentative, hesitant, and, sensing his need, she took several hasty steps towards him and clasped it firmly. Leigh's fingers curled around hers tightly as he went on.

'In the middle of that week I was supposed to be at some high-flying dinner party, but I just couldn't face it. The only person I wanted to be with was you—so I found myself here, sitting on that appallingly uncomfortable settee, drinking very flat cider and loving every minute of it. I'd spent all afternoon putting on the public face for that reporter, but with you I could relax—I didn't have to play a part any more.'

That was the night he should have been at Anna's, Jassy recalled, and shivered as she remembered the actress's words. 'If you're wise, you'll get out now, before you regret it for the rest of your life.' At the time she had thought that Anna was simply referring to her belief that Leigh could never love anyone, but, hearing those words in her mind in the light of tonight's events, she saw them for what they really were—a threat that Anna had carried out to devastating effect.

'But you were so different from the other women I knew, and I didn't know how to handle them.' Leigh seemed not to have noticed Jassy's momentary abstraction. 'Looking back, I think I avoided anyone who might threaten the way I thought I wanted to live my life, so I knew only the Gemma Morgans of the world, which reinforced my prejudiced view of the female sex. And I was so used to holding back, not letting people see too much, that I didn't know how to tell you what I was feeling. And I was impatient; I wanted to grab you, hold you any way I could. Suddenly the film didn't matter, success didn't matter, without you, it was all empty—nothing. Then, just when I thought that maybe you felt something too, you turned up at that bloody audition and I went completely crazy, thinking you'd just used me. I wanted to lash out, destroy everything that was important to me—and I damn nearly succeeded!'

Leigh turned to Jassy, his eyes very dark and intense.

'You couldn't have loved me then.'

'But I did,' Jassy assured him confidently. 'I never stopped loving you.'

'You mean, even in the middle of that whole bloody mess... Hell, I could kill Anna!'

The ferocity of Leigh's expression frightened Jassy, but it was not that that made her heart lurch painfully. She had known that, inevitably, they must come to Anna Golden, but now the time had come and she was not sure she was quite ready.

'Jassy,' Leigh said quietly, 'about Anna...'

Jassy wanted to stop him, tell him that Anna was in the past, that she didn't matter, but she knew from his face that he wouldn't accept that and, deep down, neither could she. Anna had tried to come between them, and in a way she was still there, an invisible, vindictive presence that had to be exorcised so that there would be no doubts, no questions left unanswered.

'Tell me about Anna,' she said simply.

Leigh sighed tiredly, raking his hands through his already ruffled hair.

'Anna's a very lonely woman. Underneath all that sex goddess act, she's a rather inadequate human being. She's had three husbands and none of them stayed around for more than a year, her career's a mess, she's terrified of growing old, losing her looks, being alone. I cared enough for her in the past to want to help her.'

'You're not her lover,' Jassy said, making a statement, not asking a question, but still she saw Leigh's golden head move in angry denial.

'I was once—years ago, for a very short time. It was dead before it ever hit the papers, and there had been nothing between us before she and Carrington had officially separated.'

'But he cited you——' Jassy was interrupted by Leigh's groan of self-disgust.

'I know—dear lord, I know! That was one of the biggest mistakes of my life. Look, Anna and I had a very brief affair, one that burned itself out before it had really begun—but Anna wanted a quick divorce from Carrington, so she gave him my name as her lover. I'll admit I went along with it, on the advice of my agent— the worst advice I've ever been given in my life. If I'd known what it would lead to——'

Leigh broke off, shaking his head at his own foolishness.

'Jassy, I was just twenty-two, and my career was beginning to take off. The Anna Golden affair helped my image.' Leigh's tone was wry. 'I was my agent's despair, I was being billed as the new sex symbol, but there wasn't a woman in my life—and that can start some very nasty rumours. So I let myself be seen with Anna, let the papers think there was more to it than there was just for the publicity. I was pretty bloody naïve because I never expected it to snowball as it did.' A twisted smile flickered across his mouth. 'Needless to say, I have changed agents since those days.'

'But that Sunday—when you came to my flat——' Jassy made herself say it.

'I'd been at Anna's all night?' There was a flash of the old fire in Leigh's eyes. 'Dammit, Jassy, I'm quite capable of staying the night in a friend's home without dragging her into to bed with me! And that's all Anna is—was—a friend. Oh, I know she tries to make it out to be more than that, her career's on the skids and mine is riding high, so she uses me for publicity as I once used that damned Golden Thief nickname. I put up with her play-acting because it didn't touch me—except in one way. Whenever I look at Anna I see my mother—she was about Anna's age when she died. I couldn't help her, but if being seen with me stops Anna from going the same way then it's the least I can do. My friends all knew the truth, so it didn't matter—until now.'

The muscles in Leigh's jaw tightened, drawing his mouth into a thin, hard line.

'She's never done anything like this before. I suppose she must have realised from the way I talked that you were a real threat to her position in my life. When you told me she'd come to the office that day I knew I'd have to have it out with her, tell her things couldn't go on as they had been, but I had to get those damned auditions out of the way first. Then, when we were at the theatre, I got a phone call from Benjy——'

Leigh broke off abruptly, his eyes shadowed with remembered pain so that Jassy's heart twisted inside her at the thought of how he must have felt. He had to make an obvious effort to speak again.

'But after tonight I doubt if Anna will ever want to see me again. It's just as well I was desperate to get back to you because when I found out how she'd arranged the audition to make it appear as if you were only using me I was strongly tempted to break her selfish little neck! Loving you the way I do, and thinking I'd lost you because of Anna, I felt positively murderous!'

Leigh's hands clenched convulsively at the memory, then a moment later he opened them suddenly, lifting them in a gesture that dismissed Anna from his thoughts, and, remembering the glimpse she had had of the sad, pathetic woman behind Anna's careful façade, Jassy knew that she could understand why he had tolerated her for so long, but that now she too could dismiss her from their lives.

'I do love you,' Leigh said, his eyes very dark and sincere. 'You do believe that, don't you?'

Jassy could only nod, too full of happiness to speak as Leigh drew her gently towards him.

'I have something very important to say,' he murmured, causing Jassy to glance up at him in some confusion. What could possibly be more important than hearing Leigh say he loved her?

'Marry me, Jassy,' Leigh said simply. 'Marry me and take the part of Clara. If we're together it can't fail—but I can't do it without you. I need you with me, at my side wherever I am, whatever I'm doing. Of course, if you really don't want the part, I won't force it on you. You can do anything you want if you'll only say you'll marry me and let me love you as I've wanted to from the moment I saw you.'

The tiger's eyes were intent as Leigh lifted Jassy's face towards his. He must have read her answer in her own eyes, but Jassy still had to speak because there was one thing she had to make very clear.

'On one condition,' she said quietly, refusing to let the uncertain, questioning look in his eyes distract her as she went on determinedly. 'I must have another audition for the role of Clara—and you mustn't have anything to do with it. Steve knows what you want—let him decide. I want that part desperately, but only if I'm good enough, not because you want to give it to me. All I want from you is that man you offered me. I want you for yourself, not because of who you are.'

The silence that followed her words left Jassy in no doubt that Leigh had understood the importance of what she had said. He drew a long, ragged breath, and when he spoke his voice was distinctly unsteady.

'That's a condition I have no intention of arguing with. On those terms, then, what's your answer?'

'Yes,' Jassy told him unhesitatingly. 'Yes to marriage, yes to Clara, but above all, yes to having you love me— I wouldn't want any of the others without that.'

'There's no chance of that,' Leigh declared huskily. 'I'll have myself written into your contract just to make sure.'

At last every trace of doubt and uncertainty was wiped from his face, and there was no holding back now as he pulled Jassy close up against him, his arms fastening tightly around her waist. His kiss was long, deeply passionate and completely perfect—perfect because it was the first kiss they had shared safe in the mutual certainty of each other's love. Jassy didn't know if it was minutes or hours later that Leigh lifted his head with a reluctant sigh, cradling her against his side, her cheek resting on the warm strength of his chest, his hand stroking her hair with infinite gentleness.

'I think I'd better let you get some sleep,' he said unwillingly. 'Though it hurts like hell to leave you.'

Jassy's smile came easily. Confident in his love, she gave him a soft, enticing look.

'Then don't,' she whispered cajolingly. 'Don't leave me—take me with you.'

'Don't tempt me.' Leigh's voice was a husky mutter. 'Right now, I can think of nothing I want more—but I forced the pace last time, rushed you into things though I'd said I could wait. This time will be different.'

'But you only said you'd wait until I could tell you I wanted you,' Jassy challenged lovingly, moving very slightly away from him in order to see him more clearly.

She searched his face, looking deep into his eyes, finding in them a flame of love and longing to match the one that burned in her own heart.

'I'm saying it now, Leigh, the waiting's over. Take me with you because I want you, my love—I want you more than I can say.'

Later, Jassy was to reflect that she should have known. It was inevitable that, having got their hands on a good catchphrase, the papers would be reluctant to let it go, even when it was clearly obsolete. On the morning after their wedding every popular newspaper carried a photograph of Leigh and Jassy together, their happiness clear for all the world to see, and above it ran the caption: 'The Girl Who Stole the Heart of the Golden Thief.'

Coming soon
to an easy chair near you.

FIRST CLASS is Harlequin's armchair travel plan for the incurably romantic. You'll visit a different dreamy destination every month from January through December without ever packing a bag. No jet lag, no expensive air fares and *no* lost luggage. Just First Class Harlequin Romance reading, featuring exotic settings from Tasmania to Thailand, from Egypt to Australia, and more.

FIRST CLASS romantic excursions guaranteed! Start your world tour in January. Look for the special **FIRST CLASS** destination on selected Harlequin Romance titles—there's a new one every month.

NEXT DESTINATION:
AUSTRALIA

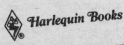 *Harlequin Books*

JTR3

HARLEQUIN
Romance®

Coming Next Month

#3109 EVERY WOMAN'S DREAM Bethany Campbell
Cal Buchanan's photograph landed on Tess's desk like manna from heaven. It
would guarantee the success of the calendar project that could launch Tess in New
York's advertising world. Only things don't work out quite that way—there
are complications....

#3110 FAIR TRIAL Elizabeth Duke
They come from two different worlds, Tanya Barrington and Simon Devlin, two
lawyers who have to work together on a case. Their clashes are inevitable—and
their attraction to each other is undeniable.

#3111 THE GIRL HE LEFT BEHIND Emma Goldrick
Molly and Tim were childhood friends, and he never knew that he'd broken Molly's
heart when he married her cousin. When Tim turns up on Molly's doorstep with his
daughter, asking for help, Molly takes them in despite the pain they bring her. And
the joy ...

#3112 AN IMPOSSIBLE PASSION Stephanie Howard
Fayiz Davidian's job offer comes just when Giselle needs it, and if he thinks she'll
refuse just because she finds him arrogant and overbearing, he's dead wrong. She
always rises to a challenge!

#3113 FIRST COMES MARRIAGE Debbie Macomber
Janine Hartman's grandfather and Zach Thomas have merged their companies.
Now Gramps wants to arrange another kind of merger—a wedding between his
unwilling granddaughter and an equally unwilling Zach!

#3114 HIDDEN HEART Jessica Steele
To protect her sister and family, Mornay shoulders the blame when wealthy
industrialist Brad Kendrick wrongly accuses her of being the hit-and-run driver
who'd landed him in the hospital. She never suspects that her heart will
become involved....

Available in March wherever paperback books are sold, or through
Harlequin Reader Service:

In the U.S.
P.O. Box 1397
Buffalo, N.Y.
14240-1397

In Canada
P.O. Box 603
Fort Erie, Ontario
L2A 5X3

You'll flip . . . your pages won't!
Read paperbacks *hands-free* with

Book Mate · I

The perfect "mate" for all your romance paperbacks

Traveling • Vacationing • At Work • In Bed • Studying • Cooking • Eating

Perfect size for all standard paperbacks, this wonderful invention makes reading a pure pleasure! Ingenious design holds paperback books OPEN and FLAT so even wind can't ruffle pages – leaves your hands free to do other things. Reinforced, wipe-clean vinyl-covered holder flexes to let you turn pages without undoing the strap . . . supports paperbacks so well, they have the strength of hardcovers!

Pages turn WITHOUT opening the strap

SEE-THROUGH STRAP

Reinforced back stays flat.

Built in bookmark

BOOK MARK

BACK COVER HOLDING STRIP

10˝ x 7¼˝ opened.
Snaps closed for easy carrying. too.

COMING IN 1991 FROM
HARLEQUIN SUPERROMANCE:

Three abandoned orphans,
one missing heiress!

Dying millionaire Owen Byrnside receives an
anonymous letter informing him that twenty-six years
ago, his son, Christopher, fathered a daughter. The
infant was abandoned at a foundling home that
subsequently burned to the ground, destroying all
records. Three young women could be Owen's long-
lost granddaughter, and Owen is determined to track
down each of them! Read their stories in

#434 HIGH STAKES (available January 1991)
#438 DARK WATERS (available February 1991)
#442 BRIGHT SECRETS (available March 1991)

Three exciting stories of intrigue and romance by
veteran Superromance author Jane Silverwood.

They went in through the terrace door. The house was dark, most of the servants were down at the circus, and only Nelbert's hired security guards were in sight. It was child's play for Blackheart to move past them, the work of two seconds to go through the solid lock on the terrace door. And then they were creeping through the darkened house, up the long curving stairs, Ferris fully as noiseless as the more experienced Blackheart.

They stopped on the second floor landing. "What if they have guns?" Ferris mouthed silently.

Blackheart shrugged. "Then duck."

"How reassuring," she responded. Footsteps directly above them signaled that the thieves were on the move, and so should they be.

For more romance, suspense and adventure, read Harlequin Intrigue. Two exciting titles each month, available wherever Harlequin Books are sold.

Everyone loves a spring wedding, and this April, Harlequin cordially invites you to read the most romantic wedding book of the year

With This Ring

ONE WEDDING—FOUR LOVE STORIES FROM YOUR FAVORITE HARLEQUIN AUTHORS!

The church is booked, the reception arranged and the invitations mailed. All Diane Bauer and Nick Granatelli have to do is walk down the aisle. Little do they realize that the most cherished day of their lives will spark so many romantic notions....

Available wherever Harlequin books are sold.